WILD CARDS VII

DEAD MAN'S HAND

The Wild Cards Universe

The Original Triad

Wild Cards

Aces High

Jokers Wild

The Puppetman Quartet

Aces Abroad

Down and Dirty

Ace in the Hole

Dead Man's Hand

The Rox Triad

One-Eyed Jacks

Jokertown Shuffle

Dealer's Choice

Double Solitaire

Turn of the Cards

The Card Sharks Triad

Card Sharks

Marked Cards

Black Trump

Deuces Down

Death Draws Five

The Committee Triad

Inside Straight

Busted Flush

Suicide Kings

The Fort Freak Triad

Fort Freak

Lowball

High Stakes

 WILD CARDS VII

DEAD MAN'S HAND

Edited by
George R. R. Martin

Assistant Editor
Melinda M. Snodgrass

Written by
George R. R. Martin
and John Jos. Miller

TOR

A TOM DOHERTY ASSOCIATES BOOK
New York

WILD CARDS VII: DEAD MAN'S HAND

Copyright © 1990 by George R. R. Martin and the Wild Card Trust

A Tor Book
Published by Tom Doherty Associates
175 Fifth Avenue
New York, NY 10010

www.tor-forge.com

Tor® is a registered trademark of Macmillan Publishing Group, LLC.

The Library of Congress Cataloging-in-Publication Data is available upon request.

ISBN 978-0-7653-3561-6 (trade paperback)
ISBN 978-1-4668-2439-3 (e-book)

Our books may be purchased in bulk for promotional, educational, or business use. Please contact your local bookseller or the Macmillan Corporate and Premium Sales Department at 1-800-221-7945, extension 5442, or by e-mail at MacmillanSpecialMarkets@macmillan.com.

First published in the United States by Bantam Spectra

First Tor Edition: June 2017

Printed in the United States of America

0 9 8 7 6 5 4 3 2 1

for Mary Mertens

DEAD MAN'S HAND

Monday
July 18, 1988

5:00 A.M.

THE TREES WERE MOVING, though there was no wind.

He did not know how long he had been walking, or how he had gotten to this place, but he was here, alone, and he was afraid. It was night, a night longer and darker than any he had ever known. Moonlight painted the landscape in shades of black and gray, but the moon was obscenely swollen, the color of rotting flesh. He looked up at it once, and for one awful moment it seemed to *pulse*. He knew he must not look again. Whatever he did, he must not look again.

He walked. On and on he walked. The gray, thin grass seemed to clutch at his bare feet with every step, to slide greasy tendrils between his toes. And the trees moved. Windless, they moved. Long cruel branches, barren of any leaves, writhed and twisted as he passed, and whispered secrets he did not want to know. If he stopped for only a moment, he would hear them clearly, he would understand. And then, surely, he would go mad. He walked.

Beneath that sickly-sweet moonlight, things that did not bear thinking of woke and stirred. Vast leathery wings beat against the air, filling the night with the smell of corruption. Gaunt spider shapes, leprous and rotten, slipped between the trees just out of sight, their legs rustling softly as they moved, never seen but never far behind him. Once a long low moan shuddered across the landscape, growing louder and louder until even the trees grew still and silent and afraid.

And then, when the feeling of dread was so thick he thought he might choke on it, he saw the subway kiosk up ahead.

It stood in the middle of the forest, bathed in that awful moonlight, but he knew it belonged, somehow. He began to run. He seemed to be moving very slowly, as if each stride took an eon. Slowly the mouth of the kiosk grew. The steps descending into the dark, the worn railing, the familiar signs; they called him home.

Finally he reached the top of the stairs, just when he felt he could run no farther. There were sounds behind him, but he dared not look around. He started down the steps, holding the handrail, faint with relief. It seemed as though he descended a long way. Trains rumbled through dark gulfs far, far below him. Still he descended. Now he could taste the fear again. The steps twisted around on themselves, spiraling down and down.

Then, well beneath him, he glimpsed another passenger, descending. He moved faster, bare feet slapping against the cold stone, down and around, and saw him again, a big man in a heavy black coat. He tried to call out to him, but here, in this place, his voice was gone. He ran even faster. He ran until his feet began to bleed. The steps had grown very narrow.

They opened suddenly, and he stepped out onto a long, narrow platform suspended over a vast blackness, a darkness that swallowed all light. The other man stood on the platform. There was something odd about his proportions, something disturbing about the way he stood there, humped and silent.

Then he turned, and Jay saw its face, a featureless white cone that tapered to a single wet red tentacle. It lifted its head and began to *howl*. Jay screamed . . .

. . . and woke, shaking, in a dark room that smelled of piss.

"God*damn*," he muttered. His heart sounded like a rock drummer on speed, his underwear was soaked with sweat, and he'd wet the bed. This had been a bad one.

Jay fumbled for the bedside lamp, and swung his legs off the side of the bed and sat waiting for the nightmare to recede.

It seemed so *real*. But it always did. He'd been having the same damned nightmare since he was a kid. When he'd started waking up screaming twice a week, his parents banned H. P. Lovecraft from the bookshelf and threw away his prized collection of E. C. Comics. It didn't help; the dream stayed with him. Sometimes it went away for months. Then, just when he thought he was rid of it forever, it would return with a fury, and haunt his sleep night after night. He would be forty-five this year, and the dream was as vivid as the first time he'd dreamt it.

It was always the same: the long walk through that nightmarish forest, the old New York City subway kiosk, the endless descent into the earth, and finally the cone-faced thing on the platform. Sometimes, just after he woke, Jay thought that there was more to the dream, that there were parts he was forgetting, but if that was truc, he didn't want to know.

Jay Ackroyd made his living as a private detective. He had a healthy respect for fear that had saved his life a time or two, but he didn't scare easily, at least not when he was awake. But he had one secret terror: that some night he would find himself standing on that platform, and the cone-faced thing would turn, and lift its head, and howl . . . and *he wouldn't wake up.*

"No fucking thanks," Jay said aloud.

He looked at the clock. A few minutes past five in the morning. No sense trying to get back to sleep. He was due at the Crystal Palace in less than two hours. Besides, after one of his dreams, nothing short of cardiac arrest would close his eyes again.

Jay stripped the bed, bundling sheets, blankets, and underwear in his hamper to take to the laundromat the next chance he got. He'd be sleeping on Crystal Palace sheets for the next week or two, however long this gig with Chrysalis lasted. He hoped like hell the nightmare went away for a little while. He didn't think Chrysalis would be too thrilled to learn her new bodyguard had a recurring nightmare that freaked him out so bad that he wet his bed. Especially if she was in the bed when he wet it. Jay had been hitting on Chrysalis for years, but she'd never succumbed to his charms. He was hoping this might be his chance. Her body was so *alive.* Beneath that transparent skin, you could see the blood rushing through her veins, the ghostly movement of half-seen muscles, the way her lungs worked under the bones of her rib cage. And she had great tits, even if they were mostly invisible.

He opened the window to air out his bedroom, although the odors wafting up the dingy airshaft to his third-floor walk-up were almost as foul as those in the room. After a long soak in his clawfoot tub, he dried himself off in a beach towel decorated with a rather threadbare picture of Opus the Penguin.

In the top drawer of his dresser, Jay found some clean boxer shorts. Black socks in the drawer below. Then he went to the closet and looked at his suits. He had a cool white linen number that was fashionably rumpled, a charcoal gray Brooks Brothers three-piece, a pinstripe from Hong Kong that had been precisely tailored to his measurements. Hiram Worchester had given him all three. Hiram was always after Jay to dress better. He'd get more respect, Hiram promised. He'd get noticed. He might even get girls. The part about the girls tempted him, but otherwise Jay was having none of it. "Hiram," he had explained, "I'm a PI. I sit in parked cars and donut shops. I shoot Polaroids through motel windows. I bribe doormen and hide in bushes. I don't *want* to be noticed. If they made a suit out of Holiday Inn wallpaper, I'd buy six of them." But every Christmas Hiram gave him another goddamned suit.

It looked like it was going to be hot. Jay picked out a short-sleeved white shirt with a button-down collar, a pair of dark brown slacks to match his hair, and a tan blazer. No tie. He hated ties.

7:00 A.M.

Brennan woke from a deep, dreamless sleep as the light from the rising sun shone through the window and touched his face. Jennifer Maloy turned over, murmuring, as he slipped silently from under the sheet that covered their futon and padded noiselessly to the chair where his clothes were laid out. He put on shorts, T-shirt, and running shoes, and went quietly through the back door that opened to the outside.

The sun was up, the land was half-awake, wet with dew and alive with the smells of a clean country morning. Brennan took a deep breath, filling his lungs with fresh air as he stretched, unlimbering his body for his daily run.

He jogged to the front of the A-frame house, slipping into a slow trot as he reached the looping gravel driveway. He turned left at the mouth of the driveway, scattering the rabbits playing on the front lawn, and passed the sign that read ARCHER LANDSCAPING AND NURSERY. He felt alive and clean, at peace with himself and the world at the beginning of another beautiful day.

♣

After his third knock went unanswered, Jay stepped inside the Crystal Palace.

The door wasn't locked. That surprised him. Chrysalis had been expecting him, yes, but she'd also been expecting trouble. Otherwise why bother to hire a bodyguard? When you're expecting trouble, you're supposed to lock your doors.

Jay poked his head into the darkened taproom. "Anyone home?" he called softly. "Chrysalis? Elmo?"

There was no answer. "Real good," he muttered under his breath. No wonder she needed a bodyguard. He considered turning on the lights, thought better of it, waited for his eyes to adjust. Slowly the outlines of the familiar room began to emerge from the gloom. Straight-back chairs upended on small round tables. The bar along one wall, rows of bottles stacked behind it against a long silver mirror. Booths across the way. And way in back, set off a little from the rest, the antique table in the private alcove where Chrysalis herself held court and sipped her amaretto.

For a moment, in the morning half-light, Jay thought he saw her sitting there, cloaked in shadow, slim ivory cigarette holder held lightly between skeletal fingers, smoke coiling lazily through the clear flesh of her throat as she tossed back her head to smile. "Chrysalis?" he said, walking slowly across the taproom. But her chair was empty when he reached it.

A strange chill went through him.

That was the moment when Jay Ackroyd knew.

He stood quietly beside the table, listening, remembering what he knew of the Crystal Palace. Chrysalis lived on the third floor, her chambers crowded with expensive Victoriana. Elmo, her dwarf bouncer, lived on the second floor. So did Sascha, the eyeless telepath who tended bar for her. All the public rooms were on the first floor. So was her office. Jay decided to start there.

The office was in the back of the building under the stairs. It had a wooden door, ornately carved, with a crystal doorknob. Jay took a rumpled handkerchief out of his pocket and turned the knob carefully with two fingers. The door swung open.

The room was windowless and black, but Jay didn't need eyes to know what he'd find inside. Death has a smell all its own. The hard coppery scent of blood, the sweaty stench of fear, the stink of shit. He'd smelled it before. The familiar miasma was there, waiting for him, and under it all was her perfume.

"Goddamn you," Jay said quietly to no one in particular. He reached over, handkerchief still in hand, and found the light switch.

Once, this room had had charm. Polished hardwood floors, a gorgeous Oriental rug, floor-to-ceiling bookcases full of leather-bound first editions, a solid oak desk older than he was, big leather armchairs that looked as though they might have come from the world's oldest men's club.

The chairs were shattered, wooden legs cracked and splintered, soft leather upholstery ripped and torn. Three of the high wooden bookcases had been toppled; one had been snapped in two. Splinters as long and pale as knives sprang from where the two halves clung together. Books were scattered everywhere.

Chrysalis lay sprawled on her back across the shattered remains of an armchair, the leather cushions and broken legs a jumble beneath her. The huge oak desk had been tipped over across the upper part of her body, hiding her face. She'd been wearing blue jeans and a plain white blouse. The front of the blouse was spattered with tiny droplets of blood. Her left leg bent the wrong way at the knee, and a jagged red piece of shinbone poked through the denim. Jay squatted by her left hand. He could see her finger bones through the ghostly outlines of tendons and the smooth, clear skin. All five fingers were shattered, the ring finger in two places; her crystalline flesh was suffused with the rosy glow of burst capillaries. Jay took her broken fingers in his own. A faint warmth still clung to her body, but she was cooling even as he held her.

After a moment, he released her hand and tried to lift the desk off her. It was heavy. He grimaced, shoved harder, and righted it with a grunt. Only when the desk was back against the wall did he look back down at Chrysalis.

Her face was gone.

Her skull hadn't been crushed as much it had been obliterated. The back cushion of her chair was sticky with dried blood. Bits of mashed brain oozed out between fragments of bone. Everything was red and wet. A small pool of blood had gathered under what was left of the chair, soaking into the Oriental rug. Jay looked up and saw more blood, a faint spray of it across the front of the desk and low on the walls, around the light socket. The patterned antique wallpaper was a gloomy purple color, very Victorian; it was hard to see the blood spatters, but they were there when you looked.

Jay stood up and tried not to feel anything. He'd seen bodies before, more than he cared to think about, and Chrysalis had been playing dangerous games for a long, long time. She knew too many secrets. Sooner or later, something like this was bound to happen.

He studied the position of the body, committing it to memory. It wasn't Chrysalis now, just dead meat, just evidence. When he'd seen all there was to see, Jay turned his attention to the rest of the room. That was when he first noticed the small rectangle of cardboard, lying beside her left thigh.

He moved around her and squatted for a closer look. He didn't touch it. He didn't have to. There wasn't a drop of blood on it, and it was lying faceup. A playing card.

The ace of spades.

"Son of a bitch," he said.

He was closing the office door behind him when he heard footsteps on the stairs. Jay pressed himself against a wall and waited. A moment later, a slender man with a pencil-thin mustache stepped into the hall. He wore slippers and a silk dressing gown, and there was an unbroken expanse of pale skin where his eyes should have been. His head turned slowly until he was looking into the shadows at Jay. "I can see your mind, Popinjay," he said.

Jay stepped out. "Call the police, Sascha," he said. "And don't call me Popinjay, dammit."

8:00 A.M.

Brennan leaned into the hill, arms pumping, breath flowing easily, sprinting up the steep grade near the end of the run that had taken him over forested hills and through dew-drenched meadows. The route he followed varied, but always ended at the unpaved county road that led him, sweaty and pleasantly winded, back to the gravel driveway with ARCHER LANDSCAPING AND NURSERY posted at the entrance.

The driveway looped around a series of gardens that were living advertisements of his horticultural skills. First was a Japanese miniature hill garden in the *tsukiyama* form, then an English shrubbery, and third a traditional flower bed blooming with a dozen different species of a dozen different hues. The driveway circled the flower bed and led past two greenhouses—one for tropical foliage, the other for desert species—and the A-frame house.

Brennan finished his run with a gut-busting sprint that brought him around behind the A-frame. He took a few minutes to cool down and calm his breathing, then folded himself comfortably into a meditative posture and gazed out over the *kare sansui*, the raked gravel bed rippling like frozen water in the morning breeze. Nested in the gravel were three rock triads. Brennan spent a timeless time sunk in the pool of *zazen*, not studying the rocks, their shadows, or the patterns of the moss that grew on them, then stood smoothly, relaxed, refreshed and ready for the day.

He went back into the bedroom that was sparsely furnished with a futon on the polished wood floor, a comfortable chair with a reading lamp and side table stacked with books, and a large wicker clothes hamper. Jennifer had gotten out of bed. He could hear water running in the shower of the connecting bathroom. Brennan took off his sweat-soaked T-shirt and dropped it in the hamper as he passed on through to the room that served as a combination living room/

office. He flicked on the television to get the morning news, then sat at his deck and fired up the PC to check his schedule.

He watched the television as the computer tracked down the proper file. Most of the news was devoted to the Democratic National Convention, convening today in Atlanta. Nothing of substance had happened yet, but the analysis and predictions already seemed overblown and overdone.

Gregg Hartmann was the favorite, but his nomination would be a struggle, particularly with the man directly opposite him in political philosophy and belief—the Reverend Leo Barnett.

Brennan distrusted all politicians, but if he could vote, he would cast his ballot for Hartmann. The man seemed honest and caring, especially when compared with the demagogue Barnett.

A lot of jokers were backing Hartmann. The news cameras panned the Atlanta public parks where they had gathered by the thousands to noisily show the nation their depth of support for the senator.

Brennan watched a few interviews with the joker on the street, then turned down the volume on the television set and turned his attention to the computer screen. He wished Hartmann and his joker supporters well, but the day was already getting old and he had his own worries.

His schedule had come up on the screen, and it promised to be a full day. Archer Landscaping was in the middle of two jobs. Brennan was building a hill garden with a *tsutaiochi*, a miniature waterfall trickling over a bed of emplaced rocks, for a Japanese-American banker who had just moved into the area, and he was also constructing a multiterraced shrubbery with a fish pond for a doctor who lived down the road. Joachim Ortiz, Brennan's foreman, would boss the crew at the doctor's while he took care of the other job. Japanese gardens were his personal specialty.

Brennan leaned back in the chair, still mildly surprised at the contentment he felt as he contemplated the upcoming day. Abandoning death and destruction and returning to the country to nurture life was the best thing he had ever done. He felt cleansed, content, and at peace for the first time in years. Sometimes he felt guilty for setting aside his vendetta against Kien and the Shadow Fist Society, but over the last few months the guilt had been coming less frequently and with less intensity.

He took his copy of *Sakuteiki*, Tachibana Toshisuna's classic treatise on garden design, from his reference shelf, but before he could look through it to get some ideas for the new job he stopped to stare at the image of a well-remembered woman that filled the television screen. He turned up the volume.

". . . mysterious woman known only as Chrysalis was found dead this morning in the office of her nightclub, the Crystal Palace. The police have so far refused comment, but an ace of spades found on her body has linked the slaying to the mysterious bow-and-arrow vigilante known as Yeoman, who was responsible for at least fifty deaths in 1986 and early 1987."

Brennan was still staring at the screen as Jennifer Maloy walked through the wall, damp from her shower, carrying two cups of tea.

"What's the matter?" she asked when she saw the expression on his face. "What happened?"

Brennan turned to her, the coldness back in his eyes, the hardness back on his face. "Chrysalis is dead."

"Dead?" she echoed, unbelievingly.

"Murdered."

"How? By who?" Jennifer asked as she sank down into the chair facing him. She handed him one of the cups. He took it mechanically and put it aside.

"Report didn't say. But her killer tried to frame me by putting an ace of spades on the body."

"Frame you? Why?"

Brennan looked at her for the first time. "I don't know. But I'm going to find out."

"The police—"

"The police think I did it."

"That's insane," Jennifer said. "We haven't been to the city for over a year."

They'd been so busy that it hadn't seemed that long since Brennan had called off his vendetta against the Shadow Fist crime lord named Kien and left New York City with Jennifer. They'd spent some time traveling, some time resting and healing and learning to love one another, then settled down outside of Goshen, a small town just north of New York City. Jennifer had begun writing what she hoped would become the definitive biography of Robert Tomlin. Brennan, weary of dealing in death, wanting to build rather than destroy, had started a landscaping business. He found that he had a genuine talent for horticulture, and Jennifer was happy researching and writing her book. They'd been quite content with their quiet, peaceful, isolated existence.

"Someone set me up," Brennan said in a low voice.

"Who?"

He looked at Jennifer. "Kien."

She leaned back, considering it. "Why?"

Brennan shrugged. "Maybe he found out that Chrysalis knew he was head of the Shadow Fists. Maybe he thought that he could get rid of her and me at the same time."

"The police would never find you if we stay here."

"Maybe," Brennan conceded. "But maybe they'll never find Chrysalis's real killer, either."

"We're building something here," Jennifer said. "We can't just let it go."

Let it go. It should be easy, Brennan told himself, to let the past go, to live for the present and the future. But he couldn't. Someone had murdered his ex-lover. He couldn't forget that. And then the murderer had framed him for it. He couldn't forgive that.

He stood up. "I'm not letting anything go. I can't."

Jennifer just looked at him. After a moment he turned and went out to the back and unlocked the shed where he kept his bows and guns. He loaded the van and sat waiting in it for several minutes, wondering if Jennifer was going to join him.

After a while he started the engine and drove away, alone.

NOON

Maseryk played the good cop, Kant played the bad cop, and both of them deserved rave reviews. Jay Ackroyd had seen the act before, though. Maseryk was lean and dark, with intense violet eyes. Kant was a hairless scaled joker with nictitating membranes and pointed teeth. As Jay ran through his story for the seventh time, he found himself wondering whether they swapped roles when the suspect was a joker. He took one look at Kant and decided not to ask.

By lunchtime, even the two detectives had gotten tired of going round the mulberry bush. "If you're playing games with us, you're going to be real sorry," Kant said, showing his incisors.

Jay gave him a *who, me?* look. "I'm sure Mr. Ackroyd's told us everything he knows, Harv," Maseryk said. "If you do happen to remember anything else that might be of use, you'll give us a call." Maseryk gave him his card, Kant told him not to leave town, and they walked him to the squad room to sign a copy of his statement.

The precinct house was full of familiar faces. The doorman from the Crystal Palace was giving a statement to a uniformed cop while a waitress that Chrysalis has fired last month sobbed loudly in the corner. Other Palace employees waited on long wooden benches by the window. He recognized three waiters, a dishwasher, and the guy who played ragtime piano in the Green Room on Thursday nights. But the most important faces were the ones he didn't see.

Lupo, the relief bartender, sat alone by an unoccupied desk. After he'd dealt with the paperwork, Jay drifted over. "Can you believe it?" the joker asked. "What's going to happen to us?" Lupo had deep-set red eyes and a wolf's face. He'd been shedding; there were hairs all over the shoulders of his denim shirt. Jay brushed them off. Lupo hardly seemed to notice. "I hear it was you found the body," he said. "Was it really the ace-of-spades guy?"

"There was a card next to the body," Jay said.

"Yeoman," Lupo muttered angrily. "Son of a bitch. I thought he was gone for good. He used to drink Tullamore Dew. I served him once or twice."

"Ever see him without the mask?"

Lupo shook his head. "No. I hope they catch the fucker." His long red tongue lolled from a corner of his mouth.

Jay looked around the room again. "Where's Elmo?"

"No one's seen him. I heard the cops got a whatchacallit, a APB, out on him."

Kant came up behind them. "Your turn, Lupo," he said, gesturing toward an interrogation room. He stared at Jay. "You still here."

"I'm going, I'm going," Jay said. "As soon as I use the little cops' room."

Kant told him where to find it. By the time Jay emerged, Kant and Maseryk and Lupo were off doing their thing. Jay went back to the captain's cubicle and walked in unannounced.

Captain Angela Ellis was behind the desk, chain-smoking as she scanned a file, flipping pages like a speed reader. She was a tiny Asian woman with green eyes, long black hair, and the toughest job in the NYPD. Her immediate predecessor had been found dead in this office, supposedly of a heart attack, but there were still people who didn't buy that. The captain before him had been murdered, too.

"So," he asked, "you have a lead on Elmo yet?"

Ellis took a drag on her cigarette and looked at him. It took her a moment to remember who he was. "Ackroyd," she finally said, with distaste. "I was just reading your statement. There are holes in your story I could drive a truck through.'"

"I can't help that, it's the only story I've got. What kind of story did you get from Sascha?"

"A short one." Ellis stood and began to pace. "He woke up, sensed a strange mind in the building, and came downstairs to find you sneaking out of Chrysalis's office."

"I didn't sneak," Jay said. "I sneak very well, I majored in sneaking in detective school, but on this particular occasion I didn't happen to be sneaking. And there's nothing strange about my mind, thank you. So you don't have a thing on Elmo yet?"

"What do you know about Elmo?" Ellis asked.

"Short guy," Jay said.

"Strong guy," Ellis mused. "Strong enough to smash a woman's head into blood pudding, maybe."

"Real good," Jay said, "only wrong. Elmo was devoted to the lady. Utterly. No way he'd hurt her."

Her laugh was hard and humorless. "Ackroyd, you may be the world's chief authority on philandering husbands, but you don't know much about killers. They don't waste the real atrocities on strangers, they save them for family and friends." She started to pace again. Ash fell off the end of her cigarette. "Maybe your friend Elmo was a little too devoted. I heard Chrysalis fucked around a lot. Maybe he got tired of seeing the parade go in and out of her bedroom, or maybe he made a pass of his own and she laughed at him."

"You setting up Elmo to take the fall?" he asked.

Ellis paused over her desk just long enough to stub out her cigarette in an ashtray overflowing with butts. "No one gets set up in this precinct."

"Since when?" Jay asked.

"Since I took over as captain," she told him. She took a pack of Camels out of her jacket, tapped one out, lit up, and resumed pacing. "You're supposed to be a detective. Look at the facts." She stopped at the wall long enough to straighten a framed diploma, then spun back toward him. "Her head looked like a cantaloupe run over by a semi. Both legs broken, every finger in her left hand snapped, her pelvis shattered in six places, massive internal hemorrhaging." She jabbed the cigarette at him for emphasis. "I had a case once, back when I was on the street, where some Gambione capos went to work on a guy with tire irons. Broke every bone in his body. Another time I saw what was left of a hooker who'd been done in by a pimp fried on angel dust. He'd used a baseball bat. Those were pretty ugly, but they looked a. lot better than Chrysalis. Those weren't normal blows. Nobody's that strong. Nobody but an ace, or a joker with super-human strength."

"A lot of people fit that description," Jay pointed out.

"Only one of them lived in the Crystal Palace," Ellis pointed out. She crossed behind the desk, sat down, opened a file folder. "Elmo was strong enough—"

"Maybe," Jay said. Elmo was way stronger than a nat, that was true enough, but there were others who made him look like a ninety-seven-pound weakling. The Harlem Hammer, Troll, Carnifex, the Oddity, even that golden asshole Jack Braun. Whether Elmo actually had the raw power to do what had been done to Chrysalis was a question Jay didn't have the expertise to answer.

Captain Ellis ignored his quibbling. "He also had the opportunity, anytime he wanted." She began rearranging a stack of files in her OUT basket, dropping ash on them in the process.

"I don't buy it," Jay said.

"If Elmo is so goddamned innocent, where is he?" Ellis asked, toying with her stapler. "We searched his room. The bed hadn't been slept in. He hasn't returned to the Palace. Where'd he go?"

Jay shrugged. "Out." She had him there, but he was damned if he was going to admit it. "Seems to me you got another candidate who's a lot riper than Elmo."

Captain Angela Ellis slammed down the stapler and blew a long plume of smoke across the room. "Ah. Right. The ace-of-spades killer." She didn't sound impressed. "We're going to find Elmo," she promised, crushing out her cigarette. "And when we do, five'll get you ten it turns out your dwarf pal dropped that card. You can buy a deck of playing cards at any five-and-ten. You're supposed to be a bright boy, Ackroyd. Figure it out for yourself."

"Maybe I will," Jay said.

Angela Ellis didn't like that one bit. Her bright green eyes narrowed as she stood up. "Lemme make one thing real clear. I don't like PIs. And I don't like aces. So you can probably guess how I feel about ace PIs. You start getting in our way on this one, you can just kiss your license good-bye."

"You're beautiful when you're angry," Jay said.

Ellis ignored him. "I don't like bodies cluttering up my precinct either."

"You must be unhappy a lot of the time," Jay said as he headed for the door. He paused in the doorway to study her little glass-walled cubicle. "This really where they killed Captain Black?" he asked innocently.

"Yes," she snapped, irritated. Jay figured he'd hit a sore point. Knowing the NYPD, they probably hadn't even gotten her a new chair. "What the hell are you doing?" she said.

"Getting a good picture of the place in my head," Jay said. He smiled crookedly and made his right hand into a gun, three fingers folded down, thumb cocked like a hammer, index finger pointed at Angela Ellis. "I'm a good boy, Captain. If I bump into your killer, I'll want to send him right here to you."

She looked puzzled for a moment, then flushed when she remembered what he could do. "Aces," she muttered. "Get the hell out of here."

He did. Kant and Maseryk were back in the squad room. "Captain on the rag?" Jay asked as he passed. They exchanged looks and watched him leave. Jay went out the front door, walked around the block, went back in, and took the steps down to the basement.

The precinct records were kept in a dimly lit, low-ceilinged room next to the boiler, part of which had been the coal cellar once upon a time. Now it held a couple of computer consoles, a xerox machine, a wall of overflowing steel filing cabinets, and one very pale, very short, very nearsighted policeman.

"Hello, Joe," Jay said.

Joe Mo turned around and sniffed at the stale air. He was just under five feet tall, stooped and potbellied, with a complexion the color of a mushroom. Tiny pink eyes peered out from behind the largest, thickest pair of tinted spectacles that Jay had ever seen. White, hairless hands rubbed together nervously. Mo had been the first joker on the NYPD, and for more than a decade he'd been the *only* joker on the NYPD. His appointment, forced through under the banner of affirmative action during Mayor Hartmann's administration in the early seventies, had drawn so much fire that the department had promptly hidden him down in Records to keep him out of public view. Joe hadn't minded. He liked Records almost as much as he liked basements. They called him Sergeant Mole.

"Popinjay," Mo said. He adjusted his glasses. The milk white of his skin was shocking against the dark blue of his uniform, and he always wore his cap, night and day, even indoors. "Is it true?"

"Yeah, it's true," Jay told him. Mo had been a pariah when he'd joined the force, even in Fort Freak. No one had wanted to partner him, and he'd been made unwelcome in the usual cop bars. He'd been doing his off-duty drinking in the Crystal Palace since its doors first opened, paying for every drink in a rather ostentatious show of rectitude, and collecting ten times his tab under the table for acting as Chrysalis's eyes and ears in the cophouse.

"I heard you were the one found the body," Joe Mo said. "Nasty business, wasn't it? Makes you wonder what Jokertown is coming to.

You'd think *she'd* be safe, if anyone was." He blinked behind the dark, thick lenses. "What can I do for you, dear boy?"

"I need to see the file on the ace-of-spades killer."

"Yeoman," Joe Mo said.

"Yeoman," Jay Ackroyd repeated thoughtfully. It came back to him then. *Yeoman, I don't care for this,* Chrysalis had said with ice in her voice, that night a year and a half ago when they'd faced off in the darkened taproom of the Palace. She was always a master of understatement. "I remember," he said.

"Why, there hasn't been a new bow-and-arrow killing in more than a year," Mo said. "You really think he's the one?"

"I hope not," Jay said. Yeoman had entered the taproom silent as smoke, and before anyone even noticed him, he'd had a hunting arrow notched and ready. But Hiram Worchester had stepped in the way in righteous indignation, and Jay had gotten the drop on the guy. Suddenly Yeoman was gone in a *pop* of in-rushing air. Jay Ackroyd was a projecting teleport. When his right hand made a gun, he could pop his targets anyplace he knew well enough to visualize.

Only he'd sent that fucker Yeoman to the wrong damn place. "I had the sonofabitch dead to rights, Joe," he said. "I could have popped him right into the Tombs. Instead I sent him to the middle of the Holland Tunnel, God knows why." Something about his tone when he'd replied to Chrysalis, maybe, or the loathing in his eyes when he glanced toward Wyrm, or maybe the fact that he'd had the decency to hesitate when Hiram stepped forward and blocked his shot. Or it could have been the girl he had with him, the masked blonde in the string bikini who seemed so fresh and innocent.

It hadn't been what you call a deliberate, conscious decision; a lot of the time Jay just went on gut instinct. But if he'd been wrong that night, then Chrysalis had paid for it with her life. "I really need to see that file," he said.

Joe Mo made a sad little clucking sound. "Why, that file's up on the captain's desk, Jay. She sent down for it right away, soon as the squeal came in. Of course, I made a xerox before I sent it up. It always pays to make a xerox. Sometimes things get misplaced, and you don't want to lose any valuable documents." He blinked slowly, looked around. "Now where did I put that? It's a wonder I ever find anything, with my eyes."

The copies were on top of the xerox machine. Jay riffled through the folder, rolled up the papers and slid them under his blazer, replaced them with two twenties. "I'm sure you'll sniff them out," he said.

"If not," Joe said, with a wide pink smile, "I can always wait till the captain returns the originals, and xerox another set." He busied himself with some filing, but when Jay opened the door to leave, he called out quietly, "Popinjay."

Jay looked back. "What?"

"Find the bastard," Joe Mo said. He took off his tinted specs, and his pale pink eyes implored. "All of us will help," he promised, and Jay knew he wasn't talking about the police.

◆

As he drove down Route 17, alone, Brennan was already missing Jennifer. He couldn't blame her for not accompanying him on a quest to find Chrysalis's murderer. And it didn't help any that she'd been right. They had a quiet, beautiful life. Why was he so ready to return to the death waiting him in the city?

It wasn't, Brennan knew, because he enjoyed the killing and the violence. He'd rather build a garden than dodge bullets in a stinking, garbage-choked alley. It all came down to what Jennifer had said about letting things go. He just couldn't get Chrysalis out of his mind. He didn't think of her often. He was too satisfied with his life with Jennifer to dwell morbidly on what might have been with another woman.

But sometimes at night he'd lie awake with Jennifer asleep beside him and remember the crystal lady. He'd remember her invisible flesh flushed to a delicate pink with the passion of their lovemaking, he'd remember her cries and moves in the dark. He'd remember and wonder what it would've been like if she'd accepted his offer of protection and love. He would look at Jennifer asleep at his side and know that he was happy and content, but he would still wonder. The memory of her was a throbbing ache that wouldn't leave him alone.

He buried the van in the Tomlin International parking lot and caught a taxi to Manhattan, where he took a room in a cheap but dirty hotel on the fringe of Jokertown. The first thing to do, he decided, was visit the Crystal Palace. He slipped on his mask for the first time in over a year and left the hotel carrying his bow case.

3:00 P.M.

ACE-OF-SPADES KILLER SLAYS JOKERTOWN BARKEEP, the *Post* screamed.

The *Jokertown Cry* was less generic. CHRYSALIS MURDERED, it said beside a two-column picture. The *Cry* was the only paper in the city that regularly ran photographs of jokers.

JOKERS DESCEND ON ATLANTA AS DEMOCRATS CONVENE, said the front page of the *Times*. Thousands of them had headed south in support of Senator Gregg Hartmann, the presidential frontrunner. But in this year's crowded Democratic field, nobody was even close to a majority, and a brokered convention was being predicted. There were widespread fears of violence should Hartmann be denied the nomination. Already there were reports of ugly clashes between Hartmann's jokers and the fundamentalist supporters of Reverend Leo Barnett.

Jay usually ranked politicians right alongside used-car salesmen, pimps, and the guy who invented pay toilets, but Hartmann did seem to be a breed apart. He'd met the candidate a few times at the fundraisers Hiram had hosted at Aces High. Hiram was a big Hartmann supporter, and Jay never could resist the lure of free food and drink. Senator Gregg seemed intelligent, effective, and compassionate. If somebody had to be president, it might as well be him. He probably didn't stand a joker's chance of getting anywhere near the nomination.

The political bullshit took up the whole front page; he couldn't find any mention of Chrysalis anywhere. Knowing the *Times*, Jay figured tomorrow's edition would have a brief obit and that'd be it. Brutal joker murders weren't the kind of news that's fit to print. That made Jay angriest of all.

"How do you know when a joker's been dead about three days?"

the news vendor asked him. His voice was flat and lifeless, the voice of a man grimly going through a ritual that had lost its meaning. Jay looked up from the headlines.

Jube Benson had been a fixture on the corners of Hester Street and the Bowery for as long as there had been a Jokertown. Walrus, they called him. He was a joker himself, three hundred pounds of greasy blue-black flesh, big curved tusks at the corners of his mouth, a broad domed skull covered with tufts of stiff red hair. Jube's wardrobe seemed to consist exclusively of Hawaiian shirts. This afternoon he was wearing a magenta item in a tasteful pineapple-and-banana print. Jay wondered what Hiram would say.

Jube knew more joker jokes than anyone else in Jokertown, but this time Jay had the punch line. "He smells a lot better," he said wearily. "That one's older than your hat, Walrus."

Jube took the battered porkpie hat off his head and turned it over self-consciously in his thick, three-fingered hands. "I never made her laugh," he said. "All those years, I came by the Palace every night, always with a new joke. I never got a single laugh out of her."

"She didn't think being a joker was very funny," said Jay.

"You got to laugh," Jube said. "What else is there?" He put his hat back on. "I hear you were the one that found her."

"Word gets around quick," Jay said.

"It gets around quick," Jube agreed.

"She phoned me last night," Jay told him. "She wanted to take me on as a bodyguard. I asked her how long and she couldn't tell me. Maybe she wouldn't tell me. I asked her what she was scared of. She laughed it off and said I'd found her out, it was just a ruse, she was really hot for my body. That was when I realized how shaky she was. She was trying her damnedest to sound wry and cool and British, like nothing was wrong, but her accent kept slipping. Something had frightened her badly. I want to know what, Jube."

"All I know is what I read in the papers," Jube said.

Jay just gave him a look. As long as Chrysalis had been brokering information, the Walrus had been one of her chief snitches. All day long Jube stood in his kiosk, watching and listening, joking and gossiping with everyone who stopped to buy a paper. "C'mon," Jay said impatiently.

Jube glanced nervously up and down the street. No one was near them. "Not here," the fat joker said. "Let me close up. We'll go to my place."

♠

Brennan watched with wry amusement as the armless joker pick-pocket worked the gawkers who had gathered around the Crystal Palace. The dipper was dressed in threadbare, but carefully patched clothes. His pants were specially tailored to fit his third, centrally located leg that ended in an oddly configured foot whose toes were more dexterous than most people's fingers. He was using this limb to pick the pockets of his unsuspecting victims.

A bright yellow crime-scene ribbon roped off the Palace's cano-pied entrance. The crowd gathered before it was gossiping—mostly wildly and inaccurately—about the Crystal Palace and its mysteri-ous proprietress. Newsies and street merchants were working the crowd along with the pickpocket, who suddenly turned with the sixth sense of the often-hunted and looked right at Brennan.

Brennan nodded back and the three-legged joker cut through the crowd and headed toward him, lurching in a peculiar rocking gait, sometimes placing his third "foot" on the ground to balance him-self.

"Hello, Mr. Y," he murmured.

Brennan nodded again. The joker's name was Tripod. He was a hustler, a small-time grifter who lived on the edge of the law. During Brennan's last stay in the city he'd been one of his best sources of information. He was dependable for a snitch. He didn't have a drug habit and he was loyal. When he was bought, he stayed bought.

"Pretty awful, what happened, Mr. Y," he offered in his quiet, def-erential manner. If he wondered about Brennan's sudden reappear-ance after a year's absence, he said nothing.

Brennan nodded. "You hear the police think I killed her?"

Tripod shrugged. It was a peculiar gesture for a man who had no arms.

"Maybe, Mr. Y, but it wasn't done in your style."

"How do you know how she was killed?"

"Man over there," Tripod said, gesturing at a derelict who sat on the curb by a hotdog cart, "said he saw her body when they brung her out to the coroner's wagon."

Brennan glanced at the cart. SAUERKRAUT SAM THE HOTDOG MAN was lettered on its side. It was manned by a joker who was continuously dispensing dogs, making change, and slapping mustard, catsup, sauerkraut, and relish on waiting buns with his extra sets of arms. The derelict sitting on the curb was bloated and alcoholic, but seemed to be a nat. He'd stationed himself next to the cart to cadge coins while endlessly repeating his story to all who would listen. Brennan nodded at Tripod and they joined the gawkers who were munching hot dogs and listening to the old man.

"I was in the back when they brung her out. I was there all right. I got a nice place to sleep right by the dumpster and the ambulance woke me up. I was scared. I didn't know what all the fuss was about, but pretty soon they brung her out. I could see it was Chrysalis. I seen her a lot of times and it was her. She was dead, all right." He lowered his voice and leaned forward to whisper conspiratorially to his two dozen or so listeners. "Her head was squashed. Just squashed. If it weren't for her invisible skin, you couldn't tell who it was. Squashed, just like a watermelon dropped from a ten-story building." He nodded with some satisfaction at his simile. "I was there all right. I saw her when they brung her out. . . ."

Brennan, impotent anger knotting his stomach, turned away from the cart as a cop came up and hassled the vendor about his license. Sauerkraut Sam complained in a loud voice with angry gesticulations of all his arms, but it didn't seem to get him anywhere.

Brennan and Tripod stood silently for a moment, watching the cop run off the hotdog vendor, who was wheeling his cart with four arms and still angrily gesturing with the others.

Chrysalis had been killed by someone—an ace—strong enough to smash her utterly. That was at least a place to start an investigation. But Brennan knew he could use more information. A lot more information.

"You seen Elmo or Sascha around?" Brennan asked Tripod, after the crowd that'd been munching hot dogs and listening to the derelict had dispersed.

The joker shook his head. "They're gone, Mr. Y. Ain't seen 'em, ain't heard of 'em all day."

Brennan sighed to himself. He knew, right away, that this was not going to be easy. He took two twenties out of his pocket and surreptitiously dropped them on the sidewalk. Tripod's bare foot closed over them. His nimble toes picked them up and stuffed them in one of the pockets he'd sewn on the bottom of his pant leg.

"Keep an eye out for them. For anything about the killing. You can get in touch with me at the Victoria. I'm registered as Archer."

"Yessir." Tripod watched Brennan for a moment. "Good to see you again, Mr. Y."

"I wish I could say it was good to be back."

Tripod nodded once, then started down the street with his peculiar lurching gait. Brennan watched him go, then turned back to the Palace. The crowd of gawkers was still there. He wanted to get a good look at the crime scene, but now obviously wasn't the time for that. He'd come back when it was quiet and dark.

Now he had other avenues to explore. He wasn't convinced that Kien was actually behind Chrysalis's death, but it was as good a place as any to start his investigation. Kien, of course, wouldn't have done the killing himself, but the Shadow Fists had plenty of hired muscle capable of doing the job. Wyrm, for example, Kien's extraordinarily strong bodyguard, whom Brennan had witnessed threaten Chrysalis two Wild Card Days ago.

Of course, he'd been out of touch a long time. Things had probably changed, but there were people he could talk to, people who would be willing to pass on the latest information. Brennan hefted his bow case and started down the street.

The hunter had returned to the city.

4:00 P.M.

Jube lived in the basement of a rooming house on Eldridge, in an apartment with bare brick walls and a lingering odor of rotting meat. His living room featured a lot of second-hand furniture and some kind of weird modern sculpture, an imposing floor-to-ceiling construct with angles out of Escher and a bowling ball at its center. Every now and then the bowling ball seemed to glow.

"I call it *Joker Lust*," Jube told him. "You think that's strange looking, you ought to meet the girl who modeled for it. Don't look too long, it'll give you a headache. Want a drink?"

St. Elmo's fire flickered disturbingly across the surface of the construct. Jay sat down on the edge of the couch. "I'll take a scotch and soda," he said. "Go easy on the soda."

"All I've got is rum," Jube said, waddling into his kitchen.

"Yum," Jay said, deadpan. "Sure."

Jube brought him a water tumbler half-full of dark rum, with a single ice cube floating on the surface. "The papers say it was the ace-of-spades killer," he said as he eased his bulk into a recliner, his own glass of rum in hand. His was decorated with a little paper parasol. "The *Post* and the *Cry* both."

"There was an ace of spades next to the body," Jay agreed, sipping his drink. "The cops don't buy it."

"How about you?"

He shrugged. "I don't know." He'd spent the last couple of hours reading the police file on the yahoo who signed himself "Yeoman." Now he wasn't sure what to think. "The M.O. is all wrong. Our friend likes to litter the landscape with corpses, but most of them have arrows sticking out of sensitive parts of their anatomy."

"I remember the papers used to call him the bow-and-arrow killer, too," Jube said.

Jay nodded. "Not that he isn't flexible. If he can't put a razor-tipped broadhead through your eye, he'll strangle you with a bowstring or use an arrow with an explosive tip to blow you to hell. The cops have him down for one job with a knife and two with bare hands, but those have question marks next to them. Mostly he goes in for theme murders. He's got a real grudge against Orientals, too, judging from the number he's offed. But he's not fussy, he'll kill anyone in a pinch." Jay sighed. "The only problem is, Chrysalis was beaten to death by someone who was inhumanly strong, and our friend with the playing-card fetish is a nat."

"How can you be sure?" Jube asked.

"I took a crack at archery once," Jay said. "It's hard. You'd need to work at it for years to get good, and this psycho is a lot better than good. Why bother, if you're an ace?"

Jube plucked thoughtfully at one of his tusks. "Yeah," he said, "only . . ." The fat little joker hesitated.

"What?" Jay prompted.

"Well," Jube said reluctantly, "I think maybe Chrysalis *was* frightened of the guy."

"Tell me," Jay said.

"The last ace-of-spades murder was something like a year ago," Jube said. "Then they just stopped. It was about the same time that Chrysalis changed. I'm sure of it."

"Changed how?" Jay asked.

"It's hard to explain. She tried to act the same, but if you saw her every night like I did, you could see she wasn't. She was too . . . too *interested*, if you know what I mean. Before, when you came to her with some information to sell, she always acted a little bored, like she didn't care one way or the other, but this last year, it was like she didn't want to miss any little piece of information, no matter how trivial. And she was especially desperate for any kind of word on Yeoman. She offered to pay extra."

"Shit," Jay said. This put him back at square one.

"You couldn't exactly tell if she was frightened, not with Chrysalis," Jube said. "You know how she was. She always had to be in control. But Digger was jumpy enough for both of them."

"Digger?" Jay asked.

"Thomas Downs," Jube said. "That reporter from *Aces* magazine. Everyone calls him Digger. He's been hanging around the Crystal Palace ever since he and Chrysalis came back from that round-the-world tour last year. Two, three nights a week. He'd come in, she'd see him, and they'd go upstairs."

"Was he getting any?" Jay asked.

"He stayed past closing all the time," Jube said. "Maybe Elmo or Sascha could tell you if he was still there in the morning." He scratched at one of the stiff red bristles on the side of his head. "Elmo, anyway."

That comment struck Jay as odd. "Why not Sascha? He's the telepath. He'd know who she was fucking if anyone would."

"Sascha wasn't spending as much time around the Palace as he used to. He's been seeing this woman. A Haitian, I hear, lives down by the East River. Word is she's some kind of hooker. One of the roomers here, Reginald, works night security at a warehouse near there. He says Sascha comes and goes a lot. Sometimes he doesn't leave until dawn."

"Not good," Jay said. He was starting to get an inkling of why Chrysalis thought she needed a bodyguard. Sascha had never been a major-league telepath, only a skimmer plucking random thoughts off the surface of a mind, but for years his abilities had sufficed to give Chrysalis early warning of any approaching trouble. But if Sascha had been spending a lot of nights out . . .

"There's something else," Jube said. Thick blue-black fingers worried at a tusk again. "About ten, eleven months ago, Chrysalis had a whole new security system installed. Cost a fortune, all state-of-the-art-stuff. I know a man who works for the company that did the work. According to what I heard, Chrysalis wanted them to design— now get this—some kind of defense to kill anybody who tried to *walk through her walls!*"

Jay picked up the glass. The ice cube had melted. He didn't like the taste of rum anyway. He drained the glass in one long swallow, feeling more and more angry with himself.

Yeoman had come in through the front door, that night at the Crystal Palace. None of them heard him enter, but when they looked up he was there. But his girlfriend, the sexy little blond bimbo in the black string bikini . . . *she* came in through a wall, stepping out of the mirror behind the bar, and ducking out the same way after Jay sent Yeoman off to play in traffic.

"What's wrong?" Jube asked.

"Nothing but my goddamned instincts," Jay said bitterly. "Did they build her the trap she wanted?"

"They told her there was no such thing," Jube replied.

"Pity," Jay said. "Pity."

♥

The Church of Our Lady of Perpetual Misery was nearly empty. A few scattered penitents were kneeling on the scarred wooden pews, head—or heads—bowed in silent prayer to the god who was more real to them than the clean-featured Jesus of the old Bible. The hunchback called Quasiman was puttering about the altar, humming to himself as he dusted the tabernacle. Dressed in a sharply pressed lumberjack shirt and clean jeans, he moved in a stiff, jerky manner, dragging his left leg behind him. The wild card virus had twisted his body, but had also given him extraordinary physical strength and the ability to teleport. He put the tabernacle down and watched Brennan as he approached the altar.

"Hello," Brennan said. "I'm here to see Father Squid."

"Hello." Quasiman's eyes were dark and soulful, his voice soft and deep. "He's in the chancellery."

"Thanks—" Brennan began to say, but stopped when he realized that Quasiman was staring at him with unfocused eyes. The joker's jaw was slack and a line of spittle drooled down his chin. It was obvious that his mind was wandering. Brennan simply nodded to him and went through the door at which he still pointed.

Father Squid was sitting behind his battered wooden desk, reading a book. He looked up and smiled when Brennan knocked on the open door. Or at least he looked as though he smiled.

Father Squid was an immense, squat man in a plain cassock that covered his massive torso like a tent. His skin was gray, thick, and hairless. His eyes were large and bright, and gleamed wetly behind their nictitating membranes. His mouth was masked by a fall of short tentacles that dangled like a constantly twitching mustache. His hands, closing the book and setting it on the desk before him, were large, with long, slim, attenuated fingers. Rows of circular pads—vestigial suckers—lined his palm. He smelled faintly, not unpleasantly, of the sea.

"Come in, sit down." He regarded Brennan with the benign affection with which he usually faced the world. "Here I am reading the words of an old friend"—he gestured at the book, *A Year in One Man's Life: The Journal of Xavier Desmond*—"and another old friend appears. Though"—he wiggled his long fingers in reproach—"it would have been nice if you had dropped by to see me before you vanished. I was somewhat worried about you."

Brennan smiled with little humor. "Sorry, Father. I told Tachyon my plans, trusting he'd pass the word to those who cared. I hadn't figured on ever returning to the city, but recent events have made me change my mind."

Father Squid looked troubled. "I can guess. The death of Chrysalis. I knew that you two were . . . close . . . at one time."

"The police say I killed her."

"Yes, I'd heard."

"And not believed?"

Father Squid shook his head. "No, my son. You would never have killed Chrysalis. While I can't say that I approve of some of the things you've done, only he who is without sin should cast the first stone, and I'm afraid that the antics of a far from unblemished youth have left me unable to claim spiritual purity." Father Squid sighed. "Chrysalis, poor girl, was a sad soul searching for salvation. I hope that now she has at least found peace."

"I hope so, too," Brennan said. "And I'll find her killer."

"The police—" Father Squid began.

"Think I did it."

The priest shrugged massive shoulders. "Perhaps. Perhaps for now they are grasping at straws, but will eventually set their feet upon the proper path. I'll not deny you my help if you are determined to proceed on your own. If, that is, I know anything of value." He rubbed the spot where his nasal tentacles gathered. "Although I cannot conceive what I would know that would be useful in tracking her killer."

"Maybe you can help me find someone who does know something."

"Who?"

"Sascha. He does belong to your church, doesn't he?"

"Sascha Starfin is a faithful churchgoer," the priest said, "though, upon thinking about it, it has been quite a while since he's partaken of Communion."

"He's disappeared," Brennan said, more concerned with tracking down Sascha's body than with the state of his soul. "You know that he lived at the Palace. I think he's gone into hiding because he witnessed the murder."

Father Squid nodded. "That may be. Have you tried his mother's apartment?"

"No," Brennan said. "Where is it?"

"The Russian section of Brighton Beach," Father Squid said, giving specifics.

"Thanks. You've been a big help." Brennan rose to leave, then hesitated and turned back to the priest. "One last thing. Do you know where Quasiman was early this morning?"

Father Squid looked solemnly at Brennan. "Surely you don't suspect him? He has the gentlest of souls."

"And very strong hands."

Father Squid nodded. "That is true. But you can take his name off your list of suspects. As you may know, it has become something of a nat fad to acquire joker remains—bodies, skeletons, what have you—as conversation pieces. Quasiman was guarding our cemetery last night. At least I hope he was. He forgets things, you know."

"I've heard. Was he there all night?"

"All night."

"Alone?"

Father Squid hesitated a beat. "Well, yes."

Brennan nodded. "Thanks again."

Father Squid raised his hand in benediction. "God go with you. I shall say a prayer for you. And," he added quietly as Brennan left, "for Chrysalis's murderer. With you on his trail, he shall certainly need someone to pray for the repose of his soul."

7:00 P.M.

A small crowd had gathered on the sidewalks outside the Crystal Palace, and four police cruisers were parked out in front, a fifth by the alley in back.

As Jay climbed out of the cab, he recognized Maseryk standing beside one of the cop cars, talking on the police radio. The building was sealed off. The steps up to the main entrance had been blocked with sawhorses, and a yellow crime-scene banner was draped across the door. There were lights in the third-floor windows. He figured they were giving her private rooms a real good hard look. A couple of uniforms prowled through the rubble-strewn lot next door, shining flashlights into holes, looking for God knows what.

The gawkers watched everything with interest, muttering to each other all the while. It was the usual Jokertown street crowd, mostly jokers, with a slumming nat or two standing nervously on the fringe. Hookers cruised the sidewalk across the street, soliciting right under the noses of the cops. Off to one side, four Werewolves in gang colors and Mae West masks were having a fine old time cracking wise to each other. A few Crystal Palace regulars stood looking on.

Maseryk hung up the phone. Jay walked over. "So," he said, "the murderer return to the scene of the crime yet?"

"You're here," Maseryk pointed out.

"Droll," Jay said. "Find any prints?"

"Plenty. So far we've got yours, hers, Elmo's, Sascha's, Lupo's, you name it. What we're not finding are the files."

"Ah," said Jay noncommittally.

"There's such a thing as knowing too much for your own good. Kant thinks our motive is somewhere in those secret files."

"Real good," Jay said, watching a very nice rear end in a tight leather miniskirt sway past. "For a lizard." He was turning back to Maseryk when he noticed a hooded shape standing in the mouth of an alley half a block away.

"I'll tell him you said that," Maseryk said, with the barest hint of a smile.

"The thing of it is," Jay said, "if Kant finds that cache of information, he may get more than he bargained for. Motives are like fingerprints, too many are as bad as none at all." He glanced back toward the alley. The hooded man stood in shadow, watching the Palace. His head turned, and Jay caught a brief flash of metal as the light reflected off the steel-mesh fencing mask beneath the hood.

"I'm sure he'll be grateful for that hint. Any other words of advice you want me to pass on to him?"

"Yeah," Jay said. "Tell him it's not Elmo." He looked back at Maseryk again. "Sascha at home?"

"He's rooming with his mother until we're done going over the building. Not that it's any business of yours. Didn't Ellis tell you to stay the hell away from this?"

"I'm staying away," Jay said. He caught a hint of motion out of the corner of his eye and glanced aside just in time to see the hooded man melt back into the shadows of the alley. "All the good clues are inside," he continued without missing a beat. "You see me going inside?" Jay held up his hands, palms out. "But hey, I'm easy. In fact, I'm going. See? Bye, now."

Maseryk frowned at him as he backed off, then shrugged, turned, and went back inside the Crystal Palace. When he was gone, Jay spun and elbowed his way through the crowd to the alley.

He was too late. The man in the fencing mask and black hood was gone. Except "man" wasn't quite right. Under that dusky black cloth, the talk on the street said, the massive body of the Oddity was male and female both.

But whatever else the joker was, one thing was certain. It was *strong*.

8:00 P.M.

A little old woman, tiny as an ancient sparrow, opened the door a crack when Brennan knocked.

"Is Sascha in?" Brennan asked.

"No."

Brennan put his foot in the door, holding it open as she pushed to close it. He had seen a flash of movement in the room beyond the door, and he knew who it was.

"Sascha, I don't want to hurt you," he called out. "I just want to talk."

The old woman struggled to close the door, pushing valiantly but uselessly against Brennan's weight, then a weary voice called out, "It's all right, Ma. Let him in." There was a long sigh, then Sascha added, "I couldn't hide from him for very long, anyway."

Sascha's mother backed away from the door and let him enter. She had a worried expression on her wrinkled face as she glanced from Sascha, who'd collapsed on the living-room sofa, back to Brennan.

"It's all right, Ma. Why don't you go brew some tea?"

She nodded and bustled off to the kitchen as Brennan looked at Sascha with concern. The bartender had always been thin, but now he was no more than muscle and bone. He looked deathly tired and his face was lined and pale.

"What's going on?" Brennan asked.

"Not a damn thing." Sascha shook his head tiredly. There was pain and loss in his voice, and an unconcealed bitterness that Brennan had never heard before.

"Why are you hiding out? Did you recognize Chrysalis's murderer telepathically?"

Sascha just sat there. For a while Brennan thought he wouldn't say anything, but then he nodded. "I heard someone," he finally said.

"Who?"

"That PI, that Popinjay character."

Jay Ackroyd, Brennan thought. He'd had a run-in with the ace before, but he couldn't conceive of him as a murderer. "What was he doing at the Palace?"

Sascha said nothing, just shrugged.

"What about Elmo?" Brennan asked.

The bartender shook his head. "She'd sent him out late the night before on some kind of secret errand. Didn't tell me anything about it." The bitterness came back, this time edged with fear. "He never got back to the Palace. I heard that the cops are looking for him."

"Do they think he did it?"

Sascha laughed. "Maybe. What a joke. Do you think the dwarf would ever hurt her? He loved her. It's almost as funny as thinking you killed her."

"You don't know anything more? Nothing specific about the murder?"

Sascha fidgeted nervously and picked at an ugly scab on the side of his neck. "How about who did it?" he asked in a frantic burst of words. "I was getting a drink at Freakers this afternoon, and everyone was talking about it."

"About what?"

"About Bludgeon! He did it! He killed Chrysalis. He's been bragging about it."

"Why would Bludgeon kill Chrysalis?"

Sascha shrugged. "Who knows why he does anything? He's crazy mean. But I heard he's trying to get back with the Fists. I guess he's had hard times since the Mafia got busted up."

Brennan nodded grimly. It made sense. Bludgeon was nothing but muscle. He was strong but stupid, and he'd proven to be even too brutal for the Shadow Fists, who'd cut him loose a couple of years ago. He'd hooked on with the Mafia, but the Mafia had been crushed in a vicious gang war with the Fists last year. If Kien and the Fists had put a contract on Chrysalis, Bludgeon was certainly capable of beating her to death to ingratiate himself with them.

Sascha's mother returned from the kitchen with a tea tray. Brennan watched as Sascha lifted a steaming cup with shaking hands.

"I have to go," he said. "Take care of yourself, Sascha." He nodded to the old woman as he left her apartment. If the rumor was around town as Sascha said it was, Tripod would pick up on it and find Bludgeon. At any rate, Bludgeon was only the muscle. He may have done the killing—and if he did, Brennan wanted him—but he wanted the one who had sicced him on Chrysalis even more.

He had a truce with Kien. He had called off his vendetta against his old enemy, but if Kien—or anyone in Kien's organization—had ordered Chrysalis's death, the Fists were going to bleed.

9:00 P.M.

The apartment was a loft over a bankrupt print shop, in a century-old cast-iron building a block off the river. Over the door a sign, faded almost to illegibility, said BLACKWELL PRINTING COMPANY. Jay peered through a windowpane, but the grime covered it like a coat of gray paint, and he could get no hint of the interior.

He shoved his hands into the pockets of his blazer and walked slowly up and down the sidewalk. As far as he could see, there were two ways into the loft. An old iron fire escape clung to the back side of the structure. He could probably pull the ladder down and climb in through a window. Or he could just ring the bell.

He could see lights in the loft windows. To hell with it, he thought. He went around to the steel-reinforced door by the alley. There was no name on the bell. Jay jabbed it with his thumb.

After a moment there was a metallic rasping noise, and the lock on the steel door disengaged. That was easy, Jay thought as he pushed his way inside. He found himself at the bottom of a narrow flight of stairs in a ghastly little hallway that smelled of mold and printer's ink. A light bulb dangled from the ceiling, swaying slightly from side to side as moths fluttered around it. The bulb was hot and bright, probably way too high a voltage for the old wiring in this firetrap, but it did light up the place. One of the moths brushed against it and fell, smoking, at his feet. Its burned wings beat a frantic tattoo against the bare wood floor. Jay stepped on it and felt it crunch as he ground it into the floor with his heel. He wondered what the hell Sascha saw in a place like this.

A door opened on the landing above him. "Aren't you coming up?" a woman's voice called down.

Jay had no idea whom she was expecting, but he didn't figure it was him. "I'm looking for Sascha," he said as he started up the steps. They were so cramped and steep it was hard going.

"Sascha is not here." The woman came out of the loft and stood on the top step, smiling down at him. "I am all alone."

Jay looked up. He stopped right where he was. He stared.

The woman ran the tip of her tongue across full, pouty lips. She was dressed in a short red teddy that barely reached her hips. No panties. Her pubic hair was black and thick, and when she stood with her legs apart like that, he could see a lot more than just hair. Her skin was a light brown color, the kind Hiram would call café au lait. A tangle of wild black hair fell across her shoulders and back, longer than her teddy. Under the wisp of fabric was the most magnificent pair of tits that Jay Ackroyd had ever seen. "Come on," she said to him. Her accent was as provocative as the rest of her. "Come *on*," she repeated, with more insistence.

Jay resisted the urge to look over his shoulder to see if somebody else was on the steps behind him. He couldn't take his eyes off her anyway. When Jube had said that Sascha was seeing a Haitian prostitute, he'd expected some gaunt, pockmarked girl with hungry eyes and needle tracks along her arms. He cleared his throat and tried to sound like he ran into half-naked women all the time. "Ah," he managed, "Sascha, ah—"

"Sascha bores me," the woman said. "I am Ezili. Come." She smiled again and held out her hand.

"I'm Jay Ackroyd," Jay said. "I'm a friend of Chrysalis," he added. "Sascha too," he went on. "I need to talk to him again," he explained. "About her," he clarified. "Chrysalis, that is." All the time walking up the stairs. Ezili just listened, nodding, smiling, nodding. Jay was two steps below her when he saw that her eyes matched her lingerie, two small black irises surrounded by a sea of liquid red. "Your eyes," Jay blurted out, stopping suddenly.

Ezili reached down, took his hand, and put it between her legs. Her heat was like a living thing. Moisture ran over his fingers and down the inside of her coffee-colored thighs. She moved against him, and gasped as his fingers slipped up inside her, moving almost of their own accord. She had her first climax right there on the stairs, grinding her hips furiously against his hand. Afterward she licked his fingers like a greedy child, sucking the fluids off them one by one, then drew him wordlessly into the apartment.

By then Jay had forgotten all about her eyes.

10:00 P.M.

There was never a Werewolf around when you needed one. Egrets were scarce, too. Brennan pounded the streets for two hours before he spotted one of the gang members, a Werewolf, staggering out of Freakers.

The Werewolf was big, hairy, and muscular. He wore faded and torn jeans and enough chains and leather straps and cords to fill Michael Jackson's closet. The plastic Mae West mask that covered his face added more than a touch of incongruity to his appearance. He stopped on the street in front of Freakers to extort a few bucks from some slumming nat tourists who were trying to decide whether or not to go into the bar, then lurched past them into an alley half a block down the street. Brennan followed him.

The alley was suitably dark and isolated. The joker was urinating against a brick wall and singing "I'm So Lonesome I Could Die" to himself, lowly and badly. He was zipping up his fly when Brennan laid the edge of his knife against his throat and said conversation-ally, "I think your voice would sound a lot better if I cut you right here. What do you think?"

The joker stood paralyzed until Brennan stepped back, then he turned around slowly, carefully holding his hands out and away from his sides.

"You some kind of crazy nat?" the joker finally asked.

"Just visiting the big bad city to check on some of my old friends." Brennan reached into the pocket of his denim jacket with his left hand. "My card," he said, holding up an ace of spades.

The huge joker seemed to shrink back into himself. "You the real thing, man?"

"Try me," Brennan offered, but the joker just shook his head. "I don't want to dance," Brennan said. "I just want to talk. I'm look-ing for one of the bigger fish. Warlock. Lazy Dragon. Maybe Fade-out. Seen any of them tonight?"

"I seen Dragon earlier. He said he was going to be spending the night at Chickadee's, but he wasn't too happy about it. He was body-guarding some Fist wheel, so he couldn't party."

Brennan nodded. Lazy Dragon was a freelance ace who worked part-time for the Fists, often directly for a Shadow Fist lieutenant named Philip Cunningham, who was fairly high in the organization. Cunningham, who was also called Fadeout because of his ability to turn invisible, would know if Kien had put out a contract on Chrysalis. Brennan had once worked for Fadeout himself when he'd joined the Fists undercover in an attempt to bring them down from within. In fact he'd saved Fadeout's life when the Mafia had attacked his headquarters. Perhaps they could come to some kind of accom-modation.

"Okay," Brennan said. He gestured with his knife. "That the model the Werewolves are wearing this week?"

"Huh?"

"Your mask."

"Sure."

"Give it to me."

Brennan watched the Werewolf carefully. The common mask the gang wore was their symbol, their badge of belonging. Some fanatic

Werewolves would kill before giving it up. This one visibly tensed, then sighed and relaxed. He obviously knew Brennan's reputation, and despite his size and ferocious appearance had no wish to tangle with the man who had decimated Shadow Fist ranks the year before.

He slipped the mask off and gave it to Brennan, turning his face down and away. Brennan took the mask, glanced at the man's face, and said nothing. He'd seen worse, a lot worse, though he could understand why the fierce-looking Werewolf was ashamed of his face. It looked as if it had stopped growing during the man's first year. It was a baby's face, soft and beautiful, perched grotesquely in the middle of his oversized head. It contrasted weirdly with the joker's savage, metal-and-leather appearance.

Brennan stepped back and the Werewolf edged around him and backed away, face still averted. He started off down the alley.

"Your fly's still undone," Brennan called out after him.

♣

"Sleep," Ezili whispered to him, afterward.

He *was* very drowsy. He felt as though he could just surrender, settle slowly into the deep soft pile of the carpet beneath him, close his eyes, and drift peacefully. Until this moment, he hadn't realized how exhausted he was.

Ezili was smiling down at him, the soft weight of her breast against his arm. They'd never even bothered to turn on a light, but he could see her dimly by the light from the street lamp outside, filtering through softly blowing curtains. Her nipples were large and dark, the color of bittersweet chocolate. He remembered the taste of them. He reached out a hand, stroked the soft skin on the underside of her breast, but this time her fingers caught his wrist and gently took his hand away. "No," she whispered, "just sleep. Close your eyes, little boy. Dream." She kissed his brow. "Dream of Ezili-je-rouge."

Some part of Jay realized how crazy this was, but the rest of him didn't care. He wondered if Ezili was going to try and hit him up for money. She was supposed to be a hooker, after all. He didn't care. Whatever she charged, she was worth it. "How much for all night?" he whispered drowsily.

Ezili seemed to find that amusing. She laughed a light, musical laugh and began to stroke his forehead with languid, knowing fingers. It was incredibly soothing. The room was warm and dark. He closed his eyes and let the world begin to drift away. Ezili's fingers touched and gentled. Far off he heard her talking to herself, murmuring, "All night, all night," as if it were the funniest thing anyone had ever said. There were other noises, too, more distant, a door opening somewhere, a rustling of clothing, as if there were someone else there with them, but Jay was too tired to care. He was floating, sinking into a warm sea of sleep, and tonight he knew his nightmare would not come.

Then the outer door slammed open with a loud *bang*, and someone screamed, "Where *is* he?"

Bright light from the hallway fell across Jay's face, jolting him awake. He sat up groggily and put a hand in front of his eyes. Through his fingers, he saw a man outlined in the doorway, indistinct against the glare. "Shit," he complained, before he quite remembered where he was.

Ezili was on her feet, screaming at the intruder in French. Jay didn't speak a word of French, but he could tell from her tone that you wouldn't find many of *those* words in your basic French–English dictionaries. He heard a muffled noise behind him and turned just in time to glimpse a dark shape vanish through a bedroom door. A child, he thought, with some kind of humpback or twisted spine, but in the dim light it was hard to be sure. Whoever it was slammed the door behind them.

"I couldn't help it," the man in the doorway said. His voice was hoarse and shaky. Ezili spat more venom at him in French. "I didn't know," he pleaded. "Please, I can't wait. Ezili, I need the kiss, I need it bad. Listen to me."

Jay knew that voice. He got to his knees, bumped into the edge of the couch, fumbled for a lamp, and turned on some light.

"You don't understand what I've been through," Sascha said.

"Shut up, fool," Ezili said in English. "You have a visitor."

Sascha's head turned slowly, until it faced Jay. "You."

Jay suddenly remembered that he was naked. His clothes were scattered all over the room, pants over the back of the couch, boxer shorts dangling from the lampshade, socks and shoes God knows where. Ezili was just as naked.

Of course, Sascha had no eyes. Somehow Jay didn't think it mattered. "Me," Jay admitted, a little sheepishly. He snatched his boxer shorts off the lamp, climbed into them, and tried to think what else to say. *Pardon me, Sascha, I came here to talk to you, but wound up fucking your girl on the living-room carpet, and by the way, she is one terrific piece of ass. . . .* No, he couldn't say that. Of course, he'd just *thought* that, and Sascha was a telepath, which meant that he already . . .

"Coward," Ezili snarled at Sascha. "Weakling. Why should you have the kiss? You don't deserve it."

Jay looked at her, a little shocked. This was a whole different side to Ezili, and she sure as hell didn't sound like a hooker talking to a well-heeled customer. She stood with her fists balled on her hips, naked and furious, and Jay noticed for the first time that she had a big, crusty brown scab on the side of her neck. He thought of various venereal diseases, then of AIDS, remembered that she was supposed to be Haitian, and felt like a total idiot. "Where the fuck is my shirt?" he said angrily, louder than he'd intended.

Ezili and Sascha both looked at him. Ezili muttered something in French, spun on a bare foot, and stalked off toward the bedroom. She slammed the door behind her. Jay heard it lock.

Sascha looked as though he was going to cry, although Jay wasn't at all sure you *could* cry, without eyes. He sagged into an armchair and lifted his head to favor Jay with his eyeless stare. "Well?" Sascha said bitterly. "What do you want?"

Jay, struggling into his pants, felt at a certain disadvantage, but he tried not to let on. "I'm looking for Elmo," he said, zipping up his fly.

"Everyone's looking for Elmo," Sascha complained. He looked like shit, Jay thought, except that he'd never seen shit look as pale and sweaty and trembly as Sascha looked right now. "Well, I don't know where he is. He went off to run an errand and he didn't come back." Sascha giggled. It was a thin, high, frightening sound, on the edge of hysteria. "The dwarf who never returned, that's Elmo. Good for him. They'll hang him for it, you know. Wait and see. He's only a joker."

Jay couldn't find one of his socks. He shoved the other one in a pocket and sat on the edge of the couch to lace up his shoes. The couch was new, expensive, upholstered in plush wine-colored velvet. Jay gave the apartment a good once-over, really seeing it for the first time. The floors were covered by deep-pile wall-to-wall carpeting, as white as snow. On the far side of the pass-through was a modern kitchen where rows of copper-bottomed pots hung between a towering bronze refrigerator-freezer and a microwave that could double as a hangar for small planes. The living room was full of weird but expensive-looking primitive art that Jay figured must be Haitian. Elaborate painted symbols covered the walls. Off to his left, the loft had been subdivided into a maze of smaller rooms; it looked like there could be five or six bedrooms back there.

"What is this place?" Jay said, a little baffled.

"It's a place you don't belong," Sascha said. "Why don't you just leave me alone?"

"I will. As soon as you've answered a few questions."

That made Sascha furious. "No!" he shouted. "Now. I told you, I can't wait, damn it, you get out of here, I need the kiss, I don't want you here, I don't want you bothering me."

Jay had never seen Sascha this way. "What the hell is wrong with you?" he asked. "Sascha, are you hooked on something?"

Sascha's rage suddenly changed to giggles again. "Oh, yes," he said. "Kisses, oh, kisses sweeter than wine."

Jay stood up, frowning. "Kisses," he repeated sourly. Ezili was *real* good in bed, but if this is what a long-term relationship with her did to you, he'd settle for a one-night stand. "Sascha, I don't give a damn about your love life, I just need to find Elmo. He knows me well enough to know I won't turn him in. I just want to talk. He might know something that could help me figure out who killed Chrysalis."

Sascha stroked his little pencil-thin mustache in a motion that was almost furtive. "But we know who killed her, don't we? He left his calling card, didn't he? Yes, I see you remember, I can see the picture in your head right now."

It made Jay feel a little creepy to have Sascha fooling around in his mind. "Someone dropped an ace of spades on the body," he said, "but I'm not convinced it was Yeoman, he—"

"It was him!" Sascha interrupted. He surged to his feet angrily. "Yeoman! That's who it was! There's your murderer, Popinjay, oh yes. He's back in town. I just saw him."

Jay was unsure. "You saw him?"

Sascha nodded rapidly. "Out at Brighton Beach. My mother's place. He came looking for me. He's after Elmo, too."

"Why?" Jay demanded. "Why would he kill Chrysalis?"

Sascha looked around the room, as if to make sure that no one else was listening, then leaned forward and whispered, "She knew his real name." He giggled. "Would you like to hear it? If I tell you, will you go away and leave me alone?"

"You know it, too?"

Sascha nodded eagerly. "She never said it aloud, but sometimes she *thought* it. I picked it right out of her mind one day. If Yeoman knew, he'd kill me, too. Do you want it?"

"Tell me," Jay said.

"You promise you'll go away? You won't bother me anymore? You won't pry into my affairs?"

"I promise," Jay said impatiently.

"Daniel Brennan," Sascha said. "Now get out."

Jay looked back once on the way out as he pulled the door of the apartment shut behind him. Sascha was kneeling by the bedroom door, eyeless face pressed up against the wood, pleading for a kiss.

11:00 P.M.

Chickadee's was located in the heart of the Bowery. Its exterior was plain, almost severe, greystone, with no sign, canopy, or doorman to announce its existence. Chickadee's didn't have to advertise. Word of mouth was enough.

Brennan went up the steps empty-handed, having stashed his bow case in a rental locker, and was met in the bordello's anteroom by a joker with the approximate size and musculature of a male gorilla. The joker gave him the once-over, and sniffed, a little put off by Brennan's jeans and T-shirt. Nevertheless he open the antechamber's inner door, leading, as Chickadee's thousands of satisfied customers thought, to paradise.

Twelve-Finger Jake was playing the piano in the corner of the greeting parlor, pounding out the complicated chords of the super-syncopated music he called j-jazz—joker jazz—that took all twelve of his fingers to play properly. Johns, dressed mostly in expensive-looking three-piece suits, were sitting on the parlor's comfortable chairs and sofas, drinking and chatting with the girls. The women of the house ran the gamut of races and colors. All were beautiful, but since this was Jokertown some of them had decidedly unusual attributes.

A nat hostess met Brennan at the door. At least she looked like a nat, and the garter belt, nylons, and high heels she wore could have done very little to conceal joker deformities. It was true, though, that some of the girls at Chickadee's were different in very subtle ways.

"Hello, Joe," she said. "I'm Lori. Want to party?"

Brennan smiled. "I'm looking for a man," he began.

"Wrong place, Joe. We got all kinds of girls—white ones, black ones, brown ones, ones like you never seen before, but if you want a man—"

"A friend, I mean," Brennan added hastily. "Lazy Dragon—"

"Oh." Lori nodded. She linked arms with Brennan and drew him toward her. Her sleek hip pressed against Brennan's, her long, lean silk-covered thigh brushed against his as they walked. "I should have guessed with the mask and all. Marilyn Monroe, right? She's one of my favorites. I'll take you up myself. I can use another taste."

"Sure."

Brennan followed, somewhat mystified, but satisfied that his minimal disguise was doing its job. They went through the parlor area, raucous with the j-jazz flowing from Twelve-Finger Jake's nimble digits and the chatter of thirty girls and fifty prospective johns, up a flight of stairs, and down a corridor ending in closed double doors guarded by a couple of Werewolves wearing Mae West masks identical to Brennan's.

"What's up?" one of them asked as Brennan and the girl approached.

Brennan nodded. "Relief. Let me check in with Dragon."

"Just one of you? Who gets off?"

Brennan shrugged. "Not my decision."

The Werewolf grunted, stood aside, and Brennan and Lori went through the doors.

Inside was a large room decorated with the exuberantly lavish taste one might expect in an establishment like Chickadee's. Half the walls were wallpapered in a silver-and-gold paisley pattern, the other half were mirrored, making the room seem much bigger than it really was. The overstuffed couches and fat hassocks scattered about the room were all occupied by house girls and men wearing suits that were as tasteful as the wallpaper.

A naked girl was lying languorously on one of the couches with lines of what looked like cocaine laid out on her body between and over her ample breasts, up her sleek legs, and converging at the juncture of her thighs. Three men were taking turns snorting lines leading to their favorite body parts. Other girls wearing mostly makeup were circulating with trays with drinks and little silver bowls filled with powders or pills of various sorts.

Lori said, "See you later, hon," and moved off into the drift.

Lazy Dragon was sitting in a corner of the room, sipping a drink from a long-stemmed glass. As Brennan watched he virtuously turned down a bowl of white powder offered him by a sleek black woman whose body was covered by fluffy feathers.

"What do you want?" Dragon asked as Brennan approached. He was a young man, Asian, small and trim looking. He was also a potent ace who could animate then possess animal figurines he carved or folded out of paper. Right now he didn't appear to be in a good humor.

"No rest for the wicked, is there?"

Dragon stiffened at the sound of Brennan's voice, half rose, then sank down in his chair. "What the hell are you doing here, Cowboy?" he said, using the name Brennan had taken when he'd gone undercover and joined the Fists.

Brennan shrugged. "Looks like a fun party. I'd hate to see anything break it up." He looked steadily at Dragon. "What's going on, anyway?"

Dragon looked at him for a long time before answering. "The guy over there," he said, indicating a tall, thin, wasted-looking man in white linen trousers, jacket, and shirt, "is Quinn the Eskimo. You've heard of him."

Brennan nodded. Quinn the Eskimo—his real name was Thomas Quincey—was head of the scientific arm of the Shadow Fists. He specialized in the development of synthetic drugs with extraordinary special effects.

"Trying out a new product?" Brennan asked.

As Brennan watched, Lori approached Quinn and spoke to him. He smiled and handed her a vial of blue powder, some of which she snorted, some of which she rubbed on her nipples and breasts, turning them the same bright blue color of the powder. Quinn and the men standing around him laughed. At Quinn's urging one of the men started to lick her breasts. She closed her eyes and leaned up against a nearby wall, and, as the man sucked her nipples, came to an obvious, powerful orgasm.

"What the hell was that?" Brennan asked.

Dragon shrugged. "The new product. Demonstrating for the distributors. What do you want, anyway?"

Brennan looked back down at Dragon. "A friend of mine was killed, Dragon. You heard."

"Chrysalis?"

Brennan nodded. "And I heard that someone is bragging around town that he did it to get in good with the Fists."

Dragon shook his head. "I didn't know the Fists wanted her dead."

"You don't make policy. I want to talk to someone who does. Fadeout."

"He's not happy with you, Cowboy. You really fucked us over."

Brennan shrugged. "That's life," he said. "Fadeout will talk to me, or the Fists will bleed."

Dragon stood up slowly, carefully. "You don't want to start anything here, Cowboy. I'm head of security for this party—"

Brennan nodded, smiled under his Mae West mask, and backed away. "And I wouldn't want you to have a black mark on your record. Just tell Fadeout I want to talk."

They stared at each other until Brennan backed out of the room.

"So?" one of the Werewolf guards in the corridor asked Brennan.

"So what?"

"Who's going off duty?"

"Oh." Brennan stripped off the Mae West mask and tossed it at the astonished Werewolf, who caught it against his chest. "I am."

"What the hell?" the other one growled angrily. "That's not fair."

"Life's a bitch," Brennan told him. "Then you die."

The Werewolves recognized the danger in his voice. They watched him as he went down the corridor, wondering who he was, deciding that it would probably be better if they never found out.

♣   ♦   ♠   ♥

Tuesday
July 19, 1988

2:00 A.M.

THE STALE AIR TRAPPED inside the unused sewer line that Chrysalis had converted to a secret Palace entrance stank of mold and rot. It was dark but for the beam from Brennan's flashlight, quiet but for the infrequent noises he made as he crept toward the Palace. Once he passed a side tunnel that Chrysalis hadn't told him about. He thought he heard something moving in it, but decided that now was not the time to indulge idle curiosity.

The sewer line led to a tunnel of more recent construction, that led in turn to a dark basement storeroom. The room was packed with stacks of liquor cases, piles of aluminum beer kegs, and cardboard boxes filled with potato chips, pretzels, pork rinds, and other junk food.

Brennan moved through the storeroom silently and went up the flight of stairs to the first floor. He waited for a moment, but neither saw, nor heard, nor smelled anything to indicate that anyone else was in the Palace. He hadn't figured there would be. He went down the corridor to Chrysalis's office and paused at the door, strangely reluctant to enter the room.

He realized that once he saw her blood splattered on the walls, he would know without a doubt that Chrysalis was dead. She'd kept too much of herself to herself for him to have loved her, but he had shared her bed and some of her secrets. He'd known the lonely woman under the cool exterior. He hadn't loved her, but he could have. He couldn't forget that. It kept gnawing at him like the pain from an open wound, unbound and bleeding.

He remembered Chrysalis's office as a dark, quiet, charming room. It had a fabulous Oriental carpet on the floor, floor-to-ceiling bookcases full of leather-bound volumes that Chrysalis had actually read, solid oak-and-leather furniture, and dark, purple-patterned Victorian wallpaper. The room had even smelled of Chrysalis, of the exotic frangipani perfume she wore and the amaretto she drank. It had been a peaceful room, and he didn't want to see it transformed into a scene of death and destruction. But he had to. He took a deep breath, pulled away the tape that sealed the door, and entered the office.

It was worse than he had suspected. The room had been utterly devastated. Her huge oak desk was on its side halfway across the room from its usual place. Her black leather chair had been shattered. Her bookcases had been torn from the walls and the volumes scattered on the floor. The visitors' chairs had been smashed to kindling. Her wooden file cabinets had been upended and their contents strewn all over the floor and the broken furniture. Worst of all was a light spray of blood, barely visible on the patterned wallpaper, splattered low on the wall behind where her desk and chair normally stood.

Brennan had seen a lot of destruction, but this devastation filled him with anger. He took the anger and forced it down, pushing it deep inside himself until it was a glowing pinpoint in the pit of his stomach. This was no time to give in to emotion. Perhaps later he could afford to vent it, but now he needed a cool, dispassionate intellect. Not knowing yet what might constitute an important clue, he memorized the horrible scene in as much detail as he could so that he'd be able to reconstruct it in his mind later.

Brennan left the office with the room locked in his memory. He couldn't face the stuffiness of the tunnels running under the streets. He wanted to breathe fresh, clean air, as fresh and clean, anyway, as could be found in the city. He went to the stairs that led to the exits of the upper floor, and he heard a voice, the last voice he ever expected to hear again, whispering from the dark stairwell ahead of him.

"Yeoman," it said, sending shivers up his spine, "I'm waiting for you. Come to my room. I'll be waiting, my archer."

It was her voice. Chrysalis, speaking in her almost-English accent. He stood still for a moment, but heard no one or nothing move in the darkness.

Brennan didn't believe in ghosts, but the wild card made nearly anything possible. Maybe Chrysalis hadn't even been killed, maybe it was all an elaborate hoax, perhaps perpetrated by Chrysalis herself for whatever unfathomable reason. Whatever it was, he couldn't just walk away from it. He drew his Browning Hi-Power from his hip holster and crept up the stairs as quietly as a stalking cat.

The door to Chrysalis's bedroom was open, and as he peered around the jamb he could see that someone had been here before him. The intruder had been searching for something and hadn't bothered to be neat about it. Chrysalis's canopied bed had been pulled apart and its mattress shredded. All her Victorian portraits and elegantly framed antique mirrors had been stripped from the walls and lay in silver slivers scattered about the floor. The crystal decanter that usually stood on the nightstand lay shattered on the floor. A fencing mask sat in its place.

Brennan entered the room and stared about in dismay. Just as he reached the smashed bed, a bulky figure appeared at the mouth of the walk-in closet where Chrysalis had kept her extensive wardrobe. Its face was feminine and beautiful, but etched with what looked like chronic pain. Her body was grotesque, huge and blocky under her floor-length black cloak. Something was moving under the cloak. Something twisted and writhed across her chest and abdomen like a sack full of snakes. The intruder stopped short and stared at Brennan, who stared back and pointed his gun.

"You're the Oddity," Brennan finally said.

"Who are you?"

"No one you know. Call me Yeoman."

There was another silence, then the Oddity said, "We see. What are you doing here?"

"That's my question."

"We're looking for something."

Brennan's lips quirked in a grimace. "Let's not draw this out."

"Or what? Shouldn't a threat be in there somewhere?"

Brennan's voice was as cold as glacial ice, the hand holding the gun as steady as a statue's. "I don't threaten. I don't play games. I've found you in my friend's bedroom and I'm inclined to believe you had something to do with her death. If you don't want to tell me anything, fine. I'm not going to turn you over to the police. I'm going to leave you dead."

"We believe you would try," the Oddity said softly.

Brennan said nothing.

"All right." She sighed. "We had nothing to do with Chrysalis's death. When we heard about it, we came looking for something . . . some information that Chrysalis was blackmailing us with. We just wanted to recover it before the police found it."

Brennan scowled. "Blackmailing you? For money?"

The Oddity nodded, then her face suddenly screwed up in an expression of intense pain. She gasped and fell to her knees, her arms crossing over her stomach. She threw back her head, her face a rictus of suffering.

"Christ," Brennan murmured. The Oddity wasn't acting. She was in intense, uncontrollable pain. Brennan didn't know what to do or how to help her. He started to approach the helpless joker, but she held out a hand to ward him off. He stared as her features crawled from her face and slid down the side of her throat. Another set of features, swarthy and masculine, began to move around from the back of her head.

The new eyes stared at Brennan with suspicion. Even before they were properly in place, even before the Oddity finished moaning, he—as Brennan now thought of the joker—stood, grabbed the leg of the end table that stood near the bed, and threw it at Brennan with a flick of his wrist. Brennan ducked and squeezed off a shot.

He never knew if the bullet hit home, because the Oddity charged at him like a fullback blasting for the goal line, and when they collided, it felt as if he'd been smashed by a sack full of bricks.

He twisted away and placed a powerful side kick into the squirming mass that was the Oddity's torso. A feminine hand grabbed him, and it was much, much stronger than his. It pulled at him and he followed it without resistance as it whirled him around and slammed him against the wall hard enough to make his teeth clatter and his back ache.

His gun flew away. He hit the floor, rolled, and grabbed a knick-knack stand of solid oak. He swung it with all his strength and caught the Oddity in the side. The stand shattered. His arms quivered with shock and he tried unsuccessfully to shake the numbness from his hands. The Oddity hadn't even budged.

He swung at Brennan and Brennan dodged, dodged, and dodged again, dangling his hands at his side, trying to get feeling to return to them. He retreated until he felt a wall against his back and the Oddity loomed before him, scowling with ferocious anger.

He swung again and Brennan ducked, sliding down the wall as the Oddity's fist smashed through it, his arm punching into the wall cavity to the shoulder.

Brennan slipped around to the side and grabbed one of the posts that had supported the canopy of Chrysalis's demolished bed. He swung it like an oversized baseball bat and connected solidly with the Oddity's back, right over the kidneys.

The Oddity howled more in anger than pain. Brennan swung again, splintering the post into kindling.

"Christ," Brennan muttered as the Oddity cursed and wrenched at his trapped arm.

There was no sense, Brennan realized, in trying to fight the berserk joker. He dove out of the room as the Oddity pulled free, and ran down the hallway, gritting his teeth at the pain in his back.

"We'll get you, you bastard!" the Oddity cried. His voice was slurred, as if perhaps two people were fighting for control of it. "We'll get you!"

Brennan took a deep breath as he ran. No bones were broken, but his whole back felt bruised. There was no time to waste moaning. The police could arrive at any moment to investigate the commotion. He went up the stairs and out through the roof, replaying the Oddity's story in his mind.

Chrysalis might have extorted favors or information as part of the game she liked to play, but she would never blackmail anyone for money. Brennan knew that wasn't in her.

So why was the Oddity lying? And what was he—they, whatever—really looking for in the closet of Chrysalis's bedroom?

9:00 A.M.

"You've got a reporter named Thomas Downs," Jay said.

The receptionist looked at him dubiously. She was a chic little number who looked like she'd been specially bred to sit behind the high-tech chrome-and-glass reception desk. The offices of *Aces* magazine were a lot classier than Jay had anticipated. If he'd known they had two entire floors at 666 Fifth Avenue, Jay might have stopped for that shine in the subway. Obviously, there was money to be made in stories about Peregrine's love life.

"Digger didn't come in today," the receptionist said.

On the wall behind her, the magazine's logo had been burned into a chrome steel plate by Jumpin' Jack Flash. Elsewhere around the reception area, various distinguished ace visitors had transmuted a chrome ashtray into some kind of weird purple glass, twisted steel bars into new and fanciful shapes, and constructed a perpetual-motion machine that had been whirring happily away for four years now. Little brass plaques commemorated each of these feats.

"Where can I find him?" Jay asked. "It's important."

"I'm sorry," the receptionist said. "We don't give out that kind of information."

"Is there someone else I could talk to?" Jay asked.

"Not without an appointment," she said.

"I'm an ace," Jay told her.

She tried to suppress a smile, and failed. "I'm sure you are."

Jay looked around the reception area, made the gun shape with his fingers, and pointed at a long chrome-and-leather sofa. It vanished with a *pop*. He'd needed a new couch anyway. "Do I get a little brass plaque?" he asked the receptionist.

"Perhaps Mr. Lowboy could help you," she said, lifting up the phone.

The editorial floor had been partitioned off into a maze of tiny cubicles. Larger private offices, with real walls and doors, lined the outside of the building, leaving the big central space windowless. There were lots of cheerful colors and potted plants, and peppy Muzak kept the well-dressed staff busy at their computer terminals. Everything was very clean and orderly. Jay hated it.

Mr. Lowboy's corner office had no computer terminal, no cheerful colors, and no Muzak. Just a lot of wood and leather, and two huge tinted windows looking out over the Manhattan skyline. Mr. Lowboy wasn't there when they arrived, so Jay wandered around the room looking at the framed photographs on the walls. He was studying a faded black-and-white print of Jetboy shaking hands with a wizened little man who looked like an anemic gnome when Lowboy finally made his entrance.

"That's my grandfather," he said. "He and Jetboy were like that." Lowboy crossed his middle and index fingers. He was a couple of inches shorter than Jay and wore a three-piece white suit with a pastel shirt and a black knit tie.

"Why is he handing Jetboy a check?" Jay asked.

"Oh, well, truth is, he was lending the kid money all the time. Jetboy never did know how to manage his finances. Just like a lot of these modern aces." He held out his hand. "I'm Bob Lowboy. I understand you're looking for Digger." He didn't wait for an answer. "I'm afraid we can't help you," he said as they shook. "Digger's a crackerjack reporter, no doubt of it, but he's not the most reliable man we've got on staff. He took off yesterday during his coffee break, and we haven't seen him since."

"Aren't you a little concerned about that?"

"Not to worry," Lowboy assured him. "He's done it before. The last time, he showed up a week later with all the dope on the Howler's secret love child. Made the cover."

"I'll just bet it did," Jay said.

"If you'd like to leave a card with my assistant, we'll make sure Digger gets it," Lowboy promised.

Jay left a card with Mr. Lowboy's assistant and told her he'd find his own way out. He was threading his way through the labyrinth when a woman called out to him. "Mr. Ackroyd?"

She was young, early twenties maybe, dressed in a plain white shirt open at the collar, jeans, and a pin-striped gray vest. Her hair was cropped short, and round wire-rims framed her face. "Mandy told everyone about the couch," she said. "You're Popinjay." She offered her hand shyly. Her nails were trimmed down to the quick.

"I hate that name."

She looked guilty. "Oh God, that's right, it was in your file. I'm sorry, I forgot. I hope I haven't offended you. I'm Judy Scheffel. Sometimes they call me Crash."

"Crash?" Jay said dubiously.

"Don't ask. I'm Digger's research assistant. Can we talk?" She produced a key from the pocket of her vest. "The key to Digger's office," she said. "C'mon."

Downs might have been only a reporter, but clearly *Aces* valued his services. His office was a third the size of Lowboy's, but it was a real office, with walls, a door that locked, and even a single narrow window. The bookshelves along the west wall were jammed far beyond capacity and looked as though they could come cascading down at any moment. A computer work station occupied the corner by the window. Next to it was a bulletin board crowded with mug shots of people that Jay didn't recognize. "Who are they?" he asked.

Crash carefully locked the door. "Aces who are still up the sleeve," she said. "For future reference. You'd be surprised how many times Digger's been the first to break the story on a new ace. No one else comes close."

"If they haven't gone public yet, how does he know they're aces?" Jay said, studying the pictures.

"I think he has a source down at the Jokertown Clinic who tips him off whenever a new ace is diagnosed." Crash shoved some papers aside and sat on the edge of Digger's desk. "Digger's in trouble, isn't he?"

"You tell me," Jay said.

"He's in trouble," she said. "He's always been kind of jumpy, but yesterday he just *freaked*."

"Tell me about it," Jay said. He moved a box of Peregrine pinup calendars off the swivel chair and sat down.

"We were working on a story yesterday morning. About the convention—a profile of the ace delegates. Digger had this tiny little

Sony Watchman on in the background, in case any news broke on the convention floor. When they came on with the newsflash about Chrysalis, he turned white as a sheet."

"They were close," Jay said. "Maybe even lovers."

"It wasn't just grief," Crash said. "It was fear. Digger was terrified. *I gotta go*, he said. I asked him when he'd be back, but it was like he didn't hear me. He practically ran out of the office. And Mandy, up front at the desk, she told me he didn't even wait for an elevator. He took the stairs down."

Jay had to admit that didn't sound like a man going underground for a story; it sounded like a man running for his life. "Downs ever do a story on the bow-and-arrow killer?"

"No. *Aces* doesn't run a lot of crime stories."

"He ever mention Chrysalis being afraid of someone?"

She shook her head.

"Some of his stories must have pissed people off. Was there anyone in particular had it in for him?"

"Peregrine," Crash said quickly. "She and Dr. Tachyon were both angry with Digger over a story he did during the tour. He just reported what Tachyon told him."

Dr. Tachyon was one of maybe six people that Jay was reasonably certain he could beat in an arm-wrestling contest. Peri he wasn't so sure about, but both of them were down in Atlanta anyway. "You're sure he had no history with Yeoman?" he asked. When she nodded, he said, "How about the Oddity?"

She considered that for a minute. "Digger did a story on the Oddity years ago, when he first came on staff. He showed it to me once. It was very well written. Digger said it would have won a Pulitzer, but Lowboy spiked it and it never ran."

"Why?" Jay said.

Crash looked embarrassed. "It was before my time, but I guess it was because the Oddity's a joker. Lowboy is always saying that our readership doesn't want to read about jokers."

"Was the Oddity upset that the story never ran?"

"Not as much as Digger was," she said.

Jay frowned. "You have any idea where Digger might have gone?"

Crash shook her head. "All I know is he's not at home. I've phoned him a half-dozen times, but all I ever get is his machine."

"That just means he's not answering the phone. Could be hiding under his bed, for all we know." He could be dead, too, he thought, lying on the floor in a pool of his own blood, his brains leaking onto the rug. He didn't say it. "I better check." Jay looked at her thoughtfully. "Before, you said something about my file."

"Sure," she said. "We have files on all the aces."

Jay put his hand on top of the computer. "Can you get at them through this thing?"

"You can tap into our data library from any work station, if you've got the password," she said. "But I could get fired for giving unauthorized access to our files."

"No problem," Jay said. "I'm sure Digger will understand. If he's still alive."

Crash looked at him for a moment, then got up and pulled the dustcover off the computer. Jay leaned over her shoulder. She turned on the machine and typed in Digger's password.

"*Nose?*" Jay asked.

Crash shrugged. "It's his password, not mine. What file do you want to look at?"

"Chrysalis got killed by someone who was inhumanly strong. Five'll get you ten that Digger's hiding from the same guy. I want to know who that could be."

"I can call up a list of all aces on file with that power, but it's going to be awfully long. Enhanced physical strength is the third most common wild-card power, after telepathy and telekinesis."

"Do it," Jay urged.

Her fingers moved expertly over the computer keyboard. "You want just aces, or jokers, too?"

"I thought *Aces* didn't report on jokers?"

"We don't, but the library draws from all kinds of sources. SCARE reports, scientific papers, clippings from the daily press. The research department is very thorough."

"If it's strong enough to pulp a human skull, I don't care if it's an ace, a joker, or a rutabaga."

"We don't have the rutabaga data on line yet," she said, entering a series of commands. It seemed a god-awful long time before the computer completed its search.

"Three hundred nineteen cases," Crash read cheerfully from the screen. "Not as many as I thought. That's everyone we know of who's ever displayed physical strength beyond the normal human range. Want me to print out the list?"

"Three hundred nineteen suspects might be a little cumbersome," Jay said. "Is there some way to narrow it down?"

"Sure," she said. "Factor in some other parameters. Some of these people are dead. We could eliminate them."

"Dead people make lousy suspects," Jay agreed.

Crash typed in a command. "Three hundred and two," she said. "Not much of an improvement. What if I restrict it to city residents?"

Jay thought about that for a moment. "No," he said reluctantly.

"Why not?" she asked. "It would cut the list by seventy or eighty names, at least. The computer's counting aces from all over the country . . . Detroit Steel, Big Mama in Chicago, Haymaker in Kansas City. You don't think it was one of them?"

"No," Jay admitted. "I figure it's more likely our killer is somebody who actually met Chrysalis. It usually works out like that in murder cases. Problem is, there are some out-of-towners who qualify. Billy Ray and Jack Braun, for two."

"It couldn't be Golden Boy," Crash pointed out. "He's down in Atlanta. Besides, Digger was always saying what a weenie he was."

"Obviously the mere mention of Braun's name reduced him to a state of abject terror," Jay said. He put his hand on her shoulder. She didn't seem to object. "Listen, can this thing cross-index several factors at once?" he asked.

"No problem," she said.

"Real good," he said. "I want anyone with a criminal record or a history of mental illness. Hell, give me anyone who's been *arrested* for a crime, never mind whether they were convicted. Also anyone who's ever been linked to Chrysalis or the Crystal Palace. Anyone who lives in Jokertown. Or *near* Jokertown . . . the Lower East Side, Little Italy, Chinatown, the East Village, anywhere down around there. Can you do that?"

"I think so," she said.

Jay gave her shoulder a squeeze and watched her work.

When it was done, Crash leaned back in the chair, stretched, said, "Here goes nothing," and pressed the enter key.

The machine began to hum and search.

"It's working through the three hundred two candidates, name by name, taking each suspect and searching the data banks to see if any of our criteria fit," she explained. "You gave me four parameters—arrests, mental illness, ties to Chrysalis, geography. I programmed it to flag each name with stars to indicate the number of fits."

"Real good," said Jay, who hadn't thought of that.

Jay grabbed the paper as it slid out of the laser printer, still warm to the touch. Nineteen finalists had survived.

BRAUN, JACK	GOLDEN BOY	*
CRENSON, CROYD	THE SLEEPER	****
DARLINGFOOT, JOHN	DEVIL JOHN	***
DEMARCO, ERNEST	ERNIE THE LIZARD	**
DOE, JOHN	DOUGHBOY	***
JONES, MORDECAI	THE HARLEM HAMMER	**
LOCKWOOD, WILLIAM, JR.	SNOTMAN	****
MAN, MODULAR	N/A	*
MORKLE, DOUG	N/A	**
MUELLER, HOWARD	TROLL	***
O'REILLY, RADHA	ELEPHANT GIRL	*
RAY, WILLIAM	CARNIFEX	*
SCHAEFFER, ELMO	N/A	***
SEIVERS, ROBERT	BLUDGEON	***
NAME UNKNOWN	BLACK SHADOW	**
NAMES UNKNOWN	THE ODDITY	**
NAME UNKNOWN	STARSHINE	*
NAME UNKNOWN	QUASIMAN	***
NAME UNKNOWN	WYRM	****

"How does it look?" Crash asked him.

"Like a start," he said. He showed her the list. "Any of these people ever threaten to rearrange Digger's features?"

She looked over the names carefully. "Well," she said, "Billy Ray was pretty upset with him once. Digger wrote a piece on the strongest men in the world, and he said that Billy Ray was minor league compared to Golden Boy and the Harlem Hammer. Ray took it the wrong way." She turned off the computer. "But he's in Atlanta, too, isn't he?"

"He better be," Jay said, "he's Senator Hartmann's bodyguard." He folded up the list and slid it into his breast pocket. "Two more things. Digger's address." He smiled. "And your phone number."

Well, he thought afterward, one out of two wasn't bad.

◆

Brennan woke to the jangling of the phone that sat on the nightstand beside the hotel room's lumpy, sagging bed. He sat up and winced as pain lanced through his stiff shoulder and sore back where the Oddity had slammed him against the wall. "Hello."

"Morning, Mr. Y." It was Tripod. "I've found someone you may want to have a word with. Name's Bludgeon."

"You're right," Brennan said grimly. "Where are you?"

"Uncle Chowder's Clam Bar," Tripod said.

"Right." Brennan hung up. He sat for a moment on the edge of the bed. He was still tired and he ached from the beating he'd taken the night before. Worse, he missed Jennifer more than he had ever missed anyone or anything. Perhaps, he thought, he had lost too many friends and lovers down through the years and he was getting too old and weary to bear the losses anymore.

He stood carefully and stretched his sore back and shoulder cautiously.

To hell with it, he told himself. He had never given in before. He wouldn't start now. He needed rest, but there was no time. He needed food, but he could take care of that easily enough. He needed Jennifer above everything, but there was nothing he could do about that.

As he dressed he decided to leave his bow behind. There was no way he could pull it properly the way his shoulder felt. He'd lost his other weapon, his Browning, the night before, during his tussle with the Oddity.

Great, Brennan thought, just great. He had to face Bludgeon empty-handed. What a way to start the day.

Tripod was lounging against a building whose grimy brick facade was in desperate need of a sand blasting. A flashing neon sign proclaimed the ground-floor restaurant UNCLE CHOWDER'S CLAM BAR while a mollusk with a top hat and cane and pink neon smile did a fluttering dance on stick-thin legs. A picket fence of rusty iron bars screened off a stairway that led to the basement. The battered sign bolted to the fence had a pointing six-fingered hand painted on it, a sure sign that they were in Jokertown.

"Squisher's Basement," Brennan read. "Charming." He turned to Tripod. "You're sure Bludgeon's still in there?"

"I been watching," the joker said, "and he ain't come out."

Brennan nodded and pulled out a sheaf of bills from his jeans' pocket. He peeled off two twenties and gave them to Tripod.

"They don't much like nats in Squisher's," the joker said.

Brennan smiled underneath his mask. "Thanks for the warning." He went down the stairs.

Squisher's was already crowded with jokers who felt compelled to drink their breakfasts. It stank of infrequently washed bodies, spilled beer, and indifferently sopped vomit. It was dimly lit, but Brennan could see the heads of the patrons swivel to stare at him as he entered. Conversations stopped as he approached and picked up again when he passed by. Tripod had been right. This was strictly a joker hangout and it looked as if they liked it that way.

The biggest aquarium Brennan had ever seen was set behind the bar over the shelves of liquor bottles. Something floating in the dark and oily water suddenly surged against the glass and poked his head over the side, blowing water from a hole in the top of his skull. He stared at Brennan with cold, unblinking eyes.

"Don't get many of your kind in here," the joker finally said. His ghastly face was set in a hairless round head, his fish mouth was filled with rows of pointy teeth. "Nats, I mean. You are a nat, right?"

"I have business with one of your customers."

Squisher gave him the fish eye. "What kind of business?"

"It's none of yours."

Brennan could hear the jokers seated along the bar mutter among themselves.

"This is my place," Squisher said. "Whatever happens in it is my business." He glanced down into the water, reached out a long boneless arm, and caught something. Brennan saw orange scales flash as Squisher dropped a small fish into his mouth, gulped twice and swallowed, then looked back at Brennan.

Brennan removed an ace of spades from his hip pocket and held it out toward the joker.

Squisher squinted, then reached out a long sinuous arm that ended in a collection of twitching tentacles and took the card from Brennan. He brought the pasteboard close to his face, looked from it to Brennan, then silently slid under the water of his aquarium.

Brennan turned to face the room where everyone was suddenly very interested in their drinks, and spotted Bludgeon sitting alone at a table in a far, dark corner.

He recognized the joker instantly. He'd only seen him once before during a crazy, confused brawl in Times Square almost two years ago, but Bludgeon didn't have the kind of face you could easily forget.

He was seven feet of ugly, with a puckered, scarred face and a right hand that was a twisted club of muscle and bone. He was thinner than the first time Brennan had seen him, so thin that his filthy clothes hung loosely on his frame. His skin was blotchy, his hair long and greasy. He sat alone, staring at nothing and mumbling to himself as Brennan approached. The whites of his eyes were a clouded yellow shot through with scarlet veins. Brennan stared at him, unsure whether to feel pity or disgust.

"Whadda fuck you want?" Bludgeon asked after a long moment.

"Talk on the street is that you killed Chrysalis," Brennan said lowly.

A spark of animation kindled in Bludgeon's sick eyes. "Yeah," he rumbled. "It was me. I offed the cocksucking bitch. Buy me a drink and I'll tell you all about it."

"First tell me how you killed her."

Bludgeon held up his clubbed right fist. "I beat the fucking whore's brains out with my hand. It's all I ever needed. Never needed a fucking gun, never needed no goddamn knife. Just my hand."

The twitch of disgust in Brennan's face, the loathing in his eyes, went unnoticed by the drunken joker. "Where?" Brennan said softly.

"Where what?"

"Where'd you kill her?"

"In that shithole saloon of hers, man," Bludgeon mumbled. "I threw her on the bar and stuck my dick in her and fucked the living shit out of her." He laughed and a mad light shone in his sick eyes. "Then just to make sure she was dead I beat her fucking head in. Just to make sure."

"You scum," Brennan said through clenched teeth. "You shit-eating scum. I'd kill you where you sit if I didn't know that you're lying."

Bludgeon blinked, his porcine eyes staring at Brennan without comprehension. He stood up when Brennan's words finally soaked into his clouded brain, and screamed a stream of obscenities. He pushed the table at Brennan, but it only scraped slowly across the floor and Brennan sidestepped it easily.

Bludgeon howled and swung his clubbed arm. Brennan avoided the slow-motion punch and grabbed Bludgeon by his wrist and shoulder and threw him against the bar, scattering jokers right and left.

Squisher rose agitatedly from the depths of his aquarium as Brennan picked up a chair.

"My tank!" the joker screamed. "Don't break the glass!"

Bludgeon, pinned against the bar and breathing hard, looked at Brennan with fear and pain in his eyes. Brennan swung the chair, smashing him across the gut, and Bludgeon gasped like a fish out of water. Brennan swung again, catching Bludgeon on the side and slamming him down across three bar stools. Bludgeon made a feeble attempt to stand, but his slack muscles wouldn't work. He sighed, bubbling the bloody froth on his lips, and made weak swimming motions with his arms.

Brennan checked his third blow when he saw that Bludgeon had nothing left in him. He dropped the chair, the tubular metal of its back and legs twisted into an ornate abstract sculpture.

"You didn't kill her," Brennan said in a low voice. "Why say you did?"

"I need a fucking job," Bludgeon panted. "No one will touch me.

No one will give me a fucking chance. I figured . . . I just figured Fadeout or somebody in the Fists would give me a chance, you know. Just give me a fucking chance . . ."

"You pathetic lying shit," Brennan said in a low voice. He had known it wouldn't be this easy. Partly out of frustration, partly because he wanted Chrysalis's killer to know that he was on his trail, he turned to face the room and said, "I was Chrysalis's friend and I'm going to find her killer. Bet on it."

He dropped an ace of spades on Bludgeon and stalked out of the bar. Before he got out the door one of the bar's bolder patrons was stripping the leather jacket off Bludgeon's back, slapping him in the face when he protested in a sad, tremulous whine.

11:00 A.M.

Digger's apartment was a fifth floor walk-up on Horatio in the West Village. In the playground across the street, some teenagers were shooting baskets, shirts against skins. Jay stopped to watch for a few minutes. They had a couple girls playing, but they were both on the shirts side, more's the pity.

A heavyset man with a shaved head sat on the stoop of Digger's building, drinking a can of Rheingold. When Jay stepped off the sidewalk, he got up and blocked the door. "You got business here?"

The man had three inches and fifty pounds on him, not to mention an eagle tattooed on his right biceps and a gold hoop in one ear. "I'm looking for Digger Downs," Jay told him.

"He ain't home."

"I'll check for myself, thanks."

"The fuck you will. We had enough freaks comin' round for a free look."

Jay didn't like the sound of that. "You had trouble here?"

The man crushed the beer can in his fist. "Nothin' like the trouble you're gonna have."

He mulled over the idea of popping this asshole down inside an abandoned subway station, but decided to try it the easy way first.

"I want to know what happened here," he said. He took a fold of bills out of his pocket. "So does Mr. Jackson."

"I don't know no Mr. Jackson," the man said, "but you lay a tenspot on me, you can go inside and look."

Wit was a lost art, Jay decided; on the other hand, he'd just saved ten bucks, so he shouldn't complain. He unfolded a ten-dollar bill and put it in the man's thick, callused hand. "C'mon," the man said, "I ain't got all day." They went inside. The entryway was small and dark, doorbells mounted beside the mailboxes. While the big man fumbled for a key, Jay found Downs and pressed his button. There was no answer.

"You really lookin' for Digger?" his host said, grunting again, as he opened the inner security door. "Like I told you, he ain't here." They stepped through the door, and he pointed up the staircase. "You want to see the bloodstains, they're up on four and five. I been humping up and down all day, I'm sick of all them fucking steps."

"Are you going to tell me what happened here, or should we play twenty questions?"

"Fuck, I thought the whole city knew, the way the cops were crawling all over the place yesterday. You oughta read the *Post*, mister. Double murder."

"Oh, shit," Jay said, a sinking feeling in the bottom of his stomach. This iced the cake, he supposed, but the frosting was a real ugly flavor. "Downs?"

"Nah. It was Mrs. Rosenstein, she's got the apartment across the hall from Digger, and Jonesy the super."

"Let me guess," Jay said. "They were beaten to death."

"Fuck no."

It had been a long time since Jay Ackroyd had been that surprised. "No?" he said.

"Nah. They was cut to pieces, both of 'em, by some nutcase with a buzz saw. I was the one that found 'em. God, you should've seen it. I took off early yesterday, had this sum-bitch of a hangover, and when I come home, there's this shit lying right in front of my door. I'm up on three. Fuck, I almost stepped in it. It was all bloody, like something you'd find in the garbage behind a butcher shop, some piece of meat nobody wanted, y'know? So I nudge it with my foot, and I seen it had an eye in it. Know what it was?" He leaned forward, and Jay could smell the beer on his breath. "Jonesy's face! Not the whole thing, only half of it. It must of fallen down the stairwell. The rest of him was on the fourth-floor landing. I don't know how he made it that far, his whole fucking belly was cut open, and his guts was spilling out on that fag Cooper's welcome mat. His hands was all slimy from trying to stuff 'em back in, but one of them whatchacallits, intensines, it went all the way up the stairs to the fifth floor. That was where I found Mrs. Rosenstein. Betcha never knew them intensines was so long, right?" He shrugged. "Well, the cops took the bodies away, but there's still blood all over the goddamn walls. Now that fuckin' landlord is gonna *have* to hang some new wallpaper. Bet it takes him six months, though."

"What about Downs?" Jay demanded.

"Fuck if I know. He ain't been home. The cops checked his door, but it was still locked. He's just off doing some write-up for that fuckin' magazine. He's gonna be pissed when he finds out what he missed. What a laugh."

"A riot," said Jay, who didn't think Digger would be pissed at all. "Hey, you ever been in Newark city jail?"

"Fuck no," the man said, with a frown.

"Oh, good," Jay said. "I spent a night there once. It really sucks." He pointed. Air rushed into suddenly empty space with a *pop* that sounded almost like a hiccup, and Jay was alone in the hallway. He started up the stairs, smiling. That was pointless and petty, and if he kept doing stuff like that he was going to get himself sued one of these days. But sometimes it just felt so good.

He spotted red-brown traces on the third-floor landing, and droplets on the wooden banister between three and four, but the serious bloodstains began on the fourth floor. The faded wallpaper showed long dark streaks in two places, where the custodian must have staggered against the wall as he tried to flee, maimed and bleeding, holding himself together with his hands.

That was pretty bad, but the fifth-floor landing was a lot worse. There were dried brown smears where a body, or a piece of a body, had struck the wall. The carpet runner had soaked up so much blood it looked black in places. The spray had gone everywhere. The walls were spotted by it, as if the hallway had come down with measles. Over his head was a trapdoor to the roof, and even that had caught a few stray droplets.

Jay looked around and tried to reconcile what he was seeing with what he'd seen yesterday morning in the Crystal Palace. It didn't add up. A buzz saw, the asshole downstairs had said; it sure as hell looked like it. The West Village Chainsaw Massacre; no wonder the *Post* had had a field day. By comparison, Chrysalis had hardly bled at all. A few drops on her blouse, a little down low on the walls, but nothing like this.

He tried on the theory that was all coincidence, that this little exercise in atrocity had nothing to do with what had happened to Chrysalis, but every gut instinct he had told him that was bullshit. What the hell was going on here?

Disgusted, Jay turned to Digger's door. It was locked, as advertised. He opened the spring lock easily enough with a credit card, but there was a dead bolt as well. For that he needed a lock pick and a good ten minutes of work. Jay had deft, practiced hands and a real nice set of lock picks, but this was a good lock. Finally he heard the tumblers click, and the door pushed open. There was a chain, he saw as he stepped through, but it hadn't been used. Neither had the police bar, which meant the apartment had been locked from the outside.

Jay took one look around and said, "Oh shit."

The place had been trashed. Thoroughly and savagely trashed.

He moved through the cramped little rooms carefully. Things had been thrown, smashed, stepped on. At every turn he expected to find a body, or what remained of a body. The living-room floor was buried in a blizzard of paper. A gigantic old Zenith console television had been reduced to ground glass and kindling, and what might have been an impressive collection of old LPs crunched underfoot as Jay stepped on the pieces. In the bedroom, the bed was in pieces, sheets razored, stuffing torn out of the mattress and scattered, books sliced in half right down their spines. The kitchen was covered with decaying junk food, the riper bits already crawling with roaches. All the cupboards had been shattered, their contents strewn wildly about. A huge old refrigerator lay facedown on the linoleum. When Jay bent to examine it, he found a jagged gash in the thick metal of the door. "Jesus Christ," he said. He stood up.

Back in the living room, he noticed the bars on the window. He went through the apartment once again to check.

There were thick iron bars on *every* window, even in the white porcelain ruins of the bathroom. The bars looked new. Installed within the past year, Jay would be willing to bet. It looked as though Digger had been as security conscious as Chrysalis, not that it had done him much good. The windows were all locked. Whoever had done this had come in the same way Jay had, through the front door.

Unless maybe they'd come in through a wall.

Jay looked around for an ace of spades, not really expecting to find one. Yeoman might be a psychopath, but his killings had always been accomplished with a certain cool, professional efficiency. This, and the butchery out in the hall, looked like the work of some rabid animal. Jay could easily imagine the killer foaming at the mouth as he went from room to room, destroying.

He was making one final, methodical sweep through the apartment when he spotted the notebooks on the bedroom floor, jumbled up with the latest celebrity bios, a few reference books, and a wide selection of paperbacks by Anonymous with soft-focus covers of women in Victorian undergarments. Not more than one book in five was intact. The corner of one wire-bound notebook was sticking out from under a snowdrift of loose pages, and the plain cardboard cover caught his eye. He dug through the paper and found three more of them, and parts of a fourth. Reporter's notebooks, filled with a hurried, semilegible scrawl. A long diagonal chunk was missing from one book, but you could still read most of it.

Each notebook was dated. Jay sat gingerly on what remained of Digger's mattress and opened the most recent. The last article Digger had worked up was called "The Farmer of Park Avenue," about an eight-year-old girl whose miniature farm filled an entire floor in her daddy's Park Avenue town home. The farm had model houses, painted rivers, felt grass, toy cars and trucks, and an electric train that circled the property. Her farm animals were real. Cows four inches long, tiny little sheepdogs, suckling pigs the size of cockroaches, all shrunken to their present diminutive size by the freckle-faced little farmer, who just loved animals.

Somehow Jay didn't think eight-year-old Jessica von der Stadt was a likely suspect. He flipped back to older material, looking for any mention of Chrysalis, death threats, or homicidal maniacs with or without buzz saws. He found the address of a photographer who had gotten some spicy shots of Peregrine breast-feeding, bios of the government aces assigned to protect the presidential candidates, Hiram's recipe for chocolate mango pie, quotes for a cover profile of Mister Magnet, and Mistral's fond reminiscences of the day her daddy had taught her to fly.

Jay flipped the notebook aside in disgust, and found himself possessed of an overpowering urge to get the hell out of this place.

♠

Brennan sat in a booth in Hairy's Kitchen, sipping occasionally from his cup of tea and ignoring the irritated stares from the passing waitress when he refused to order anything else. He was surrounded by a litter of newspapers that he'd read looking for news about the killing. Chrysalis's death was already relegated to the back pages, pushed aside by the political craziness in Atlanta where a huge platform fight on the jokers' rights plank was brewing. Barnett was marshaling his holier-than-thou forces and the big clash between him and Hartmann was looming on the near horizon.

Chrysalis's death was already old news. Only the *Jokertown Cry* was still running the killing as a front-page item, including a photo of the detective team heading the investigation, Jokertown's own Harvey Kant, and his partner, Thomas Jan Maseryk.

Brennan put his teacup down, oblivious to another hard stare from the waitress, and looked closely at the grainy newspaper photo of two men standing outside the Crystal Palace. Kant was the joker on the left. A tall, scaly reptiloid, he reminded Brennan of his old Shadow Fist foe, Wyrm. The other was Maseryk. Brennan nodded to himself. He slid out of the booth, went to the public phone booth in the back of the restaurant, and dialed the Jokertown precinct. It took a moment for the connection to go through, and then he heard a deep, gruff, tired voice on the other end. "Maseryk."

It was definitely him. Brennan hadn't heard the voice in almost fifteen years, but he still recognized it. There was a shadow in it, a brooding, sepulchral tone that hinted at the blackness that had followed Maseryk everywhere when Brennan had known him in Nam.

"Long time no see," Brennan said quietly.

There was a short silence. Brennan could almost hear the gears whirring in Maseryk's head. "Who is this?"

"Brennan. Daniel Brennan."

"Brennan?"

"It's me."

"Christ. I guess it's been a long time. So is this a social call to renew old acquaintances?"

"Of a type," Brennan said. "I'd like to talk to you."

"About what, after all these years?"

"About Chrysalis's murder."

"What's your interest in that?"

"Personal. She was a friend of mine."

"Mmm. You always did take things personal. Okay. Where shall we have this chat?"

Brennan thought it over. He wanted to pump Maseryk for information, but Maseryk was always a closemouthed sort. It wouldn't hurt to meet in a place that might smooth Maseryk's often-touchy feelings, a place Maseryk would also be disinclined to bust up if their talk went sour. "How about over lunch at Aces High?"

"That's a little rich for a cop's pay."

"My treat."

"How can I resist?"

1:00 P.M.

"More coffee, Jay?" Flo asked him.

"Please," Jay said, pushing the cup across the Formica counter. It was his fourth cup. Flo had removed the evidence of his patty melt and fries twenty minutes ago.

"Working a puzzle?" the waitress asked as she refilled his cup. Some of the coffee slopped over into the saucer.

"Something like that," Jay admitted. The list was spread out on the counter. He'd been going over it name by name while he ate. A translucent smudge on the paper marked the spot where a bit of onion had slid out of his patty melt.

"Well, call me if you need any help," Flo said. "I work them *TV Guide* crosswords every week." She went off with her coffeepot to a booth in back, where a chicken hawk in a white linen suit was trying to recruit a blond boy fresh off the bus from St. Paul. The Java Joint was on Forty-second Street between Times Square and the Port Authority Bus Terminal, sandwiched in between the Wet Pussycat Theater and an adult bookstore. The food wasn't quite up to Aces High, but Jay liked the prices. Besides, it was a half block from his office.

He chewed on the pencil he'd bummed from Flo and looked at the list again. The original nineteen finalists were down to eleven. Snotman was in jail at the moment; he'd gone first. Most of the one-star candidates had followed in short order. Chrysalis's office wasn't big enough to hold an elephant, which eliminated Radha O'Reilly. Modular Man and Starshine had both made the list strictly on the basis of geography; neither had any particular reason to want Chrysalis dead. Carnifex had been in Atlanta, as had Jack Braun. Jay knew Elmo hadn't done it, no matter how many stars the computer had assigned him. That left the list looking like this:

~~DRAUN, JACK~~	~~GOLDEN BOY~~	~~*~~
CRENSON, CROYD	THE SLEEPER	****
DARLINGFOOT, JOHN	DEVIL JOHN	***
DEMARCO, ERNEST	ERNIE THE LIZARD	**
DOE, JOHN	DOUGHBOY	***
JONES, MORDECAI	THE HARLEM HAMMER	**
~~LOCKWOOD, WILLIAM, JR.~~	~~SNOTMAN~~	~~****~~
~~MAN, MODULAR~~	~~N/A~~	~~*~~
MORKLE, DOUG	N/A	**
MUELLER, HOWARD	TROLL	***
~~O'REILLY, RADHA~~	~~ELEPHANT GIRL~~	~~*~~
~~RAY, WILLIAM~~	~~CARNIFEX~~	~~*~~

~~SCHAEFFER, ELMO~~	~~N/A~~	~~***~~
SEIVERS, ROBERT	BLUDGEON	***
NAME UNKNOWN	BLACK SHADOW	**
NAMES UNKNOWN	THE ODDITY	**
~~NAME UNKNOWN~~	~~STARSHINE~~	~~*~~
NAME UNKNOWN	QUASIMAN	***
NAME UNKNOWN	WYRM	****

Jay considered the names that remained. Ernie the Lizard De-Marco owned a Jokertown bar, but it was strictly a neighborhood place, no competition for the Palace. He crossed him out. Devil John Darlingfoot was hired muscle with a record as long as a joker's dork, but all his strength was in one deformed leg. Maybe he kicked in Chrysalis's face? Somehow it didn't feel right. Besides, Jay had the vague impression that Devil John drew the line at murder. He crossed out that name, too. Doughboy had tremendous strength and the mind of a child. He'd become somewhat of a cause when the cops arrested him for murder a few years back. But he hadn't done that one and Jay didn't think it was very likely that he'd done this one either. He went. Mordecai Jones lived in Harlem, half a city away from Jokertown. Except for that world tour last year, he didn't move in the same circles as Chrysalis. He went, too.

He hesitated for a couple minutes over Howard Mueller, better known as Troll, the chief of security at Dr. Tachyon's Jokertown Clinic. Mueller was a Palace regular, and the nine-foot-tall joker was up there with Golden Boy and the Harlem Hammer in the strength department, but as far as Jay knew, Troll was one of the good guys. Maybe he wasn't as clean as he looked. Maybe Chrysalis had dug up some dirt on him, a secret out of his past, and tried to leverage him with it. It was possible, Jay supposed.

Of course, it was also a complete supposition. You could make the same theory fit Ernie the Lizard, the Harlem Hammer, Starshine, hell, any of them. What a great theory, one size fits all. No, that road would take him back to three hundred nineteen names in no time at all. He put pencil to paper and resolutely scratched out Troll.

That left seven little Indians. Seven real *strong* Indians: Wyrm,

Quasiman, the Oddity, Black Shadow, Bludgeon, the Sleeper, and Doug Morkle, whoever the fuck *he* was.

Wyrm was an ugly bit of business, a major player in the Shadow Fist Society. Jay had run into him once, had heard him threaten Chrysalis, in fact. That had been almost two years ago, but Wyrm looked like the kind of guy who held grudges. The only problem was the M.O. Strong as he was, Wyrm killed with his bite, pumping his victims full of venom. Jay didn't recall any bite marks on Chrysalis, but it was worth checking. The autopsy would certainly show the presence of poison in her system.

Quasiman was a caretaker at Our Lady of Perpetual Misery. Much stronger than Wyrm, the hunchback was a teleport, too. He could have gotten in and out of the Palace without being seen. He was supposed to be on the side of the angels, but every so often part of his brain drifted off to another dimension or something, and then there was no telling what he might do. An unlikely suspect, but still . . .

The Oddity was one Jay already had his suspicions about.

Black Shadow was another lunatic vigilante. Hated crime and liked to kill criminals, or maybe just break all their arms and legs if he was in a good mood. Maybe Shad had learned that Chrysalis was involved in some kind of criminal activity. Maybe she'd learned his real identity and threatened to expose him. Maybe, maybe, maybe. Again, though, the M.O. was a problem. Shad was only slightly stronger than the human norm. The whispers said he was a creature of the darkness, a vampire who drank light and heat instead of blood, that he killed by draining all the warmth from his victims. He didn't break heads. Jay crossed him off.

Bludgeon was a brutal seven-foot-tall joker whose right hand was twisted into a permanent fist. He'd been a Shadow Fist until he proved too violent and stupid even for them, and they'd cut him loose, thanks in no small part to Jay and Hiram Worchester. That deformed fist of his could mash bone and brain real easy, and Bludgeon would probably enjoy every minute of it. The only thing was, he was dumb as a stump and twice as ugly. No way he'd penetrate the Palace security on his own, and Jay couldn't imagine why Chrysalis would ever agree to meet with him. But maybe there was something Jay didn't know yet. He left Bludgeon on the list.

Croyd Crenson, the Sleeper, was a freelance operating on the fringes of the law. His powers changed every time he slept, but usually included super strength, and in the later stages of each waking period he was a speed freak given to fits of paranoid rage. Jay didn't recall that Croyd had any beef with Chrysalis, but if he was far enough gone in amphetamine psychosis, that might not matter. So if the Sleeper was awake, and if the strength had stayed with him this time, and if he'd taken enough crank to fuck up his judgment, and if Chrysalis somehow provoked him into a psychotic rage . . . Jay decided there were too damn many if's. The Sleeper got penciled out.

Then there were five. Wyrm, Quasiman, the Oddity, Bludgeon, and Doug Morkle. "Who the fuck is Doug Morkle?" he asked Flo when she came back with the coffeepot. She didn't know either.

He sighed and paid his bill, overtipping as usual. He was on his way out through the revolving door when he saw the newspaper folded up next to the punk with the green mohawk in the first booth. Jay just revolved all the way back around, walked over to the booth, and picked up the paper.

"Hey," the mohawk objected.

"Shit," Jay said, scanning down the column of newsprint, "they got Elmo." Riding the D train out to Brooklyn, the story said. A goddamn Guardian Angel made the arrest; he bet the cops really loved that part.

Jay decided that Doug Morkle would keep.

♥

Brennan had never been inside Aces High before. It was a nice place. It seemed the kind of place where two old friends—old acquaintances, at least—could sit down and have a nice, civilized chat about murder and related subjects. He hoped that Maseryk would think so, too.

He finished his drink and waved away the waiter when he tried to bring another. Outwardly he was as patient as always, though inside he was as tense as a joker at a Leo Barnett rally. Maseryk was hard and tough. There'd been whispers about him in Nam when, like Brennan, he'd commanded a long-range recondo team. But there were always a lot of strange rumors in Nam.

Brennan recognized Maseryk the moment he spotted the waiter leading him to the table. He hadn't changed much over the years. A compact man, Brennan's size and build, he moved with the same easy grace and economy of movement. He had thinning dark hair, pale skin, and intense violet eyes. He still had the air of brooding menace about him that Brennan remembered from Nam.

"Hello, Captain," Brennan said as Maseryk slid into the chair across the table from him.

Maseryk stared at him. "Do something to your face?" he asked.

When Brennan had infiltrated the Shadow Fists, he'd had Dr. Tachyon give his eyes epicanthic folds so he'd fit in better with the Asian gang. Maseryk, of course, had last seen him years before the operation.

"It's the eyes, Captain. Asian eyes are all the rage nowadays."

Maseryk grunted and sat down. "I'm just a lieutenant now."

Brennan nodded, gestured at the waiter.

"It's your party," Maseryk said.

"Two more Tullamore's, then. On ice."

"Very good, sir." The waiter bowed a precise millimeter, then left.

Brennan wondered where to begin and in the wondering they sat in silence until the waiter returned with their drinks. "Do you care to order now?" he asked, stepping a pace backward and holding his pen poised expectantly over his pad.

Maseryk glanced at the unopened menu before him on the table. "I hear the blackened redfish is pretty good, though on a cop's salary I've never had the opportunity to try it."

"It is very good, sir," the waiter said, faintly astonished that anyone could possibly think otherwise. He turned to Brennan with a raised eyebrow and poised pen. "And you, sir?"

"Seafood salad."

"Very good, sir." The waiter collected the menus and was gone.

Maseryk took a sip from his drink, set it aside. "So what's this about? Neither of us are exactly the type to get together to talk over the good old days we spent chasing Charlie through the jungle."

"Chrysalis's murder."

Maseryk grunted. "You said that. What was she to you?"

"We were lovers."

Maseryk's eyebrows rose. "Chrysalis had a lot of lovers. You the jealous kind?"

"Come off it," Brennan said flatly. "Why would I be talking to you if I killed her? You had no idea I was involved in this until I called you."

"Murderers sometimes do strange things," Maseryk said, "to call attention to themselves."

Brennan snorted. "I thought the bow-and-arrow vigilante was your prime suspect."

Maseryk looked at him carefully. "A playing card was found on her body," he admitted, "but it wasn't the ordinary kind of card he used. This was a fancy one from Chrysalis's own antique deck."

Brennan nodded. Something that had been bothering him since his break-in at the Palace suddenly clicked into place. "And the rest of the deck is missing."

"That's right," Maseryk said. "How did you know?"

Brennan smiled tightly. "Someone told me that Jay Ackroyd was at the Palace early that morning."

"That's right, too," Maseryk said. "He found the body."

"Why was he there?"

"You're awfully full of questions," Maseryk said. "You're not thinking of interfering with an ongoing police investigation, are you?"

"I want her killer brought to justice. If you find him, fine. If I do . . ." His voice trailed off and he shrugged.

"Look, Brennan," Maseryk said in a sudden, hard voice, pointing his forefinger at him, "none of this vigilante shit—"

"If you did your job," Brennan replied, in a voice just as hard, "there wouldn't be any need for this vigilante shit. I could be home where I want to be, instead of putting my ass on the line."

Maseryk was about to reply when the waiter appeared at their table and slipped their plates in front of them. He glanced from one man to the other. "Will that be all?"

Brennan tore his gaze from Maseryk's and nodded at the waiter. "For now."

"Enjoy your meal, sirs," the waiter said, and hustled away.

"If you answer my question," Brennan said in a soft, conciliatory voice, "I'll give you another one you should ask somebody."

Maseryk looked at him a long time, then finally sighed. "All right. I'll bite. The PI said Chrysalis had hired him to be her bodyguard. He did one hell of a job."

Brennan nodded thoughtfully and picked at his seafood salad.

"Well," Maseryk prompted, "what do you have for me?"

"Ask the Oddity what he, she, whatever, was looking for in Chrysalis's bedroom last night."

Maseryk scowled at his dish as Brennan speared a bit of crab. "Do you want to tell me what's going on?" he finally asked.

Brennan shook his head. "Not now. I have nothing you'd believe." He popped the crab in his mouth and chewed, his gaze far away.

Maseryk frowned. "You better not be jerking me around."

"Enjoy your meal," Brennan said.

Maseryk nodded, cut another slice. "I will. It's a damn fine fish. Damn fine."

They ate their food, saying little. Neither was much for small talk and both were absorbed in their own thoughts. Maseryk refused the waiter's offer of coffee and dessert when they had finished. Brennan ordered a cup of tea.

"I'll be in touch," Brennan said as Maseryk rose from the table.

"Don't do anything foolish," Maseryk advised him.

Brennan nodded. The waiter set a teacup in front of him and left. Brennan lifted the cup to his lips. He frowned. There was a note on the saucer. It was written on a ragged scrap of paper in a childish, impossibly tiny hand.

"If you want to no what the Shadow Fists are hidding," it read, "go to Stoney Brook, 8800 Glenhollow Rode. Be carfull."

Brennan quickly looked around the restaurant, and then immediately felt foolish for doing so. Someone had to be trailing him—or reading his mind. Someone knew as much about what he was doing as he did. It gave him a chilly, uncomfortable feeling, as if he were the hunted instead of the hunter.

He looked again at the note. It was unsigned, of course. It appeared as if it were sent by someone who was friendly, and seemed childishly innocuous with its semilegible scrawl and misspelled words. Brennan decided to check out the tip it offered, but also to follow its final hint and be very, very careful indeed.

2:00 P.M.

Kant didn't look pleased to see him. "I thought we got rid of you yesterday," he said.

"The reptile ranch was closed, so I came here," Jay said. "Where's your partner?"

"Out to lunch," Kant snapped at him. "Like you. Only with you it's a permanent condition." He showed his teeth. They were still pointed.

"Is that a joke?" Jay asked. It was, he was almost sure of it. He turned to a passing uniform. "Kant just made a joke," he said. The cop ignored him. "I don't think he was real impressed."

"You keep playing games with me, I'm going to make you real sorry," Kant promised. His moment of levity had obviously passed. "What the fuck do you want?" he asked irritably, rubbing at a big green scab under his collar. The starch must chafe his scales.

"I want to talk to Elmo," Jay said.

Kant was so surprised he stopped scratching his scab. "Get the hell out of here before I throw you out."

"You again?" Maseryk said as he sauntered up to the desk. He was chewing on a toothpick. It must have been a good lunch.

"He wants to see Elmo," Kant told his partner, in a tone that suggested it was the funniest thing imaginable.

Maseryk didn't laugh. "Why?"

Jay shrugged. "Might as well, can't dance."

"Elmo isn't talking," Maseryk said. "We told him he had the right to remain silent, and damned if he didn't take us up on it."

"He'll talk to me," Jay said.

Kant and Maseryk exchanged glances. "And you'll tell us what he said?" Maseryk suggested.

"Wouldn't be sporting," Jay said.

Kant gave him one of his sideways blinks. "Get out of here before I lose my temper. I wouldn't want you to get hurt."

"Uh-oh," Jay said. "You hear that, Maseryk? Your partner was threatening me with police brutality. Do all lizards have such nasty dispositions, or is it just him?"

Kant came around his desk. He towered over Jay, all teeth and scales. "That's it. C'mon, asshole. Let's dance."

Jay ignored him. "I've got a proposition for you," he said to Maseryk. "Why don't you tell your partner to go sun himself on a rock while we talk privately?"

Maseryk looked at Kant. "Give us a moment, Harv."

"You're going to buy into this bullshit?" Kant said.

Maseryk shrugged. "He might have something." They walked down to an empty interrogation room. Maseryk shut the door, swung a chair around, and sat down with his arms crossed on its back, studying Jay with those piercing violet eyes. "This better be good," he said.

"It's a modest little deal, but I think you'll be amused by its presumption," Jay said. "You give me ten minutes with Elmo, I'll give you the name of the ace-of-spades killer."

♣

Stony Brook—or, as the note had said, Stoney Brook—was a small suburban town in Suffolk County, Long Island. Brennan stopped at a gas station in his rented Toyota to ask directions to Glenhollow—thank heavens his unknown informant had managed to spell that right—Road. It ran nearly parallel to Long Island Sound, and in fact turned into a wandering county road through sparsely settled, heavily forested country soon after Brennan turned onto it. A few houses were directly on the road, more stood back out of sight on meandering dirt lanes.

Brennan kept looking for number 8800, but missed it the first time by. He stopped when he saw number 8880 on a mailbox next to a dirt lane, checked for nonexistent traffic, then did a careful three-point turn and headed back down the road, this time driving even slower. This time he passed number 8700 without finding the address he was looking for, but remembered going by an unnumbered lane that could have been the missing 8800.

Brennan pulled over to the side on a relatively wide section of the road. He parked, got out of the car, and went to the trunk where he had stashed his bow case. He glanced up and down the road. There was still no traffic. He opened the bow case and with practiced, assured ease, assembled his compound bow. He drew the string smoothly. His shoulder burned, but he decided he could handle the pain. He slipped his hood over his head and then faded into the trees crowding the roadside, the hunter returned to the forest.

◆

The lockup in Fort Freak had special cells for special customers. Elmo rated a windowless cubicle with a reinforced steel door. There were unseemly bulges in the metal where some previous tenant had tried to punch his way out.

When they entered, Elmo was seated on the narrow bed, feet dangling a foot off the floor. His arms were locked in the most massive pair of handcuffs Jay had ever seen. "Custom design," Maseryk told him. "For perps with more muscles than mother nature intended." He was using his bad-cop voice, hard-edged and nasty. Maybe he and Kant really did swap roles with jokers.

"Take them off," Jay said.

"That wasn't part of our deal," Maseryk said. "You've got ten minutes." He locked the cell behind him. They listened as his footsteps receded down the corridor.

Elmo looked up for the first time. "Popinjay," the dwarf said. He was about four feet tall and almost as wide. His arms and legs were short but massive, thick with cords of muscle.

"They tell me you're not talking."

"Nothing to say. I still got my phone call coming. Know any lawyers?"

"Try Dr. Pretorius," Jay said.

"He any good?"

"He's a pain in the ass, but yeah, he's good. And he's had lots of practice defending scapegoats."

"You don't think I did it?"

Jay sat down on the toilet. "She was scared. No offense, Elmo, but I can't imagine her being scared of you. She hired me as extra security, told me I'd start the next day. That make any sense if the guy you're scared of lives downstairs?"

The dwarf's normally stolid features twisted in pain. "I was her bodyguard," he said. "For years. I never let nothing happen to her. This is my fault. I should have been there."

"Why weren't you?"

Elmo studied his hands. His fingers were blunt and stubby, ridged with calluses. "She sent me on an errand."

"Then it's not your fault. You did what she told you to do. What kind of errand?"

Elmo shook his head. "Can't say. Her business."

"She's dead," Jay pointed out, "and you're going to take the fall for killing her. You think Jokertown is bad? You ought to see how jokers get treated up in Attica. Talk to me, Elmo. Give me something to work with."

Elmo looked around the cell. "I delivered a sealed envelope and an airline ticket to a man in a warehouse," he said after a while. "The meeting went off without a hitch, but when I got back to the Palace, there were cop cars out front. I didn't like the looks of that, so I figured I'd lay low until I found out what was going on. When I heard over the radio, I decided it'd be healthier to leave town. I didn't have nothing to go back for anyway."

"Who was the man?" Jay asked.

Elmo closed his hand into a fist. "Don't know."

"What did he look like?"

Elmo opened his fingers again. "It was dark, and he wore a mask. A bear mask. Black, with big teeth."

Jay scowled. "He look strong?"

Elmo laughed. "We didn't do any arm wrestling. I delivered an envelope, that's all." Then he fell silent, staring at his fingers as he opened and closed his hand.

"What else?" Jay prompted. He got no reply. "C'mon, Elmo, we've only got ten minutes. Help me."

The dwarfs face was expressionless for a moment, his eyes locked on Jay's. Then he nodded slowly and looked away. "Yeah," he said. "Okay. It's hard. She . . ." Elmo groped for words. "She didn't tell me not to say nothing, but she never had to. I knew when to keep my mouth shut. If you didn't, you didn't stay around the Palace for long. But now it don't matter, does it? She's gone."

"Tell me about the meeting."

"The envelope was full of money. A *lot* of money. She was buying a hit. I knew it. She knew I knew. We both pretended otherwise. That was the way she liked to do things." He looked up at Jay. "He must have hit her first, that's all I can figure."

Chrysalis had never been a model citizen, Jay knew. She made her own rules. Murder, though . . . that didn't sound like the woman he'd known. "Who did she want dead?"

"In the envelope with the money was a folded-up piece of paper with a name on it," Elmo told him. "I never saw it, but when the guy in the bear mask read it, he made a crack. He said, *Shit. Never ask for anything small*. Then I knew. The money in the envelope was *way* more than the going price for a hit, and that was only part of the payment. And that airline ticket? Round-trip to Atlanta."

"Atlanta?" Jay said. For a moment he wondered who the hell Chrysalis could possibly know in Atlanta. Then he got it, and a cold sick feeling spread over him. "Oh shit," he said.

"She was never interested in politics until last year," Elmo confided. "Then she got *real* interested. I figured, I don't know, maybe some of the stuff she'd seen on the tour. She wasn't like old Des or some of those other joker politicos, but she *was* a joker."

"Leo Barnett?" Jay said.

Elmo nodded. "Gotta be."

"Great," Jay said. "Just fucking *great!*" For a moment he couldn't think. "Tell me about the hit man," he said.

"Tall, skinny. Wore gloves. Cheap suit, didn't fit too well. On the ticket, the name was George Kerby, but that was just something Chrysalis made up."

"George Kerby," Jay repeated. The name sounded vaguely familiar. "When was this flight?"

"Today," Elmo said.

"Shit," Jay said. "Shit shit shit." He glanced at his watch. His time was almost up. "Maseryk will be here in a minute to chase me out, we need to hurry. Tell me about Yeoman."

"Yeoman? He's history," Elmo said bluntly. "He's been gone for, what, a year now? Nobody knew where, not even Chrysalis. She tried like hell to find him. I think she was afraid the Fists had iced him. There was bad blood between Yeoman and the Fists. But it couldn't have been him. He was only a nat."

"The Oddity?" Jay asked.

Elmo shrugged. "If they had dealings, it wasn't anything she told me about."

"Who else?" Jay asked. "Enemies, rejected lovers, greedy heirs, anyone who had a reason to want her dead?"

"She had a silent partner," Elmo told him. "A joker named Charles Dutton. He helped her buy the Palace, way back when she started. I guess the joint is his now."

"I'll talk to him," Jay promised. "Anything else?"

Elmo hesitated.

"C'mon," Jay urged. "Spill it."

"I don't know what it means," Elmo said, "but last year, in the spring, I had to get rid of a body."

"A body?" Jay said.

Elmo nodded. "A woman. Young, dark-skinned, might have been pretty once, before, but not when I saw her. She'd been butchered, cut all to hell. Her breasts cut off, her face sliced to ribbons, one arm flayed, it made me sick. I'd never seen Chrysalis so scared as she was that night. It was my night off, but she found me, called me back. When I got there, Digger Downs was dry-heaving in the men's room, and Chrysalis was in her office, just sitting there smoking and staring at that body. Her hand was trembling, but she couldn't seem to look away until I covered it up with a sheet. She told me to clean it all up. So I did. I didn't ask no questions and she didn't tell me nothing. After, she never spoke about it."

"What did you do with the body?" Jay asked.

"Put it in a garbage bag and left it in the basement. The next morning it was gone. The neighbors—"

They both heard the footsteps at the same time.

"The neighbors?" Jay prompted.

"Next door," Elmo started to say as a key turned in the lock. "Any bodies we left for them. They were good at stuff like that." He shut up and looked sullenly at the floor.

The cell door swung open. Next to Maseryk was Captain Ellis herself, puffing on a cigarette and bouncing from heel to heel. "Get the hell out of there."

"I was just leaving," Jay said. He gave Elmo a reassuring pat on the arm as he walked past. The dwarf didn't even look up.

"I want you to know that Maseryk made this little arrangement without my permission," Ellis snapped. "But now that it's done, you damn well better deliver that name, and it damn well better pan out, or you and your friend Elmo could be sharing a cell."

Jay couldn't even work up the energy to sass her. "Daniel Brennan," he said.

Maseryk shot him a look like someone had just slipped an ice cube down his pants. Ellis just snorted, and wrote down the name. "Have a nice day," Jay told them, walking out.

♠

There were no walls, fences, or other barriers to keep Brennan off the grounds of 8800 Glenhollow Road. A few trees had posted signs on them, prohibiting hunting, fishing, or any other trespass under the full extent of the law, but Brennan didn't let them stop him. He moved cautiously through the trees, as quietly and carefully as if he were back in Vietnam and the forest was crawling with the enemy.

He finally broke through the screen of trees and found himself facing a rolling lawn that was as smooth as a putting green. Past the beautifully manicured lawn was an extensive flower garden. Past the flower garden was a high hedge. Past the hedge was a house, two stories. The first floor was hidden by the hedge, but four windows on the second floor looked directly upon the lawn.

Brennan took a deep breath and sprinted across the open lawn, feeling completely naked and vulnerable to anyone who might be watching from the house. He hurtled the first row of flowers, landing lightly in a crouched position, and caught his breath and listened. Nothing. He looked around. Nothing but flowers.

He scuttled into the garden in a crouch, keeping out of sight of the second-story windows, recognizing many of the flowers as he moved through the garden. There were roses and chrysanthemums, snapdragons and sunflowers, but planted side by side with them were poppies, like those he had seen growing in plantations in Vietnam and Thailand, and datura, which he recognized from his boyhood days in the Southwest, and, in cool, deep-shaded bowers, mushrooms of a dozen colors and shapes, none of which looked suitable for sautéing and eating with steak.

The innocent-looking flower garden, Brennan realized, was a drug chemist's dream with enough raw material to concoct almost any kind of stimulant, depressant, or hallucinogen. But, Brennan noted with a professional landscaper's eye, it was also a place of beautiful serenity, laid out with an eye toward the perfect blending of colors, shapes, and textures. Even the occasional ornaments interspersed between the rows of plants were pleasing and harmonious, if at times a little outré.

Like the four-foot-high concrete mushroom and the hookah-smoking caterpillar curled up on it. Not your typical garden ornament, certainly, but it fit the theme of this one.

Brennan smiled, and then the caterpillar turned and looked at him. Its cheeks puffed out and blew a hazy cloud of smoke, which engulfed Brennan before he could shut his mouth. He sucked in a deep lungful of sweet-tasting smoke, turned, and managed to stagger three steps. His head was swimming in unstoppable circles and his eyes were rolling up in back of his head as he fell heavily on the thick grass. It felt cool on his cheek as the caterpillar spoke in a naggingly familiar voice through mechanical lips.

"Welcome to the magic kingdom," it said as Brennan's eyes closed.

8:00 P.M.

The cops had the funeral home staked out to hell and gone. Jay spotted the first one selling franks from a pushcart on the corner, two more sitting in a parked car halfway down the block, a fourth on a roof across the street. Either they weren't completely convinced that Elmo was their man, or they were hoping for Yeoman to show up and pay his last respects.

Cosgrove's Mortuary was a sprawling three-story Victorian

monstrosity that looked like a shipwreck from another time. It had a great round turret in one corner, a tall Gothic tower in another; a wide wooden porch that girdled the entire house, jigsaw carpentry everywhere. Chrysalis would have loved the place.

He was climbing the steps when the door banged open and Lupo came stalking out. "A bloody farce, that's what it is," he snarled when he saw Jay. His ears were flat against his skull in anger. "Who the hell does he think he is?" He didn't wait for an answer. Jay shrugged and went on in.

The foyer was darkly papered and full of antiques. The daily directory, in a glass case mounted on the wall, announced three viewings. Wideman was in the East Parlor, Jory in the West Parlor, Moore upstairs in the Round Room. Jay realized that he didn't know Chrysalis's real name.

"Oh," said a soft voice beside him. "Mr. Ackroyd, it's so good of you to come."

Waldo Cosgrove was a round, soft man in his seventies, bald as an egg, with tiny moist hands. Waldo dressed impeccably enough to please even Hiram, smelled like he'd bathed in perfume, looked like he'd been rolled in talcum powder. Jay had done some work for him the year before, when a pair of particularly grotesque joker corpses had been stolen from the mortuary. The whole thing had upset Waldo dreadfully, and Waldo wasn't used to being upset. Mostly Waldo was sorry. He was better at being sorry than anyone Jay had ever met. "Hello, Waldo," Jay said. "Which one is Chrysalis?"

"Miss Jory is laid out in the West Parlor. It's our nicest room, you know, not to mention the largest, and she had so many friends. I was so *sorry* to hear about this dreadful business."

The words were right, but Jay had heard Waldo sound a lot sorrier. Something was upsetting the senior Cosgrove. "What's going on?" he asked. "Why was Lupo so pissed off?"

Waldo Cosgrove *tsked*. "It's not our fault. Mr. Jory was quite insistent, and after all, he was her father, but some people are taking it the wrong way. I don't know what they expect us to do. I assure you, we've spared no expense."

"I'm sure Mr. Jory will realize that, too, once he gets your bill," Jay said. "Have I gotten any phone calls?"

"Phone calls? For you? Here?"

"I've been trying to reach Hiram Worchester down in Atlanta," Jay explained. "I've been leaving messages with his hotel. If he calls, let me know."

"Oh, certainly," Waldo Cosgrove said. Another group of mourners was leaving. Jay recognized a hostess from the Crystal Palace. She didn't look too happy either. He decided to see what was going on.

The West Parlor was a long, somber, high-ceilinged room full of flowers. So many floral arrangements had been sent that some of them had been crowded out into the hall. A sign-in book had been placed by the door. Yin-Yang stood beside it, expressing condolences to a big, robust man in his sixties who could only be Chrysalis's father. Jory wore a white shirt and a black suit, and there was something about him that made you think, yes, this was definitely a black-and-white kind of man. Right now he looked uncomfortable. Maybe it was the suit. Maybe it was the occasion. Maybe it was Yin-Yang, both of whose heads were talking at once, as usual.

When the joker finally shuffled into the parlor, Jay stepped up and offered a hand. "Mr. Jory, I'm deeply sorry about your daughter," he said. "She was an extraordinary woman."

"Yes," Jory replied. He had a firm handshake and a distinct twang in his voice that was utterly at odds with his daughter's carefully cultivated British accent. "Debra-Jo was a fine girl. Did you know her well, Mister . . . ?"

Jay ignored the question. Jory would undoubtedly recognize the name, and they'd get into the whole thing about how he found the body, a can of worms Jay didn't especially care to open. "Not well enough to know her real name, I'm afraid."

"Debra-Jo," Jory said. "She was named after my great grandmother. Real pioneer stock, she was, a genuine sooner."

"You from Oklahoma?"

Jory nodded. "Tulsa. New York's not much to my taste."

"Chrysalis loved the city," Jay said quietly. "I knew her well enough to know that much. It was her home."

"Her home was Tulsa," Jory said stiffly, "and no offense, sir, but I'd thank you not to call her by that name." He turned at the sound of footsteps, and Jay saw the revulsion in his eyes as they beheld Jube

Benson waddling through the door, a stack of newspapers under one arm. Then his manners got the better of his distaste, and Jory forced a smile and extended a hand.

Jay went inside the parlor.

There were enough folding chairs to accommodate a hundred people. A third were occupied, while another dozen mourners milled around, talking in soft whispers in the corners of the room. Eight out of every ten faces belonged to jokers. Yin-Yang knelt beside Mushface Mona at the casket. The Floater bobbed against the ceiling, talking quietly with Troll, whose huge green hands brushed lightly against the chandelier when he gestured, making the crystals ring like wind chimes. Hot Momma Miller wept copiously, her hands smoking as she clutched a lace handkerchief, her small face wrinkled as a prune. Beside her, Father Squid murmured consolations. Another plainclothes cop, out of place as a grape in a box of raisins, sat by an ashtray, smoking a cigarette.

The Oddity was seated in the last row.

Jay thought that was real interesting. He stared, glimpsed motion beneath the black cloth. It looked like some animal under there squirming to get out, but it was only the joker's body reshaping itself, a metamorphosis that never ended. The hooded face turned, until Jay looked straight into the steel-mesh fencing mask. He could feel eyes looking back from beneath the mesh.

Jay crossed the room to where Chrysalis had been laid out. Yin-Yang was just getting up. Jay stopped in shock.

The casket was open.

That can't be, he thought wildly.

Then he saw Cosmo seated in a folding chair, back in the shadows of the alcove where the casket had been placed, so still and quiet that he was almost invisible in the riot of funeral wreaths, and suddenly Jay understood.

Three Cosgrove brothers had inherited the family mortuary. Waldo, who was very sorry, was the front man. Titus, who was never seen, was the embalmer. Cosmo, the youngest, was the family joker. He was a frail, thin man in his fifties, bald as his brother, but patches of grayish fungus grew all over his skin and clothing and anything he touched, and even a daily scraping couldn't quite keep the growth in check. But Cosmo had a power, too, a little deuce that made Cosgrove's the preeminent mortuary in Jokertown. He made the dead look good. He made them look better than they had in life.

Jay stepped up to the casket and looked down at her.

Sleeping beauty, he thought, and knew why Lupo and the others had been so upset.

She wore a simple dark dress, demure but stylish, an antique cameo fastened at her throat. Her hands were folded just under her breasts, clasping a Bible. She was lovely. Long blond hair spread out across a satin pillow, eyes closed peacefully in sleep, a hint of blush on her smooth pink cheeks. Chrysalis had been on the downhill side of thirty-five, Jay knew; she looked ten years younger now. Her skin looked as soft as the lining of the casket, so alive that you wanted to touch it, to caress it with your fingertips, to feel the warmth you knew was there.

But you didn't want to do that. Cosmo could fool the eye, but not the hand. Reach down into the casket, try to stroke that blushing cheek, and God knows what your fingers would find. Not even the Cosgroves could make a head out of chunks of bone and brain.

"A sad day," Father Squid said as he stepped up beside Jay. The pastor of Our Lady of Perpetual Misery made a liquid squishing sound when he walked. "Jokertown will be a different place without her. A darker place, I fear. Do you realize it was a year ago that Xavier Desmond passed away?"

"Almost to the day," Jay agreed. "But when Des was in here, the line of mourners went clear around the block."

"Chrysalis was well respected in the community," Father Squid said. "Even feared. Des was loved. He wore his heart on his sleeve. She guarded hers jealously." He put a hand on Jay's shoulder. "The talk is, you hunt her killer."

"Might as well," Jay said, "can't dance. Tell me, Father, how much do you know about our pal the Oddity over there?"

"Three tortured souls in search of salvation," the priest replied. "Surely you do not think—"

"I don't know what to think," Jay said. Waldo Cosgrove was standing in the door and gesturing at him. "Excuse me, Father, I have to take a phone call."

Waldo let Jay use his office in the back of the mortuary. It was dark, quiet, private. He waited until Waldo had closed the door before he picked up the receiver. "Hello, Hiram?"

The other end of the line was very noisy, but Hiram Worchester was a big man with a big voice. "Popinjay? The hotel said you'd called six times. Might I ask what could possibly be so urgent?"

"Hiram, we got big trouble. Where are you? It sounds like you're having a party."

"I'm phoning from Senator Hartmann's campaign trailer," Hiram said. "This platform fight is dragging on and on. The least you could do is watch the convention on television. It's only the future of the country that's at stake."

"Don't give me a hard time," Jay said. "I'm dressed real nice, how much more do you want? Listen, I'm poking around trying to find out who killed Chrysalis—"

"I thought that was settled," Hiram interrupted. "It was that ace-of-spades fellow. The psychopath who tried to steal those stamps from us that night in the Crystal Palace."

"Yeah, well, I don't think it was him," Jay said.

Hiram cleared his throat noncommittally, then said, "You're the sleuth, but I think you're wasting your time."

"It won't be the first time," Jay admitted. "Hiram, listen to me, and be careful what you say. Little politicos have big ears. Before she died, Chrysalis hired an assassin to kill Leo Barnett. He's probably in Atlanta already."

For a long moment there was nothing on the phone but the sound of Hartmann staffers shouting strategy into walkie-talkies. Then, in a hoarse voice, Hiram finally managed, "Barnett? Are you sure?"

"It's the only thing that makes sense," Jay said. "Barnett's the candidate who wants to put jokers in concentration camps. Chrysalis was a joker. Last time I looked, two plus two still added up to four." Or did it? Assassinate Barnett and you might just guarantee the triumph of Barnett's ideas. Hadn't Chrysalis been more subtle than that? Maybe two plus two equaled . . . what?

Hiram was talking. ". . . Barnett's done everything he can to emasculate the jokers' rights plank. I deplore everything the man stands for, but assassination can't be tolerated. Jay, you have to go to the authorities."

"Oh, that'd be real good," Jay said. "Just tell them that two jokers conspired to send an assassin, who's probably an ace, to knock off Leo Barnett because they didn't like his politics. Once the press gets wind of that, you might as well just inaugurate the fucker, save us from all those campaign commercials."

"God," Hiram swore. He was whispering now. "You're right, of course. Jay, what are we going to do?"

"Somehow we have to keep Barnett alive without blowing the lid off this story. I'll leave the details up to you."

"Thanks," Hiram said dryly. "Ever so much."

"Get help," Jay said. "Someone you can trust. Tachyon, maybe. Be subtle, but be careful, too. See if you can come up with some way to tighten security around Barnett."

"Around *all* the candidates," Hiram suggested.

"Fine," Jay said. "I'll keep digging on this end."

"Jay, listen to me, you'd be more valuable down here. Chrysalis is dead, this quixotic investigation of yours won't bring her back. Start your meter and catch the next flight to Atlanta. I'm hiring you. I'll want you to be Senator Hartmann's bodyguard."

"The last body I was supposed to guard wound up short a head," Jay pointed out. "Besides, I thought each candidate had a government ace assigned to baby-sit?"

"Carnifex is an incompetent braggart," Hiram said. "Nothing more than a street brawler, really, and not terribly bright. I have more faith in the Secret Service, but they're only men. At least Barnett has Lady Black attached to him, but Gregg is terribly vulnerable. We need your help, Jay."

"Yeah, well, get in line," Jay said. "Hiram, I got to go. I'll keep in touch. Be careful. Do what you can."

"Popinjay, will you listen to reason for once?" Hiram insisted.

"Nah," Jay said, "it might become a habit." He hung up before Hiram could reply, and headed for the door.

No sooner did he step out of the office than the phone started ringing behind him. Jay leaned back against the office door and counted the rings. Hiram didn't give up easily, he had to give him that. On the ninth ring, he sighed, went back into the darkened office, and scooped up the phone. "Look, Hiram," he said, "I'm not going to Atlanta, goddamn it. If Senator Gregg needs another baby-sitter, do it yourself, you can't just—"

"My archer needs help," a woman's voice said quietly on the other end of the line.

A cold chill went up Jay's spine. He knew that voice. The timbre of it, the cadences, the crisp British accent. "Chrysalis?" he said, in a stunned whisper.

"Go to him," Chrysalis said. "Before it's too late."

"You're dead," he said hoarsely. Standing in the dark, the phone clutched in a sweaty hand, Jay suddenly felt like the world had been pulled out from under his feet.

"The eskimo . . ." Chrysalis began.

"The *eskimo?*" Jay interrupted. This was getting weirder and weirder; he felt like he'd slipped down a rabbit hole. Chrysalis was lying dead in her coffin a few rooms away, and here she was on the phone talking to him about eskimos. All of a sudden he got real suspicious. "Who the hell is this anyway?" he asked.

There was a long silence. "Chrysalis," the voice said at last.

It sure as hell sounded like her. "My God," Jay said with all the awe he could muster. "You're alive. My darling . . . my lover . . . is it really you, sweet one?"

Another hesitation. "Yes," the voice whispered at last. "It's me, darling. Listen. You must save my archer, he—"

"Yeah, I know, he's been kidnapped by eskimos," Jay said. "Maybe you think this is funny, but I don't. You do a damn good impression, but you're not Chrysalis. So why don't you take your eskimos, put Prince Albert back in the can, and go fuck yourself, okay?" He slammed down the receiver so hard it rang.,

Then he sat there in the dark for a long time, fuming, staring at the phone, daring it to ring again. It stayed silent.

9.00 P.M.

Ann-Marie was eight months pregnant with their child. They made love slowly and gently, Brennan kneeling before her, Ann-Marie lying on her side with one leg straight out, the other drawn upward.

She was a slight, slim woman, now swollen to ripeness with the child in her womb. Her small breasts were heavy with milk, their nipples dark, pointed, and excruciatingly sensitive to the touch of his fingertips, the caress of his lips. Her face favored her Vietnamese ancestry more than her French, and she was beautiful, beautiful and hungry for Brennan's touch.

They made love in languorous slow motion, every minute movement of their bodies perfectly mated in rhythm and cadence, and as they made love Ann-Marie changed. Brennan watched her skin fade and flesh disappear, until he could see the network of blood vessels that laced throughout her body, and the bones and organs underneath their son in her womb. Then the baby melted away and changed and Ann-Marie did, too. She became larger, stronger, with wider hips and larger breasts, invisible but for the veins coursing through them and their dark nipples. Somehow they'd changed positions and Brennan was on his back and Chrysalis was atop him, dreamy passion on her enigmatic face, her nipples bobbing on their invisible pads of flesh as she rode Brennan, grinding her pelvis against his in long, slow, hard strokes that made him groan with each thrust.

He reached out to grasp her warm, soft invisible breasts, and they faded like smoke. Chrysalis slowly vanished, but he could still feel her warmth and wetness on his loins, and then like a ghost she slowly coalesced again, but her flesh was opaque, her breasts were small and hard, her body long, lean, and muscular.

"Jennifer," Brennan whispered, and she smiled sadly at him and pulled away, taking all her warmth and leaving him alone and naked. He wept as the pain of her leaving stung him again and again and she slowly faded from his sight in a haze of anguish and tears.

He squinted through the blur. There was a face swimming in the mist, peering closely at him.

"Jennifer," he croaked. His lips were dry, his throat tight and choked.

"About time you woke up," the face said in a naggingly familiar voice. "Let's see if we can bring you all the way out of it."

Brennan couldn't move his arms or legs, but he still had feeling in them. He felt the man grab his upper arm, and then pain shot through it as needles lanced into his flesh in what felt like three or four separate places. Brennan opened his mouth to protest, but couldn't get his tongue or lips to work together. He mumbled something unintelligible, not even understanding himself what he was trying to say. A moment or two passed and suddenly Brennan felt his heart starting to beat faster and faster. His vision cycled in and out, from misty to excruciatingly clear focus, pulsing like a strobe light. He wanted to stand, to shout, to run, but realized suddenly that he was bound in a chair with leather straps. He wrenched at the straps, but they were strong. He gritted his teeth and yanked back and forth, but the chair wouldn't budge and the leather straps only cut into his flesh. He howled, panting in savage, unreasonable rage. He had to stand up and the goddamned chair wouldn't let him! He'd get free, he had to! He concentrated all his strength in his right arm and yanked again and again, trying to pull free. He felt blood run down his arm, but he only redoubled his efforts.

"Sorry," someone said. "Sometimes it's difficult to judge the strength of the dosage."

He smiled reassuringly and all of a sudden Brennan felt calm and peace flow from the man's friendly grip into himself. Brennan recognized him. He'd seen him the day before in Chickadee's. It was Quincey, Kien's chemist. Quinn the Eskimo. He seemed like a nice man. When Quinn the Eskimo comes around, everybody's gonna jump for joy. Brennan looked at his right arm and wondered why it was bleeding.

"That's better," Quincey said approvingly. He smiled, and withdrew his hand from Brennan's upper arm. As he did, Brennan could see that three of his fingers had sharp needles protruding from their tips. As he watched they suddenly slipped back out of sight into Quincey's fingertips. "Welcome to Xanadu, Mr. Yeoman."

Brennan focused on him. "What am I doing here?"

Quincey shrugged. "You would know the answer to that better than me. One of my mechanical sentries caught you skulking in the garden."

"The caterpillar on the mushroom," Brennan said, suddenly remembering.

"Yes," Quincey said. "One of my favorites. Cost me a fortune to hire the animatronic engineers away from Disneyland, but if one can't have what one wants in one's own pleasure dome, what good is it?"

Brennan shook his head. He remembered it all now. The strange note he'd gotten at Aces High, the garden, the caterpillar, his capture, the dream. The dream.

He closed his eyes. It had all been so real. Ann-Marie. The last time they'd made love before she and their unborn child had been killed by Kien's assassins. Chrysalis alive again. Jennifer.

"So what did you want?" Quincey asked.

Brennan opened his eyes. "Chrysalis's killer."

"Oh my," Quincey said. "Well, you won't find such a person here. This is my pleasure dome. Violence rarely intrudes."

Brennan looked around. They were the only people in the room, which looked like something out of an Arabian Nights' fantasy. There were rich, colorful carpets on the floor, and brocaded silk tapestries, half of them featuring maidens, half featuring slim young men in Grecian outfits—or nothing at all—cavorting in pairs or in groups. There were numerous sculptures in a similar vein scattered around the room on delicate, expensive furniture, and the bed was canopied, with silk and velvet cushions, and throw pillows scattered around.

"I'm afraid, though," Quincey said thoughtfully, "this is going to have to be one of those times. I'm putting the finishing touches on an important project. We can't have you nosing about. Excuse me while I make a call."

The needles extruded smoothly from his fingertips again. They were white as bone—which they probably were—Brennan realized, and hollow. After a moment a clear fluid oozed from the central one, and Quincey plunged them into Brennan's arm again.

"It'll only hurt for a moment," he confided.

♥

It seemed very quiet in the house as Jay headed back to the wake. He was surprised to find that Jory had abandoned his post by the door. Instead Waldo Cosgrove stood there, wringing his damp little hands and looking very sorry indeed. Jay went past him, stepping into a strained, icy silence.

The mourners had backed off discreetly from the two men in the center of the room, but everyone was watching them.

Jory stood in the aisle between rows of folding chairs, his face dark with anger. "What did you say, sir?" he asked.

A newcomer stood over the casket, looking like death incarnate. Tall and slender, he wore a hooded cloak over a black wool suit. At first glance Jay thought he was in a mask; given the occasion, a singularly tasteless mask, too. Then he spoke, and Jay realized that the death's-head—yellowed and noseless, teeth bared in an eternal grin—was his real face. "I said," the joker repeated in a deep, chilly voice, "that *this* is not Chrysalis," He waved a gloved hand over the young woman in the casket.

His words made Jay's stomach do a sudden lurch. If it *wasn't* Chrysalis in the coffin, if somehow he'd been mistaken about the body he'd found, then maybe she was still alive somewhere, and the voice on the phone . . .

"I don't recall asking for your opinion," Jory said, his accent deepening under the stress of the moment. "Sir, you're causing a disruption, and I'd thank you to leave."

"I think not," the man in the black cloak replied. "I came here to see Chrysalis one last time, to make my farewells. And what do I find? Some nat fantasy lying in a coffin, and a roomful of people forbidden to speak her name."

"Her name was Debra-Jo Jory, and she was my daughter!" A vein in Jory's neck had begun to throb.

"Her name," the joker replied coldly, "was Chrysalis."

Father Squid moved close to him. "Charles, he's from Oklahoma, he knows no better. We must respect his grief."

"Then let him respect ours."

"He does not mean to give offense," the priest said.

"That makes this charade no less offensive." The joker's eyes, deep-set in his skull face, had never left Jory.

Waldo Cosgrove hurried forward nervously. "Gentlemen, gentlemen, please don't quarrel. This is not the time or the place, is it? Our dearly beloved Chrysalis, oh, ah, Debra-Jo, that is, well, surely she would not have wanted—"

"What I want," Jory said suddenly, "is for you to throw out this ugly sonofabitch, Cosgrove. You hear that? Either you call what passes for the law hereabouts, or I will, but either way this asshole is going out onto the street."

Waldo looked helplessly around the room, searching for some way out of this mess. Jay felt sorry for him. Finally, meekly, the funeral director turned to the joker and said, "Charles, please, it's customary in these matters to honor the family's wishes."

"Yes," Charles said. He made a gesture that took in all the jokers in the room. "And we are her family, Waldo. Not him. He doesn't even know what her name was." He turned his back on Jory and walked to where Cosmo sat on his chair. Cosmo looked up and adjusted his round, wire-rim spectacles. There was fungus growing on the back of his hand and a gray five o'clock shadow beneath his jaw. He said nothing. "I want to see her, Cosmo," Charles told him. "Show her to me. Show her to me the way she really was."

"No!" Jory shouted. "I forbid it!" He stormed forward, jammed a finger at Cosmo. "You hear me, boy?"

Cosmo looked at him, said nothing, looked back at Charles.

Someone gasped. All eyes went to the casket.

The color had begun to bleach from Debra-Jo's soft skin.

"Goddamn you," Jory swore at Cosmo. He spun around to face Waldo. "You there! Call the police! *Now!*"

Waldo's chin trembled as his mouth worked silently.

In the casket, the smooth pink flesh and hints of rose had faded. Her skin was bone white, as smooth and pale as milk. Here and there, it began to turn waxy and translucent.

"I'll do it myself then," Jory said. He started for the phone.

There was a sound like a stack of two-by-fours might make if you broke them all at once. Everything stopped. Jory looked up, and up, and up. Into red eyes that stared down from beneath a huge, swollen brow ridge. From his nine-foot vantage, Troll gazed down at Jory, cracked his knuckles once more, then closed his huge green hand into a fist the size of a country ham. "I don't think that would be such a good idea," Troll said, in a voice that sounded like it came from the bottom of the world's deepest gravel pit.

All around the room, the mourners mumbled agreement.

Her skin had gone all the color of wax paper, and you could see the tracery of veins now, and dark shadows of bones and organs beneath the fading flesh.

Jory whirled back to the casket and slammed the lid down hard. "Get out of here!" he screamed, distraught beyond words. "All of you, out of here." He looked around at all the joker faces with loathing. "You people," he said. "You all stick together, don't you. Damn you. You did this to her, you rotten—"

Jay took his hand out of his pocket, pointed. Jory vanished.

When the mourners realized what had happened, the tension drained from the room with a rush. Father Squid shook his head, facial tentacles bouncing from side to side with the motion. "Where did you send him, my son?" he asked.

"Aces High," Jay said. "A good meal, a few drinks, maybe he'll feel better. It was getting too damn ugly."

The joker called Charles stepped up to the casket and opened the lid. Chrysalis lay there now. Skin as clear as the finest glass, perfectly transparent, ghostly pale wisps of muscle and tendon beneath, and under that bones and organs and the blue and red spiderweb of blood vessels.

It was as much an illusion as the other had been, but it was the one they wanted. It was Chrysalis as she'd looked in life.

Jay's last lingering doubts vanished as he stared at the body, and with them any last lingering hopes. Chrysalis was dead; the voice on the phone had been an imposter's.

Charles looked at her for a long moment, then turned away, satisfied. He patted Cosmo on the shoulder before he walked off. Hot Mamma dropped to her knees, smoking hands waving in the air, and began to weep again. Others pressed close around the casket, quiet and reverent. The Oddity stood in the corner, watching.

Jay caught up to the skull-faced joker as he stepped out of the parlor. "Charles Dutton, I presume."

Death turned and looked him in the eye. "Yes."

"Jay Ackroyd," he said, offering a hand. "I'd like to ask you a few questions."

10:00 P.M.

"I'm afraid there's not much I can tell you, Mr. Ackroyd," Charles Dutton said. A hot July wind gusted down the Bowery, flapping the joker's long black cloak behind him as they walked. "Chrysalis and I were business associates, but I can't claim to have known her well. She liked her little secrets."

"You should know, you were one of them," Jay said. "How come no one knew Chrysalis had a partner?" He had to walk quickly to keep up with Dutton's long-legged strides.

They passed the Chaos Club, and Dutton waved politely to the doorman. "The limelight suited Chrysalis, and I prefer to avoid it," he said. "Tonight was something of an exception. I'd intended to quietly pay my last respects, but when I saw what that posturing fool had done, I couldn't help but get emotional."

"Jory was her father," Jay said.

"Her beloved father," Dutton agreed, "who made her a prisoner in her own home for years, because he was so deeply embarrassed by the way she looked. You see, I do know a little of her history. It was not something she liked to talk about, but when she first came to Jokertown, she needed my help to open the Crystal Palace, and I insist on knowing the background of my business associates."

"You lent her money?"

Dutton nodded. "She arrived in the city with a considerable fortune in bearer bonds. However, she wanted to buy almost half a block, not only the building that became the Crystal Palace but the adjoining properties as well, all that debris. I don't imagine I have to tell you that Manhattan real estate is expensive, even in Jokertown. There were other costs as well. The restoration, fixtures and furnishings, the liquor license . . ."

"Bribes," Jay suggested. A car passed them, going the other way up the Bowery. Jay watched its lights recede in the long plate-glass window of the laundromat they were passing.

"The city inspectors work so hard," Dutton said, "as do our police and firefighters. Periodic tokens of esteem are always a wise policy, particularly for a joker. Costly, though."

"So you lent her a lot of bucks," Jay said. He was still keeping an eye on the reflections in the laundromat window. "How much of the joint did you own?"

"A third," Dutton said. "She held the controlling interest."

"Don't stop and don't look behind you," Jay said quietly. "We're being followed."

"Really?" Dutton was good; his pace didn't even falter.

"He's across the street, maybe a half block back, trying to slink from doorway to doorway," Jay said. "Real amateur hour. He would have flunked slinking in detective school. He's avoiding the street lamps, but the headlights pick him up every time a car passes."

"Do you know who it is?" Dutton asked.

"The Oddity," Jay told him. "Friend of yours?"

"I'm afraid not. I know him only by reputation."

"You got any kick-ass powers you haven't mentioned, or is it up to me?" Jay asked.

Dutton laughed. "Does wealth count as a power?"

"Maybe," Jay said. "If the Oddity attacks us, try throwing some hundred-dollar bills at him, we'll see how it works."

"I have a better idea," Dutton said. He stopped suddenly.

They were in front of the Famous Bowery Wild Card Dime Museum. Dutton went up to the doors. "What the hell are you doing?" Jay asked. "The place is closed."

"I have a key," Dutton said. He opened one of the doors and motioned Jay inside. "The management won't mind."

"You own the place?" Jay guessed as Dutton relocked the door.

"I'm afraid so," Dutton said. He punched some numbers into a key box on the wall. A blinking red light went out, and a green one came on. "We're clear," Dutton said. "Come with me."

The interior of the museum was dim and cool. They went through a swinging door and down a service corridor. "This place do good business?" Jay asked.

"Fair," Dutton said. "You've been here, of course?"

"A long time ago," Jay said. "When I was very young. The only thing I remember is the jars. Dozen of big jars, with deformed joker babies floating inside. It really freaked me out." The memory had been buried for a long time, but the moment he spoke, it came back so vividly Jay could taste it: endless small bodies, twisted and terrible, floating in formaldehyde behind a wall of glass. One of them, bigger than the others and especially grotesque, had been mounted on a rotating pedestal, and Jay could still remember his fear as its face slowly turned toward him. It was going to open its eyes and *look* at him, he had screamed, and nothing his father had said had calmed him down. "It gave me nightmares," Jay said, astonished by the sudden realization. He couldn't quite repress a shudder. "Jesus," he said to Dutton. "Those are long gone, right?"

"Sadly, no," Dutton said. "The Monstrous Joker Babies were one of the original exhibits. The tourists have come to expect them. But I have made considerable efforts to turn this into a legitimate museum since acquiring it from its original owners, and our new attractions are quite different. Let me show you."

He led Jay through an access door. "Here," Dutton said. "This is our Syrian diorama."

Jay peered through the glass at a dramatic waxwork tableau. In the foreground, Carnifex was wrenching an Uzi away from a terrorist, while a pregnant Peregrine raked his face with metal talons. Tachyon, dressed like a color-blind Arab fop, was out cold on the floor. Elsewhere, Jack Braun raced toward a gunman, bullets whining off his body. One of the richochets had struck Senator Hartmann; you could see the blood seeping through his sport coat. Way in back, Hiram Worchester glared up at a giant economy-sized Arab Rambo, while a woman in a black chador held a bloody knife over a fallen prophet.

"I'm sure you recall the incident," Dutton said.

"Yeah," Jay said. "From the tour. Getting wounded did wonders for Hartmann's presidential campaign."

"It never hurts to be a hero," Dutton agreed.

Jay indicated a panel of buttons in front of the diorama. "What are these?"

"Our new exhibits are state-of-the-art," Dutton said. "Sound effects, dramatic lighting, animatronics. One button lights up Braun's golden force field, another turns on the Nur's green glow. That one at the end will actually make Sayyid fall. He's the giant. Worchester made him too heavy to support his own weight."

"I didn't know waxworks could move," Jay said.

"We've been moving away from wax on the animated exhibits," Dutton said. "Sayyid is three-quarters plastic."

"Doesn't he crush those other figures?"

"He never hits the ground," Dutton said. "The children love it. They all squeeze their little fists, pretending to be aces."

"Hiram will be *so* thrilled," Jay said dryly.

"Come, let me give you the tour," Dutton said.

"Only if we skip the Monstrous Joker Babies," Jay said. "I got enough problems without running into them again."

Dutton laughed, and escorted him through a maze of dim-lit corridors where heroes and villains of years gone by watched from the shadows. They passed Jetboy, the Four Aces, the Lizard King. Hard-hat and the Radical stood locked in eternal combat, while a squad from the Joker Brigade stood off Charlie in some hellforsaken part of Nam. In the Hall of Infamy, the Astronomer hung from a wall, embedded in the brick with only his face and hands visible. The mortar had turned red with his blood. Nearby Gary Gilmore stood surrounded by pillars of salt, and Gimli exhorted a maddened crowd with upraised fist. The dwarf's glass eyes seemed to follow them.

"Great waxwork," Jay said. "Looks real."

"It is," Dutton said. "Gimli's empty skin was found in an alley not far from here. There was no family, so we, ah, acquired the remains."

Jay gave him a look. "You *stuffed* him." He'd heard that story on the streets somewhere, but somehow he'd forgotten.

Dutton cleared his throat. "Yes. Well. He has been quite a popular attraction."

"I think I've seen enough," Jay told him.

"Fine." Dutton took him across a cavernous hall where the Turtle's old shells hung suspended from the ceiling. The adjoining gallery was still under construction. Dutton guided Jay through the tangle of ladders, tarps, and sawhorses to a snack-room square in the center of the building. He turned on the lights and stood in front of a bank of vending machines.

"Would you prefer coffee or a soft drink?" he asked.

It was chilly in here, Jay realized suddenly. They must use the air-conditioning even at night on account of the waxworks. "Coffee would be real good," he admitted.

Dutton fed quarters into the coffee machine and came to the table with two cardboard cups. He gave one to Jay. They sat. "So what do you think of my little museum now?"

"Museums are like graveyards," Jay said. "Full of dead things. Dead things depress me."

"The Famous Bowery Wild Card Dime Museum is a Jokertown institution."

Jay blew on his coffee. "The Palace is an institution, too."

"Yes," Dutton said. "Of a different sort."

"And now you own it, too."

"Under the terms of our partnership agreement, the surviving partner assumes full ownership of the Crystal Palace, yes."

"That why you had her killed?" Jay suggested casually.

♣

Dreams came again, but this time they were vague, formless things that chased Brennan through a cloying mist as he tried to find his way back to a home that didn't exist. The landscape was silent but for the unknowable twitterings of the things chasing him; then he heard someone softly, but insistently, calling his name. It was a woman's voice. It was Jennifer.

He felt her cool hands on his face, and she was kneeling before him. She was dressed in a bathing suit this time, and she was softly saying his name over and over again. He tried to reach out to her, but he was still tied to his chair. She reached out and touched his bonds, and they dissolved. He tumbled forward. She broke his fall and they both landed on the floor, Brennan on top.

She was beautiful. He kissed her for a long, long moment, but then she squirmed away.

"We have to get away, Daniel, we have to get out of here before they come back."

Brennan nodded. "We will," he said, "we will," and tried to kiss her again.

She pushed him away. He fell off her to the floor and looked at her with hurt in his eyes. "Just like my other dream," he said, and had an overwhelming urge to cry.

"This isn't a dream," Jennifer said firmly, but lowly. "This is real."

She grabbed Brennan's hand and held it. Her hands were warm and solid. Brennan reached out and touched her face.

"You *are* real," Brennan said wonderingly.

"I am." She stood, and pulled on Brennan's arm.

He tried to stand too, and immediately was struck by an intense attack of vertigo. He leaned on Jennifer, who staggered, but started him shuffling toward the door.

"What are you doing here?" he asked.

"Rescuing you. No time to talk now."

Brennan's bow and quiver was by the door, as were assorted knives and other items Quincey had taken from him. They stopped to pick up the bow and quiver, but there was no time for anything else.

It was dark outside. Brennan wondered foggily how long he'd been unconscious. They just managed to stumble behind a tall, thick hedge when they saw Fadeout enter the front door accompanied by a brace of Werewolves. Brennan took a deep breath. The night air seemed to help revive him, or perhaps the drugs had simply worked through his system. He followed Jennifer under his own power through the garden. They were past the lawn and into the trees before they heard an alarm raised back at the house.

"My car's this way," Brennan said.

"I know. I'm parked next to it."

"How did you find me?" Brennan asked.

Jennifer glanced at him as they made their way through the trees, their path lit by the light of a nearly full moon.

"It took some doing. I spent a good part of yesterday and most of today looking through your old haunts, and finally tracked you down to the hotel. But you were gone, of course, and I'd never have found you if it hadn't been for the phone call."

"Phone call?"

"Yes. She said you were here, that you'd been captured."

They broke out of the trees to the roadside. Brennan's keys were gone, so they piled into Jennifer's car and roared off down the road with Jennifer behind the wheel.

Brennan ran through a breathing exercise, trying to clear his head. Jennifer kept her eyes on the road, occasionally glancing at him.

"The funny thing," she said, "about the phone call."

She fell silent and glanced at Brennan again.

"Yes?" he prompted.

"I could swear that it was Chrysalis on the other end of the line."

Brennan slumped back in the car seat. There were a thousand things he wanted to say to Jennifer, but he couldn't speak. His head whirled with her revelations and the aftereffects of the drugs Quincey had pumped into his system. Something was wrong here, very wrong, and there was perhaps only one person who could set them straight, only one person who would know for certain if it was Chrysalis's shattered body that'd been found in her office.

The man who had discovered it.

◆

Dutton sipped from his cardboard cup very calmly. "Would you prefer that I spill my coffee in shock or just quietly turn pale with guilt?"

"Either one, just so you confess," Jay said, "I'm not fussy."

"Assuming that I was guilty, isn't it a bit naive to expect that I'd own up the moment I'm accused?"

"Hey, it always works for Perry Mason," Jay said. "You can't blame a guy for trying."

Dutton put down the coffee, took off his cloak, and draped it over the back of a chair. Beneath the banks of fluorescent light, his skin was a ghastly shade of yellow, here and there mottled with dry, dead patches of brown. "I happen to look like the popular image of the grim reaper," the joker said. "Sometimes that causes people to make unfortunate assumptions about me. I did not kill Chrysalis."

"Not personally," Jay said, "but you had the bucks to hire it done. And you had the motive."

"Did I?" Dutton seemed amused. "The land on which the Palace stands is worth quite a bit, agreed. The saloon itself is a good tax loss. I may keep it open and I may not, but I'd hardly kill for it."

"Her other business was *real* profitable," Jay pointed out. "Tax-free, too." He took a sip of coffee. It was so hot it burned the back of his mouth going down. "You own part of that one, too?"

"No," Dutton said. "Oh, she willingly shared certain pieces of information whenever she heard anything that might affect my business interests, and there was never any charge to me. That was part of our arrangement. But otherwise her little hobby was her own."

"Only now it's yours by default," Jay suggested. "You wouldn't want to put all those snitches out of work."

"Perhaps not," Dutton said. "Undoubtedly her files contain items of considerable interest, and others of considerable value; I won't pretend otherwise. Still, it's nothing I'd bloody my hands for. I could have bought and sold Chrysalis a dozen times over, I didn't need to murder her."

"So who did?" Jay asked.

"I'm mystified," Dutton said. "She was privy to a great deal of dangerous information, of course, but that very thing kept her safe. Alive, she could be dealt with. Kill her, and who knows what skeletons may come out of the closet."

"There are a lot of closets in the Crystal Palace," said Jay.

"You take my meaning then," Dutton said. He shrugged. "I wish I could give you something more to work on. Truly I do."

"It's okay," Jay said. He took a last swallow of coffee and stood up. "Well, time to shuffle home to bed. You got a back door on this place?"

"A side exit on the alley," Dutton said, rising. "Come, let me show you."

The joker led him back through the labyrinth of silent wax, their footsteps echoing down the long corridors. They were crossing a small rotunda when Jay heard something behind them.

He stopped, looked back. Nothing moving. "Are we alone here?"

"Quite," Dutton said. "Is something wrong?"

"I heard something," Jay said. "And I've got a funny feeling. Like we're being watched."

Dutton smiled. "That's very common. It's the waxworks. People say their eyes follow you around the room."

Jay glanced around. They were passing through the Gallery

of Beauty. In the shadows he glimpsed Peregrine, Aurora, Circe. "Peregrine's eyes can follow me anywhere," he quipped, but somehow he didn't think that was it.

"This way," Dutton said.

They turned a corner. Jay took Dutton firmly but quietly by the arm and pulled him back into a dark alcove beside a towering metal-and-wax likeness of Detroit Steel. Jay held a finger to his lips. Dutton gave a small, quick nod.

In the stillness, Jay heard soft padding footfalls.

Coming toward them.

It couldn't be the Oddity. Whatever it was was light-footed as a cat. And barefoot by the sound of it.

Jay shaped his hand into a gun.

A shadow darted past them, faster than Jay thought possible. It was small, no more than knee high, and it was out of sight before Jay could react. He jumped out of hiding, saw it—a hairless gray monkey thing, with too many arms—and pointed. Only it was faster than he was. It skittered up the front of a diorama, sliding over the glass quick as a lizard, and Jay popped a waxwork joker right out of his orgy and into the Aces High meat locker.

"*Damn*," he swore. He pointed again, but the monkey thing jumped before he drew a bead, swung on a fluorescent lighting fixture, and somersaulted right over Jay's head. He turned to give chase and bumped into Dutton. "Where did it go?" he said.

"Into the rotunda," the joker said, "but . . ."

Jay ran. It was gone when he hit the rotunda, but he caught a glimpse of motion down one corridor. He sprinted after it, turning the corner just in time to see it grab hold of an overhead pipe. It paused long enough to hiss like a feral cat, then ran down the pipe into a pitch dark room. Jay went after it. He was looking up at the ceiling pipes, running flat out. He never saw the display pedestal.

It was like running into a telephone pole. Jay clutched his stomach and sat down hard, gasping with pain. The pedestal wobbled back and forth, and toppled over on top of him. Glass shattered. Liquid drenched him, and something soft and pale and slimy flopped onto his chest with a wet squish. There was an overwhelming smell of formaldehyde. He closed his eyes.

There were footsteps behind him. "Are you all right?" Dutton's voice asked.

"No," Jay said.

"I tried to warn you," Dutton said. He flicked on the lights.

"Am I where I think I am?" Jay asked, eyes still closed. He thought he sounded surprisingly calm, all things considered.

"I'm afraid so," Dutton replied. "Welcome to the Monstrous Joker Babies. Can I do anything for you?"

"Yes," Jay said. "You can *get it off me!*"

By the time he did, the monkey was long gone.

11:00 P.M.

Brennan smelled Ackroyd even before he opened his apartment door. Moving with sure, swift grace, he caught him by the elbow, propelled him in a half circle, and slammed him against the wall. Jennifer materialized from nowhere and shut the door.

"Keep quiet and don't move," Brennan ordered. He had Ackroyd in a painful wrist lock, grinding the detective's forearm into the small of his back.

"Jesus Christ," Ackroyd muttered aggrievedly, his face mashed up against the wall. "I think you broke my goddamn nose."

Brennan's own nose twitched. "What the hell have you been drinking? You smell like you've been dipped in a vat of bad booze."

"Close," Ackroyd muttered as Jennifer looped a rope on his free wrist and twisted it gently to his back where she tied his hands together.

Brennan turned Ackroyd around and shoved him onto a plush chrome-and-leather sofa that looked wildly out of place in Ackroyd's shabby apartment.

The PI fell onto the couch with a loud "Oooof" and wiggled around uncomfortably on his hands. He sniffed and held his head back, trying to keep the blood that was seeping out of his nose from dripping onto his chest. He squinted at Brennan. "Yeoman, I presume. Since we're all such good friends, can I call you Dan?"

"How do you know my name?" Brennan said quietly.

Ackroyd shrugged. It was difficult to do that and keep the blood from running onto his shirt. "One of the first things I learned in detective school was how to find out stuff. Like the names of masked vigilantes."

"Why don't you just answer my question?"

"Or what?" Ackroyd said angrily. He struggled to find a comfortable position on the sofa. "You think you can just come in here and—"

Jennifer stepped between them. "We don't 'think,' Mr. Ackroyd, we *have*," she said practically. She found a bunch of Kleenex in her handbag and stanched the flow of blood coming from his nose. She felt it gingerly and Ackroyd winced. "It doesn't seem to be broken." She made a face herself and stepped out of close smelling range.

"Thanks," Ackroyd muttered grudgingly.

Jennifer gave Brennan a significant look. He took a deep, calming breath and began again.

"Mentioning my real name to the wrong parties would cause me no end of trouble—"

"Trouble," Ackroyd interrupted. "What about the 'trouble' you caused all those people you killed? How many was it? Do you even remember?"

"Every face," Brennan said in a slow, hard voice. He sank down on his haunches so that he and Ackroyd were eye to eye, and stared at the detective. "You don't like me or what I do, and I couldn't care less. I do what I have to."

"Ambushing innocent—"

"I can't point my finger at people and make them go away," Brennan said in the same hard voice. "And no one I killed was innocent. Maybe not everyone deserved to die for what they'd done, but they were playing the game, consciously and willingly. I'm not to blame if they were too stupid to realize the consequences of their involvement."

"Game?" Ackroyd asked. "What the hell are you talking about?"

Brennan gestured angrily. "I'm not going to justify myself to you. I'll just say this. It is"—he stopped, looked at Jennifer and corrected himself—"was me against the Shadow Fists. One man against hundreds. I did what I had to do. I don't regret any of it. Nor have I forgotten any of it."

"What you had to—"

"That's that," Brennan said flatly. "We have more important things to discuss. We don't have to be friends. We don't have to like each other. We don't have to work together. But we should talk."

Ackroyd nodded, but gestured stubbornly with his bound hands. "I'm not saying anything tied up like this."

"All right." Brennan drew a knife from his ankle sheath and slashed Ackroyd's bonds. The two men stared at each other for a long moment as Ackroyd rubbed his wrists angrily and then tenderly felt his nose.

"My name," Brennan prompted.

Ackroyd shrugged. "All right. Sascha gave it to me. He said he'd plucked it from Chrysalis's mind. Said you were probably involved in the murder, though I figure he was lying. Something had him really scared. Why all this mystery about your real identity, anyway? Other than the fact that you're wanted for multiple homicides, of course."

Brennan looked at him coolly. "I'm in the country illegally. Maybe I'll explain it someday when we have a couple of spare hours. Only Wraith"—he nodded at Jennifer—"and my enemy knew my name. Apparently also Chrysalis."

"You're wanted by the feds?"

"I deserted from the army. It's complicated and it doesn't have anything to do with Chrysalis's death. If she's really dead," Brennan said significantly.

"If?" Ackroyd said. "What do you mean 'if'? I found her body."

"Are you sure?"

"Sure? She was not merely dead, she was most sincerely dead."

Brennan sighed, rubbed his face tiredly. "I don't know. . . ." he said softly.

"Look, are you crazier than I think, or what? I saw her—"

"And I heard her voice. Yesterday."

"What?" Ackroyd asked quietly.

"And I heard her voice today," Jennifer added.

Brennan looked at him closely. "What is it?"

"I heard it, too," Ackroyd admitted quietly. Then he looked at Brennan and shook his head. "But it couldn't have been *her* voice.

Christ, I was just at the funeral parlor where she was lying in her coffin."

"You're certain, one hundred percent certain, that it was Chrysalis in the coffin?"

"Do you know anyone else with invisible skin?" Ackroyd said. "It was her body I found. Besides, the wiseguy who called me had to be an imposter. She didn't know the, uh, real story of the relationship between me and Chrysalis and she was telling me all kinds of screwy stuff. Claimed you'd been captured by eskimos."

Brennan sighed and shook his head. "Well, she was right about that." He held up his hand, forestalling any more questions on Ackroyd's part. "All right. So you're convinced she's dead. Do you have any suspects, any idea at all who killed her?"

Ackroyd looked at him for a long moment before he spoke. "Suspects I got." He fished a sheet of paper out of the inside breast pocket of his battered jacket and handed it to Brennan. It was soggy and had the same horrible smell that Ackroyd had. It was a list of names, most of them crossed off.

"These are your candidates?" Brennan asked as Jennifer peered at the list over his shoulder.

Ackroyd nodded. "Those that are left. I crossed the others off because of my years of experience as a trained investigator and my keen insights into the human psyche."

"Hmmm," Brennan said. "Well, you can also cross off Bludgeon. I beat the hell out of him this morning in a place called Squisher's Basement."

"You?"

"Don't look so surprised," Brennan said with something of a smile. "Actually, something's wrong with him. He's obviously sick. He claimed that he killed Chrysalis, but he didn't know enough details to make his claim convincing. It was all just a pathetic attempt to rebuild his reputation."

"Okay." Ackroyd produced a pen and struck a line through Bludgeon's name. "I'll take your word for it. That still leaves us with four prime suspects."

Brennan nodded. "I know Wyrm."

"What about him?" Ackroyd asked.

Brennan and Jennifer exchanged glances. "We've gone *mano a mano* a few times. He's strong, but I don't know if he's strong enough to do what Chrysalis's killer did to her. Also, bludgeoning isn't his ordinary M.O."

"I thought about that already," Ackroyd interjected. "He likes to use his fangs, doesn't he?"

Brennan unconsciously rubbed the side of his neck. "That's right."

"But all of us heard him threaten Chrysalis," Jennifer said.

"Right. And he is one of Kien's chief lieutenants, high in the Shadow Fist Society."

"Kien?" Ackroyd asked.

"Why don't you just leave Wyrm to me?" Brennan suggested.

Ackroyd looked at him, shrugged. "Okay. You want the lizard, he's yours."

"What makes Quasiman a suspect?" Jennifer asked.

"You mean besides the fact that his brain has more holes in it than a Swiss cheese? Well, Barnett saved his life with a faith healing. Brought him back from the dead through the power of prayer. Or so some of Barnett's people claim."

"And?" Brennan prompted.

"And Chrysalis hired someone to do in the Bible thumper."

Brennan frowned. "Are you sure?"

"Reasonably. Elmo gave some hired muscle her order to make a hit on one of the politicos in Atlanta."

"Why?" Jennifer asked.

Ackroyd shrugged. "I'm not sure. Because she was afraid of Barnett's politics?"

Brennan shook his head. "She wasn't stupid. She'd realize something like that would push the country right into his hands. But," he said thoughtfully, "perhaps you're not the only one who misinterpreted Elmo's mission. Perhaps one of Barnett's people also found out about it and told Quasiman. At any rate, we should look into it." He glanced at Jennifer. "Perhaps we should have Father Squid lend us Quasiman for a while."

"For what reason?" Jennifer asked.

"Ostensibly in case we run into the Oddity again."

"The Oddity?" Ackroyd echoed.

"I found him trashing Chrysalis's bedroom. He said that he was looking for something that Chrysalis was using to blackmail him. But I didn't buy it. Chrysalis never extorted money from anyone."

"You're right," Ackroyd said.

"That leaves just one name," Jennifer prompted.

Brennan looked down at the list. "Who the hell is Doug Morkle?"

Ackroyd shook his head. "Beats me. Let me know if you find out."

"All right." Brennan looked at Jennifer, then back at Ackroyd. "That's all you've got?"

"Yup. Except for a few questions."

"Like?"

"Like did you know that Chrysalis had taken up with Digger Downs?"

"Who's he?"

"He masquerades as a reporter for *Aces* magazine."

"I wouldn't know," Brennan said. "I haven't seen or spoken to Chrysalis since October '86."

Ackroyd nodded. "Elmo said she was desperate for info on you." He watched Brennan closely. "Well. We all know you're pretty good with a bow, but how about a chain saw?"

Brennan scowled. "Is that supposed to be a joke?"

Ackroyd shrugged. "No. Not really. One last thing. What do you know about the Palace's neighbors?"

Brennan was tired of Ackroyd's bizarre questions. "The Palace has no neighbors," he said flatly. "It's alone on the block."

"That's right," Ackroyd said. "That's entirely right."

Brennan took Jennifer by the arm. "We're even," he said as they turned to go.

"Just so you know," Ackroyd said as they stopped by the door. "I didn't pop you into the Tombs this time, but our next meeting will be an entirely new matter."

"Next time," Brennan said, nodding and smiling. "I'll look forward to it."

"Good-bye," Jennifer said. She blew Ackroyd a kiss and went through the door.

Brennan stopped to open it and turned to look at Ackroyd a final time. "Take my advice," he told the PI, "and either cut down on your drinking or switch to a better brand. You smell like you've been swimming in formaldehyde."

"Real good," Ackroyd said. "You could almost be a detective."

Wednesday
July 20, 1988

5:00 A.M

THE SIGN BEFORE THE rambling three-story Victorian house said COSGROVE MORTUARY, COSMO, TITUS, AND WALDO COSGROVE, PROPRIETORS, in suitably somber, Gothic-style lettering. The building was as quiet as death, as dark as the tomb. Brennan crept onto the wooded porch that encircled the house, moving slowly and carefully lest one of the ancient floorboards reveal his presence by creaking in the silent night.

He jimmied a window and stepped through it into the lobby. He paused for a moment and shone his pocket flashlight around the small room. It had dark wallpaper and was cluttered with antique furniture and bric-a-brac. Chrysalis, he thought, would have loved it.

The directory, hanging in a glass case on the wall, listed several viewings. The one he wanted—Jory—was in the West Parlor. He clicked off the flashlight and gave his eyes a few moments to readjust to the darkness, then moved into the bowels of the mortuary.

There was a peculiar odor to the place, a curious mixture of chemicals and death. The silence was oppressive, unbroken by any sounds of movement or life. Brennan had to force himself to move slowly and quietly. He badly wanted to get an answer to his question and then get the hell out into the dirty, but living, city air.

The West Parlor was a long, high-ceilinged room, still choked with scores of flower arrangements. The flowers, like everything in this place, were dead and wilted. Their scent was stultifying in the enclosed dark. They had been placed all over the room, the most were clustered around the closed coffin that was still in place against one wall. Brennan let out a deep sigh of relief when he spotted the coffin. He was afraid that he might be too late, that it might have already been moved to the church. That would have complicated things.

Brennan approached the coffin silently, stopped before it, stared at it. For a moment he couldn't bring himself to open the lid. But he had to know if it was Chrysalis in the coffin, he had to see with his own eyes.

He lifted the lid and held it high. The darkness made it impossible to see any details, but Brennan thought that was a good thing. He kept his pencil flashlight off.

The corpse was wearing a demure dress that covered it from neck to ankles. Above the neck was nothing. The head was totally missing, apparently obliterated beyond any possible hope of reconstruction. The hands, though, holding a Bible on the sunken stomach, were clear, invisible, dead flesh. They were her hands, Chrysalis's hands, of that Brennan was sure, though blood no longer surged through their pulsing arteries. Whatever fluid that now filled them was clear and unmoving.

"It was a difficult job," a soft voice said behind Brennan.

Brennan started, almost dropping the coffin lid. He barely managed to maintain his hold on it while he turned on his flashlight and swung it around.

There was the sound of something moving swiftly away from the light, and the voice spoke again. "Please, the light is painful to me."

The voice was so authentically gentle and sad that Brennan couldn't help but comply with it. "All right," he said, and flicked off the flash.

The speaker moved out from behind the straight-backed sofa. He was a vague pale blur in the darkness, very white, very tall, and very thin. He smelled of strange, powerful chemicals, but his voice was as sweet as a young boy's.

"You work here?" Brennan asked.

"Oh yes. I do the embalming. Light is injurious to me, so I do most of my work at night. I was just stopping by to say good-bye to Chrysalis—it was a difficult job, but I did the best I could."

"This may sound strange," Brennan said, "but you are sure that it's Chrysalis in that coffin?"

"Certainly," the pale man said in his sweet voice. "Why do you ask?"

Brennan shook his head. "Never mind. I was just making sure."

The pale man nodded in turn. "I'll leave you to your private good-byes. Even though it's past our regular visiting hours." He turned to go, stopped, and looked back at Brennan. Brennan could see his small pink eyes shine with light reflected from his flash. "I tried to put her head back together, you know, but her killer had been terribly thorough. There weren't enough pieces to work with. I've repaired the results of many violent killings, but this was one of the most savage. Her murderer deserves to be caught. To be caught and punished, Mr. Yeoman."

"I know," Brennan said, looking down at what was left of Chrysalis, "I know."

6:00 A.M

In the still, sick moonlight, the fingers of the trees reached out for him hungrily as he passed.

He did not look up at that grim starless sky where the moon pulsed like a thing alive, glistening palely with all the colors of corruption. He knew better than to look, or to listen to the terrible secrets the trees whispered in the rustling of branches as bare and thin as whips. He walked through a land black and barren, where dead gray grasses grasped at his feet, and the fear grew in his soul like a black worm.

Huge wings of dry cracked skin stirred the dead air. Eight-legged hunters, lean and cruel as any hound, slid from tree to tree just out of the range of his sight. The endless, deep ululation sounded behind him, promising an eon of terror, an eternity of pain. He knew this place; that was the most frightening thing of all.

When he saw the subway kiosk up ahead, he began to run. So

slowly he ran, each stride consuming an hour, but at last he reached it and started down the stairs. He held the railing tight as he descended. Trains roared through mindless gulfs far below him. Still he descended, down and around on steps that spiraled round forever, until he saw the other passenger. He began to chase him, down steps that grew narrow and cruel, and so cold that his bare feet stuck fast, and each step ripped away more bloody flesh.

And he was there again, on that platform, hanging out over the endless subterranean dark, and there was the man before him. Don't turn, he pleaded silently, while inside he gibbered in fear, oh please don't turn.

He turned, and Jay saw that white, featureless face, tapering to one long red tentacle. It lifted its head and began to *howl*. Jay screamed . . .

. . . and grunted in pain as he fell out of bed, cracking his elbow hard against the hardwood floor. He doubled over and clutched the elbow, making a whimpering sound deep in his throat. It hurt like a motherfucker, but he was almost grateful. There was nothing like a good sharp pain to chase away the nightmare.

He lay there for a good five minutes, until the throbbing in his elbow had finally subsided. Figuring out that his childhood trauma in the Dime Museum had caused the nightmare didn't seem to have cured him of it. He'd wet the bed anyway. At least this time he'd had the sense to sleep in the nude.

He started the water running in the tub, then went to the kitchen, spooned some Taster's Choice into a cup, and waited for the kettle to boil. When the coffee was ready, he took it back to the bathroom. The tub was just about full. Jay set the coffee on the rim, turned off the faucets, and stepped in gingerly. The bathwater felt as hot as the coffee, but he forced himself to stand there until the heat started to feel good. He stretched out in the scalding water and drank his coffee. It made him feel clean again.

Otherwise he felt like shit. Both his elbows hurt, one from falling out of bed, the other from where that psychopath son of a bitch Yeoman had twisted his arm. His nose was still sore from getting mashed against the wall. He had a big bruise on his stomach where he'd gotten mugged by the Monstrous Joker Baby.

He drank his coffee and considered what to do with this good early start he'd made. He had his list, down to four names now: Wyrm, Quasiman, the Oddity, and Doug Morkle. It had to be one of them. So why didn't he believe it?

The problem was, none of his four finalists seemed real tied in with all this other crap that kept turning up, the assassins and eskimos and imposters, and the agile little homunculus that Jay had chased futilely through the Dime Museum.

He sat nursing his coffee until the bathwater was tepid, but all he came up with were more questions. It sure as hell looked like he was dealing with at least two different killers, the strongman who'd done Chrysalis and the chainsaw psycho who'd butchered Digger's neighbors just for the hell of it. Were they working together? That suggested a conspiracy.

Or maybe it was just one lunatic with lots of different powers, like the late, great Astronomer. Someone ought to go dig up the old man's grave and see if he was still in it. But it wasn't going to be Jay; he'd been there the night the Astronomer dropped by Aces High to have dessert and kill a few people, and he was perfectly willing to let someone else swing that spade.

Besides, if he started considering dead suspects, he'd wind up checking where Jetboy had been the night of the murder.

Chrysalis had hired George Kerby to go assassinate Leo Barnett. If Barnett had found out, maybe the killers were working for him. Except what ace in his right mind would work for Leo Barnett? Quasiman? Presuming he could even *remember* that Barnett had saved his life? Okay, so somehow Quasiman stayed smart long enough to do Chrysalis, so what about the chainsaw man and the body in the trash bag that Elmo had left for the neighbors last year, who was that, Friend o' Quasiman? Jay tried to picture Father Squid whipping a chainsaw out from under his cassock, but the thought just gave him a headache.

Digger Downs was the key. But Digger Downs was missing, maybe dead. It was a real big city out there, and a bigger country beyond it. He could be anywhere.

On the other hand, there was sure as hell one place he *wasn't*, and that was here in Jay's bathroom. He took one last swig of ice-cold coffee, grimaced, set the cup aside, and climbed out of the tub to towel himself dry.

9:00 A.M

When Brennan awoke, Jennifer was still asleep in the rumpled bed beside him. He was so tired that he felt as if he hadn't slept at all, and his back and shoulders were still aching from the pounding he'd taken from the Oddity. He wondered if age were creeping up on him, or if it was just that he was already bone weary of the city.

He sat up and swung his feet off the bed, planting them on the threadbare carpeting of the cheap hotel room.

It didn't matter. He couldn't leave until he'd found Chrysalis's killer. He was clear of the murder, but now Elmo was the patsy. He couldn't trust the police to get it right. Of course, Ackroyd was also on the case, but Brennan had never relied on anyone to do what had to be done.

He felt cool hands run gently over his shoulders and glanced backward. Jennifer was awake. She looked at him seriously as she caressed his bruised and aching back. Her hair was damp with perspiration. Her small breasts and rib cage shone with it. She had wanted to accompany him to the funeral home the night before, but Brennan felt that that was a job he had to do alone. She'd been asleep when he'd returned to the hotel, and he'd been careful not to wake her.

"How's your back?" she asked him.

He shrugged experimentally, then grimaced. "Sore. But I can deal with it. How about you?"

"Sore," she said, "but trying to deal with it."

She moved away from him, lay back down on the bed.

"I missed you."

"I missed you, too," Jennifer said. "Enough at least to come and find you. You could have given me more time to think about things."

"You're right."

Jennifer nodded, as if almost satisfied. "So. Did you find out about Chrysalis? Is she really dead?"

Brennan frowned. "She's in a coffin in Cosgrove's Mortuary, all right."

"Then the voices we both heard could be, what? Mimics? Her ghost?"

"Could be . . ." Brennan said softly, his voice trailing away.

"Then what's on for today?" Jennifer asked, reaching out and touching his shoulder gently.

He looked down at her. "Her funeral is this afternoon. I thought we should attend."

Jennifer nodded again. "What about now?"

"Now?"

Jennifer pulled him down to her. She was slick with perspiration and desire. Her breasts tasted salty, her tongue moist and sweet.

11:00 A.M

It was beginning to dawn on Jay Ackroyd that he'd wasted the entire morning. He hung up the receiver once again and contemplated his dreary little two-room office. The air-conditioning was broken, the window was painted shut, and it was hot as hell. Jay was hungry and tired and sweaty, and he knew more about Digger Downs than any human being could conceivably want to know. "Except where he is," he told his secretary.

His secretary stared at him with her mouth puckered in a round little O of surprise. Her name was Oral Amy and her mouth was always puckered in a round little O of surprise. The manager of Boytoys had given her to Jay after he'd figured out which of the employees was putting the pin holes in the French ticklers, and he'd installed her at the front desk by his answering machine. She didn't take dictation, but at least she was blond.

"I've got a real bitch of a headache," he told Oral Amy. She looked at him with her face all wrinkled up in sympathy. Well, either sympathy or a slow leak.

All morning he'd been dialing the phone, asking for favors, and calling in old markers. All morning he'd been lying and shucking and posing as people he wasn't to convince reluctant voices on the other end of the line that they ought to tell him what he wanted to know.

The good news was, there was no one fitting Digger's description in the morgue or any of the city hospitals. The rest was bad.

Digger hadn't booked a flight on any airline Jay could find. He hadn't taken Amtrak or Greyhound either. He carried a MasterCard, two Visas, and a Discover, but the last charge on any of them was a Friday-night dinner at an Italian restaurant two blocks away from his digs on Horatio. The bill came to $63.19, and he'd stiffed the waiter. If Digger had hit the road, he'd been smart enough not to pay his tolls with plastic.

Of course, he might have bought a plane ticket under an assumed name, and paid cash. Or boarded the Metroliner to D.C. and bought a ticket from the conductor. Or escaped to the wilds of Jersey on a commuter bus out of Port Authority, exact change only. Or walked across the goddamn Brooklyn Bridge. There were eight million ways to leave the naked city, and some you just couldn't check.

There were eight million places to stay in the naked city, too. Jay called a half-random, half-cunning selection of motels and hotels that struck him as Digger's kind of place. He even tried a few that definitely *weren't* Digger's kind of place, just in case Downs had tried to be clever. Digger wasn't registered anywhere.

He did find Digger's aged mother in Oakland, who told him that she hadn't heard from Tommy since he sent the flowers on Mother's Day, but she was still real proud of her boy the journalist. She kept scrapbooks with every word Tommy had ever written, even the little articles he used to do for his high-school newspaper, and said Jay was welcome to look at them the next time he was in the Bay area. Jay thanked her very much and left his number in case she heard from Tommy. Mrs. Downs read it back to him very carefully and suggested he might phone Peregrine, seeing as how she was Tommy's girlfriend and all. Jay mentioned that this was news to him. Mrs. Downs said it was a secret, on account of Peregrine's image.

His sister in Salt Lake City didn't know where he was.

Neither did either of his ex-wives. Wife number one asked if he was in trouble, and said, "Oh, good," when Jay admitted that he was.

Wife number two offered to engage Jay's services on a little matter of alimony. He took it under advisement.

His college roommate didn't remember him.

The journalism professor he'd listed as a reference on his job application was entirely fictitious.

The phone company had no record of any calls from his home number yesterday.

Jay tried Crash at *Aces* just in case, but no, there hadn't been word one from Digger. Mr. Lowboy still wasn't worried. He was telling them to save space in the August issue for a real Digger Downs blockbuster. "Real good," Jay said glumly, wondering if the news of Digger's grisly death would fit Lowboy's definition of blockbuster. This time maybe Digger was *really* going underground for a story. Crash asked him if he was having any luck.

"Lots of it," Jay told her. "All bad. I don't suppose he had any friends on the staff there? One of the other reporters, maybe? A poker buddy, a drinking companion, the best man at his weddings, that kind of thing? Somebody who'd let him crash on his couch until all this blew over?"

"No," Crash said. "He was too good. The other reporters resented the way he always got the big assignments and the cover stories. You should have heard them gripe when Lowboy sent him on that tour around the world. Digger can be charming when he wants, but he's very competitive when he's going after a story."

"Damn," Jay said. "Did the guy have *any* friends at all?"

"Well," Crash said, thinking, "he must have."

"Famous last words," Jay said.

"I know a lot of people thought Digger was a pain in the neck. He could be very abrasive, but he had a sweet side, too. You'd be surprised. A lot of the people he wrote up just loved him." She paused thoughtfully. "Well, at least until the stories came out," she amended.

"Terrific," Jay said with a minimum of enthusiasm. "Listen," he started, "maybe you can—" His mind went off on a tangent, and the words stopped coming.

"Jay?" Crash asked after a moment of silence. "You okay?"

"Fine," he said. "But I just had this *real* weird idea."

NOON

The sun was a shiny coin flung high in the sky, obscured by a haze of pollution and a sheath of angry clouds that were motionless in the thick air. The heat and humidity made it hard to breathe as Brennan and Jennifer waited patiently in the queue that was shuffling forward into Our Lady Of Perpetual Misery. Jokertown always took care of its own and Chrysalis was going to have a fine send-off.

People walked, crawled, hopped, and slithered into the church past a couple of bored cops who were stationed at the entrance. At least the city had enough sense to assign Kant, their tame joker cop, to this duty, but Brennan wondered what the police were supposed to detect in a gathering where masks were common. They barely glanced at Brennan, who was wearing a full-face mask, reserving most of their attention for Jennifer, who looked a lot better in black than Brennan.

The church was packed. The pews already full, Brennan and Jennifer found standing room in the back next to the droning fans that were trying to move the stifling air. Chrysalis's casket sat near the altar, covered with a carpet of flowers. There was a vast, hurried mumbling as the Living Rosary Society told their beads as they said their prayers for the repose of Chrysalis's soul.

The procession began after the final paternoster. A joker altar boy led the way, bearing a bronze helix hung with Joker Jesus. He was followed by two others—an altar boy with no visible mouth and an altar girl with too many—swinging censers that sent clouds of sickly-sweet incense billowing into the already redolent air. Other servitors followed, including priests who would assist at the funerary Mass. Father Squid brought up the rear, wearing his finest surplice. It was embroidered with a scene depicting a nat Madonna turning her back on Joker Jesus while a pair of jokers and a small, delicate, red-haired man wearing a white lab coat took Him from the helix and wrapped Him in funerary cerements.

They passed the front pew where the principal mourners sat. Tachyon, wearing a brilliant scarlet and gold waistcoat, sat next to a tanned, uncomfortable-looking man in a black suit. Next to them was a man with a death's-head face. This last, Brennan realized, was

Charles Dutton, Chrysalis's silent partner in the Palace. Various Palace employees sat in the pew behind them, but neither Elmo nor Sascha were present.

Father Squid reached the altar, set his missal in place, then turned to the crowd and raised his arms wide and said in his sad, soft voice, "Let us pray."

The Mass began. It was similar to the infrequent Catholic masses Brennan had attended as a child, but with some unfamiliar twists of symbolism and ritual. Everyone took off their masks with the first prayer. Brennan looked around apprehensively for the cops, but either they'd never entered the church or were off in another part of the congregation. He and Jennifer removed their masks and no one gave them a second glance.

During the Mass there were only a few references, veiled in strange symbolism, to the Mother, reflecting the ambiguous role she played in the Church of Jesus Christ, Joker, theology. Praise for the Father was effusive and tainted with an air of placation, as if He were the vengeful God of the Old Testament, the God who saved with one hand and damned with the other.

During Communion the altar boys and girls went out into the congregation bearing small hampers that had been blessed by Father Squid. The hampers contained loaves of bread that the servers passed out to the people sitting at the heads of the pews, who broke off bits for themselves before sending them on.

After Communion Father Squid summoned Tachyon to the altar to deliver the eulogy. As Tachyon approached the rail Brennan suddenly realized that the church's father, the small, delicately featured man with red hair, looked exactly like Tachyon. That, he thought, would make any man feel strange, but the alien's vast ego was probably capable of dealing with it.

The only somber element about Tachyon's clothing was a black ribbon tied around his upper right arm. His scarlet coat, hung with gold braid and piping like tinsel on a Christmas tree, looked out of place at a funeral. But, Brennan reminded himself, Tachyon was heir to an alien culture that had all kinds of odd sensibilities.

Tachyon took his place behind the lectern and pulled out a handkerchief to wipe at his eyes. It was hot in the church and Tachyon's velvet coat looked stifling. He was red-faced from the heat and his coppery curls were damp from perspiration. His eyes, too, were red, and Brennan realized that he'd been crying. Tachyon's emotional displays made some think less of him, but not Brennan. More than once Brennan had seen the iron underneath Tachyon's foppish exterior and in fact he envied Tachyon his ability to show emotion.

Tachyon looked out over the congregation. His expression was solemn; his husky voice was so soft that it was difficult to hear him over the thrum of the fans.

"Exactly one year ago on the twentieth of July, 1987, we gathered in this church to bury Xavier Desmond. I spoke his eulogy, as I shall speak Chrysalis's. And I am honored to do so, but the melancholy truth is that I am weary of burying my friends. Jokertown is a poorer place because of their passing, and my life—and yours—is diminished by their loss." He paused for a moment, gathering his thoughts.

"A eulogy is a speech in praise of a person, but I am finding this one to be very difficult. I called myself Chrysalis's friend. I saw her frequently. I even traveled around the world with her. But I realize now that I *didn't really know her*. I knew she called herself Chrysalis and that she lived in Jokertown, but I didn't know her natal name or where she'd been born. I knew she played at being British, but I never knew why. I knew she liked to drink amaretto, but I never knew what made her laugh. I knew she liked secrets, liked to be in control, liked to appear cool and untouched, but I never knew what made her that way.

"I thought about all of this on the plane from Atlanta and decided that if I couldn't speak in praise of *her*, at least I could speak in praise of her deeds. A year ago, when war waged in our streets and our children were in danger, Chrysalis offered her place—her Palace— as a refuge and fortress. It was dangerous for her, but danger never disturbed Chrysalis.

"She was a joker who refused to act like a joker. The crystal lady never wore a mask. You took her as you found her, or you could just be damned. In this way, perhaps, she taught some nats tolerance and some jokers courage." Tachyon stopped again to wipe at the tears that suddenly ran down his cheeks, then continued with a brighter, louder voice that gained strength as he spoke.

"Because we worship our ancestors, Takisian funerals are even more important than births. We believe our dead stay close by to guide their foolish descendants, a belief that can be terrifying or comforting, depending on the personality of the ancestors. Chrysalis's presence, I think, will be more terrifying than comforting because she will require much of us.

"Someone murdered her. This should not go unpunished.

"Hate rises like a smothering tide in this country. We must resist it.

"Our neighbors are poor and hungry, frightened and destitute. We must feed and shelter and comfort and aid them.

"*She* will expect all this from us."

He paused, his gaze sweeping over the congregation, his eyes shiny with tears, but also, Brennan thought, with strength and hope that he had somehow imparted to those gathered to mourn Chrysalis's death. A bank of votive candles burned near the lectern. Tachyon went to it, then turned to face the congregation again.

"In one year," he said, "Jokertown has lost two of its most important leaders. We are frightened and saddened and confused by the loss. But I say they are still here, still with us. Let us be worthy of them. Win honor in their memories. *Never* forget."

Tachyon held out his right hand and cut the pad of his forefinger with a knife he pulled from a boot sheath. He held his finger over the flame of a candle, extinguishing it with a drop of his blood.

"Farewell, Chrysalis."

Tachyon stepped from the podium and made his way back to his place in the pew and Brennan suddenly realized that, like Tachyon, tears were running down his cheeks, too.

1:00 P.M.

When the doorbell played "Old McDonald Had a Farm," Jay knew he had the right place.

A housekeeper opened the door. "Yes?" she asked.

Jay smiled his most ingratiating smile. "Bob Lowboy," he said, holding out a hand, "from *Aces* magazine."

"Nobody's home," she told him. "Jessica's at school, and Mr. von der Stadt won't be back from work till seven."

"No problem," Jay told her. He held up the camera he'd borrowed from his favorite pawnbroker. "I just need to get a few more shots of the farm for our story on Miss Jessica and her little animals."

The housekeeper looked suspicious. "That other reporter, Mr. Downs, he took all kinds of pictures."

"Ruined," Jay said. "A little accident in the darkroom. These things happen." He glanced at his watch. "Look, won't take me more than ten minutes, but I have to get a move on."

She frowned. "Maybe I ought to phone Mr. von der Stadt at the brokerage," she said.

"Be my guest," Jay said, "but I'm due at the next shoot in thirty minutes, and you know what crosstown traffic is like this time of day. We'll just run the story without art."

The housekeeper's frown deepened. "Well," she said, "maybe it would be all right. Just for a minute."

"Real good," said Jay. He stepped into the house.

She led him upstairs. The farm was on the top floor. Rather, the farm *was* the top floor. "You be careful you stay on the path now," the housekeeper warned him as she unlocked the special fire door. "That Mr. Downs, he almost stomped on one of the horses."

"That's Digger for you," Jay said.

The door swung open, and Jay looked around in astonishment. Digger hadn't exaggerated. It was Iowa in an attic. To his right, a herd of cows munched away on a handful of real grass tossed down in the middle of a fake-grass field. To his left, alone behind a chicken-wire fence, a bull the size of an especially husky mouse snorted threateningly. Beyond them were other fields, other animals. "That's an elephant," Jay said.

"He was Miss Jessica's Christmas present," the housekeeper said. "How come you're not taking any pictures?"

Jay turned and looked at her. "Photography is an art, you know. You don't expect me to work with you right here looking over my shoulder, do you?"

It actually worked. "Well, okay," the old woman said. "No more than ten minutes, mind you." She closed the door behind her.

Jay took the footpath across the fields toward the complex of farm buildings under the windows, past a flock of sheep and some very short sheepdogs, a muddy trough crawling with pigs, toy tractors, and plastic farmer figurines, and a ramshackle henhouse. Chickens the size of marbles squawked and fluttered at his approach. The animals weren't all to scale, but he supposed he shouldn't be picky.

The house stood surrounded by haystacks, next to the traditional red barn and a tall grain silo. It was a painstaking replica of an old-fashioned woodframe farmhouse, as lovingly detailed as any doll-house. It had painted wooden shutters, a bronze weathervane that moved when he touched it, and real cloth curtains in the windows. On the porch swing, a plastic hired hand sat with his arm around a plastic farmer's daughter. An iced pitcher of lemonade stood on the little table beside them.

Jay got on his knees and pushed open the front door with his fingers. He peered in just long enough to glimpse a living room full of antique miniatures before a tiny collie rushed out and began to bark at him wildly. "Sonofabitch," Jay said. The dog snapped at his nose. "Nice dog," he said, pulling his head back quickly. "Shut the fuck up, nice dog." The collie kept on barking. If only he'd brought a bone.

"*Digger,*" he whispered urgently. "You there?"

He thought he heard a rustle of movement from one of the upper stories, but it was hard to be sure with the racket the collie was making. Jay peeked in one of the third-story windows. He saw a woman's bedroom, all lace and frills, pale blue walls covered with butterflies, a canopied four-poster bed. Nothing moved. It was a little dusty. How do you clean the inside of a dollhouse anyway?

Jay thought about that for a moment, while Lassie danced around him and yapped. He considered seeing how far he could punt the collie with a nice hard finger flick, but restrained himself. Instead he bent over the farmhouse and lifted off the roof.

Digger Downs, all three inches of him, was huddled on the floor of a tiny, windowless closet, trying to hide under a pile of doll clothes. He screamed when he saw Jay staring down at him, leaped up, and made a run for a staircase. Jay got him on the third step, lifting him into the air by his collar.

"*Don't kill me,*" Digger shrieked in a tiny shrill voice, arms flailing as he dangled between Jay's fingers. "Oh God, please don't kill me."

"I only pick on guys my own size," Jay said. "Nobody's going to kill you. We're getting out of here. Be quiet."

He dropped Digger into his coat pocket barely an instant before the housekeeper returned. "Mr. Lowboy," she said, in a disapproving tone, "I have Mr. von der Stadt on the line, and he'd like a word with you."

"No can do," Jay said. "Gotta run." The collie was barking up a storm, jumping around on his shoe, trying to climb up his pant leg to the pocket where Digger was hidden. "You think she's trying to tell us something?" Jay asked innocently.

♠

Chrysalis's only pallbearer was a green, nine-foot-tall joker who easily lifted her coffin and, cradling it in his arms as if it were a shoe box, led the procession into the churchyard.

By the time Brennan and Jennifer had followed the crowd of mourners into the tiny graveyard, the joker and Quasiman were lowering the coffin into the open grave. Father Squid blessed the grave with incense and holy water, said the final prayers for the dead, and stepped back as Jokertown buried another of its own. A long line snaked around the grave. Each person dropped a handful, pawful, or clawful of dirt onto the coffin, then paid their condolences to Father Squid, Tachyon, and the uncomfortable-looking man who'd been sitting with Tachyon in the front pew. He was a big man with a weathered face that was florid under his tan. He was sweating from the heat and twitching from the private storm of emotions that was raging, barely checked, inside him.

"Hello, Father," Brennan said, taking the hand of the priest.

"Good to see you again, Daniel," Father Squid said, returning his handshake with his powerful, but friendly grip.

Tachyon threw himself at Brennan, hugging him with naked emotion that Brennan tolerated with good grace. He drew back after a long moment and held Brennan at arms' length, examining him critically. "We must talk. Come."

Tachyon led Brennan deeper into the graveyard until the only ones who could hear them were the carven angels on the tombstones surrounding them. Tachyon glanced back at Jennifer, who was watching them curiously from Chrysalis's graveside.

"The beautiful blonde must be Jennifer," Tachyon said.

"Yes."

"I'd say you're a lucky man, but that would seem less than apt when you're being framed for murder. Is that what brought you back?"

"Partly," Brennan said. "Mostly I'm here to find who killed her."

"And how are you progressing?"

"Not too well," Brennan admitted.

"Any theories?"

"I thought Kien might have done it," Brennan said doubtfully.

Tachyon seemed even less thrilled by the notion. "That makes no sense. We had a deal that took you out of the city and ended the war. Why would he risk restarting the whole killing cycle?"

"Who knows?" Brennan shrugged. "I'm just going to keep poking until something jumps."

"Just make sure it doesn't jump on you," Tachyon admonished. "I wish I could aid you, but I must return to Atlanta. You will keep in touch?"

Brennan shook his head. "No. Once I finish this, Jennifer and I are leaving New York, and this time it will be for good."

"If you won't keep in touch, at least be careful."

"That I can agree to."

They clasped hands, then wandered back over to the grave site. The man standing in the receiving line next to Father Squid cleared his throat, and Father Squid glanced at him.

"Ah yes," the priest said, "Mr. Jory, meet, ah—"

"Archer," Brennan said softly.

"Yes, Daniel Archer and Jennifer Maloy. Daniel was a, um, close friend of your daughter. Daniel and Jennifer, this is Joe Jory, Chrysalis's father."

Jory glanced aggrievedly at Father Squid before turning to Brennan and putting out a large, meaty hand. "Nice to meet you, Mr. Archer. It's good to know that my little Debra-Jo had some normal-looking friends."

Brennan's sympathetic expression went cold. Father Squid and Tachyon pretended to look elsewhere.

"Chrysalis was an extraordinary woman with many friends," Brennan finally said in a hard, even voice.

"Her name was Debra-Jo—" Jory began, but Father Squid stepped between them and put a hand on Brennan's arm.

"As executor of the estate," the priest said, "I'll be reading her will tonight at the church. I think you should attend."

Brennan took his eyes from Jory and looked at Father Squid. "I'll be there," he said evenly. "Sorry we have to run." He looked at Jory again. "As I said, Chrysalis was an extraordinary woman. No one, as Dr. Tachyon so elegantly stated, knew much about her, though I knew more about her and her loving family than most. I promise you one thing, Mr. Jory. Her killer will be brought to justice. Not to make you feel better. But for her."

Brennan turned, and Jennifer followed him as they left the churchyard. A black cat with jade green eyes was waiting for them on the street outside. It meowed as Jennifer and Brennan approached, stood on its hind paws, and offered Brennan an envelope.

Jennifer stared at Brennan as he hunkered down until he was almost at eye level with the cat. The two looked at each other silently for a long moment, then Brennan took the envelope. "Hello, Lazy Dragon," he said. "How've you been?"

"Mmmmwell," the cat said, licked its shoulder, and then turned and ran up the street.

"Did you know that cat?" Jennifer asked.

"I worked with him once before, when he was a mouse." Brennan unfolded the sheet of paper that was inside the envelope, scanned the message on it, then handed it to Jennifer.

The message was short and to the point.

"Hello, Cowboy," it read. "Let's talk."

It was signed Fadeout, and there was a phone number next to the name.

2:00 P.M.

"It seemed like a good idea at the time," Digger said. He was sitting on a stapler, next to a Coke can that was taller than he was. The pizza carton took up most of the desktop. Jay hadn't been able to manage more than three slices, and Digger was still working on a pepperoni. In his hands it looked like a greasy red manhole cover.

"The story hadn't even run yet," Digger went on. "Nobody knew about Jessica but me, and that big farmhouse looked so *cozy*, y'know? I knew the kid'd always wanted a little farmer, but Daddy wouldn't allow it, so I figured, what the hey, nobody would know but me and Jessica, and she'd never tell. It seemed like the perfect hideout."

"Why the hell didn't you just leave town?" Jay asked him.

Digger shook his head gloomily. "Man, I wanted to, but it wasn't safe. What if they were staking out the airport, just waiting for me to make a break for it?" He grimaced.

"There's three airports," Jay pointed out. "Not to mention Penn Station, Grand Central, Port Authority. How many people were after you?"

"Who the hell knows?" Digger said darkly. "There's no telling who might be in on this—cops, FBI, CIA, maybe all of them. Besides, say there was only one, and I guessed wrong." He shuddered. "I got to Jessica in her school playground, and she *loved* the idea. Shrunk me down right there and took me home in a Flintstones lunchbox. By then I was having second thoughts, but it was too late, she was determined to keep me. The little snot-nosed brat wanted me to do *chores*. And that farmhouse—maybe it looks comfortable, but everything's made of plastic. There's no *plumbing*!"

"There's worse things." Jay told him about the carnage at his apartment building and Digger got very quiet.

"Holy shit," he said softly when Jay had finished. "Jonesy and Mrs. Rosenstein, *Jesus*. But *why*? They didn't know a damned thing."

"They were there," Jay said. "You weren't."

Digger dropped the half-eaten pepperoni and wiped his greasy palms off on his pants. "You got to believe me, I had no idea. I knew he was crazy, man, but I never—"

"You knew *who* was crazy?" Jay asked pointedly.

Digger looked around the office. There was no one watching but Oral Amy, who looked even more surprised than usual. "Mack the Knife," he croaked in a low, scared whisper. "Mackie Messer. You think the scene in the stairway was bad, man? You don't know *nothing*. I seen him kill. He did the Syrian chick right in front of us, made us watch the whole show."

"The *Syrian* chick?" Jay was confused.

"Misha," Downs told him. "The Kahina. You know, the Nur al-Allah's sister, the one who sliced his throat open." His tiny hands were trembling. He looked down at them and laughed. The laugh was thin and bitter, on the edge of hysterical. "His hands shake, too," he said. "Oh, man, do they shake, like a blur, and then they go right through you. He touched her, you know, like he was going to play with her tit, but his fingers went right in, and the blood started. He just sliced it off, right in front of us, he sliced off her tit, and then he giggled and threw it at me. I puked my guts up. Chrysalis, she just sat watching, you know how she was. It was getting to her, too, but she never liked to look weak. This is her fault, I know it. She did something stupid, right? She wasn't talking much these last few weeks, but I'm pretty good at reading people. What'd she do?"

"She sent a hired assassin to Atlanta," Jay said.

"Damn," Digger said. "Damn it. Yeah, it figures. She knew the score, but I guess she just couldn't stomach it no more. If we exposed him, we were dead meat, he'd warned us about that. She must of decided to kill him first."

"Maybe she just couldn't live with the idea of Leo Barnett as president," Jay suggested.

Digger looked at him oddly. "Barnett?" he said. "What does Barnett have to do with it?"

Jay just stared at him.

"Not Barnett," Digger said quietly. "Gregg Hartmann."

"*Hartmann?*" Jay said, incredulous.

Digger nodded.

The office was hot, airless, but Jay felt cold fingers tracing a path up his spine. "Maybe you better start at the beginning," he said.

♥

"Fadeout," Brennan said into the phone.

There was a short silence, then a voice that Brennan remembered quite well said, cautiously, "Speaking."

"How did you find me?" Brennan asked.

There was another silence, then Fadeout said, "Good to hear from you so soon, Cowboy. Or should I call you Yeoman?"

"Call me whatever you like. Just tell me how you tracked me down."

"A little bird told me you were at the church."

"Lazy Dragon?"

"Exactly. I had him covering the funeral just in case anything interesting happened. When he told me you were there, I thought I'd avail myself of your offer to discuss things, so I had him deliver my message."

"I'm glad you did," Brennan said. "I didn't think a Shadow Fist captain would want to talk to me."

Brennan had infiltrated the Shadow Fist Society to gather evidence to bring Kien to justice. His scheme probably would have worked, but he had been forced to blow his cover to save Tachyon's life when the Fists had taken over Tachyon's clinic.

"I'm not one to dwell in the past," Fadeout said expansively. "You caused me a few problems, but, as I said, I think we can help each other."

"Uh-huh. What would Kien say to all this?"

"Well . . ." Brennan could picture Fadeout's insincere smile. "He doesn't know every little thing that I do. We should talk in more detail. Not over the phone. Actually, we missed an opportunity to discuss things yesterday. That was you at Quinn's, wasn't it?"

"Yes. Sorry I didn't hang around, but I wasn't sure of the reception I'd get."

"Oh, you don't have to worry about me. I think it's very possible that we can be a big help to one another."

"I see." Evidently Fadeout was an ambitious man. He might make a helpful, if not totally trustworthy ally. Brennan checked his watch.

He desperately needed a few hours' rest, then he had the will reading to attend in the evening. "I'll call you about midnight with a place where we can meet."

There was a long pause as Fadeout thought it over. "All right," he finally said.

Brennan hung up, sighing tiredly. He leaned back on the sagging hotel bed and rubbed his eyes.

"Can we trust him?" Jennifer asked.

"Not too far. It sounds as if he wants to move up in the organization and he thinks I can help him. That gives us something of a basis for working together. He doesn't know everything the Fists do, but he's high enough in the organization to know about something as big as Chrysalis's murder."

Jennifer nodded. "He can give us a line on Wyrm. Bludgeon's been eliminated as a suspect, but there's still Quasiman and the Oddity."

"I have an idea how we can deal with Quasiman," Brennan said thoughtfully, "but the Oddity's still a problem. There's nothing to link him to Chrysalis, other than the fact I caught him in the Palace after the murder."

"Rummaging through her closet."

Brennan shook his head. "I can't see Chrysalis hiding anything important in such an obvious place." He shook his head in bafflement. "And we're forgetting someone. Doug Morkle. Whoever he is."

Jennifer massaged the knotted muscles in Brennan's shoulders and neck. "It's not getting any clearer, is it?"

"No. And I have the feeling that if we don't catch the killer soon, he'll be long gone and out of the reach of any earthly justice."

♣

Hartmann's an ace," Digger began. "I knew it the minute I met him, at the press conference before that WHO tour took off."

"How?" Jay demanded.

Downs touched the side of his nose with a tiny finger. "The smell," he said. "I got this thing, my own little ace in the hole. I can smell wild cards. Aces, jokers, latents, it don't matter, they all smell the same. Kind of spicy sweet. Nats don't have the scent. I'm never wrong.

The nose knows, and it's gotten me some big stories, too. Anyway, when I got a whiff of Senator Gregg, man oh man, I figured I'd just hooked the mother of all bylines. A secret ace in the U.S. Senate, with one eye on the White House!

"So I started asking some questions. Chrysalis got wind of it, and before long we were working together. We dug up a few interesting rumors, but nothing hard, nothing I could go to press with. Until Gimli dropped the whole story right into our hands."

"Gimli?" Jay said skeptically. "Not a real reliable source where Hartmann is concerned." The joker terrorist's hatred of Hartmann had been common knowledge.

"I know, I know. Just listen up, it all makes sense. This was last year, just a few weeks after the tour came home. Gimli meets secretly with Chrysalis. In Syria, when the Nur's sister slit his throat, all kinds of bullets were flying. One of them richocheted off the Golden Weenie and clipped Gregg in the shoulder. Went right through, a clean wound, but they had to strip off his jacket to see how serious it was. The jacket got left behind when we pulled out. Well, that was what Gimli brought to Chrysalis, that jacket, with a bullet tear in the shoulder just soaked with Hartmann's blood."

"Gimli wasn't anywhere near Syria," Jay pointed out. "He was in Berlin, conspiring to snatch Hartmann later in the trip. How the hell would he get hold of Hartmann's jacket?"

"From Misha," Downs explained. "After she gave her brother that second smile, she couldn't believe what she'd done. She got the jacket and had some blood tests run. They told her what I already knew. Senator Gregg's an ace. She came to the States incognito, with her evidence. She was working with Gimli."

Jay gave the three-inch-tall reporter a dubious look. "With *Gimli?*" he said. "We talking about the same Gimli now? Real name Tom Miller? A joker dwarf with a nasty disposition and a big mouth? I thought the Nur's people all hated jokers."

"Yeah, yeah, the abominations of Allah, don't ask me why they were working together. They were. They wanted revenge but they knew nobody would believe them. So Gimli gave the jacket to Chrysalis. He wanted her to check it out and then go public with it. She had the credibility they didn't, right?"

"I'm with you so far."

"Yeah, well, Gimli got croaked right after that. They found his skin in an alley and he wound up stuffed and mounted in the Dime Museum. Meanwhile, Chrysalis had some tests run on the quiet, and they confirmed everything the little asshole had said. The blood type matched Gregg's, the jacket was his size, and the test showed the presence of the wild card in the blood. We had him dead."

"So why didn't you go public?" Jay asked.

Downs looked unhappy. He got up off the stapler, stuck his hands in his pants pockets, paced restlessly around the pizza, then glared up at Jay. "Okay, okay, we got too fucking smart for our own good. The thing that Gimli didn't realize was that Chrysalis had her own priorities. She didn't want to *destroy* Hartmann, she just liked the idea of maybe having a little leverage over our next president. And me, I got to thinking, too. I mean, I write the story, it's a big sensation, maybe I win a Pulitzer, but a year from now, who cares? Maybe there was a better way. Presidents need press secretaries, right? I could do that, get a little respect. I wouldn't have Tachyon pouring drinks over my head or irate boyfriends punching me in the mouth. I might even get a decent table at Aces High." He sighed. "You got to remember, we knew Hartmann was an ace, we even guessed he had some kind of hinky mind control, but that was it. So maybe he made Kahina slice her brother's throat from ear to ear that day in Syria, so what? Better his neck than mine, right? And the Nur was going to off all of us."

"So you thought Hartmann was a good guy," Jay prompted.

Downs nodded. "We set up a meeting," he said gloomily. He looked off into the distance, toward Oral Amy, remembering. "We thought we had the situation under control. We were wrong." His voice had gotten very somber. "Oh, man, were we wrong," he said. "That was when Gregg and Mackie Messer put on their little show. Hartmann knew everything, don't ask me how. The hunchback delivered Kahina in a tarp, naked, covered with blood. He told us how he'd already raped her in the ass, and he went to work on her, humming 'Mack the Knife' the whole time. When he was done, he walked out through a wall." Even talking about it made Downs go shaky.

"If Hartmann's everything you say, why didn't he have his killer eliminate you and Chrysalis right then?"

"Well, he didn't want two more deaths to explain. Instead he put us in charge of the cover-up. He told Chrysalis to get rid of the body and warned me that if anything appeared in the press even *hinting* that he was an ace, Mackie would come for me."

"And you went along with this shit?" Jay could maybe believe it of Digger, but Chrysalis hated being told what to do. He couldn't imagine her being easy to intimidate.

"You weren't there!" Digger snapped. "Hartmann's little leather boy *walks through walls*, man! I checked up on him afterward. He's German, part of the gang who grabbed Hartmann in Berlin, but somehow Gregg turned him around and made a house pet of him. Five'll getcha ten he's the one made sushi of the other kidnappers. Interpol's still hunting his twisted little ass."

"Then why not tell the cops?"

Digger laughed bitterly. "Oh, yeah. Go tell them that the former chairman of SCARE is in league with the terrorist who helped kidnap him, right. And pray that word don't leak to Gregg. Except it always does, somehow. Either he's a mind reader or he's got one working for him, I don't know. The point is, we couldn't trust no one. Chrysalis had some idea about getting Yeoman to help us out, but she was never able to get in touch with him. So we just played along and stayed alive."

"Until Monday," Jay said. "The name George Kerby mean anything to you?"

Downs shook his head. "She wasn't talking to *anybody* near the end. I don't even think she trusted *me*."

It made sense, Jay thought. The fewer people who knew, the fewer people who could betray her. But if Digger was telling the truth, someone had betrayed her anyway. And *fast*—she'd barely set her plan in motion and she'd been lying dead on her office floor. Hartmann, if that was who it was, didn't waste any time. "What about the jacket?" Jay asked.

"The jacket," Digger said. He snapped his fingers. "She kept it. Hidden somewhere. It was her last line of defense, she said. It was like a stalemate. If we went public with all we had, we'd be killed.

But Hartmann had to watch out, too. If he left us with nothing to lose, we could use the jacket and bring him down."

"Real good," said Jay. "So where is this jacket?"

"In a safe place," Downs said, with a helpless shrug. "That's all she'd say. I told you, she didn't trust no one. Have you checked her closets?"

"No," said Jay, remembering what Brennan had told him, "but I know someone who has. How much do you know about the Oddity?"

7:00 P.M.

Father Squid was standing in front of Our Lady of Perpetual Misery when Brennan and Jennifer arrived.

"You're the last," the priest told them. "If you'll follow me, we can begin the reading while Quasiman guards against unwanted interruptions."

"Fine," Brennan said, "but before we go in, I have a favor to ask of Quasiman. Where is he?"

Father Squid pointed up.

The crippled joker was standing at the top of the steeple, casually leaning against the metal spiral that projected from the base of the spire. He was looking far away at things neither Brennan nor Jennifer nor Father Squid could see.

"Can you get him down?" Brennan asked.

Father Squid shrugged massive shoulders. "I can try."

He looked up, cupped his hands around his mouth, and shouted, "Quasiman!"

The joker made no sign that he heard. Father Squid sighed and shouted again, louder. This time Quasiman looked down. He let go of the spiral, waved, and started to slip down the steeply inclined surface of the steeple.

Jennifer gasped, but just as Quasiman slid off into empty space, he disappeared. There was a distinct popping sound, then he was standing next to Brennan and Jennifer on the sidewalk in front of the church.

"Yes?" he said.

Brennan stared at him for a moment. "I wanted to ask you a favor," he finally said.

"A favor?" Quasiman repeated.

"Yes. You know that I'm trying to find out who killed Chrysalis. Well, I'm having a problem with an ace. An extraordinarily strong ace. I may need your help in handling him."

Quasiman glanced at Father Squid, who nodded almost imperceptibly. "All right."

"Thanks." Brennan held up a small electronic unit, the size and thickness of a folded wallet. "When—if—we need you, we'd be able to call you with this."

Quasiman took the receiver dubiously. "All right." He looked at the unit, his look lengthening into a stare as his mind drifted away to wherever it went when he phased out.

"You know," Father Squid said, "Quasiman is not the most reliable of men."

"He'll have to do. There's no one else to turn to."

Brennan didn't mention the other reason he wanted Quasiman to carry the receiver. It was also a sensitive sending unit. He planned to monitor Quasiman to see if he had any contact with someone who might have wanted Chrysalis dead.

"Very well," Father Squid said as Quasiman suddenly returned to normal. "But now, the will."

They went into the church, leaving Quasiman outside on the sidewalk.

The first four rows of pews were filled with people who worked at the Crystal Palace, from Jo-jo the microcephalic joker who swept out the place, to Charles Dutton, the skull-faced man who was Chrysalis's silent partner. Only Elmo and Sascha were missing, Elmo because he was still being held by the police. Joe Jory was also present. As Brennan and Jennifer approached the pew where Jory sat by himself, he knocked back a drink from a silver pocket flask. Brennan couldn't tell if grief was making him drink to excess or the thought of being so close to so many jokers. Either way Brennan found it hard to be sorry for him.

Father Squid settled his immense bulk down behind the table set up before the rail and looked around expectantly as all whispered conversations stopped.

"I'm glad that you could all come to hear Chrysalis's last will and testament. This reading is not for outsiders. The lawyers weren't told of it, neither were the police. Those formalities will be taken care of later. Tonight is for Chrysalis's family."

Father Squid picked up a manila envelope, slipped out a sheaf of papers, and tapped them together into a neat stack.

"As was my duty, I have already gone over Chrysalis's will once in private. I will read it to you now." He cleared his throat, then began.

"I, Chrysalis, being of sound mind and as sound a body as I've had since the wild card changed me, give you my last will and testament. I have numerous bequests to make, Father, so please gather together everyone connected with the Crystal Palace, and a few others whom I know you know, but will be nameless here.

"First, to Father Squid and the Church of Jesus Christ, Joker, I leave the contents of the luggage locker that fits the key which you'll find in this envelope. I know you will put it to good use." Father Squid looked up. "This has already been taken care of.

"Second, to Elmo Schaeffer, my right hand since I first came alone to the city, I give you what I could not give you in life: my love. If ever there was a man who deserved it, it was you." The priest sighed, cleared his throat again, and went on.

"Third, to Charles Dutton, I give outright my share of the Crystal Palace." There was an audible intake of collective breath and half a dozen conversations broke out that Father Squid's powerful voice hushed. "*With* the proviso that everything stays exactly as it is and everyone keeps their jobs as long as they shall live."

Dutton inclined his head and a wave of relief swept over the room.

"Fourth, to Digger Downs I leave the coat. Wear it in good health, or use it as you will."

Perhaps, Brennan thought, the Oddity was searching for this coat in Chrysalis's closet. Though what role a coat could play in Chrysalis's murder was utterly beyond Brennan.

"Fifth, to my loving father, if he has bothered to attend this reading . . ." Father Squid stood and passed a large manila envelope to Jory. He took it with shaking hands, broke the seal, and slipped out a sheet of heavy paper, eight by ten inches. Brennan could see from where he was sitting that it was the famous Annie Leibowitz photograph of Chrysalis. She was naked from the waist up and you could almost see her blood race, her lungs pump, her heart throb to the pulse of her life. ". . . so that you'll remember your darling little girl, day in and day out," the priest continued in his remorseless voice, "as long as you shall live."

It was a gift with a sharp, but just, edge to it, Brennan thought. Once, in what was probably the most vulnerable mood he'd ever seen her in, Chrysalis had told him that the virus had manifested itself in her at puberty. Her family had then locked her away in a wing of their mansion. They'd kept her hidden in their shame and disgust until she'd managed to escape six years later.

Father Squid sat back down behind his table. The church was silent but for the sobbing that Jory couldn't muffle by covering his face with his shaking hands.

"Sixth, to my archer, if he has heard of my death and cared enough to attend this meeting, I leave two things. The first . . ." Brennan stood and reached out a steady hand to take the small envelope that the priest held out. He opened it. Inside was a small bit of plastic-laminated paper, two and a quarter by three and a half inches, a brand-new, crisp, clean ace of spades. ". . . to place on the body of my murderer. The second to toast to offers I should have accepted, promises I should have made."

Father Squid picked up a box from the floor and placed it on the table.

"I'm sorry," he said in his gentle voice. "It seems that a vandal broke into Chrysalis's bedroom and smashed most everything, this included. I can dispose of it if you'd like."

It was the decanter she'd kept by her bedside filled with the Irish whiskey that Brennan favored.

"Thank you, Father. I'll take it."

There were more bequests. Most everyone was given a little something that they needed, or perhaps just something that they wanted but could never have afforded. Everyone was touched by the depths of feeling there was to the woman who had known everything, it seemed, and shown nothing. Brennan wondered again, Jennifer's hand a comforting presence on his right forearm, what would have happened if Chrysalis had taken the offer of his protection, had given him the promise of her love. He looked at Jennifer, wondering if she could read the questions in his eyes.

The reading ended. There were tears of sadness and genuine grief as Father Squid moved among the Palace employees, comforting them with his gentle, stolid presence. Jory had ceased sobbing and had passed out drunk. Father Squid detailed Lupo to get him to his hotel room.

As everyone stood about chatting, Brennan thought he felt eyes on him, as if someone were waiting in ambush in the rear of the church. He glanced back and saw a huge, bulky figure dressed in a floor-length cloak slip out of the back of the choir loft. He handed the box with the broken decanter in it to Jennifer.

"Take this to the room and wait for me. There's someone I have to see right now."

She nodded and took the package from him. "Be careful," she said, but Brennan was already out in the night, following the Oddity as that mysterious entity went on its mysterious rounds.

9:00 P.M.

The Oddity wasn't listed in the phone book or the city directory. At least not under "Oddity."

The joker had other names: Evan, Patti, John. That much Digger had remembered from that story that Mr. Lowboy had refused to print. The Oddity wasn't one person but three, two men and a woman. They'd been roommates and lovers, Digger told him, a ménage à trois, until the wild card had fused them into a single nightmare creature, three minds sharing one massive body, its flesh alive with the agony of perpetual transformation. Evan, Patti, John; but no surnames.

As for an address, the best that Downs could recall was that they lived down in Jokertown somewhere. That much Jay could have guessed by himself.

He took a cab to Jokertown and hit the streets, making the rounds until his feet began to hurt. The snitches at Freakers gave him some leads, after he'd dropped a few bills, but nothing had panned out. The Oddity didn't drink in any of the usual gin joints, eat in any of the usual greasy spoons, or get his or her ashes hauled in any of the usual cathouses. Jay finally tried the cophouse, ducking in through the side entrance to avoid his buddies Maseryk and Kant. There had been rumors about the Oddity, Sergeant Mole told him, but no complaints, no arrests, and no address on file.

After that, he walked the streets at random, in the half-assed hope of bumping into his quarry. When he hadn't been looking for the Oddity, the asshole had been showing up everywhere; now he couldn't find him for a prayer.

It must have been old habit that made Jay turn down Henry Street toward the Crystal Palace. He was half a block away when he remembered the Palace was closed.

Except, he saw when he got closer, that it wasn't.

Jay shoved in through the front door, following a pair of slumming yuppies. The taproom was as crowded as he'd ever seen it. All the tables and booths were full, and patrons were lined up two deep along the bar, clamoring for service. Jay moved through the press with a couple of feints and a deft elbow, to belly up to the rail. Lupo was the only bartender. His fur was slick with sweat, and he looked harassed. "I got his *poisse café* for him right here," he snapped at a waitress, grabbing his crotch. He drew a beer and set it on her tray. "Here, give him this, if he doesn't like it, tell him Squisher makes the best *poisse café* in town over in the Basement."

The bartender caught sight of Jay from the corner of his eye. He threw together a scotch and soda and brought it down, walking right past four nat barflies who were trying to get his attention. "Son of a fucking bitch," he complained as he set down the drink on a soggy coaster in front of Jay.

"Busy tonight," Jay said.

"Tell me about it," Lupo said. "Nothing like a murder to goose up business. I never seen three quarters of these geeks before. Lemme tell you, they don't know jack about tipping neither."

"*Hey!*" one of the nats screamed from three stools down. "Hey, furface, I want some fuckin' *service!*"

Lupo turned his head and snarled, baring long yellow teeth. The nat cringed and almost fell off his stool. For a second it got very quiet along the bar. Lupo turned back to Jay. "You were saying?"

"Where's Sascha?" Jay asked.

"Good question," Lupo said. "This is *his* goddamn shift, only nobody can find him. Maybe if I was a telepath I'd know when to get lost, too."

"New boss on the premises?"

Lupo nodded, moving off as a waitress hailed him from the far end of the bar. "Try the red room," he said.

The red room was quieter than the main taproom, but all the booths were occupied, red velvet curtains drawn around each for privacy. Jay stopped a waitress and asked about Dutton. She pointed to the booth on the end.

He carried his scotch over and stuck his head through the curtain. "Peekaboo," he said.

Jube jumped like someone had given him a hotfoot and looked nervous until he saw who it was. Charles Dutton seemed unperturbed. "Have a seat, Mr. Ackroyd," he said calmly.

Jay slid into the booth and let the curtain fall closed behind him, shutting them into a soft red womb. It felt good to sit down.

Dutton was nursing a cognac. The Walrus had a huge piña colada with a pineapple ring floating on top, but he pushed it away and maneuvered his bulk out of the booth. "I got to sell some papers," he said. "Catch you later."

Jay waited till he was gone. "Picking up the pieces?"

Deep-sunk cold eyes regarded him frankly. "You might say that. I've decided to keep the business going."

"Great," Jay said. "I'll be your first customer."

"What would you like to know? If the price is right, I'm sure we can do business."

"I get my usual generous discount, right?" Jay said. He went on quickly, before Dutton could say no. "I'm looking for the Oddity. Know where they live?"

"No," Dutton said.

Jay made a *tsking* sound. "Chrysalis would have," he said. "See, if you're going to be an information broker, you got to know things like that."

"Give me time to consult her informants," Dutton said.

"Sascha might know," Jay told him. "You pick up all kinds of things when you can read minds. Where is Sascha anyway?"

"I would like to know that myself. He hasn't returned to his room since the murder. His mother hasn't seen him either. She's quite worried."

"He's probably with his girlfriend," Jay said. "Trust me, she's not the kind of girl you bring home to Mom." He finished his drink. "Guess you haven't found those secret files yet."

"No, more's the pity," Dutton told him. "I can assure you, however, that they're nowhere in this building." Dutton pulled his hood over his face and stood up.

"Don't tell me you're tired of my company already?" Jay said.

"I'm afraid I have business to attend to."

"Me too." Jay got to his feet. He was thinking about Sascha. The last time he'd paid a call, he'd gotten laid and lied to. Maybe it was time they had another chat.

10:00 P.M.

It was a cinch to follow the Oddity, no matter how crowded or how empty the streets. The joker didn't move very fast, and he certainly had a conspicuous silhouette. Things got a little trickier when the Oddity took to the deserted back alleys where there were no other pedestrians to blend in with. But the alleys were also darker than the streets and allowed Brennan to move from shadow to shadow with the stealth of a stalking cat.

The Oddity finally stopped before a back service entrance of a dark brick building and let himself in with a key. Brennan followed him as closely as he dared. He stopped before the metal door, pausing to read the legend stenciled on it:

SERVICE ENTRANCE
FAMOUS BOWERY WILD CARD DIME MUSEUM

Brennan frowned, wondering what connection the Oddity could have with the wild card museum. He went to work on the door, knowing that he wouldn't find any answers out there in the alley.

Inside, the museum was dimly lit by security lights that threw the various exhibits into shadowy relief. Brennan felt a touch of strangeness as he moved by the silent, dimly lit replicas of aces and jokers and aliens. It was a relief finally to hear the sound of clumping feet that put him back on the Oddity's trail.

He caught up to the Oddity as the joker was disappearing down a flight of stairs that led to the bowels of the museum. Brennan followed him down the stairs and caught up with him again as he entered what looked like a basement workroom. The joker had flicked on all the lights, so Brennan cautiously hid behind a tarp-covered something that was being stored in the wide hallway. From his vantage point he could peer around the doorjamb and see into most of the room, which was largely filled with half-completed wax replicas.

The Oddity was pacing before one of the wax sculptures. Brennan leaned further into the light and saw that it was a nude study of Chrysalis. Her torso was just starting to take form with bones and organs gleaming under wispy musculature. Her head was still a formless blob.

The Oddity suddenly took off his fencing mask and hurled it across the room with an anguished howl. It made a loud clatter as it smashed into a pile of pots and pails that was sitting near the wall. The Oddity, now wearing the sensitive features of a handsome black man whose face was twisted by intense emotion, continued to pace before the sculpture.

Brennan was so engrossed in watching the joker that he almost didn't hear the footsteps on the stairs. He managed to jerk back into the darkness just as Charles Dutton came down the hallway and went into the workroom where the Oddity was pacing.

"I thought it was you," Brennan heard Dutton say. There was a long silence, then Dutton added, "There's no sense brooding over it, Evan."

Brennan heard the Oddity suck in a long, angry breath. "She's dead, Charles, beaten to a pulp by some lousy ace. I'll never finish it now." There was the sound of more angry pacing, then the Oddity— Evan—said, "I'd love to get my hands on the neck of the son of a bitch who did it to her. I would! I really would!"

"Now, Evan," Dutton said placatingly, "That's not like you at all. Sounds more like John. We have plenty of other things to worry about. The police are on the case, and so is Ackroyd. *Someone* will find the murderer. Let's concentrate on the files."

"I know, Charles," Evan said as Brennan silently backed away down the hall. "I know. But why Chrysalis? Who could have done such a thing?"

Brennan went back up the stairs, through the museum, and out into the alley by the back door.

There'd been no mistaking the pain and anguish in the Oddity's voice, though Brennan was unsure if he was more upset about Chrysalis's death or his unfinished waxwork. In any case, unless the Oddity was even more schizoid than Brennan figured, it was obvious that he hadn't killed Chrysalis.

The Oddity was innocent, Brennan thought. So was Bludgeon. The Shadow Fists were looking better and better. He checked his wristwatch as he moved off into the night.

Time to call a man, he thought, about a visit to a graveyard.

◆

This time Jay decided not to ring the doorbell. Just thinking of Ezili gave him a hard-on, but last visit things had gotten entirely too messy for his taste.

He pushed an empty dumpster down the alley and climbed on top. From there his fingers could brush the lowest rung of the ladder that hung down from the old cast-iron fire escape. He stretched, grabbed the metal with one hand, and tried to yank it down. It didn't want to come. Meanwhile the dumpster rolled out from under him, leaving him dangling from the ladder by one hand. Jay grunted, caught the rung with his other hand, chinned himself up, and began to climb. It was at times like this he wished he could teleport himself as easily as he did his targets. But no, he had to do it the hard way. He hunkered down on the fire escape to catch his breath, sniffing dubiously at the air. Something smelled bad.

All the lights were out in Sascha's loft. Jay moved stealthily along the fire escape toward the window. Climbing he could live without, but sneaking was his middle name. It was even easier when you didn't have to juggle a camera.

The window opened on a bedroom. Jay took a quick peek, saw no one. He took out a glass cutter, carefully removed a section of the upper pane, and reached through to open the lock. When the glass came out, the smell got stronger. Jay eased open the window and climbed in, avoiding a window box where odd-looking herbs and flowers fought for space with weeds. It smelled foul inside the room.

By then Jay was pretty sure that he wouldn't be finding either Sascha or Ezili at home. At least not alive. He moved quietly to the bedroom door, opened it a crack, listened for any sounds, heard none, and moved out into the hallway.

The subdivided loft was a lot bigger than he'd supposed. There was the living room, the lavish kitchen, two baths, and six bedrooms. The closer he got to the back, the worse it smelled. When he opened the door to the back bathroom, he gagged and retreated.

The dressing table in the adjoining bedroom offered a dozen different perfumes. Jay found a lace handkerchief in a drawer, doused it liberally, and held it over his mouth and nose. Then he went back to the bathroom to see who'd died.

Streetlight poured wanly through a small frosted-glass window onto the tiled floor. Jay could see the tiny pale shapes of the maggots swarming over the corpse. Even through the handkerchief, the smell was overwhelming. Jay forced himself to turn on the lights.

It was a child. A boy, he guessed, though there was barely enough left to tell. Bigger than the weird little monkey thing he'd chased through the Dime Museum, but way too small to be Sascha or Ezili. Jay remembered seeing someone small and somehow misshapen run for the bedroom when Sascha had burst in on him and Ezili. Maybe it was her kid. . . . But would a mother just go off and leave her dead child's corpse to rot on the bathroom floor?

The body was too far gone in putrefaction for close inspection, and the maggots reminded him unpleasantly of the white cone-faced thing in his dream. But he made himself stare at the decaying flesh. Definitely a joker. He was naked, and at first he seemed to have too many limbs, but Jay finally decided that the long swollen thing between his legs was a tail. The body lay facedown, and Jay couldn't make out his features, but there was a huge open sore on the side of his neck, writhing with maggots.

Jay had seen enough. He turned off the light, shut the door, and stood in the darkened hallway, considering his options. He could call the cops. Only this time he wasn't there by invitation. This time he'd done a little breaking and entering. Jay decided he'd let somebody else claim the prize for once. He jammed the handkerchief back into his pocket and began to search the apartment.

No one was home. No one had been home for some time. Except for the dead boy in the john, the tenants had cleared out in a hurry. Jay found open drawers where clothing had been pulled out and packed in a big rush. The furniture had been left behind, along with the strange Haitian shit that he'd noticed on his last visit, but most of the personal effects had been removed.

But not all. Enough remained to make Jay pretty damn certain that Ezili, Sascha, and the dead kid hadn't lived here alone. In one bedroom, he found a stack of weight-lifting magazines beside the bare mattress on the floor, along with a set of barbells that showed signs of hard use. Somehow he couldn't imagine Sascha pumping iron.

Another room had been sealed, its windows bricked shut, then fixed up like some kind of medieval torture chamber. Iron manacles hung from soundproofed walls, and a long dissection table stood in the center of the room, with deep grooves for the runoff of blood. Behind the closet doors, Jay found a rolling instrument cart, carefully hung with knives, pliers, thumbscrews, and other toys, even an antique dentist's drill, its bit still crusted with dried blood.

There were used syringes and scattered pills on the floor of a third bedroom, among bean-bag chairs and throw pillows that reminded him of a hippie crash pad in the sixties. The linen closet had been turned into a wine cellar. Even Jay knew enough about wine to realize that Chateau Lafitte Rothschild cost a few bucks, and some of the other labels looked kind of pricey, too.

In the fridge Jay found bottles of Dom Perignon, a can of beluga caviar, and other imported delicacies. Everything looked scumptious, but somehow he wasn't very hungry.

The hall closet was full of winter clothing that the tenants had forgotten in their haste. A linen jacket dangled from a hook inside the door, and the rack was crammed. There were women's coats in mink and Russian sable and something spotted that was probably an endangered species, plus a leather aviator's jacket and some very expensive-looking items in cashmere, suede, and camel's hair, mixed right in with denim and polyester, men's stuff and women's stuff together, in a range of sizes that went all the way to the extremes. No gray-checked sport jackets with bullet tears in the shoulder, though; Jay looked. He was standing there contemplating the coats when the phone rang.

A chill went through him. He remembered the funeral home, the strange call from the woman who spoke with Chrysalis's voice. No, he thought, not this time. No one knows I'm here. Wrapping the damp, perfumed handkerchief around his hand, he picked up the receiver and held it to his ear.

"I been calling all day, where the hell you been?" a man's voice said. "I got to have the kiss, you hear me? I *need* it. You don't know the kind of pressure I'm under here." It all came out in one long breathless rush; only then did the speaker seem to realize that he hadn't heard a hello yet. "Ezili, is it you?"

Jay spoke through the handkerchief and tried to disguise his voice. "She's not here," he said. "Who's this?"

There was a moment of silence. "Who am I talking to?" the caller asked, in a sharp voice that was eerily familiar.

"Sascha," Jay said, trying to talk like Sascha.

"You're not Sascha," the man said.

So much for that plan. Jay decided his best policy was to shut up and listen.

"Who is this?" the caller demanded. "You play games with me, you're in big trouble."

That did it. He knew the voice. And all of a sudden Jay was deeply grateful that he hadn't phoned the police. He dropped the receiver back into its cradle and got up fast. Kant could have a cruiser here in minutes. Jay had to move.

He'd taken two steps when he noticed the message pad beside the phone. He went back. The top sheet had been ripped off, but he could still see the impressions on the sheet below. Two columns of numbers marched down the sheet in parallel. Times.

Jay pocketed the pad and retreated back to the fire escape. You didn't need to graduate with honors from detective school to figure this one out. Flight times. Sascha wasn't going to be coming to work anytime soon, and Jay had a funny hunch he knew what city the bartender had fled to.

Thursday
July 21, 1988

1:00 A.M.

"YOU'RE TALLER," JAY SAID to Digger. Only a little, but when you start at three inches, an inch or two makes a difference.

"Yeah, yeah," Downs said, from where he was perched in Oral Amy's lap. "The brat had to come in every morning before school and reshrink the ones needed it most. Otherwise you grow."

"Slowly," Jay said, locking the office door behind him.

"Slowly," Digger admitted gloomily. "Where the hell you been? I figured Hartmann had gotten to you for sure."

"Hartmann's in Atlanta," Jay pointed out. "I doubt he even knows I'm alive."

"Don't bet on it," the reporter said, his tone gloomy. "So what's going on? You blow the whistle?"

"No," Jay said. He went on into the back room, turned on the lights and the fan, sat down at his desk.

Digger jumped down off Oral Amy and came trotting after him, his little feet pitter-pattering on the hardwood floor. "What the hell you waiting for, an engraved invitation from the White House?" he said in an aggrieved voice. "They've started balloting down in Atlanta, Hartmann could win the nomination while you're shuffling around picking your nose. You going to let the guy who had Chrysalis killed become president?"

Jay picked up the reporter by his collar. "Do me a favor, Downs, and shut the fuck up," he said, dropping the little man in his waste-basket.

Downs landed among the remains of the pizza and squawked in protest. "What the hell's wrong with you, Popinjay?"

"I found another body," Jay told him.

"Jesus," Digger said. "Who?"

"Damned if I know."

"Was it one of Mackie's?" Downs wanted to know.

"I don't think so," Jay said. "This one was pretty ripe, but all the pieces were still attached."

Downs climbed up the pizza box, teetered on the edge of the wastebasket for a moment, and jumped down to the floor. He landed with a grunt. "We got to get Hartmann before he gets us," he said. "I told you how he works. . . ."

"Yeah, you told me," Jay admitted. "It's a great story. It better be, it's all we've got. Your word against his. A presidential candidate versus the guy who broke the story about the Howler's secret love child. Wonder who they'll believe? Of course, you got substantiation— Chrysalis, Kahina, Gimli, hell yes. Too bad they're all dead."

"The jacket!" Digger insisted. "That's your proof!"

"Maybe," Jay admitted. "If we had the jacket. Which we don't. You wouldn't happen to know where Chrysalis hid her stash of secrets, would you?"

Downs shook his head.

"Too bad," Jay said. "What can you tell me about Sascha?"

"Sascha?" Digger looked thoughtful. "Well, he's a telepath. Does that help? He just skims off surface thoughts, you know? But if he was to leak what he picked up . . . Christ, you don't think Sascha was tied with Hartmann, do you?"

"The notion did cross my mind," Jay admitted.

"Jesus," Digger repeated. "I never paid much attention to Sascha . . . I mean, he was just kind of *there*, you know? But he was there a lot . . . if he was reporting to Hartmann . . . she *trusted* him, god-dammit. Him and Elmo, she counted on them. Sascha could pick up on trouble before it happened, and Elmo would handle it."

"Unless Sascha was part of the trouble," Jay pointed out. "Chrysalis ever say anything about Sascha's girlfriend?"

Digger seemed astonished. "What girlfriend?"

Jay sighed. "Never mind," he said. He got up.

"Where you going?" Digger asked.

"Out," Jay said.

"When are you coming back?"

"Later," Jay said as he unlocked the door. He needed a quiet drink. Some food would be nice, too. Not to mention sleep, but somehow he didn't think sleep was part of tonight's program.

♠

Brennan tossed and turned on the lumpy bed, half-asleep and half-awake, tormented by dreams that he couldn't separate from reality. He kicked off the confining, sweat-soaked sheets and glanced over at Jennifer. She was still soundly asleep. The clock on the bedstand beside her said that he had about two and a half hours before his meeting with Fadeout. He needed more sleep, but he doubted that it would come.

The memory of Chrysalis was a dull ache in his mind. Like Tachyon had said, her ghost was a demanding one. He fantasized dropping the card she'd given him on the body of the man or woman, ace or joker, who'd killed her. The only problem was that he could only conjure a big blank spot for the identity of the murderer.

It wasn't Bludgeon, it wasn't the Oddity. He couldn't really picture Quasiman in the role of cold-blooded killer. That left Wyrm and Doug Morkle as the final possibilities from Ackroyd's list. Wyrm, maybe. Morkle, who the hell knew?

He turned again restlessly toward the window, and froze. He wondered if he were still dreaming, or if he was just hallucinating.

The window seemed to have grown to gigantic proportions, lending credence to the notion that he was only dreaming that he was awake. It was framing Chrysalis from the neck up. He'd recognize her anywhere. It was her gleaming skull, her blue eyes, her red, pouting lips.

He stared for a good five seconds, then closed and rubbed his eyes. When he opened them, she was gone.

He lay there in bed staring at the now-empty window, telling himself to get up and go to it, but he was afraid.

He lay there and closed his eyes and told himself that it was only a dream, and after a while he'd almost convinced himself that that was true.

3:00 A.M.

"Coffee, Jay?" Vi asked him.

He'd grabbed a booth by the window. The counter drew a lot of strange people during the graveyard shift, and Jay wasn't feeling real sociable. "Yeah, please," he said. "And give me a patty melt, too. Extra onions, side of fries."

"Gotcha." Vi poured his coffee and left to place his order.

Someone had left a rumpled *Daily News* in the booth. Jay smoothed it out and read the lead story. The Democrats had started voting down in Atlanta. Hartmann had broken well in front, and he was gaining strength with each ballot. Leo Barnett was several hundred votes behind, followed by Jackson, Dukakis, and Gore. Much as he hated to admit it, Digger was right. He had to do something. But what?

He pushed aside the newspaper, took his list from his pocket, and looked at the names again. Wyrm, Quasiman, Bludgeon, the Oddity, and Doug Morkle. Yeoman swore it wasn't Bludgeon. If the mystery player was really Hartmann and not Barnett, that deep-sixed Quasiman's motive. Jay hadn't turned up a damn thing pointing at the Shadow Fists, and the M.O. was all wrong for Wyrm anyway. He still didn't know who the fuck Doug Morkle was, but by now he didn't care. It had to be the Oddity. Didn't it?

Jay dug out the list of flight times he'd swiped off the scratch pad by Ezili's phone. He took a sip of coffee. "Fuck it," he said aloud. It didn't have to be the Oddity.

Atlanta was too damn close. It looked like the flight time averaged about two hours, nonstop. The earliest departure left at 6:55 in the morning, and got into Atlanta at 9:07. The killer could have caught the last plane out of Atlanta Sunday night, dropped by the Crystal Palace in the early hours of the morning to murder Chrysalis, and still made it back to Georgia in time for the opening of the convention. Which meant that some of the other names on the list deserved a second look.

If Downs was telling the truth, Chrysalis had sent her assassin after Gregg Hartmann. She hadn't told anyone, yet somehow Hartmann had found out. The leak *had* to be Sascha. Elmo had been hiring the assassin just about the same time Chrysalis was getting killed, which meant somebody had known what she was going to do *before* she did it. New York had too damn many telepaths as far as Jay was concerned, but Sascha was the only one who was close to Chrysalis.

Jay took a swallow of coffee, grimaced, and cursed himself for a fool. He should have seen it much earlier. Sascha had been there when Jay found the body; even without eyes, he'd sensed an intruder in the building. So why hadn't he sensed the killer?

Or had he?

Okay, so Sascha picks the assassination plot out of Chrysalis's mind and leaks it to Hartmann, who sends Mackie Messer to make sushi out of Digger Downs, and someone else, someone with superhuman strength, to take Chrysalis out of the game. The Oddity? Maybe . . .

But Jack Braun was a Hartmann supporter, and Billy Ray was the senator's bodyguard. The brutality of the murder seemed out of character for Braun. Carnifex had a nasty reputation . . . but maybe that didn't matter. According to Downs, the Syrian girl claimed Hartmann *made* her slit her brother's throat, so maybe he compelled Braun to do his dirty work the same way.

Vi came bustling up with his patty melt in one hand and a fresh pot of coffee in the other. She set down the plate and refilled Jay's cup. He folded up his papers and put them away. "Who you like for president, Vi?" he asked the waitress.

She snorted. "They're all crooks," she said as she walked off. "I wouldn't vote for none of them."

Jay stared at his patty melt. The onions were grilled almost black, just the way he liked them. He tried a french fry. It needed ketchup.

"Hey, Vi," he called out, but by then she was back behind the counter, waiting on a couple of hookers who'd just strolled in off Forty-second Street.

The Oddity was still a better candidate than Golden Boy or Carnifex, Jay decided. Hartmann would have had to have learned of the assassination the night before to get either Braun or Ray on a plane on time, but if he *had* known that far in advance, why the hell did it take him so long to send Mackie after Digger Downs? And why not have Mackie take care of Chrysalis, too? Why use *two* killers, either of whom could implicate him? And why dispatch someone from Atlanta when he had local talent on the scene? That is, assuming Mackie *had* been on the scene. Maybe he'd been in Atlanta, too. That would explain why it had taken him so long to make his try for Downs.

The hell of it was, if Hartmann was an ace, every name on the goddamned list would need a second look; Troll, Ernie the Lizard, Doughboy, hell, they were probably *all* Hartmann fans. None of them seemed to have any particular motive for killing Chrysalis, but maybe they didn't need one, maybe they were Hartmann's unwilling pawns, like Kahina. So where the fuck did that leave him? Jay took a bite of his patty melt and chewed thoughtfully.

Was Hartmann a secret ace? Digger said so, him and his goddamned nose. Some evidence; a smell that no one else could smell. The cops would just *love* that. The only way to prove Digger's story was to find that jacket. Jay tried to think where he might hide if he was a jacket, but the only thing that came to mind was a closet, and all the obvious closets had been checked pretty thoroughly.

The patty melt needed ketchup too. "Vi," Jay called loudly.

She came over with the coffeepot in hand and stopped when she saw his cup was still full. "Whatcha need, honey?"

"Ketchup," Jay said.

Vi looked disgusted. "Honest to Christ," she said. "What do you think that is?" She pointed.

Jay blinked. The ketchup bottle was right there on the table, over against the window between the napkin dispenser and the salt-and-pepper shakers. Vi gave a put-upon sigh and walked off. Jay picked up the bottle, unscrewed the top, and poured a good-sized puddle on his plate. How stupid could he get, the damn thing was right there in front of him all the time.

Then it hit him.

4:00 A.M.

The forgotten cemetery, left untended for several decades, had become a pocket wilderness in the city. Many of its graves had collapsed during the years of neglect. Its weathered tombstones, most bearing names as forgotten as the cemetery itself, were canted crookedly throughout the rank undergrowth. The graveyard had an air of melancholy decay about it, but Brennan didn't mind. He liked its silent darkness. It was almost as quiet and peaceful as the country.

He wore dark clothes and carried his compound bow, assembled and ready for use. The bow was the proper weapon for this place, stained as dark as the night that hid Brennan and as quiet as the corpses that kept him company as he waited.

The silence was finally broken by the approach of a car that Brennan heard but couldn't see from his hiding place in the bushes. He could hear the driver park outside the crumbling brick wall that surrounded the graveyard and kill the engine. Doors opened and slammed shut, and there was silence again.

Then Brennan heard something heavy move through the undergrowth.

He froze. From the sounds it made, Brennan could tell that it was big. He took a deep breath, but could smell nothing beside the annoying city odors that penetrated even here. He stood still, holding his breath in a night so quiet that he could hear the blood rushing through the capillaries in his ears. He heard it move through the bushes and high grass, searching for him.

He ran through the undergrowth, moving away from the thing as silently as he could. It paused and took a great snuffling breath as it tasted the air for his scent.

He kept moving, circling around the deteriorating mausoleum where once he'd ambushed a group of Immaculate Egrets who were using an alien teleportation device to smuggle heroin into the city. He paused a moment when he heard a vast, satisfied hissing, as if a dozen steam pipes had burst and were happy about it. The thing hunting him had found his trail.

Faster now, careless of sound, Brennan bounded over the broken tombstones and through a tangle of lilac and wild rose, his way lit by a late-setting moon a few days short of full. He pushed through the undergrowth, ignoring the thorns that tore at him, and reached the base of the crumbling brick wall that surrounded the cemetery.

There was a loud crash at his back as something long and sinuous smashed through the stand of lilac and wild rose and stood shining in the night, moonlight glistening off its silver and gold scales.

It was a twenty-foot-long dragon, slender as a snake. Its four feet bore razor-sharp talons; its face was an elaborate Oriental mask with knifelike teeth, bulging red eyes, and clouds of steam puffing from its flaring nostrils.

It had to be Lazy Dragon. Fadeout had sent him to the meeting as something far removed from a mouse or a cute little kitty cat. Brennan automatically reached for the quiver velcroed to his belt, though he doubted that even his most powerful explosive arrow could harm such a formidable-looking beast.

♥

The locks were nothing special. Caution made the job take three times as long as it should have, but finally he managed to slide back the dead bolt. Jay opened the door a crack and moved inside the cool, dark interior of the Famous Bowery Wild Card Dime Museum.

A red light blinked silently in the key box mounted on the wall. Jay went to it and punched in the sequence of numbers he'd seen Dutton enter on Tuesday night. He had a good memory for things like that; the flashing red light was replaced by a steady green.

The interior of the museum was even creepier now that he was alone than it had been when Dutton had led him through it. The wax figures stared at him as he crept down the halls, and he kept imagining Monstrous Joker Babies lurking in every shadow. He got lost twice before he finally found the Syrian diorama.

All the lights were out. Jay could barely make out the outlines of the wax figures behind the glass, each frozen in a moment of time; Sayyid poised on the brink of collapse, Hiram squeezing his fist, poor lost Kahina with the bloodstained knife in her hands. Somewhere in the middle was Hartmann.

It was too dark to see the senator clearly. There had to be some way inside. He looked over the row of special-effects buttons, picked one, and pressed. Inside the diorama, hidden lights bathed Jack Braun in a golden glow. Long dusky shadows grew from the wax figures. The dim light stained Carnifex's white costume yellow as a dandelion, glittered off Peregrine's metal talons. Off to one side, barely visible against the painted backdrop, Jay saw the faint outline of a door.

He released the button and looked around until he found a door marked EMPLOYEES ONLY. The accessway was pitch black, airless, and narrow. Jay lit a match and fumbled his way along with one hand on the wall. The door to Syria was unlocked.

Jay dropped the burnt-out match and lit another. Its reflected twin burned faintly in the dark glass, and the flame made the wax figures seem to twist and move. Jay stepped carefully over Dr. Tachyon, unconscious on the ground in his Arab finery, edged between Golden Boy and the Oddity, and passed under Sayyid's awesome looming presence to where Gregg Hartmann stood.

Hartmann's tie was deftly knotted, his dress shirt pressed and starched. He was in his shirt sleeves. Jay blinked in confusion. Then he heard the soft footfall behind him.

He turned just in time to see the huge black-cloaked figure looming over him, and glimpse the fist whistling out of darkness. The first blow nearly took his head off. The second smashed him square in the chest, and he stopped breathing. Somewhere in there he lost the match. A fist like a cinder block caught him along the side of his head and knocked him sideways. Jay bumped into a wax terrorist and went down hard.

It dawned on him, as he lay dazed, that the Oddity hadn't gone on that WHO tour.

He didn't have to think about it long. Jay felt hands grab him, fingers like steel cable digging into his flesh. He was jerked upward, and then he was flying. Glass shattered all around him, and something hard and cold came up to smash into him. He thought maybe it was the floor.

♣

Brennan suddenly realized that he was about to shoot at the wrong target. He swiveled, grabbed the top of the crumbling brick wall that surrounded the cemetery, and pulled himself up.

Fadeout was leaning against the hood of the car parked in front of the cemetery gate, smoking a cigarette. Brennan scowled, grabbed an arrow, and raised his bow and fired.

Fadeout did a double take as the arrow punched through the hood of his car, penetrating deep into the engine.

"Jesus Christ!" He stared at the shaft for a moment, turned, and looked into the night. "Yeoman?"

"Call off Dragon," Brennan answered, "or the next one goes into your right eye."

Fadeout hesitated.

"I mean it!" Brennan shouted, calculating his chances of releasing the shaft he had nocked to his bowstring, finding an explosive arrow in his quiver, stringing it, and hitting the dragon before the beast pulped him.

His fingers twitched, ready to release the arrow he had aimed at Fadeout; then the Shadow Fist captain called out, "Okay, it's okay. I just wanted him to scout the cemetery. Dragon, go back to your body! Now!"

Brennan stared at the creature. It looked back impassively and then started to twist and shrivel, collapsing upon itself until it was only a small bit of intricately folded paper that blew away on the night wind. A moment passed, then Lazy Dragon got out of the back of the car and stood by Fadeout.

Brennan relaxed the tension on his bowstring. "Come in through the gate," he called, "if you're done playing games and want to talk."

Fadeout and Dragon exchanged glances. Fadeout was older, taller, a fit-looking man in an expensive-looking suit. Dragon was a young Asian, smaller, frailer looking, but he had the more dangerous ace power of the two. Fadeout, though, was the boss, and Dragon would take his cue from him.

"You can't blame me for being cautious," Fadeout said, leading the way into the cemetery through the sagging wrought-iron gate. "You killed a lot of Fists at Tachyon's clinic."

Brennan jumped down lightly from the top of the wall.

"Do you really care about that?" he asked.

"No," Fadeout admitted. He looked around, suppressing a shiver. "But I was, well, a little concerned about meeting in this godforsaken place. It gives me the creeps."

"I like it. Dark. Quiet. Plenty of cover." Brennan was suddenly tired of all the small talk. "Let's talk about Chrysalis."

Fadeout glanced at Lazy Dragon, who was watching impassively. "I know that you're looking for Chrysalis's murderer. You caused quite a scene at Squisher's Basement. I'm afraid that you totally ruined Bludgeon's reputation."

"It wasn't hard. He wasn't the same old Bludgeon."

Fadeout nodded. "He's dying of AIDS. That's not a fate I'd wish on anyone, but I can't say that I'm too sorry. The man was a disgusting brute. Now he's disgusting and pathetic."

"I didn't call this meeting to discuss Bludgeon's health problems."

"Right. I want to help."

"Help?"

"Yes. Help find Chrysalis's killer."

"I see." Brennan smoothed his mustache thoughtfully. "And in return?"

Fadeout shrugged. "I want nothing more than you want. I want Kien removed."

Brennan smiled slowly.

"I don't know what you have against him," Fadeout continued. "But I know that you want him bad. As for me, well, let's say that I could envision the Shadow Fists doing quite nicely with a new leader."

Brennan glanced at Lazy Dragon. "And a new chief lieutenant?"

"I'm very generous," Fadeout said, "to those who help me. I've been generous to Lazy Dragon. I was generous to you in the past and can be again."

"The only thing I need," Brennan said, "is information."

"Ask away."

"Did Wyrm kill Chrysalis?"

"Well, you cut right to the heart of the matter, don't you?" Fadeout said, shaking his head.

"That's right."

"Well," Fadeout said carefully, "we all know that Wyrm has a violent temper, and he's totally devoted to Kien. Chrysalis, of course, knew that Kien is head of the Fists, but she'd kept quiet about it. If, however, she found out something that threatened Kien, Wyrm might have had the initiative to do something on his own."

"Like finding out about Kien's new designer drug?"

"Rapture?" Fadeout asked. "Yes, you've learned about our new head candy, haven't you?"

"Something about it."

"Perhaps Chrysalis learned something about it, too."

"And Wyrm killed her."

Fadeout shrugged again. "I make no accusations. It is a thought, however. I can make a few discrete inquiries on the subject."

Brennan nodded. "All right. I'll be in touch."

"One thing," Fadeout said as Brennan turned away, "you might keep your eyes open for. Chrysalis's secret files."

"Secret files?"

"Her information cache. The talk is that she kept meticulous records concerning everything she'd ever discovered on everybody in the city, and those records didn't turn up when the police searched the Palace. And you can bet that the police had orders to search very thoroughly."

"What do you want with these files?"

Fadeout smiled. "Someone has to take Chrysalis's place."

Brennan shook his head. "You're an ambitious man. First you want to replace Kien. Now you want to replace Chrysalis."

Fadeout shrugged. "A man has to stay busy."

"All right," Brennan said. "I'll keep my eyes open for them. I may want to have a look at them myself."

"Fine," Fadeout said with a smile. "Have fun catching Chrysalis's killer. Then come after Kien. I'll be there to help you."

"We'll see." Brennan turned, stopped, turned back to Fadeout and

Lazy Dragon. "One last thing. Ever hear of an ace named Doug Morkle?"

Fadeout and Dragon exchanged glances. "No. Should I have?"

"Beats me," Brennan admitted. "He's on my list of suspects, but no one has ever heard of the bastard."

"Morkle. Strange name. I'll ask around."

Brennan nodded, turned again, and faded into the night, leaving Fadeout and Dragon to deal with a car whose radiator fluid was now an oily green puddle on the street.

6:00 A.M.

Jay opened his eyes and closed them again quickly.

The light made his headache unbearable. The pounding behind his eyelids was like thunder, the left side of his face was a single dull mass of pain, and he could taste blood in his mouth. Somebody had yanked his hands behind his back and tied them together.

When he tried to get up, something ground together inside his chest, and the pain was excruciating. A feeble groan escaped his lips. He rolled back and tried to lie very still. Maybe he should just go back to sleep.

"I heard him," a deep voice muttered, somewhere far away. "He moaned. He's coming to."

"Bring him here, John," someone else said. The second voice was vaguely familiar.

Massive hands lifted him as easily as a grown man might lift a child, carried him across the room, and propped him up in a chair. The hands were not gentle. Jay had to stifle a scream.

"Open your eyes, Mr. Ackroyd," the second voice said.

Reluctantly, Jay tried. His left eye was swollen almost shut.

The grim reaper sat staring at him across an antique desk.

"Dutton," Jay managed, through cracked, bloody lips.

The reaper nodded.

A shadow fell across Jay. He forced himself to turn his head. It wasn't until you got really close to the Oddity that you realized how *big* the fucker was. He could hear labored breathing from behind the fencing mask and feel the weight of eyes staring down implacably through the steel mesh.

"You said you didn't know the Oddity," Jay said to Dutton.

"I lied," Dutton told him.

Jay tried to think of a wisecrack, but his mind wasn't in it. He closed his eyes again, forced them open. He felt like his head was going to explode. "I don't," he said, "don't suppose you got any aspirin you could let me have?"

"John," Dutton said, "there's a bottle of aspirin in my toilet. If you wouldn't mind?"

"Let him hurt," the Oddity rumbled. "He doesn't care how much we hurt, does he? Let him bleed for a while."

"I understand the sentiment," Dutton replied. "But we do want his cooperation, after all. Please."

Grumbling, the Oddity shuffled through the bathroom door in the back of the office. Jay heard the medicine cabinet open with a bang, then the sound of water splashing into a sink.

"My apologies," Dutton said. "John's temper often gets the better of him, and I'm afraid he does not like you."

The Oddity returned with a handful of aspirin tablets in one hand and a glass of water in the other. With his hands still tied behind his back, Jay could only open his mouth. The Oddity stuffed in a half-dozen aspirin, then lifted the water to his lips. Jay swallowed until he began choking.

The Oddity grunted, stood up, and watched Jay sputter for breath. The joker's right hand, the one that held the water glass, was big and rough, coarse dark hair covering the knuckles. The left was much smaller, more delicate, a woman's hand, its fingernails long and pointed. Under the thick, dark clothing, Jay could see the swell of breasts. "Thanks," he managed.

"Fuck you," the Oddity snarled.

Jay turned back to Dutton. "You knew I was coming," he said. It wasn't a question.

"You or someone like you," Dutton replied. "How much is Barnett paying you to betray your own people?"

For a moment Jay didn't think he'd heard him right. "Barnett?" he said groggily. "What the fuck are you talking about?"

"Don't try my patience, Mr. Ackroyd," Dutton said wearily. "Why do aces insist on treating jokers as though we were retarded children? I didn't get where I am by being stupid."

"You may be the smartest guy in the world, for all I know," Jay said. "But you're still wrong."

"Am I?" Dutton said. "Then why are you here?"

Jay hesitated. "You know the jacket is the real McCoy?"

"Yes." Dutton regarded him from eyes deep sunk in that ghastly yellow face. "Chrysalis hinted as much when she gave it to me to incorporate into our diorama."

"The purloined letter," Jay said. "Hide the goods in plain sight, where hundreds of tourists will see it every day and assume it's just a replica of itself. Not bad at all. Only she didn't tell you *why* she wanted it hidden, did she?"

"No," Dutton admitted. "It did pique my curiosity, but I had learned not to press her. After her death, I got the whole story."

"From us," the Oddity put in. "We told him, after you left, that night you led us here. You aces think jokers have shit for brains, but this time the joke's on you."

"Then you know about Hartmann?" Jay asked Dutton.

"That he's a wild card?" Dutton said. "What of it? He remains the last best hope we jokers have. Yes, he hides his condition. In the present political climate a sane man has no other choice. The public will never vote for a wild card, not even a latent like Hartmann, not when there's a chance the virus will express and turn him into one of *us*. That's why Leo Barnett wants the jacket."

"I'm not working for Leo Barnett—" Jay started.

"*Liar*," the Oddity snarled. "You're taking his goddamned nat money to help him destroy Gregg."

"You're wrong," Jay said. "Hartmann's a killer ace, he—"

The Oddity moved faster than Jay would ever have guessed, grabbing him by the hair, slamming his head back against the chair, and slapping him hard enough to rattle teeth. "Shut up! Gregg's the only friend the jokers *have*!"

Jay had a mouthful of blood from his split lip. He spat it feebly at the fencing mask and called out to Dutton. "You just going to sit there and watch the Holy Trinity here beat me into ground chuck, or you want to hear me out?"

"Let him alone, John," Dutton said. "I want to hear what he has to say." Reluctantly, the Oddity let go of Jay's hair and stepped back away from the chair. The joker's massive body shuddered. The fingers of its left hand seemed to be thickening and its breasts were shrinking visibly.

"I don't even *know* Leo Barnett," Jay began.

"You're an ace who sells his services for money. I doubt that Barnett hired you personally. Nonetheless, you're working in his interests. Why else would you want the jacket?"

"That jacket got Chrysalis murdered," Jay said. "And I hate to mention this, especially when I'm sitting here trussed up like a Christmas goose, but this great joker hero of yours is looking more and more like the one who did the trick."

"That's not true," the Oddity said. The voice was softer than before, gentler, unmistakably a woman's voice. And now the left hand was the one that was blunt and callused. The fingers of the right had grown longer and lost their hair, and the skin had turned a deep chocolate brown. "Why should we want to hurt Chrysalis?"

"Because Gregg Hartmann told you to, and you just *love* Senator Gregg, don't you?" Jay snapped.

"Gregg is a good man," the Oddity said. Jay thought the joker sounded a little defensive.

"The Oddity couldn't possibly have killed Chrysalis," Dutton said patiently. "If you were a patron of the arts, Ackroyd, you'd know that Evan is a sculptor. Once he worked in clay, bronze, marble. These days, he sculpts in wax. But Patti and John lack the talent, so Evan can only work during the brief times when his mind and at least one of his hands emerge from the Oddity. He seizes those moments when they come, day or night." Dutton sounded almost sad as he dropped the other shoe. "Evan was right here during the murder, working on a new Mistral for our Gallery of Beauty. What does that do to your theory?"

Jay was suddenly aware of the blinding pain behind his eyes again, and all he wanted to do was go home and be sick. "Shit," he managed. "Then Hartmann must have sent someone else. Carnifex maybe, or Braun. Or maybe this guy Doug Morkle, I don't know."

"You're reaching, Ackroyd," Dutton said. He looked over at the Oddity. "Why don't you tell us what really happened, Patti?"

The Oddity turned toward Jay. Even the way the joker moved seemed different now, subtly feminine. "No joker would have hurt Chrysalis. She was one of us. The killer had to be working for Barnett, looking for the jacket. Maybe he was only trying to beat the secret out of Chrysalis, but he went too far." The Oddity sounded utterly sincere.

"That so?" Jay said. "Mind telling me the guy's name?"

"There's no way to be certain," the Oddity said, the woman's voice somehow eerie and frightening coming from the huge, misshapen body. "Perhaps Quasiman. He's a poor simple-minded thing who does as he is told, and he owes his life to Reverend Barnett." The Oddity's right hand gestured daintily in the air. It was a man's hand, the nails bitten right down to the quick. "Or perhaps some ace who sells himself for money, the way you do."

"You're telling me Chrysalis died to protect Hartmann, 'cause he's such a great friend of the jokers, right?" Jay looked first at Dutton, then over at the Oddity. "Then answer me this. If she was so fucking concerned about keeping Hartmann's little secrets, *why didn't she destroy the jacket a year ago?*"

The perpetual grin on Dutton's yellowed face pulled into a momentary grimace. "That question troubled me as well," he said, "but my partner's plans were often subtle, and her motives were sometimes obscure. No doubt she was playing some game."

"That jacket was her life insurance," Jay said. "Now that she's dead, it's time to cash in the policy."

"Do you have any idea what's going on down in Atlanta?" Dutton asked him patiently. "Thousands of jokers have gone south to peacefully demonstrate in support of Hartmann. They've been welcomed with arrests, street brawls, attacks by the Klan. Yesterday there was a near riot when a hundred men in Confederate uniforms fired on the crowd. Barnett has already managed to pull the teeth out of our jokers' rights plank, and if he's elected, the good reverend will put us all in camps. Many people believe that Gregg Hartmann is the only thing that stands between this country and joker genocide."

"A lot of people believed in Hitler, too," Jay said.

Dutton sighed. "This conversation is as pointless as your quest, I'm afraid. You see, it really doesn't matter who you're working for, Mr. Ackroyd. You're too late. Much as I hated to damage a genuine historic artifact, too much was at stake to take any chances. Go back to your employers and tell them it's over. We burnt the jacket."

"Ashes to ashes," the Oddity said. "You can't hurt Gregg now."

"The tainted blood is gone," Dutton told Jay, "and if God is merciful, Gregg Hartmann is going to be the next president of the United States."

8:00 A M.

Squisher's Basement was still as crowded, still as dark, still as smelly as it was when Brennan had discovered it a few days before. The same bartender was behind the bar and mostly the same customers were scattered about the room, though this time around Bludgeon was absent. A couple of the regulars greeted Brennan jovially and one asked him if he was going to slap around another ace.

"Not today," Brennan said with a smile. "Just a drink and a few words with a friend." Tripod was perched on the edge of a bar stool at the end of the bar, his pelvic arrangement making it impossible to sit on the chair in a normal manner.

"What'll it be?" the mouthless bartender asked, his voice rasping from a small hole cut at the base of his throat.

"Irish whiskey. Tullamore."

The bartender continued to wipe glasses with a rag that Brennan wouldn't have used to wipe his nose.

Brennan sighed. All right. Scotch."

"Scotch we got," the bartender said, taking down the bottle of Importer's from the wall and pouring a shot.

Squisher peered cautiously from his aquarium. "How's it going, big guy?"

"All right," Brennan said, pulling a roll of bills from his pocket and peeling off a five.

"Hey," Squisher said, "your money's no good here. Friends of Squisher drink for free."

Brennan nodded and put the money back in his pocket. "Thanks. I'll remember that."

Brennan took his drink and joined Tripod at the end of the bar, where he was sipping a mug of beer through a straw.

The joker asked, polite as always, "What's up, Mr. Y?"

"Anything new?" Brennan asked quietly.

Tripod pursed his lips. "Nothing, Mr. Y. I been wearing my feet off, but Sascha's gone, man. He's lying low somewhere, and I can't find him."

Brennan nodded, took a sip from his drink. "Something new has cropped up. It may be connected with the murder, but I'm not sure yet. You know anything about a drug called rapture?"

"Oh yeah." Tripod nodded. "Very new. Very chic. They say that it makes everything feel real good, you know, better than ever. Food. Sex. Other drugs. Even pain."

"Pain?"

"Yeah. Like some R-heads might take a razor blade to themselves 'cause it feels so good. It doesn't feel too good when they come down, though."

Brennan nodded. "Maybe Chrysalis discovered something about the drug that led to her death. It had to be something big, something awful, not just knowledge that the drug existed."

"You know," Tripod said thoughtfully, "Sascha's girlfriend was a rap-head. At least I seen her around with blue lips sometimes."

"Girlfriend?" Brennan said. "Sascha had a girlfriend?"

"Yah. You didn't know about her? She's a real hot babe by the name of Ezili Rouge. But it's not as if she's real close to the blind boy. She's got a lot of boyfriends. Girlfriends too. I hear she's even real fond of puppy dogs and like that."

Brennan frowned. "Is she a hooker?"

"Probably. She gets dough from somewhere and she's got a lot of it."

"Do you know where she lives?"

"Hey, she's not in my league. I've seen her around. Face of an angel gone bad. Weird red eyes and a body that'd tempt a saint to sin. I'd give a leg to get a piece. 'Course, I got more legs than I know what to do with anyway."

"What about the police? Was she ever mixed up with them?"

Tripod shrugged. "Maybe. She's spent a bundle on drugs. You gotta figure the police have been at least interested."

"What kind of drugs?"

"You name it, she's bought it. H, crack, coke, speed, ludes, pot, PKD, dust, designer stuff like rapture. Christ, if the rumors are half-true she's bought enough dope to send an army up the highway to heaven."

Brennan frowned. Perhaps Sascha had gotten hooked on something that'd put him under Ezili's control. Perhaps he'd let slip something to Ezili, who told Quincey, who told Wyrm. Perhaps, perhaps, perhaps. "Where does she hang out?"

"Couple places." Tripod gave him the names of some clubs, none of which had savory reputations.

Brennan finished his drink, put the glass down on the bar, and surreptitiously dropped two twenties on the floor.

"Thanks." He turned to leave, stopped, looked back at Tripod, who was slipping the bills into his ankle pocket with the oddly articulated toes of his middle foot. "One last thing. Ever hear of an ace named Doug Morkle?"

"Morkle? What the hell kind of name is that for an ace?"

Brennan shook his head. "Damned if I know."

◆

The back half of Dr. Finn looked like a palomino pony; the front half looked too young to be a doctor. "What happened?" Finn asked as he taped up Jay's ribs.

"I was looking for a sport jacket," Jay said morosely.

"Remind me never to use your tailor," Finn replied. He finished the taping. "There. How's that feel?"

"Tight," Jay complained. He tried to flex his arm and winced at the pain. "Makes it hard to move."

"Good," Finn said. "I wouldn't want you doing too much moving until that rib knits. You're very lucky, Mr. Ackroyd. A few more inches, and the bone might have punctured a lung."

"What about my head?"

"The X-rays show only a very mild concussion," Finn told him. "Nothing to worry about, as long as you take it easy."

"Might as well," Jay said, "can't dance."

"Too bad," Finn said. He grinned and did a quick little four-legged softshoe. "I cut quite a rug myself."

"I'll just bet. Do I get anything for the pain? This headache would be killing me if I wasn't so distracted by my rib."

Finn took a pad out of his pocket and scrawled a prescription. "Here," he said, ripping off the top sheet and handing it to Jay. "This ought to help."

"Thanks." Jay hopped down off the examination table. It was a mistake, and the broken rib let him know that right away. "Oh shit," he said, gritting his teeth.

"Don't want to go around jarring yourself that way," Finn said, altogether too cheerfully for Jay's taste. "I wouldn't drive in your condition either. Do you have a ride home?"

"I'll take a cab," Jay said. Charles Dutton had taken him to the clinic, after he'd satisfied himself that Jay had nothing more of value to tell him, but he didn't imagine that the joker had hung around in the waiting room. Even if he had, Jay figured he'd had more than enough of Dutton and the Oddity for today. "You did the autopsy on Chrysalis, didn't you?" he asked.

"Yes," Finn replied. "The police always call us in on joker autopsies. The coroner doesn't feel qualified to deal with our unique joker physiology." The little centaur looked away and shuffled his feet uncomfortably. "A terrible thing. We see a lot of murder victims here in the clinic and it's never pretty, but the way her body was mutilated . . ." Finn shook his head.

"Yeah." Jay touched his bruised and swollen face, thinking that he knew just how she must have felt.

5:00 P.M.

Brennan awoke still soaked with sweat and numb from a half-remembered dream in which all of his friends and lovers were killed slowly and excruciatingly by some unseen agency he was powerless to stop. He was reassured somewhat when he spotted Jennifer sitting in the room's only chair, listening distractedly to the transmitter they'd planted on Quasiman. She heard Brennan stir, turned to watch him sit up and run his hands through his hair.

"About time you woke up," she said. "I'm suffering from terminal boredom listening to Quasiman stumble through his day."

"Nothing to link him to the murder?"

She shook her head. "Either he's incredibly clever, which frankly I doubt, or he has no connection with Barnett's crowd."

"What'd he do today?" Brennan asked.

"Got up early. It took him a while to figure out how to use the mop, then he washed the church's floors. Went up on the roof for a coffee break and forgot to come down. Father Squid called up to him to remind him to mow the lawn in the graveyard. That was a tough one. By the time he figured out the lawn mower, it was lunch. He spent the afternoon mowing and trimming. Once the transmitter stopped sending for forty-five minutes. I think it accompanied Quasiman into whatever alien dimension it is that he slips into.

"You ask me, he's just what he appears to be. A sweet, terribly afflicted church handyman."

"Figures." Brennan picked his jeans up off the floor and slid into them, then rummaged through the bureau for a fresh T-shirt. "I got a possible line on Sascha this morning from Tripod. It seems he has a girlfriend—"

He stopped and stared at the plain white envelope that was lying on the worn carpet just inside the door to the hotel room.

"How long has that been there?" he asked Jennifer.

She turned, looked at the envelope, and frowned. "I don't know. I didn't notice it before."

Brennan crossed the room and picked up the envelope. It was unsealed and unaddressed. He opened it and took out the single piece of paper it held with a message scrawled in a familiar childish hand.

"Sorry how things turned out befour," it read. "I only want to help you. If you want to find a reel rap-head, go to Chickadee's."

"Damn," Brennan muttered to himself. "Just what the hell is going on here?"

6:00 P.M.

"Jesus," Digger said. "What's wrong with your face?"

Jay closed the office door behind him and looked down at the reporter. Digger was almost eight inches tall now. In a couple more days he might be able to pass for a dwarf. "I'm disguised as a guy who got the shit beat out of him," he said. He moved slowly across the office and sat down. The radio was babbling something about the convention. It made his head hurt even more. He turned it off.

"*God*, it hurts just to look at you," Digger said. "You realize that half your face is purple?"

"Good thing I don't wear a tie. The colors might clash."

"Don't worry about it, in a day or two the swelling will go down and the bruise'll turn green." Downs sounded like a man who had been there himself; sometimes the public didn't appreciate crusading journalists. "Where the hell you been?"

"Sleeping," Jay said. The painkillers made him groggy.

"*Sleeping?* Jesus, Ackroyd. All hell is breaking loose down in Atlanta, Hartmann's something like three hundred votes from the nomination, and you decide to take a nap?"

"Downs," Jay warned, "I just woke up, my head feels like it's stuffed with cotton, I've got a concussion and a broken rib but I don't dare take any more painkillers because I can't think straight when I do, and I lost the goddamned jacket, so if you don't shut the fuck up *right now*, I'm going to pop you to the middle of the Holland Tunnel to play in traffic, okay?"

Digger made a noise like a man whose aged grandmother had just been run over by a semi. *"You lost the jacket!"* he screeched.

Jay sighed. "Dutton destroyed the damned thing before I could get to it," he said wearily.

"Jesus," Digger said, his irritating little voice in a panic. "Jesus-jesusjesus, what are we gonna *do?*"

"We're running out of options," Jay admitted. "Not to mention time." He tried to think. It wasn't easy, the way his head was pounding. "Look, maybe Kahina had something else beside the jacket. Blood tests. Letters. Anything. I know, it's a long shot, but what else is there? How much do you know about her?"

"I did a little digging after . . . after she died," Digger said. "Very low key, y'know? I didn't want to stir nothing up. The chick was in the country illegally, I know that much. With her background, I didn't think it was likely she smuggled herself in, so she must have had help, but whoever did it was a pro, covered up her trail real nice."

"What about after she got here?"

Digger shrugged. "She was living in Jokertown under an assumed name. You shoulda seen where she was staying, a real dump. The girl had guts, I'll give her that, but it wasn't like she knew what she was doing. She couldn't of been more conspicuous if she tried. The day she arrived, she was even wearing one of them black Moslem things, you know, whatchacallit, a *chador.* She switched to American clothes pretty quick but it didn't help much, she was still the only nat in the hotel, and it was obvious she just *loathed* jokers."

"Then what the hell was she doing working with Gimli and Chrysalis?" Jay said bluntly.

"*She* wasn't working with Chrysalis," Digger said. "That was Gimli's idea, Kahina was against it all the way. They had some huge fight about it. They fought all the time. Religion, politics, strategy, they didn't agree on anything." He shrugged. "Hey, politics makes strange bedfellows, right?"

Jay frowned. "How do you know all this?"

"Chrysalis told me," Digger admitted. "Gimli had a leak in his little conspiracy, and you know how it was, if anything leaked anywhere in Jokertown, you could bet your sweet ass that Chrysalis would hear it."

"Yeah," said Jay thoughtfully. He got slowly to his feet.

"Where you going now?" Digger asked.

"Jokertown," Jay said. "I got an urge to see Kahina's last known address for myself."

7:00 P.M.

Brennan looked around Chickadee's helplessly, wondering what to do now that he was here, alone. Jennifer was waiting for him outside, this not being the type of club where she could go and not attract attention. He went up to the bar and ordered a Tullamore. He was nursing it silently, letting thoughts crawl lazily, fruitlessly through his mind, when a slurred, drunken voice said, "You're the one was my little girl's friend."

He glanced down annoyedly, did a double take, and stared. The man who had spoken looked like Joe Jory, but he had been changed. His chin was virtually gone. His nose had been turned into a pig snout, and two-inch-long incisors protruded from his helplessly grinning mouth. His eyes were beady and red, as if he'd been drinking, or weeping, for hours.

"What happened?" Brennan asked.

Jory gave a helpless shrug, as if nothing mattered anymore. "I don't know. I went to a bar last night. It was in an alley and the doorman was dressed all in black. He smiled a real strange smile and let me in for nothing, he said, nothing at all. I told some of the people inside about my little girl, about how beautiful she'd been and what the virus done to her, and they brought me drinks and told me how sorry they were that my child was a joker and they told me to tell everyone about it. I got up on a stage and told everyone how awful it was, how we didn't have jokers in Oklahoma and people *laughed* at me. They laughed and laughed and someone yelled, 'You do now!' and this ugly bouncer threw me out of the bar. I went to another place and people still laughed at me and I realized that something horrible had happened, like someone put a mask on my face but I couldn't take it off. I drank till I passed out and in the morning I went back to the bar to make them turn my face back so I could be a real person again, but *the bar was gone*. It wasn't there. . . ."

His voice ran down into racking sobs, and despite himself Brennan was touched with pity for the bewildered man who was so far out of his depth. He'd run into a place Brennan had only heard whispers of; Jokers Wild in Rat's Alley, where the dead men lose their bones, where no one who enters is safe, where most anyone who enters is changed, never for the better.

"Help me. . . ." Jory sobbed.

"What do you want from me?" Brennan asked quietly.

"Give me my face back," Jory asked, but Brennan shook his head.

"Can't do that," he said in the same soft voice.

"Then buy me a bottle. They took all my money last night. All my money, and my face."

Brennan stared at him a moment longer, then signaled the bartender and put a twenty on the counter. When the bottle came, Jory took it and clutched it to his chest and scurried away. Brennan watched him disappear into the crowded room. It was then that he saw the girl with the blue mouth.

She was with a man down the bar, drinking with him and laughing a little too loudly whenever he spoke. She was standing so close to him that her bare knees were pressing against his thigh, and she was toying with his hair, making little loose ringlets of it with her middle finger. Brennan thought she looked familiar, then realized that she was Lori, the hostess who'd escorted him to Quinn's suite the night the Eskimo was having his coming-out party for rapture. She was one of the demonstrators who had shown how safe and easy it was to take the drug.

Brennan took his Tullamore's and moved off down the bar. He stopped before the man, crowding him so that he had to look up. He smiled down at him.

"I'd like to talk to the lady."

The man looked as if he were going to dispute things, then thought better of it. "Sure, buddy," he said. "Plenty of babes in this place."

He slid off the stool and Brennan took his place. Lori watched the john hurry off, then switched her attention to Brennan. She smiled. Her blue gums and tongue made her smile look sinister against her white teeth and red lips.

"You look like a man who likes to party," she said hopefully. She obviously didn't recognize Brennan, which was perfectly understandable since he had been wearing a Mae West mask the last time she saw him.

"I do."

"Good." Her smile grew wider, her eyes brighter. "Let's go upstairs, honey. I can show you something you've never seen before."

"You can?"

"Sure. Trust me." She urged Brennan off the stool. Her palms were sweaty, her body had a vaguely sour odor about it, an odor of perspiration drowned in cheap body scent.

Her room was a small cubicle with a messily made bed. She closed the door after them and smiled with insincere coyness at Brennan.

"Let's get the business out of the way, honey. Then we can be friends. Now," she went on, after Brennan had nodded, "it's gonna cost a hundred. *But* for only a hundred and fifty I can give you something really special. Something really different."

"What's that?" Brennan asked.

She was already pulling open the drawer of her cluttered, rickety vanity. "It's called rapture, honey, and it's sheer heaven."

She held up a small vial of blue powder, much like the one Brennan had seen the night of the party. But as soon as she drew it out, she became fixated on it. She stared at it with a growing blankness and her hands began to shake a little. She unstoppered it and stared at it like it held the keys to the kingdom.

"What's it do?" Brennan asked, watching her closely.

"Do?" As if unable to resist any longer, she dipped her forefinger into the vial and then put it in her mouth, rubbing it swiftly across her already stained gums. She smiled, and sucked her now-blue fingertip daintily, as if it'd been dipped in some sort of delicious sauce. "It makes everything so fresh and tasty and *good* feeling. Let me rub a little on your cock, honey, and it will be out of this world."

"Is it dangerous?"

Lori laughed and shook her head. "No way. I've been taking it for weeks now." She leaned closer and smiled confidentially. "Me and the guy who made it are like this," she said, entwining two fingers.

"I'll bet." Brennan moved closer and she smiled in unfocused ecstasy, her hand dropping to the crotch of his jeans and fumbling there. He smiled at her. "No thanks," he said, and smoothly took the vial of rapture away from her.

"Hey!"

"Why can't we do it without the rapture?" he asked.

"Because it's so good with it."

"I like it plain."

"But it's better, it really is," she said with increasing frenzy.

He remembered what Quincey had said about it a couple of days before, a drug that was so good that it makes a whore like sex.

"What's it like without the rapture?" he asked, holding the vial away as she snatched for it.

"Like always," she spat. "Boring. Dead. Unfeeling."

"How about food? What's that like without a dose?"

She made a face. "Cardboard and paste. Rotting compost."

"Wine? Champagne?"

"Tepid water with shit floating in it. Give me that!"

Brennan held it up and away from her, shaking his head. "I need it. I have a friend who might want to have a look at this."

"I'll scream," she said.

Brennan shook his head. "No, you won't. I'm going to give you a dose, then I'm going to tie you up and you can tell everyone that I robbed you."

"Give me two doses. One for later," she panted.

"Sure."

Lori nodded frantically and turned back to her vanity. She gave Brennan a small tin box into which he tipped a shot of the powder. Then she handed him a small mirror. He laid out a line and she found a straw somewhere and took it all in through her nose with a long snort. She leaned back and smiled.

"What's it like when you do it that way?" he asked curiously.

"Good thoughts," Lori said dreamily. "Only good thoughts."

He nodded and led her to the bed. She sat down obediently as he tore the sheet into strips, bound and gagged her. He left her room wondering what kind of thoughts she'd have after the rapture wore off.

10:00 P.M.

Digger Downs had been right about one thing: the hotel where Kahina had spent her final weeks was a real pit.

A half-dozen elderly jokers sat in the lobby, watching an ancient black-and-white Philco while they waited to die. When Jay entered, they all looked at him with dim incurious eyes. No one spoke. The jokers, like the lobby, smelled of decay.

The night clerk was a stout woman in her sixties with her hair worn in a bun. Her breath smelled of gin and she didn't know nothing about no Ay-rab girl, but she was perfectly willing to let Jay have a look at the files, once he'd slipped her a ten.

The records were in just as shitty a shape as the rest of the building, but after thirty minutes with the registration cards and receipt books from May and June of 1987, Jay found what he was looking for. She'd paid two months in advance, in cash, for a room on the third floor. Less than three weeks later, the same room had been re-rented, to someone listed only as Stig.

Jay showed the cards and the receipt book to the night clerk. "Her," he said, pointing out the name.

The corner of a ten-dollar bill was just visible under the registration card; it did wonders for the old woman's memory. "Oh, yeah, she was the pretty one. I only saw her once or twice, thought she looked kind of Jewish. You mean she was an Ay-rab?"

"A Syrian," Jay said. "What happened to her?"

The woman shrugged. "They come, they go."

"Who's this Stig?" Jay asked.

"Stigmata," the old woman said. She made a face. "Disgusting. Makes me sick just to look at him, but Joe, he says even jokers need a place to stay. If it was up to me . . . honestly, these people are like animals. Anyway, Stig didn't pay his rent and Joe evicted him, good riddance to bad rubbish, and we rented his room to the Ay-rab girl. But then a few weeks later Stig had the money he owed us and he says he wants his room back. We hadn't seen that girl for a week or so, so we let him back in."

"Did the woman leave any personal effects?"

"Personal *what*?"

"Any stuff," Jay said impatiently. "Letters, papers, a passport. Luggage. Clothing. She just up and vanished one day, right? What did you find when you cleared out her room?"

The night clerk licked her lower lip. "Yeah, now that I think about it, she had some stuff." She studied him greedily. "You family? I don't think I can give you her stuff unless you're family. Wouldn't be right."

"Of course not," Jay said. "But it so happens that Mr. Jackson is a very close relative of hers."

"Huh?" she said, eyes blank with confusion.

Jay sighed a deep, put-upon sigh. "How about I give you twenty bucks for her stuff?" he said wearily.

That she understood at once. She took a key off the pegboard behind her and led Jay down to a damp, chilly basement. A dozen cardboard boxes were stacked unevenly behind the water heater, each marked with a room number. The boxes on the bottom were green with fungus and half-collapsed, their numbers all but illegible, but Kahina's legacy was on top.

He went through the carton in a deserted corner of the lobby. There wasn't much: an English-language edition of the Koran, a street map of Manhattan, a paperback copy of *The Making of the President 1976* with the chapters on Gregg Hartmann dog-eared and underlined, some odd bits of clothing, a box of Tampax. Jay sorted through it twice, then carried the carton back to the desk. "Where's the rest of it?"

"That's it. Ain't no more."

Jay slammed the carton down on the desk, hard. The woman jumped and Jay winced as his broken rib made him pay the price for the gesture. "You've got forty bucks of my money and all I've got is a box of trash. You telling me this woman flew in from Syria with nothing but a few tampons in a U-Haul box? Gimme a fucking break! Where's her luggage? Where's her clothing? Did she have any cash, any jewelry, a wallet, a passport . . . *anything*?"

"Nothing," the old woman said. "Just what's in the box, that's all we found. These jokers, they don't take care of their things like you and me. The way they live, it's disgusting."

"Show me her room."

Her eyes narrowed. "What's in it for me?"

That did it. Jay shaped his fingers into a gun and pointed. "Ta-ta," he said, popping her away to the runway at Freakers. Thursday night was all-nude female-joker mud wrestling. He hoped she was in better shape than she looked.

The soft *pop* of her disappearance made a few of the jokers across the lobby look up. If they wondered what Jay was doing behind the desk, rummaging among the keys, they didn't wonder enough to do anything about it.

Of course, there was no elevator in the building. Jay trudged up three flights of stairs, grateful that it wasn't five, and then up and down the poorly lit hallway until he found the right door. His head was pounding and his side hurt like a sonofabitch. There was light flooding through the transom, he saw, and the noise of a television from within. Jay was in a rotten mood by then. He didn't bother knocking.

When he pushed the door open, the room's lone resident jumped off the bed in alarm. "What do you want?" It was suffocatingly hot in the room, with no hint of a breeze coming through the open window. The gaunt, wasted-looking joker was dressed in a pair of gray jockey shorts that might once have been white. A black rag was knotted around his temple like a crude bandage. The palms of his hands were wrapped in black, too. So were the soles of his feet. Wider strips of black cloth wound round and round his abdomen. The bandages were crusty with dried blood. There were more clots in his thinning hair, and a red-brown stain on the front of his jockey shorts.

Jay felt his anger drain away from him. "I need to ask you a few questions, Stig," he said.

Stigmata looked at him warily. "Questions? That's all?" When Jay nodded, the joker seemed to relax. He edged over toward his television. It was a big new color Sony. Stigmata turned down the sound, but kept the picture on. On the screen a man was falling, arms and legs wheeling as he plummeted down, past floor after floor, in the vast interior atrium of some building. A golden light played around him as he fell.

Jay stared. "That's Jack Braun," he said. Uninvited, he sat down on the edge on the edge of the bed.

"There was an assassin," Stig volunteered, almost eagerly. "Didn't you hear? It was on all the channels. Some ace. Pitched the weenie right off the balcony."

Jay went cold. Golden Boy was the nearest thing there was to an invincible ace, but a fall from that height . . . "Is he dead?"

"Dan Rather said the fat guy saved him. Made him light."

"Hiram." Jay breathed a sigh of relief. Hiram and his gravity power. Jay had been there the night the Astronomer had flung Water Lily from the top of the Empire State Building. Hiram had saved her life by making her lighter than air. Now it looked like he'd done it again. "The assassin . . ." Jay began.

"He was like a buzz saw. I bet he was after Hartmann." The joker's voice was bitter. "They won't *let* him win. Just you wait and see. It'll be Barnett, or one of them other fuckers. I wish they would all just eat shit and die. They don't care about us." Just talking about it got him angry. "What do you want anyway?" he demanded. "You got no call just walking in here. You nats think you can just walk in anyplace. This is *my* room."

"I know it is," Jay said, placatingly. "Look, I need to know a few things about the woman who had the room before you—"

Stig didn't give him the chance to finish. "It was my room first!" he interrupted. "They kicked me out, just 'cause I got a few months behind. Nine years I was here, and they just kick me out and give my room away. Welfare was the ones screwed up, it wasn't my fault I didn't have the money. They kicked me out of my own room and locked up my stuff, where was I going to go?"

"The woman," Jay said, trying to get him off the world's injustice and back on Kahina. "Do you know who she was?"

Stigmata sat down on the bed and examined one of his hands, picking at the black, bloodstained fabric. "She was one of us. She didn't look like a joker, but she was, she had fits. I saw one." He looked at Jay. "What happened to her?" he asked.

"She was murdered," Jay said.

Stig averted his eyes. "Another dead joker," he said. Scrawny fingers toyed with the bandage across his palm, scratching away the dried blood. "Who cares about another dead joker?"

"What happened to her things?" Jay asked.

The joker's eyes flicked up nervously, met Jay's, looked away again.

"Ask downstairs. They took it, I bet. They locked up *my* stuff. Nine years and they lock me out and take my stuff, it's not right." All the while his fingers played at his scabs.

"You're kind of nervous, aren't you?" Jay asked.

Stigmata jumped up. "I am not!" he said. "I don't have to answer these questions. Who do you think you are? This is Jokertown, you stinkin' nats don't have no business here."

Jay was looking at his hands. At the bandages. Plain cotton, dyed black, torn in ragged strips to bind his wounds. "I'm not a nat," he said, putting a little ice in his voice. "I'm an ace, Stiggy." He made a gun with his fingers.

Pink droplets of moisture ran down Stigmata's forehead, blood mingling with his sweat. "I didn't do nothing," the joker said, but his voice cracked in midsentence.

"That's a nice TV," Jay said. On the screen was a police composite of the suspected assassin, a scrawny teenage hunchback dressed in leather. "How'd you pay for that TV, Stig? Looks kind of expensive. Where'd you get the money to pay your back rent, Stig?"

Stigmata opened and closed his mouth.

"The cheapskates who own this dump never change the locks, do they?" Jay said quietly.

The look in Stig's eyes was all the confirmation he needed. The joker backed away from him. Some aces could shoot fire from their hands, toss bolts of lightning, spray acid. Stigmata had no way of knowing what Jay's finger could do. "She was *gone*," he pleaded. "I never hurt her. Please, mister, it's the truth."

"No," Jay said. "You didn't hurt her. You just robbed her. You still had your key. So after she was dead, you just came in here and helped yourself. She must have had a nice chunk of cash. Enough to pay off your back rent and buy you a new television set, at least. What else did she have? Luggage, jewelry, *what?*"

Stigmata didn't answer.

Jay smiled, aimed, and pulled back his thumb like a hammer.

"No jewels," Stigmata said as beads of blood left pink trails down his forehead. "Just her luggage, and a bunch of clothes, that's all. Honest, it's the truth. Please."

"Where is it?" Jay asked.

"I sold it," Stigmata said. "It was all girl's clothes, it wasn't no good to me, I sold it. The suitcases, too."

It was the answer Jay had expected. "Yeah," he said, disgusted. "Figures. You sold it. Except for the *chadors*. Not much market for used *chadors* in Jokertown, right? So you kept those." He pointed at the joker's hands. "She must have had quite a few, if you're still ripping them up for bandages a year later."

Stigmata gave a tiny, guilty nod.

Jay sighed and put his hands in his pocket.

"You're not going to hurt me?" Stig said.

"Nothing I could do would hurt you any more than the wild card has done already," Jay told him. "You poor sad sorry son of a bitch." He turned to leave.

He actually had his hand on the doorknob when the joker, out of some strange sense of relief and gratitude, said, "There's one other thing. You can have it if you want. They wouldn't give me nothing for it at the Goodwill."

Jay turned back. "What?" he said impatiently.

"A sport jacket," Stig said, "but I don't think it's your size. Anyhow it's no good. It's got a tear in the shoulder, and someone got blood on it."

"Blood?" Jay said.

Stigmata must have thought he was angry. "It wasn't me!" he added quickly.

Jay could have kissed him.

11:00 P.M.

Maseryk paused halfway into his apartment with his hand still on the light switch, glancing around his dark living room with the tightly wired instincts of the hunter.

"Hope you don't mind me just dropping in like this," Brennan said from the sofa, "but it's time to trade info again."

Maseryk flicked on the light and snorted. "I don't see you for almost fifteen years, now I can't get rid of you."

"I've got something you want to hear. I guarantee it."

Maseryk sighed, shook his head. He closed the door behind him and stood with his back to it. "All right," he said. "I'll bite."

Brennan looked at him closely. His mood seemed dark and somber even for Maseryk. His eyes were sunken and there were dark circles under them. The investigation into Chrysalis's murder, Brennan guessed, probably wasn't going very well. "Ever hear of a woman named Ezili Rouge?"

"Ezili Rouge? What's she got to do with anything?"

"So you've heard of her. Got an address?"

"What am I, the telephone book?"

"Well, do you know anything about her? Is she clean?"

"Clean? Christ, I guess so. Other than the fact that every man who sees her wants to hump her—and most do, from what I hear—she's clean as the goddamn driven snow."

"You sure?" Brennan asked.

"Yes, I'm sure," Maseryk grumbled. "We checked her out when she first made the scene—the boys drew straws for the privilege—and she checked out clean."

"Someone reliable do the checking?"

"Of course. My partner, Kant."

Pure as the driven snow? Brennan thought. That's not exactly what Tripod had told him. Something here didn't add up. Kant either wasn't as good a cop as Maseryk thought, or wasn't as trustworthy.

"All right," Maseryk grumbled. "What's this big thing I'm supposed to be getting all excited about?"

Brennan reached into the pocket of his denim jacket and tossed Maseryk the vial of rapture he'd taken from Lori. "Know what that is?"

Maseryk grunted. "From its pretty blue color I'd say it's that new designer drug that hit the streets this week. Most of the other samples we've managed to score have been impure. Cut with everything from dry milk to strychnine."

"You know that it enhances sensation. Food, drink, sex—it's supposed to turn near anything into an ecstatic experience."

"Yeah, we know all that."

"What you don't know about is the side effect," Brennan said. "After you take that stuff for a couple of weeks, you *need* it. You really need it. Anything without it—food, sex, whatever—is tasteless and sensationless, or worse, actually revolting."

Maseryk sighed and sank back into his chair. "So it quickly becomes addictive?"

"Horribly addictive. You can confirm this with a girl at Chickadee's named Lori. She's easy to spot. She's got a blue mouth from taking this shit. Apparently she's been one of Quincey's human guinea pigs, so she's been at it longer than most."

"How long before this addiction takes root?"

Brennan shrugged. "I don't know. A few weeks, maybe."

"Well, this is valuable news. Makes what I have to do more difficult."

Maseryk locked eyes with Brennan, who returned the stare with a frown. "What's that, Maseryk?"

The cop sighed and shook his head. "You couldn't leave things well enough alone. You couldn't stay retired, could you? You had to come back and play vigilante again."

Brennan had a sudden, sharp inspiration. "Ackroyd told you that I'm Yeoman."

Maseryk nodded. "I should have guessed after our first conversation. I suppose I halfway did, but I didn't want to think it through. Then that damned PI rubbed our noses in it. Now we have to take you in."

"No, you don't," Brennan said quietly.

"It's my job," Maseryk said. "I'm sure you can appreciate that."

Brennan nodded. "I appreciate the fact that you have duties. I hope you realize that I do, too."

Maseryk stood up straight, away from the door. "Let's not get into that," he said.

Jennifer ghosted out of the wall next to Maseryk, quiet as smoke, and put the barrel of a suddenly solid pistol against his head. Maseryk froze and stared at her from the corner of his eye.

"The accomplice?" he asked, his hands held out from his sides.

Brennan got up from the sofa. "I learned the value of backup in Nam," he told Maseryk. "It's something I haven't forgotten." He walked by the cop and opened the door.

"We'll be looking for you now," Maseryk told him.

"Your time would be better spent finding Chrysalis's killer and stopping the rapture trade," Brennan said as he went out the door.

As the door slammed behind him, Maseryk whirled, grabbing the barrel of the gun. Wraith surrendered it with a laugh. He tried to grab her, too, but she was already smoke, drifting through the wall on an unseen, unfelt wind.

Friday
July 22, 1988

BRENNAN WAS ALREADY AWAKE and sitting in the chair by the bed when Jennifer turned and, finding him gone, woke up. She yawned and mumbled something sleepily.

"Good morning," Brennan said, leaning over and kissing her on her forehead as she rubbed the sleep from her eyes.

"Is it morning?"

"Just about."

"Need a shower," Jennifer said, sitting up, still half-wrapped in the twisted sheet. "Care to join me?"

"Sure." Brennan still felt tired, too, and already sticky with sweat despite the earliness of the hour. "Go ahead. I have to make a quick phone call."

"All right." She stood and shed the sheet. "If you hurry, I'll soap your favorite parts."

Brennan smiled, reached for the phone, and dialed a number given him by a cat as Jennifer walked naked to the bathroom.

The phone rang three times before it was picked up and an annoyed voice said, "Yes."

"This is Yeoman."

"Christ, do you know what time it is?"

"It's early," Brennan said, cutting through Fadeout's grumbling. "You said you'd help, and I need some information."

"All right, all right." Fadeout was obviously still annoyed, but asked grumpily, "What is it?"

"Do you know anything about a joker cop named Kant."

"Oh, him. Wyrm's evil twin."

"What?"

"Nothing. A joke. They both look like they escaped from the reptile house. What do you want to know about him?"

"Is he honest?"

"Well, I wouldn't exactly say honest. He used to be one of F. X. Black's boys. He did a little extracurricular arm twisting, but nothing really serious until lately. He's taken up with some foreign whore and been seen sampling the less-than-legal delights at some of the kinkier nightclubs. Rumor has it he's been supplying her with drugs."

"Is this woman's name Ezili Rouge?"

"Something like that," Fadeout said.

"What do you know about her?"

"Not much. Black, but light-skinned. Likes drugs. Likes men. Kant's not the only one on her string."

"Do you have an address?"

"No. Look around. She's hard to miss."

"I have."

"Well," Fadeout said, "I'm sorry I can't help. Tell you what, give me her phone number when you get it. I'd like to check her out myself."

"Sure. Do you have anything else for me?"

"I turned up something on that Morkle guy through our union connections. He's a longshoreman, a heavy-equipment operator. Works the early-morning shift at the Fulton Street docks. But the big news has to do with Wyrm."

"What about him?"

"Well, no one will say anything concrete, you understand, but there are whispers that he did an important job for Kien a couple of days ago, a job that no one else would handle." And, after a few moments of silence, Fadeout said, "Hello, you still there? Hello?"

"Yes."

"Oh. Okay. If you want to discuss things with him personally, he'll be at Lin's Curio Emporium later this morning, about eleven or so."

"The Chinese art shop on Mulberry?"

"That's right. You've heard of it?"

Brennan grunted a noncommittal reply. Lin's was famous in the art world for its antiquities, and in the drug world as a notorious pickup spot where high-class clientele could get whatever they wanted in the way of illegal pharmaceuticals.

"Say, what's all this about that Ezili chick, anyway?" Fadeout asked.

"I'll be in touch," Brennan said, then hung up. Wyrm. It had to be Wyrm. But this Morkle guy had been a thorn in his side since the start of the investigation. If Morkle worked the night shift at the docks, now would be the time to go after him. Wyrm would keep for a while.

The small shower stall was crowded when Brennan entered. The water was cool against his body. Suddenly he wasn't so tired when Jennifer began to massage him with soapy hands.

Tension and frustration swirled down the drain with the sweat and grime that had layered his body. First he'd run down the mysterious Doug Morkle, then Wyrm. But now it was just him and Jennifer. They kissed, their soapy bodies entangling as they made languorous love under the cool, soothing spray of the shower.

♠

"It's fine if you carry on your garment bag," the woman behind the Delta ticket counter told Jay, "but I'm afraid that your animal will have to be checked."

"Yeah, sure," Jay said wearily. He lifted the cat carrier onto the luggage scale, too tired to argue. He'd been up half the night finding the damn thing.

The Delta agent stapled a claim check onto his ticket envelope and handed it across the counter. "Here you are," she said. "Non-smoking window. The flight is already boarding."

"Thanks," Jay said. He watched as she fixed a luggage tag to the handle of the gray plastic box and shifted it to the moving belt behind her. Jay had carefully lined the interior with old newspaper so no-body could see through the air holes. There didn't seem any point in waving good-bye.

When the cat carrier had vanished into the depths of La Guardia, Jay headed down the concourse toward his gate. Even at this hour of the morning, the airport was crowded, and he had to stand in line at security. A large sign by the X-ray machine warned that guns and bombs were no joking matter; Jay decided they wouldn't be amused if he mentioned that he had dynamite in his garment bag.

The flight, scheduled for 6:55, departed forty-five minutes late. Jay slept all the way to Atlanta.

9:00 A.M.

The Fulton Street docks and the fish-rendering plants and warehouses surrounding them were swarming with activity in which a man could hide out through doomsday.

"Did Fadeout say what this Morkle looks like?" Jennifer asked.

"Just that he's a heavy-equipment operator." Brennan looked around with a frustrated frown. "Must drive a forklift or something. We can eventually pinpoint him through Fadeout's union connec-tions, but I'd hoped we'd be able to run him down today. I'd hoped."

"Let's give it a try."

They searched the docks for an hour before a man with a blue knit cap, a drooping mustache, and tattooed biceps as big as softballs nod-ded when Brennan mentioned the name.

"Morkle? Yeah, I think I know him. Strange fellow. He works down on Wharf 47."

"Would he be there now?"

The longshoreman shrugged. "Could be. I think he usually works the night shift."

"Thanks," Brennan said. "One last thing. How'll we spot him?"

"Can't miss him. He's the guy without the forklift."

"Without the forklift," Brennan repeated as the stevedore trundled his hand truck down the street. He looked at Jennifer and shrugged.

The ship unloading at Wharf 47 was larger than most. A steady stream of large wooden boxes was wending its way down the gangplank and heading to the processing stations and market stalls bordering the docks. The stevedore had been right. Doug Morkle was easy to spot.

He was five feet tall and almost as broad, with an immense chest and short, thick limbs. His face, Brennan thought, was oddly out of proportion to his body. It was long and narrow, with delicate, almost feminine features. It took Brennan several moments before he realized that the longshoreman looked like, of all people, Tachyon.

He was carrying one of the huge crates without strain, balancing it with one hand atop his head. In that posture he resembled photographs Brennan had seen of African women carrying pots of water, but pots of water didn't weigh close to half a ton. He walked steadily and easily, seemingly not at all encumbered by his massive burden.

"Doug Morkle?" Brennan asked.

The man glanced at him, kept walking.

"No. My name is Doug Morkle," he grunted, the weight of his load making it difficult to speak clearly.

"Ah, yes. Your name's not Morkle?"

"No. It's Morkle. *Morkle.*"

Brennan glanced at Jennifer helplessly, and she gave it a try. "Could you spell that please, Mr., uh, Morkle."

He flashed Jennifer an angry look, stopped, and quickly shifted the crate, slamming it down to the dock.

"What do you people want? My papers are in order. I have a green card." He fumbled angrily in the pocket of his coveralls. He spoke perfect English, but with a peculiar accent that Brennan had never heard before.

He shoved a piece of paper at Brennan. It had his photo and the name "Durg at'Morakh bo Zabb Vayawandsa" printed under it. He was born, it said, on Takis. The name on his union ID card, which he also handed to Brennan, had been Americanized to Doug Morkle.

"Everything is in order," he said, his anger turned to smugness.

"Yes, I see," Brennan temporized. This was utterly unexpected.

Brennan remembered that Tachyon had once mentioned the Takisian who'd been marooned on Earth back during the Swarm troubles. Expert martial artist and casual killer, he was certainly capable of murdering Chrysalis. But what motive would he possibly have for killing her? "It, uh, says here on your union card that you're a heavy-equipment operator."

Morkle stared at him through slitted eyes. "Are you from the union office?"

"That's right," Brennan lied.

"My exemption has been filed," Morkle said, triumph in his voice. "There is nothing wrong with my papers. The proper box is checked."

"Uh-huh." Brennan looked again at the card, scanning it carefully. The special "ace exemption" box had indeed been checked, "Giving the bearer the right to function as a heavy-equipment operator with or without the actual physical presence of such equipment as long as he/she is remunerated at commensurate rates of compensation."

"Of course," Brennan said.

"I must return to work. My shift is almost over." Morkle held out a hand the size of a shovel. "My papers please."

"Do you always work the midnight-to-eight shift?"

The Takisian nodded impatiently and hoisted his burden.

"Last Monday, too?"

He nodded again, his anger obviously building.

"Well, thanks, Mister . . . Morkle."

"That's Morkle!" He pronounced it with a liquid lilt at the end of the word. "Ideal! Will you Earthers ever learn how to speak correctly?"

"Do we believe him?" Jennifer asked as they watched him stroll off with his burden.

"It looks like an iron-clad alibi."

"Another dead end?"

Brennan sighed. "I'm afraid so."

But that just made Wyrm look more and more like the prime candidate. It was time to interview him personally. First, though, Brennan decided, it would be sensible to return to the hotel room and pick up more firepower. He wasn't about to waltz into the Curio Emporium bare-handed.

10:00 A.M.

"What the hell do you *mean* it never got put on the plane?"

"I'm sorry, sir." The Delta luggage clerk wasn't nearly as good at being sorry as Waldo Cosgrove was. "Our next flight from La Guardia is due in about twenty minutes, I'm sure your luggage will be on that one." Behind her on the wall was a large poster covered with drawings of suitcases. "If you could indicate the type of luggage," she said, "it would help us to locate the missing bags."

"It wasn't a suitcase," Jay said. "It was a cat carrier. Gray plastic, brand new, I just bought the damn thing. You have any idea how hard it is to find a twenty-four-hour pet shop, even in Manhattan?" He sighed. "My, uh, cat's going to be pissed."

"Oh, the poor thing," the woman said. "I have five cats myself, I understand how you must feel. We'll find it, don't worry. If you give me your Atlanta address, I'll have your cat delivered."

"Great," Jay said. He thought for a moment. "I don't know where I'll be. The convention has booked all the big hotels solid, I hear. Tell you what, deliver it to the Marriott Marquis. To Hiram Worchester." He spelled it for her.

"Our pleasure," she said as she completed the lost-luggage form and handed it across the counter for signature. "What's the little fellow's name?"

"Digger," Jay said. At least he hadn't checked the garment bag. He slung it over a shoulder and went out to look for a cab.

♥

"There's an envelope on your bow case," Jennifer said, looking at it as if it were some kind of poisonous reptile.

"What?" Brennan called out from the bathroom. "Another message?"

"Apparently."

Brennan came out of the bathroom, drying his hands on a towel. He joined Jennifer, who was staring at his bow case and the small, plain white envelope resting on it.

"This is getting weird," Brennan said.

"Getting?"

Brennan grunted and picked up the envelope. Inside was a single sheet of paper with a message written in the now-familiar tiny hand, complete with its usual quota of spelling errors.

" 'For yur own safety,' " he read, " 'stay away frum the Cristal Palace.' "

"Why?" Jennifer asked.

Brennan shook his head. "Your guess is as good as mine. Our secret informant hasn't lied so far. It's been spooky as hell and gotten me into trouble a few times, but it's always told the truth."

"Were you planning on going to the Palace?" Jennifer asked.

"No. Right now I'm planning on heightening my appreciation of Chinese art." He folded the note and put it in his pocket, then hefted his bow case. "Let's go."

♣

They stopped him the moment he stepped out of the revolving doors into the lobby of the Marriott Marquis. "May I see your room key, sir?" a black man in a security blazer asked him, none too politely.

Jay gave him his most apologetic smile. "Don't have one yet," he said. "I'm just checking in." He tried to walk briskly around him, the garment bag slung over his shoulder.

The guard sidestepped, planting himself squarely in Jay's path. "Hotel's full," he said. "We're not authorized to admit anyone but guests. Can I see some identification?"

"I've got business with one of your guests," Jay said. "Hiram Worchester. He's in the New York delegation."

"Is he expecting you?"

"Well," Jay admitted, "not exactly."

"Then I suggest you phone him. The desk will be glad to take a message. If he wants to see you, we'll arrange a pass."

Jay slapped his forehead and let his mouth hang open. "A *pass?* You know, Hiram *gave* me a pass, how could I be so stupid? God, isn't that funny? You thinking I'm trying to get in without a pass, and here I've got one all the time?"

"Hilarious," the man in the security blazer said.

"Where did I put it?" Jay fumbled in his pocket for a moment, shaped his hand into a gun, drew it out. "*Here's* my pass," he said happily, looking up. Two tall men in dark suits were flanking the guy in the blazer, dark glasses hiding their eyes. Neither of them was smiling.

"I don't see a pass," the guard said. "I just see you pointing at me, asshole."

Jay looked at his finger. Then he looked at the men. There were three of them. The two on the ends had bulges under their jackets. He put his hand back into his pocket and took a step backward. The dark suits moved in, crowding him toward the wall. "No, really, I was wearing my pass just a moment ago," Jay explained. "In all this crush, somebody must have brushed against me, knocked it off. . . ."

"That so?" The man looked at his partner and smirked.

"You know," Jay said, snapping his fingers, "come to think of it, I just remembered. My friend's in the *Hyatt*, not the Marriott. How could I be so stupid?" Scuttling backward like a crab, grinning like a moron, he edged back through the revolving doors into the July heat of Atlanta. The feds watched him carefully every step of the way.

11:00 A.M.

Lin's Curio Emporium was located near the nebulous boundary between Jokertown and Chinatown. It was surrounded by other quality stores and expensive restaurants. Outside it didn't really look like much. Inside it was understated elegance.

The carpeting was deep, rich red. The lighting was subdued and intimate. The curio cases scattered on the floor were antiques themselves. The screens and silks and statues displayed on the walls and in the cases were superb examples of Oriental art dating as far back as the Shang dynasty, more than a thousand years before Christ.

Brennan was impressed by their wares. He was also impressed by the elegant floor clerk, who was as beautiful as any of the artifacts on display. She kept a watchful, if discreet, eye on Brennan since he entered the shop.

Lin's collection of artifacts was really extraordinary. Brennan had almost lost himself in contemplation of a case full of intricately carved jade censers when he looked up to see Jennifer hovering behind the salesclerk and making urgent gestures toward the rear of the building. It was time to go to work.

He approached the clerk, who asked in a musical, lilting voice, "Can I help you?"

Brennan laid his case flat atop one of the waist-high curio cabinets and smiled at her. "I believe so." He opened it and reached inside. "I would like to get this silk painting appraised."

"Ah, yes," she said, leaning forward. A frown creased her exquisite features as Brennan pulled out a gun and pointed it at her.

"Sorry," Brennan said.

She looked at him quizzically as Jennifer materialized behind her and chopped her across the back of her neck. Brennan reached out and caught her before she hit the floor.

"No flirting with the help," Jennifer said as Brennan lowered her to the floor behind the counter.

He ignored her statement. "What's going on in back?"

"Wyrm's in the back office, in conference with a small, middle-aged Chinese woman."

"Sui Ma," Brennan said.

"Who?"

"Kien's sister." He went past Jennifer and patted her cheek. "Lock the front door," he said. "It would be embarrassing if someone walked in on us."

Brennan got his bow out and assembled it as Jennifer locked the front door and put out the CLOSED sign. He went through the bead curtain that separated the shop's floor from the rear of the building, and down the hallway beyond. The elegant ambience disappeared as he entered what was obviously a shipping and receiving area. It was deserted now, though dozens of boxes were lying around waiting to be packed or unpacked.

There was a small, glassed-off office in one corner of the shipping area. Sui Ma was sitting behind a desk in the office and Wyrm was standing before her, packing a small suitcase.

Fadeout hadn't mentioned Sui Ma, Brennan thought. She was Kien's sister, and head of the Immaculate Egrets, the Chinatown street gang that ran the Fists' drug enterprises. She was plain and innocuous looking, but as wily as her brother.

Brennan went silently through the shipping area, creeping closer to the office until he could hear what Wyrrn was saying.

". . . with her dead the sssecret isss sssafffe," Wyrm said.

There was no doubt in Brennan's mind as to whom Wyrm was referring. Anger burned brightly in him as he suddenly stood in the doorway, arrow drawn and aimed at the back of Wyrm's head.

It was a startling entrance. Sui Ma gaped at him in astonishment, then Wyrm also turned to stare. Brennan realized that Wyrm was packing plastic bags of blue powder into the false bottom of the suitcase. A small pile of clothes sat on the desk next to the suitcase. What looked like Wyrm's passport was balanced precariously atop the pile.

"Yeoman!" Sui Ma said sharply. She didn't blubber or bluster, but cut right to the heart of the matter. "I thought that you and my brother had a truce!"

"We did," Brennan replied, "until Wyrm killed Chrysalis."

"What?" burst from both Sui Ma and Wyrm at the same time. Their feigned ignorance seemed almost believable.

"Who told you that Wyrm killed Chrysalis?" Sui Ma demanded.

"I have my sources," Brennan replied. "Besides, what were you talking about when I just came in? Whose death, and what secrets?"

Sui Ma burst out laughing. "*Live for Tomorrow.*"

Confused, Brennan lowered his bow slightly. "What?"

"*Live for Tomorrow,*" Sui Ma repeated. "It's a soap opera," she said.

Brennan felt a sense of immense dislocation. "Soap opera?"

"Yes. You see, Janice was killed in a car crash in yesterday's episode, so Jason's secret of actually being her love child is safe and he can marry Veronica."

"A soap opera?"

"Yes. Wyrm had missed a few episodes. I was filling him in while he packed his, uh, delivery."

"Sure," Brennan said mockingly. He turned to Wyrm. "So you watch soap operas?"

The hatred was still in Wyrm's eyes, but also something of a shameful expression, as if it'd just been revealed that he was some kind of hideous pervert. "Ssssometimesss," he said defensively.

Brennan increased the tension on the bowstring and aimed right between Wym's angry eyes. "That's possibly the stupidest lie I ever heard. You'd better start talking or you're one dead lizard. Right now."

"About what?" Wyrm hissed angrily.

"About Chrysalis!" Brennan shouted. "Why did you kill her?"

Wyrm was about to make an angry reply when Jennifer suddenly stepped into the office through the wall. "Wait," she said. "We'd better check this soap-opera stuff." She turned to Wyrm as Brennan lowered his bow a little. Wyrm stared at her with the hate and anger that he usually reserved for Brennan. "So you watch *Live for Tomorrow?*" she asked.

"That'ssss right!" Wyrm spat out.

"Well then, who's Erica married to?"

Wyrm gave her a cold look. "She just married Colby lasssst month," he said, "but what she doesn't know isss that Ralph, her first husss-band, isss not dead. He hasss amnesia, and isss being exploited by terroristsss, who have convinced him that he issss Prince Rupert, a Takisian lordling, who hasss come to Earth to cure the virusss, but isss really—"

"All right," Brennan interrupted. He turned to Jennifer. "Is that crap right?"

Jennifer nodded silently.

"Christ!" Brennan lowered his bow. His feeling of frustration re-doubled, he fixed his attention on the bag Wyrm was packing. "Where are you taking that?"

"Havana," Wyrm said sullenly.

"Step away from the desk."

As Wyrm did, Brennan edged forward carefully. He released the tension on the bowstring so that he could hold the arrow on the string with one hand, and picked up Wyrm's passport from the desk. He looked at the last stamped page. Apparently this wouldn't be Wyrm's first trip smuggling rapture to Havana. He'd been in Cuba the day Chrysalis had been killed.

"Damn," Brennan said, throwing the passport back on the desk. Brennan's anger flared to an uncontrollable peak. He drew back the arrow he had ready. Wyrm hissed as it flashed by him, and then whirled to see that it had skewered a rat that had been sitting by the wall and eagerly observing the confrontation. When Wyrm looked back at Brennan, the archer had another arrow nocked and ready.

"It appears," Brennan said angrily, "that I got some bad information. The truce is still on."

Wyrm hissed angrily as Brennan backed up out of the office. Jennifer followed him, watching Lazy Dragon's rat as it shrank and turned into a hunk of soap pinned to the office wall by Brennan's arrow.

NOON

"What's going on?" Jay said when the jokers fell in beside him. No one answered. No one even seemed to hear him. There were a dozen or more, grim-faced, quiet, sober. An old man was sobbing, very softly, to himself. Jay looked back over his shoulder and saw more jokers following behind them. Everyone seemed to be headed in the same direction.

The garment bag was awkward. Jay moved it to his other shoulder, dropped back, fell in alongside a hulking joker whose green translucent flesh shimmied like lime Jell-O as he walked. "Where's everybody going?" Jay asked him.

"The Omni," the Jell-O man said.

A woman bobbed in the air above him. She had no legs, no arms. She floated like a helium balloon, her pretty face red from crying. "She lost the baby," she told Jay. Then she flew on up ahead.

Jay let himself be swept up in the human tide that flowed through the streets of Atlanta, thousands of feet all converging on the Omni Convention Center. Slowly, piece by piece, he got the story out of the jokers who walked briefly beside him. Early this morning, Ellen Hartmann, the senator's wife, had suffered a tragic fall down a flight of stairs. She had been pregnant, carrying Hartmann's child. The baby had died.

"Is Hartmann going to withdraw?" Jay asked a man in a motorized wheelchair whose ragged clothing covered his deformities.

"He's going on," the joker said defiantly. "She asked him to. Even through this, he's going on. He loves us *that much!*"

Jay couldn't think of a thing to say.

The jokers had begun drifting over as soon as the word had reached their encampments in Piedmont Park. Atlanta police and convention security watched the crowd swell with growing unease, but made no move to disperse them. Memories of the convention riots in New York in '76 and Chicago in '68 were still fresh in too many minds. By the time Jay arrived, the jokers had closed all the streets surrounding the convention. They sat on the sidewalks, covered the fenders of parked cars, filled every little patch of grass. They sat peacefully, wordlessly, under a blazing Georgia sun, with every eye fixed on the Omni. There was no shouting, no chants, no placards, no cheers, no prayers. There was no talk at all. The silence around the convention hall was profound.

Eleven thousand jokers squatted together on the hot pavement, a sea of tortured flesh pressed shoulder to shoulder in a silent vigil for Gregg Hartmann and his loss.

Jay Ackroyd moved through them gingerly. He felt fuzzy and exhausted. It was over a hundred in the shade, as humid as an armpit. Jay didn't even have a hat. The sun beat relentlessly against his head, and his headache was back screaming vengeance. His resolve had broken down and he'd swallowed a couple of painkillers, but even that hadn't done more than dull the throbbing in his side and the pounding behind his eyes.

There was nothing anyone could do for the sick feeling in his gut. All around him, the jokers sat silently, watching, waiting. Some wept openly, but tried their best to stifle the sound of their sobs. Others hid their faces behind cheap plastic masks, but somehow you could still feel their grief.

Jay found that he could scarcely bear to look at them. None of them knew who he was or what he was doing here. None of them knew what he carried in the garment bag slung awkwardly over his shoulder, or what it would do to their hopes and dreams. But Jay knew, and the knowledge was making him ill.

He took up a position across from the main doors of the Omni, where he could see the delegates and journalists come and go under the watchful eyes of security. Time seemed to pass very slowly. It got hotter and hotter. TV crews panned their minicams endlessly across the sea of faces. News choppers hovered above them, and once the Turtle glided past overhead, his passage as silent as the crowd, the shadow of his shell giving the jokers a momentary respite from the sun. Later, a small woman in black satin tails and top hat emerged briefly from inside the convention hall and surveyed the crowd through a domino mask. Jay recognized her from the news: Topper, a government acc, assigned to bodyguard Gore, probably reassigned now that her man had dropped his candidacy. He thought about trying to get her attention, handing over the bloodstained jacket, making it somebody else's dilemma. Then he remembered her colleague Carnifex, and thought again.

When Topper went back inside, a gaggle of delegates emerged through the open doors. One was a huge man with a spade-shaped beard who moved lightly in spite of his size; his impeccable white linen suit made him look cool even in this terrible heat.

Jay got to his feet. *"Hiram!"* he shouted over the heads of the jokers, waving his arm wildly despite the dull flare of pain in his side.

In the silence of the vigil, Jay's shout seemed like some obscene violation. But Hiram Worchester looked up, saw him, and made his way through the crowd, as ponderous and stately as a great white ocean liner sliding through a sea of rowboats. "Popinjay," he said when he got there, "my God, it *is* you. What happened to your face?"

"Never mind about that," Jay said. "Hiram, we got to talk."

◆

"What was all that about?" Jennifer asked.

Brennan was still seething. "A setup. A goddamned setup."

"What?"

Brennan looked at Jennifer. "We weren't set up. Wyrm and Sui Ma were."

"I see. I think."

"Let's find a phone."

There was one on the corner. Brennan dialed and Fadeout picked it up on the second ring. "Hello."

"I don't like to be lied to," Brennan said softly.

"Well, Cowboy. Nice to hear from you at a decent hour."

"Did you hear what I said?"

"Well, sure. What's it in reference to? I didn't get the dope on Morkle wrong, did I?"

"That was fine," Brennan said. "The dope on Wyrm wasn't quite as accurate."

"Oh?"

"He had nothing to do with Chrysalis's death. He was in Havana when she was killed."

"Oh. Well. Sorry."

Greasy weasel, Brennan thought. "I'm not your private executioner," Brennan said grimly.

"It was an honest mistake—"

"Don't compound the lie," Brennan said. "I'll be in touch—"

"Wait," Fadeout said before Brennan could hang up. "Anything on Chrysalis's files yet?"

Brennan put the phone down without answering.

1:00 P.M.

"It's simply not possible," Hiram said after Jay had finished telling his story. "No."

Jay unzipped the garment bag, brought out the jacket, and laid it on the table between them. "Yes," he said.

The cocktail lounge was one of those places that was as dark at noon as it was at midnight. It was well away from the convention, deserted enough to give them a little privacy. The air-conditioning was set way below arctic blast, but beads of sweat trickled down Hiram's broad forehead into his neatly trimmed beard. The booth was a tight fit for the ace's imposing bulk, his ample stomach pushing up hard against the table, but when Jay put down the jacket, Hiram seemed to squirm backward, as if he were afraid to touch it.

"This is some kind of grotesque misunderstanding. Gregg is a good man. I've known him for years, Jay. For *years!*"

Jay touched the jacket. "You were with Hartmann in Syria. Is this the jacket or isn't it?"

Hiram forced himself to look at the jacket. "It appears to be," he said. "But Jay, an off-the-rack sport coat, they manufacture them by the thousands. It has to be a fraud, it *has* to be."

"I don't think so," Jay said. "Stigmata had no reason to lie. He didn't even realize what he had. The other jacket was the fraud. Kahina never trusted Gimli. She gave him a double, probably used her own blood so a test would show the presence of the virus. That was what Gimli gave to Chrysalis. The real one Kahina kept for herself. She must have had her own plans, but Hartmann and Mackie Messer didn't give her the time to carry them out."

"Then," Hiram said hesitantly, "Chrysalis . . ."

"Died for nothing. For a phony jacket."

"The assassin she hired wasn't phony!"

"No," Jay admitted. "George Kerby is real. The hell of it is, right now I'm not sure if I'm rooting for him or against him."

"You can't mean that!" Hiram said in horror. "What Chrysalis did makes her no better than the Nur . . . murder is murder, I don't care what she knew or thought she knew. If she had charges to make, she should have come forward and made them. Doesn't Gregg deserve the opportunity to defend himself? Jay, I tell you, this is all wrong. If you knew Gregg Hartmann the way I do . . . he, he's such a fine man . . . so much courage . . . in Syria, if you'd only seen the way he stood up to the Nur al-Allah, you'd have been so proud. To accuse him of such . . . such *monstrous* crimes . . . and based on what, *what?* The testimony of Digger Downs?" Hiram was getting angry now. "The man's a professional liar, Jay! How many times have I had to throw him out of Aces High?"

"That's not the issue, Hiram," Jay said.

Hiram Worchester frowned. One hand curled into an impotent fist on the table in front of him. "Where is Downs?" Hiram demanded. "I want to look into his eyes and hear this story for myself. I'll know if he's lying, and I swear, if he is . . ."

"The airline lost him," Jay said ruefully. The cat carrier hadn't been on the flight after his, or the flight after that one either. Delta said on the next plane for sure. "Never mind."

Hiram looked confused. He drained half his Pimm's Cup in a series of long gulps. His hand was shaking when he put it back on the table. "You didn't say who you think . . . actually did the . . . the business . . . with Chrysalis, I mean."

"Let's just say I'm going to be real interested to find out what Billy Ray was doing on Sunday night and Monday morning."

"Billy Ray," Hiram said. "My God, that's absurd! He's a Justice Department operative! You can't think the whole federal government is involved in this, surely!"

Jay shrugged. "Until somebody proves otherwise, I'm not trusting anyone I don't have to."

Hiram finished his drink. He looked down at the empty glass, but his eyes had turned inward. "So many people have worked so hard. We've all . . . done so much. You saw those pour souls in the street. Gregg's their only hope. What will they do if it's true?"

"Vote Republican?" The quip was a halfhearted effort and the minute it was out, he regretted it. It was far too flip for the circumstances, for Hiram's genuine grief.

But Hiram scarcely seemed to hear it. He pulled out a black silk handkerchief from his lapel and used it to mop his brow. The huge man looked confused and lost, too weak to carry all that flesh. "There's a reporter," he said slowly. "Sara Morgenstern, she's been telling everyone that Gregg is a killer ace. No one believed her. She's not a very stable person, you know. But last night, an attempt was made on her life. By an ace, I'm sad to say. Jack Braun saved her, and would have died himself if I hadn't taken a hand."

"I saw the highlights on TV," Jay said. "The man Braun fought fits Digger's description of Mackie Messer."

"It sounds like the same man," Hiram said. "That doesn't prove he was actually working for Gregg, but I suppose . . ." He gave a long deep sigh of resignation, like a man being forced to accept something he could not stomach. "I suppose I must take this all seriously. Very well, then." For a moment he sounded like the old Hiram;

decisive, full of resolve. "I'll take you to Dr. Tachyon. He can perform the necessary blood test, and if need be, he can go into Hartmann's mind and find the truth. Whatever that truth may be." On the table, his fingers opened and closed, opened and closed. Hiram stared down at them, grimaced, forced his hand to relax. "So much is at stake," he said. "Jay, if we're wrong, think of all the people we'll hurt."

"And if we're right?" Jay asked quietly.

Hiram seemed to shrink in on himself. "If we're right," Hiram said softly, "God help us all."

♠

"Ever see anything like this before?" Brennan asked Tripod, putting the mysterious note down on the bar, careful to avoid the wetness seeping out from around the joker's beer mug.

Tripod bent down close to the bar to get a good look at it and shook his head. "Nope," he said.

"Great."

Squisher's Basement was still packed with the lunch crowd. Squisher himself was floating contentedly in his aquarium. He waved a long boneless arm at Brennan and whistled in a shrill, piping voice. "Hey, big guy, long time no see. Who's the babe?"

Brennan glanced at Jennifer. "Friend of mine."

"Hey," Squisher said, "we should all be so lucky." He winked his huge, staring eye and smiled leeringly. "Free drinks for my pals," he ordered the bartender.

"Thanks," Brennan said. He remembered the quality of their whiskey. "I'll have a beer," he told the mouthless bartender who was staring at him and Jennifer fixedly.

"White wine," Jennifer said, and the bartender continued to stare. "Uh, I'll have a beer, too."

"Right," he rasped through the small hole cut at the base of his throat.

"Find a table," Brennan told Jennifer and Tripod, "where we can talk things over."

They pushed off into the crowd. He waited for their drinks, nodded thanks to the bartender, then took them over to a small, isolated corner table. He put the drinks down. Tripod took a long sip of beer through a straw.

"So where'd you get that note, Mr. Y?" he asked. Brennan told him between sips of beer. Tripod shook his head after Brennan's story. "You got me baffled."

"Me too," Brennan admitted. "It's obvious that we're being watched. But by who?"

"Besides Lazy Dragon?" Tripod asked.

Brennan nodded. "He certainly hasn't been leaving notes. He's been watching us for Fadeout."

"Well," Tripod said. "I'll keep an eye out. Any other leads to follow?"

"We've eliminated Bludgeon, Oddity, and Wyrm," Brennan said. "Doug Morkle and Quasiman seem unlikely. But there's still two inconsistencies. Two things that still don't add up."

"Kant," Jennifer said. "He investigated Ezili Rouge and said that she was clean. That's not exactly what you told us."

"That's right," Brennan said. "And Sascha. He's still missing. He *must* know more about the murder than he told me at his mother's."

"And *he's* also connected with Ezili," Jennifer added.

"Right," Brennan said.

"Kant should be easy enough to find," Jennifer said. "I'll check with Fort Freak and see where he is." She came back from the phone in less than a minute and sat down, shaking her head. "He didn't report in this morning. No one at the station knows where he is."

"Bingo," Tripod said.

Brennan stood up, smiling grimly. "I hope we can get to him before he disappears, too."

"Try Freakers," Tripod suggested. "That's his favorite hangout. I'll circulate. Someone will know where he is."

"Right," Brennan said. He turned to Jennifer. "You wait at Freakers for him. Don't approach him if you spot him, just keep him under surveillance. I'm going to try Sascha's mother's place. She might know where her son is. If she doesn't open up, maybe I'll ask Father Squid to talk to her. He's not exactly Russian Orthodox, but he is a priest."

They all headed for the door. Squisher rose out of his aquarium and stopped them with a shrill whistle. "Hey, pal," he said to Brennan, "you got something I could put on our celebrity wall?"

He gestured toward a section of wall near the aquarium that Brennan hadn't noticed before. Tacked up on it was an amazing array of junk, from an autographed photo of a queasily smiling Tachyon standing next to Squisher's aquarium with one of the joker's boneless arms draped around his shoulders to a lacy handkerchief stained with green ichor, and a pair of crotchless panties with spaces for two crotches.

Brennan reached into his pocket for an ace of spades. "Will this do?"

"Sure," Squisher said. "Say, can you make it out to 'My good pal, Squisher'?"

3:00 P.M.

Jay could hear the voices through the door, shouting. "Maybe we ought to come back later," Hiram said weakly. "I don't think this is a good time."

"There's no good time for shit like this," Jay told him. He knocked loudly. Silence fell inside. A moment later the door to the suite was flung open. Dr. Tachyon gave them both a look like they were the last two people in the world he wanted to see right now. The little alien was ragged and weary. He had scratch marks on his face and a puffy split lip. Wordless, he looked at them for a long moment, then stepped back to let them enter.

Hiram moved heavily across the room, brushed aside the drapes, stared blindly out into the Atlanta heat. A teenage boy with painfully bright red hair was looking at Jay curiously. Ackroyd sat on the couch, the garment bag across his lap. No one seemed to want to speak, so Jay had to do it. "Lose the kid," he told Tachyon.

The boy protested. "Hey!"

"Blaise, go," said Tachyon, in a tone that brooked no arguments.

"I thought I'd forfeited the right."

"*Go*, damn you!"

"Shit, just when things were gettin' interesting." Blaise held up his hands, palms out. "Hey, no problem. I'm gone."

When the door banged shut, the quiet fell again. Tachyon made an exasperated gesture. "Hiram, what the devil is this?"

Jay answered. "You gotta run a blood test, doc. Right now."

Tachyon looked about. "What? Here?"

"Don't be dense, and don't be cute," Jay told him. "I'm too fucking tired and I hurt too much to deal with it." He unzipped the garment bag, dragged out the rag that so much blood had been shed on, for, and over. "This is Senator Hartmann's jacket from Syria."

Tachyon looked at the bloodstain as if it might leap off the jacket and devour him. "How did you come to possess this?" he asked, in a voice thickened by fear.

Jay sighed. "That's a long story, and none of us have the time. Let's just say I got it from Chrysalis. It was, well . . . sort of a legacy."

Nervously clearing his throat, Tach asked, "And just what do you think I am going to find?"

"The presence of Xenovirus Takis-A," Jay said.

The alien stumbled across the room like a zombie and made himself a drink. Jay could have used one, too, but none were being offered. "I see a jacket," Tachyon said when he was well fortified. "Anyone could buy a jacket, doctor it with virus-positive blood—"

Hiram finally spoke up. "That's what I thought. But he's been through too much. The link from Syria to this hotel room is clear. It's the sen—it's Hartmann's jacket."

Tachyon turned to look at Hiram. "Do *you* want me to do this thing?"

"Do we have any choice?"

"No," said Tachyon, with vast weariness. "I don't suppose we have."

4:00 P.M.

Mrs. Starfin was polite in a cold, gracious way. She offered Brennan tea, but no new information on her missing son. Just as Brennan was about to leave the apartment, the phone rang. Mrs. Starfin answered it and gestured at Brennan.

"It's for you," she said.

He took it, more than a little surprised. It had to be either Jennifer or Tripod, because they were the only two who knew that he was here.

It was Tripod.

"Yeoman," he said, "I've got something for you."

"What is it?" Tripod's voice was rougher than usual.

"I can't talk over the phone. Meet me at the marina off Beaumont on the south shore of Sheepshead Bay."

"All right," Brennan said. "See you there."

Brennan hung up and bade good-bye to Mrs. Starfin, who was not sorry to see him go. He couldn't get Tripod's tone of voice out of his mind. It sounded as if he'd discovered something bad. Perhaps, Brennan thought, Sascha's body? That would explain his reluctance to discuss his discovery in detail over the phone.

The Beaumont Marina was new and rather high-class. The ships tied in at the various slips were all rich-man crafts, not the skiffs of the casual, weekend sailor.

Brennan prowled among the slips for several minutes before he noticed Tripod standing alone at the end of a dock, looking out over the bay. Brennan hustled over to him. "What's up?" he asked.

Tripod turned to him. His face was battered and bruised.

"Sorry, Mr. Y," he said, "they made me make the call."

He nodded down at the boat tied into the dock's last slip. It was a sleek twin-engine yacht with the name *Asian Princess* stenciled on the side. Wyrm was standing there with a grin on his reptilian face, showing lots of teeth. He was accompanied by two Immaculate Egrets and a huge joker. The joker had normal if thick legs, but from the waist up had two torsos, two pairs of shoulders and arms, and two heads. He seemed vaguely familiar; Brennan realized he'd seen him among the crowd at Squisher's. He must have squealed to Wyrm about Tripod.

"There he is," one of the heads said with satisfaction. "I told you he'd come."

"You were right, Rick," Wyrm said, still smiling.

"I'm Mick," the head said. He jerked a thumb at his other head. "That's Rick. He didn't want to do this."

"I did, too," the other head answered.

"No you didn't. You were scared."

"Was not."

"Was too."

"Was—"

"All right," Wyrm said loudly, interrupting the squabbling heads. "Here." He proffered a roll of bills, which a hand belonging to Mick snatched before Rick could.

"That's mine!" Rick protested.

"Mine too!" Mick said. "I helped beat up the armless geek!"

"Enough!" Wyrm said. His good humor quickly turned to exasperation. He said to Brennan, "You embarrassssed me in front of Sssui Ma," he said. "Now it'ssss payback time. Join us on deck, won't you? You too," he said to Tripod.

The Egrets had their guns out, so Brennan wasn't about to argue with Wyrm. He steadied Tripod as the joker stepped onto the gently rocking boat, then followed him onto the deck.

"What do you want?" Brennan asked his old foe.

Wyrm's eyes gleamed with returned good humor. "Just a swimming contest. We're going to see if you can swim Ssssheepssshead Bay weighed down by thossse." He pointed at a pair of chains with lead weights attached, then turned to the Egrets. "Tie them up."

The Egrets did so quickly and efficiently while Wyrm covered them and Rick and Mick chatted inanely. When they were trussed up to Wyrm's satisfaction, he ordered the Egrets to take them down into the cabin for safekeeping while Wyrm went to the control console to pilot the ship into deep water. Rick and Mick went to cast off the line.

"Sorry," Tripod said again as they shuffled into the cabin. Brennan's hands and legs, and Tripod's legs, had been bound with rope, but the weighted chains hadn't been added yet.

Brennan shrugged. "There wasn't anything you could do."

The cabin was plush and expensive looking, complete with luxurious sofa, deep pile carpeting, and a wet bar.

"How about a drink?" Brennan suggested after Wyrm started the engines and the *Princess* pulled away from its slip.

One of the Egrets laughed. "You don't want to drink before going into the water," he said. "Stomach cramps. I ain't going to be swimming this afternoon, though."

Brennan turned to Tripod. "He's probably right," he said. "You can't be too careful when it comes to boats." He swung his bound hands at the closest Egret and caught him square in the throat, crushing his windpipe. As he went down choking, the other Egret whirled, reaching for the gun he'd put down while he was pouring a shot of scotch.

Brennan shuffled forward, crashing into him shoulder first, and they both fell to the floor. The Egret opened his mouth to yell, and Tripod fell on his head, muffling his screams.

Brennan picked up the Egret's gun clumsily with both hands and rammed it against his chest. He pulled the trigger and the Egret jerked once and was still.

The other was crawling about the cabin, making mewling sounds as he gasped for breath. Brennan caught up with him and clubbed him down with the barrel of the pistol, not wanting to risk alerting the others on deck with another shot.

Tripod took a deep breath. "I knew you'd get us out of this," he said in a relieved voice.

"We're not out of it yet," Brennan said.

Tripod rolled over to where Brennan was sitting on the floor, leaning against the cabin's plush sofa. "We will be in a minute." His dexterous third foot was free. He quickly untied Brennan, who returned the favor.

"What do we do now?" Tripod asked.

"How about trying our hands at piracy?"

They crept onto the deck. Wyrm was at the wheel. Rick and Mick were arguing. Wyrm said exasperatedly, "Well, if Rick thought he heard something below, you should go check it out."

"No need," Brennan said.

Startled, they turned to see Brennan standing there pointing a gun at them. Wyrm hissed in hate and frustration. Rick and Mick looked at each other.

"I told you we shouldn't get involved," Mick said.

For once, Rick said nothing.

Brennan glanced at the boat's position. They were nearing the middle of the bay, and there were no other boats in the vicinity.

"Time for the swimming contest," he said.

He gestured Wyrm away from the wheel with his gun. For a moment the joker hesitated, but then he moved.

"You're lucky," Brennan said in a hard voice, "that I decided to dispense with the chains. Over you go."

Wyrm looked like he wanted to say something, then thought better of it and swallowed his exit line. He went over the edge without a word.

Brennan turned to Rick and Mick.

"Hey," Mick said. "I didn't want to have anything to do with this."

"You're just a victim of the company you keep," Brennan suggested.

"That's right. Rick's a bad influence."

"Jump or die," Brennan said. "It makes no difference to me."

Rick and Mick looked at each other, nodded, and leaped over the side of the ship. They made a big splash when they hit the water.

Tripod let out a deep sigh of relief. "You know, Mr. Y, I think I need some time off."

"A vacation would probably be in order," Brennan said as he took the wheel. "Know anybody who buys boats?"

Tripod brightened. "There's this guy in Jersey. . . ."

6:00 P.M.

It was a hundred times more complex than a snowflake, delicate as the finest lace, like a flower made of ice. Jay stared at the image on the screen of the electron microscope for a long time. "Jesus," he said, releasing the breath he hadn't even realized he'd been holding, "it's beautiful."

Tachyon pushed back his long red hair. "Yes, I suppose it is. Trust us Takisians to create a virus to match our aesthetic ideal." He pivoted on the lab stool and suddenly yelled out, *"Ackroyd!"*

Jay turned just as Hiram started to go down in a faint. He grabbed one arm, Tach the other. Hiram's weight brought them all down with a thump. On the floor, the huge ace ran a hand across his face and said, "Sorry, must have blacked out for an instant."

Tach gave him a hit from a pocket flask, and Hiram sucked it down greedily. Jay suddenly realized how thirsty he was. "Hey, can I have a sip of that? It's been a hell of a week." Tach handed it to him wordlessly, and Jay tried a swallow. Brandy. Well, it was better than nothing.

"There can be no doubt?" Hiram was asking.

"None."

"But just because he's an ace . . . well, that proves nothing. He'd have been mad to admit to the virus. He might be a latent."

Tachyon stared up at the ceiling. He looked lost. Jay broke the silence. "So what do we do now?"

"A very good question," Tachyon said.

"You mean you don't know?"

"Contrary to popular belief, I do not have the solution to every problem."

Hiram struggled to his feet ponderously. "We've got to have more proof than this," he said.

Jay jerked a thumb at the fancy microscope. "What more proof do you want?"

"We don't know if he's done anything wrong!"

"He had Chrysalis *killed!*" Jay said, rising to face him.

"I demand *evidence* of wrongdoing." Hiram whacked a closed fist into an open palm.

Jay pointed at the screen. "*That's* evidence."

"*Stop it! Stop it!*" Tachyon yelled.

Hiram took the alien by the shoulders. "You go to him. Talk to him. There may be some logical explanation. Think of all the good he's done—"

"Oh, yeah," Jay said with all the sarcasm he could muster. He was sick and tired of hearing about Saint Gregg. He took another hit of brandy.

"Think of what we stand to lose," Hiram cried.

Sometimes Hiram's innocence was unbearable. "So he'll just lie to Tachyon," Jay said. "Where the hell does that get us?"

"He cannot lie to me," Tachyon announced portentously. Hiram took his hands away, and Tach straightened like a man trying to be tall. It didn't work very well. "If I go to him, you know what I will do," he told Hiram. "Will you accept the truth of what I read in his mind?"

"Yes," Worchester said.

"Even though it is inadmissible in a court of law?"

"Yes."

Tachyon danced around to face Jay. "As for you, Mr. Ackroyd, take the jacket. Destroy it."

Fleeting visions of the world of shit he'd lived through to find the jacket passed through Jay Ackroyd's mind, and he protested. "Hey, that's our only proof!"

"Proof? Are you really suggesting that we publicize this? *Think.* What we hold could spell the ruin of every wild card in America."

Stubbornly, Jay said, "But he killed Chrysalis, and if we don't nail him, Elmo takes the fall."

That was too much for the alien. All of a sudden Tachyon started pulling at his hair in something that looked perilously close to a hysterical frenzy. *"Damn you, damn you, damn you."*

"Look, it's not my fault," Jay said, scared that Tach was about to burst into tears. "But I'm damned if I'm going to agree to some sleazy little deal that lets Chrysalis's murderer walk."

"I swear to you upon my honor and blood that I will not let Elmo suffer."

"Yeah? What are you going to do?"

"I don't know yet!" Tachyon switched off the electron microscope, removed the slide, washed the incriminating scraps of fabric down the sink. Hiram moved to follow when the alien started to leave, but Tach stopped him. "No, Hiram. I must do this alone."

Jay pointed out the obvious objection. "And if he's got Buzz Saw Boy waiting for you?" he asked.

"That's the risk I must take."

7:00 P.M.

"It's all," Brennan told Jennifer grimly, "just a matter of patience."

For what was perhaps the tenth time in the last hour one of the Freakers patrons cruised their table, eyeing Brennan and Jennifer speculatively. For the tenth time in the past hour, Brennan gave a cold stare that made the cruiser move on without lingering.

"But," he added through gritted teeth, "I'm about all out."

He'd made it back to Freakers about an hour ago and had told Jennifer about his nautical adventures and Tripod's wise decision to go on vacation in Florida until things quieted down. He'd had quite a bankroll to finance it, because Kien's *Asian Princess* had brought a nice sum from Tripod's boat-broker acquaintance, which they'd split fifty-fifty.

A cocktail waitress with a Medusa head of twitching blind worms came up to their table.

"We're waiting for someone," Brennan said.

She smiled. "Someone in particular," she asked, "or will anyone do?"

Brennan ground his teeth together. He started to answer her, stopped, and gripped Jennifer's arm while nodding toward the bar. "Here," he said, giving the barmaid a twenty without looking at her. "Go away."

She took the bill, slipped it into her ample cleavage, and went off on her rounds.

"It's him," Jennifer whispered.

Brennan nodded. "Wait here."

Kant was at the bar. Even from across the room Brennan could see that he was highly agitated. He was questioning one of the bartenders as Brennan came up quietly behind him. The bartender was shaking his head.

"She ain't been in for a couple of days."

Kant was disheveled and had a rank, reptile-house smell about him.

"You don't understand," he told the bartender. "I need her. I need the kiss!"

A woman sitting at the bar swiveled toward him, her face hidden by a cheap, glittery mask. "You sound like you need it bad, doll."

Kant turned to her. His eyes were bloodshot, his breath was a husky rattle.

"I'll kiss you, honey," the woman said. "Anywhere you want."

Kant growled wordlessly and struck her backhanded across the face, knocking her from the bar stool. She gazed up at him in terror as he towered over her, glowering like a madman.

"I don't need a filthy whore!" he screamed. He pounded his fist on the bar, then shuddered all over like a dog throwing off water. He brought himself under control with great effort and hissed, "I need the kiss!"

He whirled and almost trampled Brennan as he lunged toward the door. No one tried to stop him. Brennan turned to signal Jennifer and saw that she was already at his side. He took his bow case from her and said quietly, "Let's go."

It was the easiest tailing job Brennan had ever done. Kant left a trail of disgruntled pedestrians in his wake as he obliviously slammed through them. The biggest problem Brennan had was keeping up with him. Kant wasn't exactly running, but he was moving with the urgency of a man who had to find a bathroom.

They followed him for half a dozen blocks to a shabby five-story apartment building. It was solid and functional looking, with no pretense toward elegance or security. Kant went in the lobby and after a moment Brennan and Jennifer followed him. They heard him pound up the stairs and then followed at a more sedate pace all the way to the top, meeting no one else on the way.

Brennan and Jennifer reached the top floor just in time to peer around the stairwell and see Kant take a key ring from his pocket and unlock the door. He entered the apartment and slammed the door so hard that it rattled in its frame.

"He's off the deep end," Brennan whispered.

Jennifer nodded. "Let's find out why."

Brennan unzipped his bow case and took out the long-barreled air pistol that had been snugged down next to the bow. It was loaded with tranquilizer darts. He didn't want to hurt Kant, and he wanted the joker able to answer his questions.

They went down the corridor and stopped in front of the door. It had rebounded out of its latch when Kant had slammed it, so that it was open a crack. Brennan nodded at Jennifer, who blew him a kiss, and then he went in fast and low, dropping the bow case and rolling to a crouch.

The living room was decorated with obvious expense, but it was not to Brennan's taste. It was brightly lit with numerous bulbs blazing in track lighting set in the ceiling, and even though it was summer, the heat was on and cranked up to the max. The furniture was all shiny leather and polished chrome. The image of a lizard sunning himself on a smooth rock flashed through Brennan's mind.

The room was empty. Brennan closed the door as Jennifer ghosted through the wall and joined him. It was quiet but tense, as if an angry beast were waiting in ambush somewhere in the apartment.

Brennan motioned down the hallway that led to the apartment's interior, and Jennifer nodded. He crept forward, passing a kitchenette that was also empty, then a hall closet whose sliding door was half-open. Brennan looked into it to make sure it wasn't hiding a crazed joker cop. It wasn't, so he moved on toward the doorway to the bedroom, listened for a moment, then cautiously peered in.

The room was dominated by a huge four-poster water bed with mirrors on the canopy and headboard. A big-screen television stood against the wall opposite the bed. Next to the television was what looked like a child's wading pool filled with sand. A pair of sunlamps were focused on the pool and Kant was in it, naked, with his eyes closed. He was rooting in the sand, mumbling aloud as he dragged himself through the grit as if he were frenziedly trying to wipe himself clean.

"Kant," Brennan said quietly.

The joker turned slowly. His face was a frozen mask of madness. There was an ugly oozing sore on his lower neck. He stared at Brennan, his mouth working wordlessly, and then he screamed and sprang, his hands outstretched, his fingers hooked into talons.

Brennan calmly shot him.

The pistol whooshed and a feathered dart flew through the air, struck Kant's naked chest, and bounced off the hard, scaly skin.

Shit, Brennan thought. Then the maniac was on him.

♥

"So close," Hiram said. He sighed hugely, got up from the couch, and went over to the wet bar to mix himself a drink. They were in

Tachyon's suite at the Marriott, waiting for his return and watching the convention on television.

"Too damn close if you ask me," Jay said. Down on the floor of the Omni, another inconclusive ballot had just been tallied. A wave of sympathy voting had pushed Gregg Hartmann to 1956 votes of the 2082 needed to nominate. Jackson and Dukakis had both lost support, and the tiny Draft Cuomo movement had melted away entirely. Only the Barnett forces were holding firm.

Hundreds of Hartmann supporters, with victory so close they could taste it, were dancing in the aisles, waving their green and gold placards, chanting, "Hart-mann, Hart-mann," over and over while the chair gaveled for order. The convention floor was a sea of Hartmann green and gold, surrounding a few stubborn islands of Jackson red, Dukakis blue, and Barnett white.

David Brinkley had just predicted that Hartmann would go over the top on the next ballot when one of Leo Barnett's people rose and moved to suspend the rules "to allow the Reverend Leo Barnett to address the convention." All of a sudden half of the hall was on its feet, screaming at the podium.

The couch whuffed in protest as Hiram sat back down. "Damn him," Hiram said, "but it's a good move. Barnett will never get to the floor, but we'll have to vote down the motion, and that will take time. It might cost us some momentum."

"Us?" Jay said, with a sidelong glance.

Hiram scowled, rubbing at the back of his neck under his collar. "Until I have *proof* that Gregg is the monster you claim, I'm still a Hartmann delegate. By rights I ought to be there right now." He looked at his watch. "What could be taking Tachyon so long?"

Mackie Messer could be cutting his liver out, Jay thought, but he didn't say it. Hiram was in bad enough shape already. Jay was trying to figure out what their next move would be if Tachyon never came back from his little showdown with Hartmann. And what if he came back and said Greggie was innocent? That would be enough for Hiram, but Jay was of a more suspicious nature. Could Hartmann's ace powers be potent enough to twist even *Tachyon* to his will? Jay didn't think so, but he'd been wrong before. He was glad he'd ignored

Tachyon's advice about the jacket; it was safely back in its garment bag, hanging in the closet.

On the tube, Hartmann's people asked for a voice vote on the motion to suspend the rules. Barnett's supporters objected, demanding a roll-call vote. A Hartmann delegate asked for a voice vote on the motion for a roll-call vote. The chair stopped to consult the parliamentarian.

Jay got up and changed the channel. The other networks were showing the same thing, as was CNN, but he found an old movie on Ted Turner's superstation. Colorized, unfortunately; Cary Grant was a strange shade of pink. Jay left it on anyway.

Hiram was annoyed. "Damn it, Popinjay," he said. "Put the convention back on."

"Gimme a break, Hiram," Jay said. "They're arguing about whether they ought to vote about how to vote on whether some guy can give a speech."

"Yes," Hiram snapped, "and it might just be crucial. If you want to see *Topper* so badly, just say so and I'll buy you a cassette. George Kerby was never that color, dead *or* alive."

Jay looked at him sharply. "What did you say?"

"I said that George Kerby was never—"

"*Shit!*" Jay swore. "Goddammit."

"What is it?" Hiram said. He came ponderously to his feet. "Jay, are you all right?"

"No," Jay said. "I'm dumb as a plank. George Kerby, George Fucking Kerby, The *assassin*, Hiram! Chrysalis was being clever. The airline ticket was made out in the name *George Kerby*."

Hiram Worchester was scarcely a slow man. "Tickets in the name of a ghost," he said.

"Yeah," said Jay. "A ghost. A specter."

"*James* Spector!" Hiram said.

"And both George Kerbys came back from the dead," Jay said. "She hired that sonofabitch Demise."

Hiram knew what Demise was capable of. "We have to let them know," he said. He crossed the room, picked up the phone, and punched for the operator. "Connect me to the Secret Service."

The door opened. Dr. Tachyon stepped quietly into the room, head bowed. Hiram looked at him with dread, the telephone momentarily forgotten in his hand. "It . . . it's not true, is it?" he said desperately. "Tell me that it's all some hideous mistake, Gregg can't be . . ."

Tachyon looked up with pity in his lilac eyes. "Hiram," the alien said softly. "My poor, poor Hiram. I saw his mind. I saw the Puppet-man." The little man shuddered. "It is a thousand times worse than we could ever have imagined." Tachyon sat on the carpet, buried his head in his hands, and began to weep.

Hiram stood there with his mouth open. Jay had never seen him look so used up, so beaten, so *fat*. He took the receiver away from his ear and stared at it as if he had never seen a telephone before, his face gray as ash. "*God forgive me*," he said, in a barely audible whisper. Then he hung up the phone.

♣

It was Brennan's day for fighting lizards. Kant was strong, but in his frenzy he forgot whatever combat techniques he knew. Brennan blocked Kant's taloned hand as it raked at his eyes, caught the cop's other wrist, and flung him hard against the bed's footboard. Kant crouched, panting, and when Brennan leapt on him, he flicked open a switchblade he'd grabbed from the heap of clothes piled next to his sand pool. Brennan changed direction in midleap, but wasn't quite fast enough. The knife slashed open his T-shirt and the skin underneath, drawing a line of blood from belly button to nipple across Brennan's stomach and chest.

Wraith walked out of the wall as Brennan flung himself to the other side of the bed. Kant saw her and his eyes bugged out of his head. He twisted frantically from side to side, trying to watch both Jennifer and Brennan at the same time.

"We're not going to hurt you," Jennifer said in her most soothing voice. "We want to help."

"Help me?" Kant asked, his voice high-pitched, hysterical, and mean. "If you want to help me, get me the goddamned kiss!"

Brennan lunged across the bed, grabbed Kant's knife wrist, and yanked hard, pulling Kant down. The knife plunged into the mattress. Brennan leaped on him and Kant twisted savagely, gutting the water bed.

Water spewed from it as if a dam had broken. Brennan and Kant tumbled apart and the cop washed up next to Jennifer, wet as a wharf rat, sputtering and spitting. He grabbed Jennifer, drew the knife back to slash. She ghosted. He swung through her, teetered off balance, and Brennan grabbed him from behind and rammed him through the screen of the television set. It exploded with a loud crash. Kant hung inside it, stunned, until Brennan pulled him out. The cop was dazed and bleeding from a dozen cuts on his face and chest. Brennan slapped the knife from his hand and kicked it away, then pushed him down and sat on his chest.

"What's this about a kiss?" Brennan asked.

Kant moaned, unconsciously licking the blood that ran from his nose and lips.

"Is it Ezili? Do you want her?"

Kant tossed his head from side to side. His eyes were stunned and glazed, but there was still a powerful need in them.

"Nooo!" he howled. "That bitch."

"What then?" Brennan demanded, shaking Kant by the shoulders.

"The Master. Ti Malice. His kiss, so sweet, so sweet."

Brennan and Jennifer exchanged baffled glances.

"Who's Malice?"

"My master."

Brennan suddenly remembered where he'd seen a sore like the one on Kant's neck. "Is he Sascha's master, too?"

Kant shook his head, still dazed and bewildered, and Brennan slapped him to get his attention. "Sascha, the bartender at the Crystal Palace. Is Malice his master, too?"

"Yes."

"Where are they?"

"I don't fucking know! They're gone. They left me behind!"

"Who did your master take with him?"

"Some mounts," Kant mumbled. "I don't know them all."

"Did he take Sascha?"

Kant sobbed wordlessly, uncontrollably.

"Christ," Brennan said.

He stood and dragged Kant to the bed. He took the pair of cuffs he found among Kant's clothes piled on the floor and chained the cop to a bedpost. Kant crouched in a puddle on the floor, weeping and picking at the sore on his neck.

Brennan took the phone on the nightstand by the bed and dialed Fort Freak. "Maseryk," he said. "This is an emergency. Life or death."

It took the detective only a moment to answer.

"This better be good," he said, his voice harsh and flat.

"It's your partner," Brennan said. "He's strung out."

There was a shocked silence. "Drugs?" Maseryk asked after a moment.

"I don't think so. Look," Brennan said, cutting off any more queries. "I think you'd better get to Kant's apartment, fast. He needs help. And Maseryk—"

"What?"

"You owe me." He hung up the phone and turned to Wraith. "Let's get the hell out of here."

◆

"What are we going to do?" Hiram asked when Tachyon's sobbing had finally begun to subside.

"Blow the whistle," Jay said.

Dr. Tachyon bounded to his feet. "No!" he said. "Are you mad, Ackroyd? The public must *never* learn the truth."

"Hartmann's a monster," Jay objected.

"No one knows that better than I," said Tachyon. "I swam in the sewer of his mind. I felt the vileness that lives inside him, the Puppetman. It *touched* me. You can't imagine what that was like."

"I'm not a telepath," Jay said. "So sue me. I'm still not going to help you whitewash Hartmann."

"You do not understand," Tachyon said. "For close to two years Leo Barnett has been filling the public ear with dire warnings about wild card violence, inflaming their fears and their mistrust of aces.

Now you propose we tell them that he was right all along, that a monstrous secret ace has indeed subverted their government. How do you think they will react?"

Jay shrugged. He was too tired and beat up for intellectual discussions. "Okay, so Barnett gets elected, big deal. So we have a right-wing dork in the White House for four years. We managed to survive Reagan for eight."

Dr. Tachyon was having none of it. "You cannot know the half of what I found in Hartmann's mind. The murders, the rapes, the atrocities, and him always at the center of his web, the Puppetman pulling his strings. I warn you, if the full story ever becomes known, the public revulsion will touch off a reign of terror that will make the persecutions of the fifties look like nothing." The alien gesticulated wildly. "He killed his own unborn child and feasted on the pain and terror of its death. And his puppets . . . aces, jokers, politicians, religious leaders, police, anyone foolish enough to touch him. If their names become known—"

"*Tachyon*," Hiram Worchester interrupted. His voice was low, but the anguish in it was as plain as nails on a blackboard.

Dr. Tachyon glanced guiltily at Hiram. It was hard to say which of them looked most frightened.

"Tell me," Hiram said. "These . . . puppets. Was . . . was I . . . one of . . ." He couldn't finish, choking on the words.

Tachyon nodded. A small quick nod, almost furtive. A single tear rolled down his cheek. Then he turned away.

Hiram considered that, his face leaden. Then he said, "In a grotesque way, it's almost funny," but he did not laugh. "Jay, he's right. This must be our secret."

Jay looked from the tiny man to the big one, feeling outnumbered. "Do what you want," he said, "just don't expect me to vote for the fucker. Even if I *was* registered."

"We must take a vow," Tachyon said. "A solemn oath, to do everything in our power to stop Hartmann, and to take this secret to our graves."

"Oh, gimme a break," Jay groaned. The last thing he needed right now was more Takisian bullshit.

"Hiram, that glass," the alien snapped. Hiram handed him the half-finished drink, and Tachyon upended the contents onto the carpet. He bent, slid a long knife out of a sheath in his boot, and held it up in front of them. "We must pledge by blood and bone," he said. And before anyone could stop him, the Takisian took the knife in his right hand and slashed straight across his left wrist. He held the wound over the glass until there was an inch of blood on the bottom, then bound his wrist in a lace hankie and passed the knife to Jay.

Jay just looked at it. "You got to be kidding."

"No," Tachyon said, face solemn.

"How about I just piss in it instead?" Jay suggested.

"The blood is the bond," Tachyon insisted.

Hiram stepped forward. "I'll do it," he said, taking the knife. He shrugged out of his white linen coat, rolled up his sleeve, and made the cut. The pain made him inhale sharply, but his hand did not hesitate.

"So deep," Tachyon muttered as bright hot blood began to spurt from Hiram's wrist. Hiram winced and held his hand above the glass. The red line crept upward.

Then they were both looking at him.

Jay sighed deeply. "So if you two are Huck and Tom, I guess that makes me Nigger Jim," he said. "Remind me to have my head examined when all of this is over." He took the knife.

It hurt like a motherfucker.

When it was done, Dr. Tachyon swirled the glass to mix the blood, then lifted it above his head and chanted in a high singsong that Jay had to assume was Takisian. "By Blood and Bone, I so vow," he finished. He threw back his head and drained a third of the glass in one long gulp.

Jay thought he was going to be sick. Even Hiram looked a little queasy as Tachyon passed him the glass. "By Blood and Bone," Hiram intoned, and took his ritual swallow.

"Am I allowed to add some tabasco, maybe a little vodka?" Jay asked when Hiram gave him what was left.

"You are not," Tachyon said stiffly.

"Pity," Jay said. "Always liked Bloody Marys." He lifted the glass, muttered, "Blood and Bone," and drank the last of the blood, feeling like an idiot. "Yum," he said afterward.

"It is done," Tachyon said. "Now we must make plans."

"I'm going back to the Omni," Hiram announced. "I was among Gregg's earliest supporters, and I daresay I am not without influence in the New York delegation. I may be able to have some impact. We *must* deny him the nomination, at all costs."

"Agreed," said Tachyon.

"I wish I knew more about Dukakis. . . ." Hiram began.

"Not Dukakis," the alien said. "Jesse Jackson. He has been court-ing us all along. I'll speak to him." He clasped hands with Hiram, bloody hankies dangling down absurdly from their wrists. "We can do it, my friend."

"Real good," Jay said. "So Greggie doesn't get to be president. Big deal. What about all his victims? Kahina, Chrysalis, the rest of them."

Dr. Tachyon glanced over. "Not Chrysalis," he said.

"What?" Jay said.

"He threatened Chrysalis, yes," the alien said. "He made her and Digger watch while his creature tortured and killed Kahina, but he never acted on that threat. When he heard of her death on Monday morning, he was as surprised as anyone."

"No fucking way," Jay said. "You got it wrong."

The little man pulled himself up to his full height. "I am a Psi Lord of Takis, trained by the finest mentats of House Ilkazam," he said. "His mind was *mine*. I did not get it wrong."

"He sent Mackie after Digger!" Jay argued.

"And he commanded the Oddity to retrieve the incriminating jacket and destroy it. Most assuredly. *After* he heard that Chrysalis was dead, he took steps to protect himself. But he had no hand in ordering that death." Tachyon put a hand on Jay's shoulder. "I'm sorry, my friend."

"Then who the fuck did it?" Jay demanded.

"We have no time to argue about this now," Hiram said impa-tiently. "The woman's dead, nothing will—"

"Quiet," Jay said urgently.

A newsflash had banished Cary Grant from the television screen. ". . . latest tragedy to strike the convention," a solemn announcer was saying. "Senator Hartmann is unharmed, repeat, *unharmed*, but reliable reports indicate that the ace assassin took the lives of two other men in his attempt to reach the senator. We are still waiting for final confirmation, but unofficial sources indicate that the killer's victims were Alex James, a Secret Service agent assigned to Senator Hartmann"—a photograph of the dead man appeared on the screen, above the announcer's shoulder—"and the chairman of Hartmann's California delegation, ace Jack Braun. The controversial Braun, who starred in feature films and TV's *Tarzan*, was better known as Golden Boy. He was considered by some to be the strongest man in the world. Braun first came to public attention . . ."

Braun's picture appeared on screen as the announcer went on and on. He was in his old fatigues, smiling crookedly, surrounded by a golden glow. He looked young, alive, invincible.

"Oh, Jack," Tachyon said. He looked like he was going to cry again.

"He *can't* be dead," Hiram said furiously. "I just saved his damnable life last night!" The television set floated off the carpet, bobbing up toward the ceiling like a balloon. Jay glanced over and saw that Hiram's hand was squeezed into a fist. "He can*not* be dead!" Hiram insisted, and all of a sudden the TV was falling. It hit the ground as if it had been dropped six stories instead of six feet, and the picture tube exploded.

"He will not have died in vain," Tachyon said inanely. He touched Hiram on the arm. "Come," he said.

After they had gone, Jay sat down on the couch. His ribs hurt, his face hurt, and now his wrist hurt, too. His mouth tasted like blood, he no longer had the remotest idea who the fuck could have killed Chrysalis, and he was too damn tired to think straight.

He fumbled the bottle of painkillers out his pocket, put four of them into his mouth, and washed them down with a good long swallow of Dr. Tachyon's best brandy. It tasted pretty damn good. The second swallow tasted even better; the third was downright delicious. After that he lost count. By the time the decanter was empty, Jay's head was swimming. He lay down on the couch. No way he could sleep, with all this going on. But maybe if he just closed his eyes for a few minutes . . .

8:00 P.M.

After the long, hard day, Jennifer slept, but Brennan could not.

He was on the edge of exhaustion, but his head felt curiously clear and light. His brain wouldn't shut off and allow him the rest he needed, so he slipped quietly out of bed, dressed, and went out into the night.

It was hot and sticky. The heat wave smothering the city was unrelenting even at night. The streets were full of people, wandering, Brennan thought, in an aimless search for answers to their own particular problems, answers as elusive as those Brennan was seeking.

A new variable had shown up to further complicate the equation of Chrysalis's murder: the mysterious master, Ti Malice, and his apparent accomplice, Ezili Rouge. Sascha was his servant, and so was Kant. The cop had used a strange term to refer to those in thrall to Malice. He had called them "mounts." Brennan couldn't even begin to guess what that meant.

A crowd had gathered in front of an all-night drugstore a few blocks from the hotel. Brennan joined them, curious as to what caused their hushed expectancy, and saw that the television set in the window was tuned to a news channel that was recapitulating the day's chaotic events in Atlanta.

Jack Braun had been murdered, the newscaster said. Brennan couldn't believe it. When he was young, Brennan had been a big fan of Golden Boy, idolizing him because he was handsome, strong, and fearless. He was everything a hero should be. He sheltered the weak and protected the helpless as a living embodiment of the heroic ideal. As Brennan had gotten older, he learned that heroes could be hollow when he realized that Golden Boy had betrayed his friends in a moment of weakness and fear. But his continuing belief in the heroic ideal had been part of what had drawn him to the military.

There Brennan had learned firsthand how difficult it was for ideals to flourish in an imperfect world. He'd been sent to defend

Vietnam. Instead, because of inefficiency and incompetence, avarice and stupidity, he'd helped devastate it. Then those in charge of the mess just walked away, leaving the Vietnamese people in the hands of the murderous thugs they'd sworn to defend them from.

Stung by the pain of that lesson, Brennan had walked away himself, had tried to isolate himself by abandoning the rest of humanity. But he discovered that old ties, always remembered, are impossible to forget, and new ties, once forged, are impossible to ignore.

Let Barnett and Hartmann, Brennan thought, play their games in Atlanta. Let them hoist placards, wear funny hats, and make speeches full of empty, impossible promises. In the end they could do little that would matter. Despite his fine intentions and noble vows, Hartmann would still be constrained by a system crippled by incompetence, inertia, and injustice. Barnett, too, would face the same roadblocks if he ever tried to put his despicable plans into operation.

In the end, Brennan thought, it came down to protecting your comrades, your friends, and your family. Brennan knew he would always be ready for that. And if, as with Chrysalis, he was too late to protect, he would make sure that anyone who harmed his people once would never do so again.

Brennan smiled wryly. Noble sentiments, he thought, but actually he wasn't getting very far in exacting retribution.

Brennan stared unseeingly at the television screen. He needed more information, but his sources had all dried up. There was nothing on the street. Sascha had disappeared, perhaps under orders from the mysterious Malice. Fadeout was obviously more interested in using Brennan to get rid of Kien and to help find Chrysalis's files. . . .

Perhaps that was the answer. Chrysalis knew everything that went on in Jokertown. Perhaps her information cache had the answers Brennan needed. But the files were well hidden. Knowing how fond she was of secrets, Brennan doubted that she told anyone where she kept them.

Except perhaps for one man. One man who was something of her confident. One man whose lips would be sealed by unbreakable vows of silence. One man who had received a strange bequest from her.

The time had come, Brennan decided, to call in all debts.

His mind made up, Brennan turned back to his hotel room and a few hours' sleep. He smiled as the cat following him also turned, darting quickly through the shadows. He considered stopping and offering him a lift, but decided that Lazy Dragon could use the exercise.

Saturday
July 23, 1988

...**WALKED FASTER, HIS FEET** bare and bloody, rushing after the heavy man in the bulky black coat. He shouted after him, but nothing broke the dreadful silence but the sound of his feet. The steps grew narrow, making it harder to keep his balance as he rushed down into the darkness. When he reached the platform suspended over that stygian gulf, the man was there ahead of him. Just the sight of that back, hunched and ominous, filled him with fear, and when the man began to turn, the terror rose inside him until he thought he would choke. The featureless white face lifted, the wet red tentacle tasted the air. Its howl and Jay's scream sounded together in a horrible cacophony. . . .

"You pissed your pants," a voice sneered. "Some ace."

Jay sat up. His suit was rumpled, his side ached, and his head was pounding. Some kid was standing across the room with a smirk on his face like Jay was the funniest thing he'd ever seen. The kid had a refined, prissy little face, a French accent, and an attitude. His hair was so red it hurt to look at it. Jay wanted to pop him to the South Bronx, but he figured he'd better not. Groggy as he was, he seemed to recall that this was Tachyon's grandson.

"Where's Gramps?" Jay asked as he lurched to his feet, ignoring the boy's gibes. There was broken glass all over the carpet; it crunched when he stepped on it. It was all over the couch, too, and a few shards fell off Jay when he stood. He noticed the shattered windows for the first time. When the hell had that happened?

The kid shrugged. "His bed wasn't slept in," he said. "Maybe he finally caught one of his bimbos."

"Figures," Jay said. "I pass out on the goddamn couch with a perfectly adequate bed empty in the next room." He went over to the bar, glass breaking under his heels, and stared at the booze for a moment until he found an unopened bottle of cognac. A little hair of the dog, he decided, real good.

"You're Popinjay." The kid was as arrogant as Tachyon. Not to mention almost as tall.

"Jay Ackroyd," Jay corrected. "So who are you, Kid Tachyon?"

"Blaise. I'm one quarter Takisian," he added proudly.

"Don't let it bother you, I'm one quarter Croat myself." Jay tossed back the cognac. It burned against the back of his throat on the way down. He splashed a little more into his glass. And kept splashing. The glass was one third full. One half. Three quarters. Jay tried to put down the bottle. He kept pouring. Filled the glass to the brim. Poured it over his head.

The liquor stung when it hit his eyes, blinding him. He tried to say sonofabitch. Instead he heard himself singing "I'm a Little Teapot," in a high falsetto voice. With all the little motions. Somewhere along there the cognac glass slipped from his fingers and rolled across the carpet.

When his vision cleared, Blaise was standing in front of him, arms crossed, smiling in satisfaction. "Takisians don't let anybody make fun of them," he told Jay. "Watch what you say. I can make you do anything I like." He laughed. "Now you're wet at both ends."

"Real good," Jay said. He smelled like cognac and piss. "You'd make some detective."

"Really?" Blaise had managed to miss the sarcasm; Jay was grateful for that much.

"No shit. Of course, you still got a few things to learn."

"Like what?" Blaise wanted to know.

"Well," said Jay, "like you really should make sure a guy is unarmed before you piss him off." He made a gun of his hand, aimed it at Blaise, winked broadly.

The boy was not impressed. "*You're* unarmed," he said.

Jay smiled sweetly.

Blaise made a nice crisp popping sound when he vanished. He didn't even have time to look surprised.

Jay was standing there with his finger pointing at empty air when the door to the suite opened and a haggard-looking Dr. Tachyon walked in, saw him, and frowned. "Doc," Jay said, trying to sound innocent, "I swear, I didn't know it was loaded."

9:00 A.M.

Brennan entered the church and watched Quasiman for a few minutes as he washed the stained-glass window that depicted the passion of Jesus Christ, Joker.

"Hello." The joker greeted Brennan cordially as Brennan approached, setting the butt of his long-handled squeegee on the floor and leaning on it as if it were a spear.

"I have to see Father Squid," Brennan said.

Quasiman dropped the squeegee as the hand holding it suddenly vanished. He calmly looked down to where it had been, as if this were something he was used to. After a moment Brennan felt a blast of cold air and caught a whiff of an unbearable stench and Quasiman's hand was back. He leaned over and picked up the squeegee.

"He's meditating in the chancellery," Quasiman said, as if nothing out of the ordinary had occurred.

Brennan nodded. "I know the way." He moved to go by, but the joker laid a hand on his forearm. It was still as cold as ice, but Quasiman either didn't notice or didn't care.

"Do you know who did it yet?" he asked.

Brennan shook his head.

"Then you still may need me?"

"Quite possibly."

Quasiman let go of Brennan's arm. "I'll be ready," he said, then added, "I hope."

I hope so, too, Brennan thought, but only nodded and went past.

In the chancellery Father Squid was in his favorite meditative posture.

"Hello, Sergeant."

The priest started. His eyes snapped open and he looked up at Brennan. He smiled slightly, quivering the tendrils that hung down over his mouth.

"I could never have snuck up on you like that in the old days," Brennan said, sitting down across the desk from the priest.

Father Squid nodded from the comfortable chair where he'd been dozing. "I'm older than I was in the old days. I also sleep a lot better."

Brennan smiled, though there was little humor in his expression. "I did, too, for a while."

"Why don't you give it up and try to find the peace I have?"

"I tried," Brennan said. "I even joined a monastery for a while. A Zen monastery." He smiled at the look of astonishment on the priest's face. "But I was never one of the better students. Violence follows me like an unwelcome shadow. I rarely seek it out, Father, but it finds me wherever I hide."

"So we're back to 'Father,' are we?"

Brennan shrugged. "Whatever you prefer. How many times did you make sergeant, anyway?"

Father Squid smiled. "Four times."

"And you were busted back to private each time."

"Well, I wasn't one for following the rules back then."

"Sometimes you had cause not to," Brennan said. "The Joker Brigade was just an excuse to kill off as many of you as possible."

"Maybe. But there were some good soldiers in it." Father Squid smiled at Brennan. "And some of the units we served with weren't so bad. You never cared if a man had feathers, fur, or hair, or whether he had tentacles on his face and rows of suckers on his hands."

"We were brothers-in-arms," Brennan said softly. "That was all that mattered."

They looked at each other for a long moment, reliving memories of fifteen years gone by.

"What did you do after the war?" Brennan finally asked.

"Not much that I'm proud of. I sold my services for a while. But everywhere I went, as bad as it was in the Joker Brigade, as bad as Jokertown was back home, I found that jokers were generally treated worse outside America." He shrugged massive shoulders. "I tried to do something about it for a while, but I fear I actually did more harm than good."

"I heard once," Brennan said, "that a man called Squidface ran with the Black Dog. I wondered if it was you."

"It was," the priest said heavily. "And much do I regret those days. Never will I be able to do enough penance to cleanse my soul of the horror of the things I did in the name of my people."

"Everyone makes mistakes," Brennan said quietly. "The bad forget them. The good try to make up for them."

"Well," the priest said, his nictitating membranes working quickly, "I'm the one who should be offering spiritual comfort, my son."

Brennan smiled. "Unlike you, I'm afraid that I may be beyond redemption. I could use your help with something else, though."

"The murder."

Brennan nodded. "I've hit a dead end. I've run out of clues and have no one to turn to. I realized last night that you were Chrysalis's confidant, maybe even her confessor. I remembered the bequest she'd left you, and some whispers I'd heard about her secret files."

Father Squid shook his head. "Her bequest was merely a suitcase full of money that she'd stashed away if she ever had to flee the city on short notice. It will do much to aid the poor of my parish, but little, I fear, to help track down her killer."

Brennan grimaced. "Then she never told you anything that might have a bearing on her death?"

"If she did, it was in the sanctity of Confession and is an unshakable confidence that can never be broken."

"Even if her murderer goes free?"

The priest sighed heavily. "Even if her murderer goes free."

Brennan stood, looked steadily at the priest. "You *have* changed," he said. "Sergeant Squidface knew when justice and honor took precedence over a rigid system of rules."

"Sometimes, Captain, I despair of my soul. Sometimes I fear I am as poor a priest as you claim to have been a student of Zen."

Brennan suddenly smiled. "Sometimes, Bob, I think we're both guilty of slinging our share of bullshit."

The priest's tentacles shook with laughter. "You are correct," he said. "Well—Chrysalis did tell me things in the sanctity of the confessional that I cannot reveal to you. But I can tell you that you are overlooking a source of information." He paused dramatically. "Her neighbors, Daniel," Father Squid said. "Her downstairs neighbors."

Brennan's expression was puzzled as Father Squid rose ponderously to his feet.

"Now, if you'll excuse me, I have to prepare for the ten o'clock Mass."

10:00 A.M.

Breakfast arrived as Jay was climbing out of the shower. He toweled himself dry, wondering what he was supposed to do about the damp bandages around his ribs, and slipped into the clothes Tachyon had loaned him. The sleeves were too short and the pants showed off two inches of pale white ankle, but otherwise the suit fit well enough. The only problem was, it was puce.

Tachyon was seated in front of the room-service tray buttering a slice of toast when Jay emerged from the bedroom. Blaise, stretched out across an armchair, looked up and sniggered. Tachyon gave his grandson a stern look. "Blaise, did you enjoy your ride on the luggage carousel?"

The boy looked sullen. "No. I felt stupid."

"Then by the Ideal, you *will* mind your manners," Tachyon told him, "or I will have Mr. Ackroyd teleport you back to the Atlanta airport."

"I can't help it if he's funny," Blaise complained. "He looks like a fruit."

"Those are *my* clothes," Tachyon pointed out stiffly. He looked at Jay. "Myself, I think it's a dramatic improvement."

"I'm with the kid," Jay said. Blaise looked surprised. Then he grinned. Jay whipped up his finger in a quick-draw move, got the boy in his sights. Blaise flinched. "Gotcha," Jay said. He smiled. So did Blaise. Popping the kid halfway across Atlanta had done wonders for their rapport.

"He's enough of a rapscallion without your encouraging him," Tachyon complained.

"Ah, he's okay," Jay said, pulling a chair over to the room-service cart. "For a Takisian." He lifted the silver dome off his plate and attacked the eggs benedict wolfishly. They weren't as good as the eggs benedict at Aces High, but he was hungry enough not to give a damn. Hiram always said Jay had a Naugahyde palate anyway.

Tachyon was fastidiously patting his lips with a napkin and Jay was mopping up the last of the yolk with a piece of toast when the knock came at the door. Tachyon stood. "Who's there?"

"Carnifex. Open up, I don't have all day."

Tachyon glanced back at Jay. "Let him in," Jay said. "Ray's tough, but there's nothing he can do against you, me, and the Cisco Kid over there." He gestured toward Blaise.

The alien nodded and opened the door. Carnifex glanced around and stepped into the suite, wearing his skintight white uniform that outlined every muscle and tendon in his body. The hood was thrown back to reveal a face that looked like it had been patched together out of spare parts. "Regs say we're supposed to stay out of the political bullshit," Ray told Tachyon with disdain. "Good for you. Otherwise I'd have to whip your ass. You been hanging around Braun too much, I guess. Some of it must have rubbed off."

Tachyon's mouth tightened. "Say what you came to say, Ray," he told the government ace. "Your opinions on political and moral issues interest me not in the slightest."

"Gregg wants to see you," Billy Ray said.

"The sentiment is not reciprocated," Tachyon said.

"You'll see him," Ray said, with a crooked smile. "Gregg said to tell you he has a proposition he wants to discuss."

"I have nothing to discuss with the senator."

"Scared?" Ray wanted to know. "Don't worry, I'll hold your hand if you want." He shrugged. "Come or don't come, either way it's no skin off my nose. But if you don't, you're going to regret it." The ace in the white suit looked around the suite: at the windows Turtle had shattered, the television Hiram had dropped, the urine stain on the sofa. "Must have been a hell of a party," he said to Tachyon. "Somebody ought to teach you to clean up after yourself, doc. This place is a mess."

He was going out the door when Jay called out. "Hey, Carny."

Ray turned around with a dangerous glint in his green eyes. "That's Carnifex, asshole."

"Carnifex Asshole," Jay repeated. "I'll try and remember. How many of those Good Humor suits you own?"

"Six or eight," Carnifex said suspiciously. "Why?"

"Must be hell to get the bloodstains out," Jay said.

Ray just stared at him. "Stay out of my way, shamus," he said, "or you'll find out firsthand." He slammed the door behind him.

"Shamus," Jay said. "He actually called me shamus. God, I'm so mortified." He turned to Tachyon. "You gonna go?"

The little man straightened. "I must."

Jay sighed. "I was afraid you were going to say something like that."

♠

Brennan dropped Jennifer off half a block from the Crystal Palace and then cruised on by. Given the mysterious note warning them about the Palace, this seemed the safest way to check out the existence of the neighbors that Father Squid had told him about. Jennifer would scout in her insubstantial form, then come and get Brennan if the coast was clear.

Brennan drove past the Palace and into the alley upon which the service entrance fronted. He killed the engine and flicked on the radio while waiting for Jennifer to return.

The news from Atlanta was more cheering than it had been the night before. Apparently the initial reports of Jack Braun's demise had been greatly exaggerated. He was still alive. Golden Boy's ace had saved him again.

Brennan's train of thought was interrupted by a suddenly blaring bullhorn that froze him behind the wheel.

"You in the car, this is the police. Come out with your hands up! We've got you covered. Come out with your hands up!"

Brennan sat behind the wheel for an instant longer, his mind racing through then discarding half a dozen escape plans. He watched through the windshield as three policemen approached. The two in uniform had pistols pointed right at him. The third, following a pace behind, was Maseryk.

He put his hands up, and then with slow, exaggerated movements opened the door and got out of the car. He stood waiting for them with no expression at all on his face.

"Couldn't keep out of it, could you?" Maseryk asked.

"How's Kant?" Brennan replied.

A shadow of something crossed Maseryk's face. "Still a little shaky, but better."

One of the uniforms had opened the back door of the car while the other kept a bead on Brennan.

"It's him," the first said excitedly. "The bow 'n' arrow killer." He brandished Brennan's bow case.

"You had the Palace staked out, waiting for her killer to return?" Brennan said.

Maseryk shrugged. "It seemed like an idea."

Brennan shook his head in disgust. *That* was what the note meant. Goddamn.

"All right," the first patrolman said. "Put your hands on the fender. Feet back and spread your legs."

Brennan put his hands down, turned to comply. He didn't move fast enough, so the cop kicked his feet further apart and padded him down, finding the knife Brennan carried in an ankle sheath.

"All right, turn around." The cop was smiling as Brennan did. "We caught him, by Jesus, we caught the big, bad vigilante. Put your hands behind your back, big guy."

"Shut up, Chris," Maseryk said wearily as Brennan complied. He continued to speak in the same weary monotone as the patrolman cuffed Brennan. "You have the right to remain silent . . ."

Brennan said nothing, nor offered any resistance. His face was hard as stone as they led him away to a patrol car parked out of sight past a turn in the alley.

♥

Tachyon was practically shaking when he flung open the bedroom door, his bright hair plastered to his forehead by a cold sweat. He looked like he was about to recycle his breakfast. Even Blaise, who'd been talking and joking with Jay, had the sense to shut up when he saw the look in his grandfather's eyes. "Mr. Ackroyd, come in here, please," Tach said. "I need to talk to you."

Jay got to his feet with a shrug. His pants rode up past his ankles. He tried to yank them down as he trailed Tachyon into the sitting room. "What did Hartmann want?" He poked around the room-service tray as he spoke, looking for something edible.

"Mr. Ackroyd, I require a favor of you."

"Sure," Jay said. "Name it."

Tachyon put a hand up. "Do not be so quick to commit yourself. Having me in your debt may not be enough to outweigh what I will ask of you."

Jay found an orange slice. "Jesus Christ, get to the point, Tachyon. All this flowery Takisian bullshit." He bit into the orange and sucked at the juice.

"Hartmann is blackmailing me. I have refused to meet his demands, but I require time. A day, two at the most, and it will be over. Hartmann will have lost the nomination." Tachyon paused for a long moment, his face morose, as if the whole notion made him weary beyond words. "You can give me that time," he concluded finally.

"The point?" Jay prodded. "The *point*?"

"You must remove a man from Atlanta. The more conventional means are closed to us."

This all got weirder every day, Jay thought. "Why?" he asked. "Who is this guy?"

Tachyon turned away from him. There was a snifter on the side table, half-full of brandy. He groped for it like a drowning man groping for a lifesaver, and drained it in a gulp. "Long ago," he said slowly, his back still turned, "I was saved from death by a man who has alternately been a devil and an angel to me."

Devils and angels, just what he needed, as if assassins and aces weren't enough. "Shit," Jay said, throwing up his hands.

"This is difficult for me," Tach whined. He stared down at the empty snifter, rolling it between his palms. Then it all came out in a rush. "In 1957 I was recruited by the KGB. It wasn't all that difficult. I would have done anything for a drink. At any rate, years passed. I proved to be less useful than originally hoped. They cut me loose and I thought I was free. Then last year the man who ran me those many long years ago reentered my life and called in the debt. He's here. In Atlanta."

Jay gaped at him. The notion of the prissy little alien prince working for the Soviets was the craziest thing he'd ever heard. He would have been less surprised if Tachyon had confessed that he was really an elf. "Why?" was all he could manage.

"Hartmann," Tach replied. "He suspected the existence of the monster. Now Hartmann has found out about him, and our connection."

"Connection?" Jay said.

"He is Blaise's tutor."

"Oh hell." Jay sat down. He didn't know whether he should laugh or cry. Laugh, probably; he could always count on Tach to take care of the weeping.

"This is the bludgeon with which Hartmann seeks to cow me," Tachyon declared. "I'm probably going to jail, Mr. Ackroyd. But I'll see him stopped before I go."

"You want me to pop this guy away."

"Yes. Already the FBI and the Secret Service have been alerted. They are combing Atlanta for George."

"Are you still a commie?" Jay asked, straight-faced.

Dr. Tachyon clutched at the little doily he wore at his throat, and drew himself up to his full height. "*I?* Consider, Mr. Ackroyd."

"Yeah," Jay said, "I get your drift." He stood up. "Well, hey, it's all ancient history to me. Let's go pop this commie somewhere."

Tachyon gave him a grave little nod and went to the bedroom. "Blaise," he called.

"You're taking him?" Jay was surprised. "I mean, he knows?"

"Of course. Come, child," he said to Blaise. The teenager shot him a venomous glance, but Tachyon missed it. "I want you to have a chance to say farewell to George."

11:00 A.M.

Captain Angela Ellis stamped out a cigarette in the overflowing ashtray and immediately lit another. She strode up and down before the chair in which Brennan sat, her frustration evident in her staccato pacing.

"How long do you think you can remain silent?" she asked Brennan.

Brennan looked directly at her for the first time in twenty minutes. "Forever," he said softly.

"Christ! Why were you sitting in a car before the Crystal Palace at ten-oh-five this morning? What had been your relationship with Chrysalis? Did you kill her?"

Brennan turned away, his face utterly blank, apparently totally devoid of feeling and emotion.

Maseryk, sitting in the rear of the room, cleared his voice. "Begging your pardon, Captain, but I don't think he'll say anything."

Ellis whirled on him. "Somebody's got to say something! Some idiot let it leak that we've collared Yeoman, the bow-and-arrow killer, and there's gotta be a hundred reporters yammering at the sergeant on the front desk, and about half a dozen federal agencies are sending agents over to 'look into the affair,' as they put it."

"As far as I know," Brennan said softly, "there's nothing illegal in sitting in a car. There's nothing illegal in carrying a bow and arrow."

"Are you saying you're innocent? Are you saying you're not this Yeoman?"

Brennan said nothing as Ellis whirled on him. "You have no identification and your description matches that of a man wanted for desertion from the United States Army."

"Superficially," Brennan said.

"Close enough," Ellis ground out, "so that we can hold you until the feds arrive with this deserter's dossier. Which includes his fingerprints."

"As you will," Brennan said, returning his gaze to infinity.

Ellis ground out her cigarette, then crumpled the empty pack. "All right," she said. She opened the door to the interrogation room and called in the patrolman who'd been standing outside. "Put him in the lockup. Maybe a few hours in a cell will loosen his tongue."

The cop nodded. "All right, tough guy, move it."

"I'm not so sure that's a good idea—" Maseryk began, but Ellis nailed him with a stare, and he fell silent.

The cop led Brennan through a warren of interrogation rooms and offices, then downstairs to the general lockup. There were more than a dozen hardcases in there, waiting for bail to be arranged or other legal papers to be processed. They were a surly, tough-looking group.

The jailer grinned as he opened the door and gestured for Brennan to enter. "Got someone famous for you guys to meet. His name's been in all the papers," he said. "You've heard of Yeoman, the bow-and-arrow vigilante? Well, here he is." He chuckled again, slammed the door, and sauntered back up the corridor.

Brennan felt their hard stares and waited for the inevitable. It didn't take very long.

"Shoot," someone said from the back of the cell. "He don't look too tough to me."

"He looks like a pussy," someone else said. "Take away his bow and arrow and he's just a pussy."

There was some low, cautious laughter. The man who spoke first pushed his way to the front of the cell where Brennan stood with his back against the bars. He was a big, tough-looking nat with tattoos crawling up and down his arms and a nose that'd been broken more than once. The second speaker was shorter than Brennan, but powerfully built. His head was bald and his face was a network of scars. They approached Brennan side by side as the others in the cell backed away.

"He is a pussy," the first said. "Here pussy, pussy, pussy. We got something for you."

Brennan watched without expression. When they came within reach, he pivoted sideways and lashed out with his right foot, catching the short one in the groin. The man went down with a gurgle and then threw up all over himself. Brennan grabbed the other by the arm and whirled him face-first against the cell's barred door.

The door shook when the thug rammed up against it. His left arm went through the bars. Brennan reached out and grabbed his hand, then yanked his arm back into the cell, wrapping it between two bars. He howled as his arm snapped. Brennan grabbed a handful of greasy hair and shoved his head forward as hard as he could. It pushed through the bars, but not without leaving a lot of skin and one ear behind.

His howling grew louder, and Brennan turned to face the rest of the cell.

"Anyone else?" he asked quietly.

There were mumbled denials, then a high, feminine voice said, "How about me?"

The mob of thugs parted like the Red Sea and there were awed, unbelieving whispers as Jennifer walked naked through the rear wall of the cell. She ran to Brennan and threw her arms around him. "Take a deep breath," she said, and they sank through the floor of the cell.

It was like nothing Brennan had ever felt before, almost like what dying might be like. They went through the floor and landed, light as feathers, on the floor of the room below the cell.

Brennan ducked out of Jennifer's arms and glanced around quickly. It was dark and quiet. They seemed to be in some kind of file-storage area.

"Let's see if we can find you some clothes somewhere," he said to Jennifer, but she didn't answer. She looked dazed and drawn, and only turned to look at him when he touched her arm. He suddenly realized what a strain it must have been ghosting him. His mass was well over anything Jennifer had ever attempted to dematerialize before. "Are you all right?" he asked.

Jennifer nodded, but even that seemed to be too much of an effort for her. She collapsed limply on the dusty floor. He bent over her. She was breathing long, shallow breaths. Her pulse was weak and thready.

She obviously needed medical attention, but Tachyon, the only doctor Brennan trusted, was in Atlanta. At any rate, he had no time to agonize over it. They had to move. They needed a place to hide and recover. They needed a sanctuary.

♣

They were being followed.

Jay looked away from the taxi's sideview mirror. "Somebody's on us," he said.

"What?" Tachyon turned all the way around and gaped out the back rear window, staring suspiciously at the Volvo immediately behind.

Jay touched his arm. "Easy. He's good. You'll never spot him that way. Cabby." The detective fished out his wallet. "There's an extra fifty in it for you if you can lose the gray Dodge. Back about three cars."

"Sure thing, mister," the cabbie said, grinning.

Jay rummaged through his billfold, found a ten and three ones, cursed under his breath. A bribe here, a bribe there, pretty soon they add up to real money. He showed the bills to Tachyon. The alien grumbled and came up with the cash, leaning forward to tuck the money into the driver's shirt pocket. The cabbie hit the gas, and the taxi turned left, squealing. Tachyon landed in Jay's lap.

In the front seat, Blaise grinned hugely. "Just like Paris, K'ijdad."

"Huh?" Jay's mind was on the car behind them.

"Never mind," said Tach. "You know enough of my secrets."

Jay glanced behind. "Still on us. Damn, he's good."

Tach was flitting about, as nervous as a bird. "What are we going to do?"

"There's probably not going to be time for any long good-byes."

The Motel 6 sign loomed ahead.

"Sara's there, too," said Tachyon.

It took Jay a moment to place the name; Sara Morgenstern, the reporter who accused Hartmann of being a monster, the one Mackie Messer had tried unsuccessfully to snuff. "Jesus Christ. You got the whole New York Philharmonic there? Maybe the Dodgers?"

"This is no laughing matter."

"No shit. Punch it, buddy. Everything she's got."

The cab gunned down the street, veered into the motel lot on two wheels. They were out before it stopped. Jay threw his last ten at the driver and ran, his broken rib screaming with every step as he dashed across the asphalt.

The door was opened by a dark, round-faced man in his sixties. Behind him on the bed, a pale blond woman clutched a pillow as she watched the tube. The Russian backed up quickly as the three of them rushed inside. Jay slammed the door and locked it. Tachyon went straight for the blonde and yanked her to her feet. Blaise hugged the Russian.

"No time to explain," Tachyon said breathlessly. "Hartmann knows. There is someone after us." He grabbed the front of the girl's dress and ripped it off her with a single sharp yank. Sara gave a shriek and tried to cover herself with her hands, looking at the alien like he'd gone nuts. "Into the shower," Tach said, pushing her toward the john. She was wearing nothing but a little lacy bit of bra. Her pubic hair was the same pale blond, Jay noted with interest. "Don't come out, and by the way, you rent by the hour." Tach got the bra off on the run. Jay had to admire his manual dexterity.

Footsteps came pounding down the hall outside.

The Russian took it calmly. "There's no time," he said, holding Blaise.

"Yes, there is," said Tach. "Jay will get you out of Atlanta. For the god's sake, Blaise, *move!*"

The Russian disentangled himself from the boy.

"Open up! Open the goddamn door!"

Jay knew the voice. Carnifex.

"*Now!*" Tachyon urged.

Jay shrugged, pointed at the Russian. There was a *pop*. All of a sudden they were short a Slav. Tach grabbed some vodka off a dresser, clutched it to his chest, and dove onto the bed.

The door shattered with a *crack*. Billy Ray stepped through the splinters, brushing aside a jagged shard of wood with the back of his head. He had a gun. A big gun, one of those Dirty Harry jobs. The white gloves he wore as part of his fighting togs made it look even bigger and blacker. He pointed it at Tachyon, which was fine with Jay. He hated guns, especially when they were pointed at him. "All right, where is he?" Ray wanted to know. "Where the fuck is he?"

"Huh?" asked Jay.

"Asshole!" Carnifex shoved at him contemptuously with the flat of his hand. Jay sat down hard. Carnifex looked around, spotted the closet, and acted like he'd made a discovery. He ripped the door off its hinges, grabbed handfuls of clothes, flung them to the floor. There was no Russian in the closet. Ray grimaced, dropped to his knees, peered under the bed. There was no Russian under the bed. He got up, swung toward the bathroom. "Get out of there. Now!"

"Wal, sugah, how many you boys there gonna be?" Sara called out from under the shower, in the worst Southern accent Jay Ackroyd had ever heard.

Frowning, Carnifex stepped into the bathroom. They heard him yank back the shower curtain. They heard Sara scream. They heard a slap. Ray came out of the bathroom with a red cheek and a wet costume, looking dour. "He was here. That goddamn Russian was here."

"Russian?" Jay looked at Tachyon, shrugged. "I don't see any Russian. Do you see a Russian? And sweetcheeks in there sure don't sound Russian. Russian costs you extra."

"Why did you try to get away from me?"

Tachyon took a long drink. "Because I was afraid you were the press, and I didn't want to be found visiting a prostitute."

"You always take a kid?" He gestured at Blaise with the .44.

"Could you put the gun away? It makes me nervous when you wave it around like that. Most fatal shootings are accidental, you know."

"This wouldn't be an accident. Answer the fucking question."

Tachyon cleared his throat. "Well, that is the matter in a nutshell. It's time the boy learned." He glanced about the motel room. "This lacks the ambience that I could wish, but she is *very* good. I tried her myself last night. Of course, nothing can compare with the woman my father gave me on my fourteenth birthday—"

Disgusted, Carnifex bulled out through the broken door.

Jay looked at Tachyon with new respect. "Fourteen?" he said. "No kidding?"

"Oh Ackroyd, *please!*"

1:00 P.M.

Brennan carried Jennifer, wrapped up in his denim jacket, down into the sewer line. She seemed to be getting worse. Her skin was feeling cool and feverish in turn, and she was murmuring gibberish that Brennan couldn't make heads or tails of.

He moved as quickly as he could through the semidarkness of the sewer. He had to stop every now and then and put Jennifer down in order to climb to the surface to check his route, but Brennan had a good sense of direction below as well as above ground. It led him with only a few false turns to his destination. Our Lady of Perpetual Misery. He carried Jennifer back up to the surface and over to the small rectory attached to the rear of the church. He kicked the door several times with his foot. Father Squid opened the door after a moment, his look of annoyance quickly turning to one of surprise and concern.

"Merciful Lord," he said, "what happened?"

"I'll tell you in a moment, Father," Brennan said, pushing past the priest. "Right now we have to get a doctor. One you can trust to keep his mouth shut. Know anybody that fits that description?"

"Well, there's Mr. Bones—"

"Get him."

"He's not a real doctor—"

"Is he good?"

Father Squid nodded. "The people around here swear by him. Sometimes I think he knows more about joker physiology than Tachyon."

Brennan nodded. "All right. Get him."

Father Squid bustled off to his bedroom to make the call, while Brennan set Jennifer down gently on the priest's beat-up old sofa and then flexed his tired arms. He knelt down by her and felt her forehead. It was cold again, although sweat was beading up and running down her forehead and high cheekbones.

As he held her hand it began to turn ghostly in his as she phased in and out of her material state, uncontrollably and unconsciously.

"Jennifer!" He tried to wake her up, but she didn't seem to hear him. He was afraid to shake her, afraid to move her at all.

Her skin was white as death, her breath infrequent and shallow.

Father Squid came back into his neat little living room, bringing a blanket that he gently draped over Jennifer. "He was in. He'll be here soon. Now, tell me, my son, what's going on here?"

"I guess I owe you that," Brennan said. He settled down tiredly on the floor next to Jennifer, refused the priest's offer of coffee, and told him what had happened that day.

While he spoke, half of his mind was condemning the obsession that had put him and Jennifer in this desperate situation, and half was wondering about the palace and Chrysalis's downstairs neighbors, and how he could get by the police surrounding the place.

When he finished the tale, there was a slow, measured knocking on the rectory door. Father Squid went to answer it and let in a tall black man who looked like a resurrectionist out of a Boris Karloff movie. Mr. Bones was old, thin, and gaunt. He wore a white shirt and an old black suit that was clean and neatly repaired, but much too short for his long, lanky limbs.

This joker wasn't severe as things went. In fact, the two feathery antennae growing out of his forehead were rather attractive. They twitched like ferns blowing in a gentle breeze as Father Squid introduced him to Brennan.

"This the patient?" Bones asked as he knelt down before Jennifer. He stripped the blanket off her. As he took her pulse he bent very close to her and moved his head up and down her body. His antennae twitched and rotated like sensitive radar receptors.

"How is she, doctor?" Brennan asked quietly.

"I'm not a doctor," Bones replied, still running his antennae over Jennifer. After a moment he rocked back on his heels and looked at Brennan and Father Squid. "Her system's had quite a shock. Right now all we can do for her is let her rest." He covered her with the blanket and stood up. "And hope for the best."

4:00 P.M.

"So, Nephi," Jay said, leaning against the hood of Jesse Jackson's limo. Tachyon was inside the Hyatt Regency, conferring with his new candidate, and Ackroyd was getting tired of waiting. "The feds pay good, or what?"

Jesse Jackson's ace bodyguard looked at him like he was some kind of canker sore. He was a tall thin Mormon with a receding hairline, a gaunt chiseled face, and the best damn posture Jay had ever seen. The press called him Straight Arrow; the nameplate over his breast pocket said NEPHI CALLENDAR. "Some of us are not interested in personal gain," he told Jay. "Some of us are just grateful for a chance to serve God and our country."

Jay smiled. "Yeah, sure. And some of you just like to beat people up, right?"

Straight Arrow frowned and looked away.

"Heard that Carnifex got in some kind of brawl Sunday night," Jay said casually. "Or maybe it was Monday morning. Really pounded the shit out of some guy."

"Is that a fact?" Callendar did not seem terribly interested. "I wouldn't know. I'm sure no more force was applied than was appropriate to the situation. Ray is an experienced agent with an outstanding record."

"A hell of a dresser, too," Jay said. "Me, I don't think I could wear all that white. It's a bitch to keep clean. I like your outfit a lot better." The Mormon ace wore a tailored gray dress uniform. It looked very crisp and proper and military, until you picked up on the Justice Department insignia on the sleeves and the dark red braid on cap and shoulder boards. His collar was fastened with a jeweled pin fashioned in the shape of a flaming arrow. "Free laundry service come with the job, or you guys have to pay the dry cleaning yourself?" Jay wanted to know.

Straight Arrow took a long pointed look at Jay's puce suit. "I'd recommend burning, not cleaning," he said.

"Funny man," Jay said. "These are Tachy's. I think he wants them back, don't ask me why."

"Why all the interest in laundry, Ackroyd?"

"When my face got rearranged, I bled all over my lucky shirt." The bruises were a delightful greenish yellow shade today. "You know how it is when you got a lucky shirt. I figured you feds might know a place where I could get it cleaned. I hear that Carnifex had blood all over him after his little fracas on Sunday night."

"You shouldn't believe everything you hear, Ackroyd," Callendar told him. "As far as I know, Ray was with Senator Hartmann Sunday night, as per his assignment. If a situation arose requiring him to use force, regulations would have required that he file a report. No such report is on file."

Before Jay could reply, Tachyon emerged through the front door of the Hyatt, Jesse Jackson at his side. The sidewalk was crowded with Jackson supporters waving bright red JESSE! signs. Straight Arrow's eyes moved restlessly, scanning the faces, as the two men clasped hands and lifted them over their heads. The black man was so much taller that Tachyon had to stand on his toes.

A ragged cheer went up, then Jackson and Tachyon headed for the limo, smiling and shaking hands as the spectators crowded in around them. Jackson pressed the flesh with practiced ease, but Tachyon looked distinctly uncomfortable.

"What now?" Jay asked Tachyon when he reached the limo.

"Jesse wants us to talk to the jokers outside the Omni," Tachyon explained. He was wilting in the Atlanta heat. "He and I together. His positions on wild-card issues are just as strong as Hartmann's, if they will only listen . . ." He gave a long deep sigh. "Jay, if you have other leads to follow up, there's really no need for you to come along."

Jay thought about it for a moment. As far as he knew, he didn't have a single lead that was worth a damn. He shrugged. "Might as well," he said, "can't dance."

Inside the limo, the air-conditioning was cranked up and cooking, but Tachyon wilted visibly once out of the public eye. Even Jay could see how much he dreaded facing the jokers who had gathered in front of the convention center, many of whom considered him a traitor for deserting Hartmann in his hour of need. "They hate me now," he said with despair, glancing through the tinted windows at the crowds.

"Only some," Jackson said as the limo came to a stop. "It's not as if you switched your support to Barnett. I'm not *that* unacceptable, am I?"

"Not to me." Tachyon squeezed Jesse's arm. Jay wasn't sure who was reassuring whom. "And you will convince them. I know it."

"Well, help me a little."

"I will do my uttermost best," Tachyon declared.

The limo doors were thrown open, and they climbed out one by one. Secret Service men in dark suits and sunglasses were watching the crowd suspiciously, and a squad of uniformed cops had cordoned off a narrow path from the limo to the flatbed truck, hung with red Jackson banners, where the microphones were waiting. Jokers pressed closely around them on all sides. Some stared in dead silence. Others grinned and yelled out their support. Still others screamed obscenities. Everyone was cooking in the heat.

"How can they hate them so?" Tachyon asked plaintively of no one in particular. "They are pitiful, and so brave. So very brave."

The cops struggled to hold back that sea of twisted humanity as the jokers surged forward. Slowly, the party began to make its way down to the truck. Hands were thrust at them from all sides, between the linked arms of the policemen, over their shoulders, around their backs. Jesse moved along one side of the line, grabbing each hand in turn, giving it a quick squeeze, then moving on to the next. Tachyon, less enthusiastic, worked the other side. An elderly man with gills spat in his face. Others tried to kiss his ring.

Jay kept his hands shoved deep in his pockets, several paces behind. Straight Arrow walked beside him, keeping a careful eye on Jackson. The ace's broad forehead was dotted with sweat.

Overhead the Turtle slid across the sky. Sometime during the night someone had painted HARTMANN! across his shell in silver letters three feet high.

A vast, pale wall of moon-faced flesh suddenly loomed up behind two policemen, broke through the cordon, and waddled toward Tachyon. Secret Service men reached for their pistols. "No, it's okay," Jay said, "that's Doughboy. He's simple-minded, but he won't hurt him." Straight Arrow weighed Jay's words, gave a curt nod. The Secret Service relaxed. Doughboy and Tachyon exchanged a few quiet words. The alien looked like he was going to break down and cry.

"I hate this," Straight Arrow muttered.

Somewhere in the crowd, a chant of "traitor!" went up. Tachyon stopped and hid his face in his hands. Jesse had to put an arm around his shoulders and whisper encouragement in his ear to get the Takisian going again. Even then, Tach's smile looked like it had been pasted on. The alien grasped the flipper of a legless joker who had thrust it up between a policeman's legs. He said a few words, smiled, moved on. More hands reached for him.

A thin teenager in worn leathers slid through the crowd, smiling, just three people down the line. How the hell could anyone wear leather in this heat? Jay wondered briefly.

He was glancing away when something—the hunger in that lean face, the bright glitter in the boy's eyes—caught his attention and held it.

Tachyon touched—oh so lightly—the twisted fingers of a foul-smelling joker whose huge boils oozed with pus. He looked a little green, but he forced a smile.

One of the boy's shoulders was higher than the other.

"NO!" Jay screamed, moving forward, hands sliding out of his pockets.

The boy grasped Tachyon's hand. "I'm Mackie Messer," Jay heard him say as the buzz saw kicked in.

◆

"I was in medical school in 1946," Mr. Bones said between sips of tea, "when the wild card came down out of the sky. My deformity was slight, but enough to get me banished from school. It was unusual enough to be a black man in medical school, but a joker black man couldn't be tolerated."

"You use your antennae in your work, don't you?" Brennan asked.

Bones nodded. "After a while I discovered that they've given me a sixth sense, somewhere between taste and smell and touch that's probably about as hard to describe as sight to a blind man. Through the years I've learned to use it to help detect wrongness in my patients."

He put down his cup and turned to Jennifer as she moaned loudly, the first sound she'd made in hours. He ran his antennae over her body, listened to her heartbeat, and said to Brennan, "Give me my bag."

Brennan brought it over and put it beside him. He reached in for a hypodermic and a bottle of clear fluid, and gave her an injection. Her breathing was fluttery and rapid, her forehead was beaded with sweat. She sat straight up and cried out, "Daniel, where are you, Daniel?" It seemed she couldn't see him even though he was standing right next to her.

Bones moved over and gestured for Brennan to take his place. He knelt down and held Jennifer. She clung to him fiercely and her skin was cold even though she was soaked with sweat.

"Daniel," she murmured, and suddenly went limp.

Brennan looked at Bones desperately, who reassuringly put a large-knuckled hand on his shoulder.

"It's all right, son, let her down gently. I think she's passed the crisis point."

Brennan held her at arms' length and looked at her. She seemed to be sleeping deeply. Her breath was firm and measured. He let her down against the pillow and she sighed and turned over.

"She needs sleep," Bones said. "I'm going to give her a sedative and I don't want her to be disturbed for at least twenty-four hours."

A vast sense of relief swept through Brennan. "She'll be all right?" he asked.

Bones nodded.

"Thanks, doctor—I mean, Mr. Bones. What do I owe you?"

Bones shrugged lean shoulders. "I don't have set fees. My patients pay what they can."

Brennan reached for his denim jacket, which was slung over a chair next to the sofa. He took a flat roll of money from a secret pocket sewn into the inside and gave it all to Bones.

"This is all I have with me," he said. "If there's anything else you ever need, call this number and I'll do what I can."

Brennan scribbled the number down on a piece of paper he took from Father Squid's secretary and handed it to him.

Bones riffled through the money Brennan had given him. "You're very generous," he said.

Brennan shook his head as he watched Jennifer sleep peacefully on the sofa. "You've done more for me than I could ever repay. I'll always be in your debt."

♠

Under the high, thin shriek of Tach's screaming was the hideous wet sound of a power saw cutting meat. Fingers and pieces of flesh and bone were flying everywhere. The boy stood there, fine drops of Tachyon's blood spattering his face and arm and leathers with a sound like summer rain, all the time smiling, his mouth open just a little, tongue moving slightly across his lower lip.

It seemed to Jay like he was moving in slow motion. His hand came up, fingers sliding into the shape of a gun. . . .

Tachyon staggered back, blood jetting from the ragged ruin of his right hand. The boy's hands were a blur. A cop grabbed him by the jacket. The leather boy sliced off his arm clean at the shoulder like it was the easiest thing in the world and turned back to Tachyon. The alien had stumbled to his knees. The boy reached down for him, almost gently, as if he were going to caress his cheek, stroke that long red hair.

But Jay was pointing. No one heard the *pop*. Too many people were screaming. But suddenly Mackie Messer was gone.

Dazed, trembling, Jay was hardly aware of the big blond man who came crashing out of the crowd an instant later, glowing as yellow as a bug light and staggering almost in a circle as he punched at an assassin who was no longer there. "*Who did that?*" he shouted. All around them people were shouting, running into each other. The Secret Service had knocked down Jesse and covered him with their bodies. "An ambulance," a distant voice was calling. "Someone get an ambulance. Dammit, dammit, someone get an ambulance." Everybody was waving guns and Straight Arrow was holding a flaming arrow up over his head. TV cameras were circling like sharks. Jay heard someone say "Ackroyd," but he wasn't sure who. The policeman was still making a hideous noise, but Tachyon had fallen silent. When Jay reached him, the little alien lay on the pavement, still as death, his eyes closed, his right arm clutched to his chest. Blood still came in short, ragged spurts from his wrist, and the ruffles of his lace shirt were as red as his hair. Jay smelled something burning somewhere behind him. Then he was shoved aside, none too gently. Straight Arrow knelt over Tachyon. Dimly, from his own haze of confusion and shock, Jay watched. The man held his hands over the raw wet stump. Pale yellow flames leapt from his fingertips, and the smell of burning flesh filled the air. Tachyon's body thrashed feebly. The stump was black and seared when Callendar stood up. A couple of paramedics lifted Tachyon onto a stretcher. Jay wasn't sure when they'd arrived.

"Ackroyd," someone said. Jay looked around. Straight Arrow was talking to him. "Where did you send him?"

Jay couldn't think straight. "Yeah," he said. His hand was still clenched tightly in its gun shape. He flexed his fingers, ran them through his hair. "Oh Jesus," he said, patting himself to make sure he was intact.

"*You!*" someone bellowed at him. It was the big blond guy. He looked almost as young as the leather boy. "Who the hell *are* you?"

"Jay Ackroyd," Straight Arrow told him. "Private cop. They call him Popinjay."

"I *had* the bastard!" The blond guy made a fist, crushing a pack of cigarettes that he didn't seem to realize he was holding. Little bits of tobacco drippled down over his pants. "I could have turned him into *Jell-O!* Aw, fuck!" He threw down the squashed cigarettes and kicked them into the crowd. Suddenly Jay recognized Golden Boy. The reports of Braun's death were obviously exaggerated. Nobody ever told him anything.

"Where'd you send him, Ackroyd?" Straight Arrow asked.

"Popped him . . ." His lips were very dry. When he licked them, Jay tasted blood.

The Mormon ace grabbed his lapels and shook him. "*Where'd you send the assassin?*"

"Oh," Jay said. "New York. The Tombs."

Straight Arrow let him go. "Good."

But Golden Boy was a lot less pleased. "*He walks through walls!*"

he yelled. He seemed to feel a need to scream everything. Jay was starting to understand why Braun had never made it as an actor. "He's *out* by now."

That made Straight Arrow very unhappy. The Mormon gave a long sigh, then turned and walked away. Jay followed him, leaving Braun alone with his histrionics. "Tachyon," Jay asked, grabbing Callendar by the arm. "Is he going to live?"

"Only God can answer that question, Ackroyd. Pray."

6:00 P.M.

Brennan sat in Father Squid's rectory, waiting for the dark. The priest was out on an errand for Brennan. Jennifer was still sleeping peacefully on the couch. Brennan had turned on the Father's small black-and-white television, and with the volume turned way down was watching with disbelief the day's events in Atlanta.

The highlight, shown repeatedly from every conceivable angle—and in excruciating slow motion—was Tachyon losing his hand. It was shown again and again until Brennan thought he was going to be sick. The latest word accompanying the footage was that Tachyon had lost a lot of blood and that he'd had such a severe shock to his system that the wound might prove fatal.

Brennan prayed that the little alien would pull through. They were friends and comrades, having fought both the Swarm and the Shadow Fists together, but also Brennan felt that Tachyon was one of the few people in the world who understood his motivations. Tachyon knew why he'd been compelled to fight Kien and the Shadow Fists. He had a sense of personal duty as deep as Brennan's.

As he watched the clip of Tachyon losing his hand for the nth time, Brennan suddenly recognized someone else in the scene. Popinjay was at Tachyon's side. What the hell was the PI doing in Atlanta? Had he abandoned Chrysalis's case, or had some clue taken him to the convention?

As Brennan was wondering about all this, Father Squid returned, carrying a gym bag and a large, flat-sided leather case. He put the bags down before Brennan and said seriously, "I don't know if I should be encouraging you in this, Daniel."

"You're not encouraging me, Father. You know that I'm doing only what must be done." He unzipped the leather case and took out his backup bow. The police had his other bow, and most of his arrows, but Brennan had some left. Enough, he hoped.

He opened up his gym bag and took out a black jumpsuit. He draped it over a chair and continued to wait for the dark.

8:00 P.M.

"I wish George was here," Blaise said.

For a moment Jay thought the boy was talking about George Bush. The hospital waiting room had two television sets, both tuned to the convention, and he'd been hearing a lot about George Bush from the commentators. He was about to tell the kid that the last thing any of them needed right now was a Republican when it dawned on him that Blaise meant his jolly old KGB uncle. "George is in New York," Jay told him. Mackie Messer was in New York, too, but he wasn't in the Tombs. Jay had phoned. Mackie had freaked out, turned a couple of his cellmates into Alpo, and walked right through the bars.

The carnage in front of the Omni kept playing and replaying in his head, like a bad splatter movie. Jack Braun was one of the champion weenies of all time, but maybe he was right, maybe Jay *had* fucked up, had inadvertently saved Mackie Messer by popping him away before Braun could get to him. Or maybe he'd saved Tachyon's life. He just wasn't sure. And whether Golden Boy could actually have gotten to Mackie or not, teleporting him into the Tombs had been a ghastly mistake. There were other places Jay could have picked, empty, deserted places where no one would have died. Mackie was psychotic, he knew that from Digger, he should have thought about what his reaction would be when he found himself in that cell. But there hadn't been *time* to think. Everything had happened so goddamned fast. . . .

A horsefly was buzzing around Jay's head. He brushed it away and sighed. This afternoon was over. There was nothing he could do about it now. Except live with it. For a long, long time.

They were the last ones left in the waiting room. A few reporters still haunted the steps outside, but only family, friends, and VIPs had been admitted to the hospital itself. There had been quite a few during the first hour of their vigil. Jokers by the score had come and gone, some bearing flowers or books or other tokens of their esteem. Hiram Worchester sat with Jay for almost an hour during the dinner recess, pale and silent. "I have to get back to the floor," he said when he finally stood to leave. "Tell him I was here." Jay had promised that he would. Leo Barnett prayed for Tachyon and the TV cameras during his visit. "Lord," the reverend had proclaimed, "Hear me now, and spare this sinner. Grant him his life, that he may come to wisdom at last, and know Your power and mercy, O Lord, and accept You into his heart as his personal savior." Carnifex had swung by briefly, flashed his badge, and grilled one of the doctors. Jay was too far away to overhear what was said, but Ray seemed satisfied. A man in a cheap rubber frog mask had stuck it out longest, pacing restlessly as they waited for word, finally leaving as quietly as he had come. He was the last; now there was only Jay and Blaise.

"You think Tisianne is going to die?" Blaise asked. He didn't sound very upset about the possibility; his tone was more one of idle curiosity than of fear.

"Nah," Jay said. "If he was going to die, he'd have done it already. We been here, what, three hours? They got to have him stabilized by now." He wasn't sure who he was trying to reassure, the boy or himself.

"If he dies, *Baby* belongs to me," Blaise mused.

"Baby?" Jay said, confused. "What baby?"

"That's his *spaceship*," the boy said, with all of a child's contempt for an adult who didn't know something he assumed everyone ought to know. "It's a stupid name. I'm going to think up a better name for her when she's mine."

"Tachyon's not dead yet," Jay said.

Blaise yawned. He was stretched out across his chair in a boneless sprawl that said he could care less, his legs thrown up carelessly on the coffee table. "Was it really as gross as they say?" he asked.

His eyes moved restlessly, tracking the fly as it circled around his head. "The Secret Service guy, the one who drove me, he said there was blood and fingers and everything just flying through the air."

"It was real ugly," Jay said. The conversation was making him distinctly uncomfortable.

"I bet he cried," Blaise said contemptuously. "He should have let me come, I could have grabbed the guy with my mind, just like *that*!" He shot his hand out suddenly and caught the fly in his fist. Jay could hear it buzzing between the boy's fingers. "I could have made him cut himself up." Blaise closed his fist hard around the fly. "That would have been something," he said casually, opening his fingers and staring at the remains of the insect with a strange little smile on his face.

Jay had a sudden image of the little hunchback killer lopping off his fingers one by one and singing "I'm a Little Teapot" as blood fountained from the stumps. "You know, Blaise," he said, "you are one weird fucking kid." Maybe he was being uncharitable. The boy might be in shock, terrified at the thought of losing his only living relative, hiding fear beneath a pose of indifference and adolescent bravado. Only somehow Jay didn't think so.

The boy looked up at him. Beneath his tousled mass of glittery red hair, his eyes regarded Jay haughtily. They were purple, Jay saw, so dark that they were almost black. Under the bright fluorescent light of the hospital waiting room, they looked like pools of violet ink. "I'm not a kid," Blaise informed Jay. "On Takis I'd be leaving the women's quarters."

"Figures," Jay said. "Just when you get old enough to want in, they throw you out."

9:00 P.M.

The tunnels were dark, deserted, and very quiet. Brennan had figured they would be. He knew that the police had staked out the Crystal Palace, but he'd hoped they didn't know about the secret underground entrance Chrysalis had built.

And they didn't. At least so far it seemed as if they didn't. Brennan had left Father Squid's rectory with the priest still watching over a sleeping Jennifer and had gone underground two blocks from the Palace. He left the main line at Henry Street and went down the tunnel he'd used to gain access to the Palace the night he'd surprised the Oddity in Chrysalis's bedroom.

There was, he remembered, a short spur off the tunnel that he'd never investigated before. He stopped before it, debating his course of action, the only light a dim beam from the flashlight he held in one hand. In the other was his bow, already assembled.

As he stood there debating with himself he heard a noise coming from the tunnel before him. It was a small, skittering noise, as of many tiny feet trying to be silent. He shone his light into the darkness with little effect.

He didn't want to keep the flashlight illuminating himself as the perfect target in the otherwise dark tunnel, but he couldn't stand the thought of turning it off and standing there in utter blackness.

He put it down at his feet and backed away, taking an arrow out of his quiver and placing it on his bowstring.

As he stepped out of the feeble circle of light cast by his flashlight, he heard a voice. Her voice.

"Daniel, my dear archer. You don't have to be afraid of me."

It was Chrysalis's voice—or her ghost's. There was no denying it.

♥

The double doors to the waiting room opened with a bang. "Are you the family?" a tired voice asked.

Jay got to his feet. "I'm a friend," he said. He jerked a thumb toward Blaise. "He's the grandson."

"Grandson?" The doctor sounded momentarily nonplussed. "Oh, that's right," he finally said. "I keep forgetting the patient is older than he looks, isn't that right?"

"The question is not how old he is," Jay said. "The question is, is he going to get any older?"

"He's suffered massive blood loss, not to mention major systemic shock," the doctor told them. "And it appears he was in a terribly weakened condition to begin with. Fortunately, first aid was applied at the scene; that made all the difference. Any more blood loss and he might have been DOA. We started him on plasma as soon as he arrived. The hand . . . I'm afraid we had to lose it. It wasn't a clean cut, you have to realize, the paramedics brought us two of the fingers, but with the way the flesh was . . . well, chewed up . . . ah, there just wasn't a hand to reattach them to. Amputation seemed the only viable op—"

"Okay," Jay snapped impatiently, "so from now on, if he loses one mitten, it's no big deal. Is he going to live?"

The doctor blinked at him, then nodded. "Yes," he said. "Yes, I believe we've pulled him through. We're listing his condition as serious but stable."

"I want to see him," Blaise said, in his most imperious tone.

"I'm afraid we don't allow visitors in the intensive-care unit," the doctor said. "Perhaps tomorrow we can move—"

"Take us to him *now*," Blaise said. Those dark purple-black eyes narrowed just a little. He grinned boyishly.

The doctor spun on his heels, straight-armed the double doors, and led them back to the ICU without another word.

A bag of plasma hung over one side of the bed, an IV bottle over the other. Tachyon had tubes in his arms and more tubes up his nose, wires attached everywhere. His eyes were closed, but Jay could see his chest rise and fall beneath the thin cotton of his hospital gown.

"He's heavily sedated," the doctor said softly. Blaise must have let him go. "For the pain."

Jay nodded and glanced over at Blaise. The boy was staring down at his grandfather with a look of ferocious intensity on his face. His eyes glistened, and for a moment Jay thought he saw a tear there. Then he realized it was only the moving readout on the monitor, reflected in the iris of his eyes. "C'mon, Blaise," he said. "There's nothing we can do here."

They passed through the waiting room again on the way out of the hospital. Up on the television screen, the convention was going crazy. Jesse Jackson was standing at the podium. People were screaming, balloons were falling from the ceiling, signs were waving madly, and the band had struck up a rousing chorus of "Happy Days Are Here Again." Jay had a bad feeling. He stopped by the nurses' station. "What's happened?" he asked the nurse on call.

"Jesse just gave a speech. You should have heard him, it brought tears to my eyes. He's throwing his delegates to Hartmann. It's all over but the voting."

Over? Jay wanted to tell her. Lady, it's just beginning. But he chewed his lip and said nothing.

Blaise stood in front of the television, looking almost happy. When Jay came back over, he looked up eagerly. "They're going to nominate Hartmann, just like George said they would."

The network cut away from the convention floor to the streets of Atlanta. Thousands of jokers were dancing in the streets. Outside the Omni the *"Hart-mann"* cry went up, louder and louder. An impromptu parade was starting on Peachtree, a conga line that grew as it moved. Piedmont Park was one huge explosion of joy. The network cut from park to convention floor to street, letting the moment speak for itself. Jay put his hand on Blaise's shoulder and was just about to say that it was time they got back to the hotel when the boy said, "Hey, look, Sascha."

Jay looked. They were showing Piedmont Park, where a dozen jokers were dancing giddily around a bonfire while fifty others watched. He was standing just behind the dancers, the flames of the fire shining off slicked dark hair, pencil-thin mustache, and that pale eyeless face.

"Sonofabitch," Jay said. He'd almost forgotten about Sascha. He shouldn't have; the skinny fuck had some answers he needed. He was about to tell Blaise to head back to the Marriott on his own when he remembered what the kid could do with his mind control. All of a sudden Jay had a better idea. "Hey, kid," he said. "Want to play detective?"

♣

Brennan didn't believe in ghosts, but whatever was approaching from down the dark tunnel and speaking in Chrysalis's voice couldn't be Chrysalis. Chrysalis was dead. He'd seen her in her coffin. The face in the window had only been a dream.

He backed away until he stood against the side of the tunnel and couldn't move anymore.

"Daniel," the voice said, "I want to help you," and the speaker stepped into the light.

Brennan lowered his bow, dumbfounded. He couldn't believe his eyes. It *was* Chrysalis. A miniature Chrysalis, perfect in every detail, but no more than eighteen inches tall. Now he knew why the window had appeared so large in what he thought was his dream.

He squatted down to see her better as she approached fearlessly. The manikin mimicked her perfectly, down to the red painted fingernails, down to the tiny perfect heart beating in the cage of her ribs, down to the off-the-shoulder wrap that left one minute breast bare, invisible but for a tiny dark nipple, smaller than an eraser on the tip of a pencil.

"Who are you?" Brennan asked.

"Come with me and I shall tell you everything." She smiled at him, turned, and walked back down the dark tunnel.

He watched her for a moment, then, knowing he wasn't going to learn anything by remaining in the darkness, followed her, stopping only to pick up his flashlight.

The corridor was short, but it took several minutes to traverse because the miniature Chrysalis took very tiny steps. Brennan shuffled slowly behind her. He directed his light to the end of the tunnel, eventually discovering that it ended in what seemed to be a blank wall. When they reached it, the little Chrysalis called out and a hidden panel slipped open. Suspicious red eyes peered out.

"I have brought the archer," she said.

"He could hurt us," the watchman said in a deep, surly voice.

"She said to trust him when his word was given." The little Chrysalis turned and looked at Brennan. "Do you promise not to hurt us?"

Mystified and bewildered, Brennan said, "I promise."

There was the sound of creaky bolts being thrown and protesting metal squeaked on rusty runners. Dim light spilled from the hidden door as it swung slowly open.

"Then enter," the watchman said.

Brennan and the little Chrysalis stood at the threshold of a corridor. There were twenty or so beings in it. None were over eighteen inches tall; some were a lot smaller. Some were perfectly formed manikins, other grotesque parodies of humanity, test models discarded by the Creator and never put into mass production. Some looked more like animals than people, but all stared at Brennan with intelligence in their eyes.

"She said to trust you. She said you would help," the watchman said from the small platform that had been bolted next to the hidden door's peephole. He was one of the human-looking ones, though his leathery skin hung in folds over his nearly naked body like an overcoat that was six sizes too big.

"Who are you?" Brennan asked in a small voice.

"We were Chrysalis's eyes and ears," the Chrysalis manikin said proudly. "We moved about the city, unseen and undreamed of by the big world, and brought her the news that she was so eager to hear. She gave us a place to live, warm and dry and out of sight." She wiped at a tear that dripped down a crystalline cheek. "But now she is dead."

"It's you," Brennan said in a soft voice, "who's been leaving me notes and calling me up."

"That's right," the tiny Chrysalis said. "We only tried to help. We stopped when we realized that we were confusing and hurting you. We were only trying to help you find out who murdered our lady. We tried to help the detective, too, but he only called us names and chased us."

"Then you don't know who killed her?" Brennan asked.

The manikin shook her head. "We never spied on the Lady. It was a rule. She liked her loneness, even if at times she was sad in it."

Brennan nodded. "But you know where she kept her files."

"She would come and knock and we would let her in. Then we would tell stories of what we'd seen, what we'd learned in our hiding places in the world outside. She would bring food and drink and we would eat as she wrote things down. Once she never came for months. We wrote ourselves, but it was no fun without the Lady."

"Where?" Brennan asked. "Where did you write?"

The tiny joker pointed a tiny finger to the chamber at the end of the corridor.

More of the tribe were in the hallway, watching Brennan with eyes that were frightened and distrustful, angry and sad. One of the jokers, who looked like a tiny monkey with too many legs, turned on a shaded lamp as Brennan approached. The more skittish of Chrysalis's tiny spies peered at them silently from the dark edges of the room.

The chamber was simply furnished with a comfortable chair, an antique desk, and a Tiffany lamp. Notebooks and binders and stacks of paper cluttered the desk. As Brennan glanced through them he saw snippets about the sex life of politicians and the drug habits of bankers, notes on alliances between cops and gang figures, and even a list of which Dodgers had trouble with high fastballs and which were suckers for curveballs in the dirt.

Brennan frowned. "Is this it?" he asked the homunculus. "How in the world did she keep track of everything? Didn't she have a computer?"

"She didn't need a computer," the Chrysalis manikin told Brennan. "She had Mother."

"Mother?"

The manikin nodded and pointed. Brennan turned to follow her gesture and saw two homunculi dragging at a pullcord attached to a dark tapestry that covered the chamber's back wall. They pulled back the tapestry and Brennan stared at what was revealed.

There was a wall of flesh growing over a trestle against the back wall. It was gray and pink and purple and pulsated with a rippling rhythm, like a swimming manta ray. It was totally featureless. A dozen or so of the manikins hung from or clung to the flesh. Some were clearly attached to the thing, growing from cords attached to their heads, limbs, or stomachs. Others were just nestling against it as if for security or comfort.

"What is it?" Brennan asked in a whisper.

"Mother," the little Chrysalis said. "We are her children. She cannot see, nor talk aloud, but she speaks with her mind. She knows, she remembers everything we whisper to it while we rest in her bosom. Our lady gave her—and us—refuge. In return she remembered for the Lady."

"She can't talk?" Brennan asked.

The homuncula shook her head. "Only through her children."

Brennan, who thought he'd seen just about every kind of joker imaginable, shook his head. He wondered where Chrysalis had found it—her, actually—and how they had made their bargain. It was a story he would like to hear, but now there was no time. Later he and the little people could sit down and puzzle it out. Now he still had a murderer to uncover.

"How can I talk to Mother?" Brennan asked.

"Through us. Or," she said, "you might find what you're looking for in the Lady's journal."

"Her journal?" Somehow that sounded easier than dealing with Mother. And she was there for questioning if the journal didn't pan out. "Where is it?"

"Right there," the homuncula said, pointing at a leather-bound volume sitting on top of the cluttered desk.

As Brennan reached for it he heard a soft scuttling step where there was no one to make it. He drew back barely in time as something invisible and metallic swung through the air, caught his cheek, and ripped it open, leaving a bloody gash. Between him and the diary a pair of brown eyes floated five and a half feet from the ground.

There was loud chittering and many of the homunculi ran for the dark corners of the room as Fadeout materialized, pointing a pistol at Brennan.

"Surprise, surprise!" he said, grinning. "Drop your damn bow."

10:00 P.M.

The park was as hot and humid as a hooker's mouth. Fires burned everywhere, and shouts and snatches of song echoed through the trees as they wandered from tent to tent, from campfire to campfire, looking for Sascha.

In this hour, this night of triumph, even supposed nats like he and Blaise were welcome. Everywhere they went, jokers shook their hands and slapped them on the back. Drinks were being thrust at them every time they turned around; Hartmann buttons were pinned on their clothing at each stop. The night was heady with aroma; sausages sizzling on a hibachi, hobo's stew simmering over a campfire, a pair of squirrels turning slowly on a spit. The sound of beer cans being popped surrounded them like a thousand aluminum crickets. People were drunk, stoned, excited, turned on, fucked up, and generally crazed, but it was a happy kind of insanity. Gregg Hartmann was going to be president; he was going to kiss it and make it better; for the jokers and all the other poor damned souls in the park, Camelot was just around the corner.

Jay wondered how they'd feel the morning they all woke up and realized that somehow Camelot had turned into Mordor.

"I want to go back to the hotel," Blaise whined yet again. "This is bor-*ring*."

"Hey," Jay told him, "this is history in the making. Look around. Taste it. Smell it."

Blaise sniffed the air suspiciously. "That's just beer," he said. "Beer and piss."

Jay had to laugh; that sounded like one of his lines. "Maybe you'll make a PI yet, kid."

"I'm tired of all these stupid jokers," Blaise said. "You should let me mind-control them. I bet they're just lying to you, I bet they all know Sascha. I could make them tell us."

"No," Jay said. "When we find Sascha, you can take him, make him tell me the truth. That's all."

They found Doughboy all alone in a field, playing with a manhole cover. He was throwing it like a Frisbee, flinging it twenty, thirty yards across the grass, then scrambling after it to throw it again. It didn't fly as well as a Frisbee, but Doughboy didn't seem to mind. There was nothing but innocent, childlike joy on his great round face. But when Jay called out, the joker stopped and looked guilty.

"We're looking for Sascha," Jay asked him. "He used to work at the Crystal Palace. Have you seen him anywhere?"

Doughboy slowly shook his head from side to side. "I wath juth playing," he said.

Blaise laughed. "I know a good game he can play," he said. Doughboy's face went waxen, and he began to take off his clothes with thick, clumsy fingers.

Jay swung around. "Let him go," he snapped.

"Why should I? You can't make me."

Jay slapped him.

Blaise stood there, his eyes hot with anger, his cheek as red as his

hair, and for a second Jay was afraid of what he might do. Then, suddenly, he looked away. "Okay," he mumbled. "I'm sorry."

"All right," Jay said, after a long moment. "It's forgotten. C'mon.
Sascha's still out there somewhere."

◆

"How did you find me here?" Brennan asked Fadeout. "Wait, don't
tell me," he added before the ace could say anything. "Lazy Dragon."

"Very astute," Fadeout said sarcastically. "He lost you when you
were grabbed by the police, but he picked you up again at the church
by running down your usual haunts."

"And you followed me here."

"Quite right." Fadeout looked around. "You do know the most
interesting people." He reached over and picked up Chrysalis's journal. "But this is what I've come for. This will give me more power
than Chrysalis ever had—because I won't be reluctant to use the
information."

Brennan couldn't believe that he'd come so close to finding what
he needed, only to have it snatched away at the last moment. He
made a move to reach for Fadeout, but the ace swung his gun up and
pointed it at Brennan's midsection. "Uh-uh, wouldn't want me to
have to shoot you?" he asked as the miniature Chrysalis moved.

She'd been standing on the desk next to Fadeout, and as he
pointed his pistol at Brennan she leaped and grabbed it by the barrel. Fadeout looked at her in shock as her weight dragged the barrel
toward the floor. He cursed and shook the gun, but she wouldn't
let go.

As Brennan shouted, "No!" he pulled the trigger.

The shot echoed loudly in the confined chamber. The bullet ripped
the miniature Chrysalis off the barrel and sent her flying through
the air. She spattered against Mother like a broken rag doll. Mother
made no sound, but extruded long, humanlike arms that cuddled the
broken body against her mattress of flesh.

Brennan kicked the gun from Fadeout's hand, and with the same
smooth motion backhanded him across the face and snatched the
diary.

Fadeout went down, blood from his crushed lip dribbling on his chin. He put a hand to his mouth to wipe it away and mumbled, "You're dead now, you bastard," and threw something at Brennan. It hit his chest and bounced onto the desktop. It looked like a carved bit of potato.

Brennan backed away as the potato expanded, taking on black bands of fur, a large, chubby body, and a round, funny face with big black circles on its eyes.

The giant panda grinned at him. It was cute as hell with its fat, furry body and comical face. It was also twice Brennan's weight and had formidable talons and bright, sharp, shining teeth.

"Kill him, Dragon," Fadeout directed.

The panda made a whining, bleating noise and carefully climbed off the desk and advanced on Brennan as the homunculi ran screaming and skittering from the chamber.

There was no way Brennan could hope to defeat the thing, and it was between him and the door. The only factor he had on his side was superior speed. The damn, roly-poly panda couldn't be as fast as him. He hoped.

He backed up further into the chamber, and the panda padded after him, a stupid grin on its amiable, clownish features. When Brennan could go no further, it reared up on its hind legs and growled as if a buzz saw were rumbling deep in its throat.

Brennan moved. He tried to dodge around the creature, but the bastard was fast, damn fast. Brennan felt a surge of agony rip through his left arm as the panda swung a huge paw and caught him squarely on the forearm.

Brennan felt bones break and flesh tear, but he was by the panda and running. Fadeout had faded, but his eyes were still visible, so he could see. He tried to stop Brennan, but Brennan stiff-armed him and knocked him on his ass as he skidded by and went out into the tunnel. He looked to the left, where the sewer line lay, and then to the right, which led to a stepladder to the basement of the Crystal Palace.

Brennan didn't want to be trapped in the underground tunnel. He had to go up.

He caught his breath at the pain that lanced through his arm.

Both bones in his forearm were broken. The radius had ripped through his flesh, and blood spurted in time with the pulses of agony surging up his arm.

Brennan breathed deeply and rhythmically to get the pain under control as he ran down the corridor and grabbed the ladder leading up to the basement. He glanced over his shoulder and saw the panda coming down the corridor a lot faster than he thought possible. He transferred the journal to the crook of his injured arm, groaning as the torn flesh and broken bones took its weight, and fumbled in his hip pocket.

He took the transmitter from his pocket, activated it. "Crystal Palace," he croaked. He dropped it as he pulled himself up the ladder with his good hand.

The trapdoor at the top of the ladder resisted his efforts at first, but opened when he banged his good shoulder against it, sending waves of agony pounding down his injured arm.

Brennan pulled himself into the storeroom and slammed the trapdoor back down. A flight of rickety wooden stairs went up to the first floor, and Brennan took them at a run, bursting into a corridor that led to the Palace's rest rooms.

A woman going down the corridor toward the bathrooms took one look at Brennan, bloody-faced and with the radius of his right arm sticking out of his flesh like a jagged spear stub, and screamed. Brennan bolted past her and burst into the taproom of the Crystal Palace.

Everyone stared at him. No one tried to stop him as he plowed into the taproom, but the press of customers formed a blockade that Brennan couldn't push through.

There came another piercing scream from the hallway, and Brennan knew that Lazy Dragon was still on his trail. And he didn't have the problem that Brennan did.

Lazy Dragon simply crashed through the crowd, scattering it like screaming tenpins. Brennan, knowing he wasn't going to outrun the panda, turned with his back against the bar, his right arm an agonizing hunk of dead meat hanging from his shoulder.

The smart customers were leaving. The slow, the curious, the drunk, and the stupefied stayed to watch as the panda closed on Brennan, its cute little face grinning a grin that exposed razor-sharp teeth capable of biting off an arm with a single chomp.

"Give me the book!" Fadeout commanded from behind the bear, but Brennan shook his head. "Take it," Fadeout ordered, and the panda advanced like slow, inescapable doom.

Brennan gathered himself for a final attempt to escape as the panda shuffled forward on his hind feet. He feinted to his left, quickly shifted low and to the right, and almost scooted away.

Almost.

The ace slammed a paw down across Brennan's back and it felt like the ceiling had fallen on him. Brennan dropped to his knees with the breath squeezed from his lungs, rolled, and came to his feet right in front of the panda. The ace slapped the journal away from him, as easily as taking candy from a child, and Fadeout retrieved it.

"Finish the job," he told Dragon.

The remaining spectators crowded as best they could to the edges of the room.

"Leave him alone."

The unexpected voice sounded calm in the hushed silence, and oddly gentle. The panda turned slowly, one gigantic paw still raised and ready to smash Brennan to jelly.

A squat, hunchbacked figure had materialized in the open area between the onlookers and Brennan and the panda. Dragon, his eyes on Quasiman, swatted at Brennan, who took the blow on his shoulder and managed to roll with it a little. He smashed against the bar with a jolt that brought tears to his eyes. Somehow he managed to pull himself to his knees and say, "We need the journal," before collapsing in agony.

Quasiman advanced slowly, dragging his stiff left leg behind him. "Give me the book," he told Fadeout, and as he switched his attention to Fadeout, the panda charged.

It struck Quasiman like a runaway train smashing into a cliff face. The two hurtled backward into the screaming spectators. It was a miracle that no one was crushed as Dragon's momentum crashed them both through the wall. Wood shattered and pipes burst and a spray of water showered the room. Brennan pulled himself to his feet as they came crashing back through the hole they'd made in the wall, the panda first, Quasiman after him.

Quasiman lifted a heavy wooden table and battered his foe. His first blow crushed the panda flat on the floor, shattering the table to kindling. The panda got to its feet and charged at Quasiman, smashing him through the bar and into the large mirror and racks of bottles behind. Lupo deserted his post with a despairing yowl as mirror and bottles burst into a million scintillating shards.

Brennan swayed on his feet, undecided. He wanted to help Quasiman, but realized there was nothing he could do against Dragon. He wanted to follow Fadeout, but the ace had already managed to disappear in the dark room filled with running, screaming people. Dragon and Quasiman smashed through the bar again and rolled about the floor like angry behemoths, punching and kicking and clawing one another.

The panda had blood on its fur, Brennan wasn't sure whose, and Quasiman's shirt had been ripped off his back, exposing the mass of bone and flesh that was his hump.

Brennan's nose twitched at a sudden foul smell in the air. It was gas, natural gas. The battling aces had broken a gas line as well as a water line when they'd smashed through the wall. Brennan had a moment of calm, coherent thought, realizing that everyone had to get out before a spark ignited the gas that had seeped into the room. He turned to shout to everyone to leave, but it was too late.

There was a muted whooshing roar and flames blossomed near the shattered wall. Someone yelled "Fire!" and the pandemonium was complete.

There was a panicked flight toward the door. Some were trampled, but cooler heads somehow dampened the frenzy. Brennan realized that it would be impossible to force his way through the crowd, so he headed to the stairway that led to the exits on the upper floors. He paused at the foot of the stairs and watched Quasiman and Dragon waltz around the floor in a clumsy dance. The panda's paws were on Quasiman's shoulders and Quasiman had his hands locked around the animal's throat. Its snarling, spitting face was only inches from Quasiman's.

"*Quasiman!*" Brennan's voice cut through the panic like a bull-horn through fog. "Break it off! Quasiman!"

He never knew if the joker heard, whether he'd decided he'd had enough, or whether his brain slipped off, wandering God alone knew where. Quasiman suddenly vanished, teleporting away just as the panda snapped its jaws shut in a bite that would have taken Quasi-man's face off. It groped around in bewilderment for its vanished foe and staggered into a pillar of flame that suddenly shot from the hole it had helped pound in the wall.

The air was suddenly speared by the scent of burned fur, and the panda tottered about, spreading the fire as it bumped into the shattered bar and the broken furniture that littered the floor. It finally stopped and plopped down on its rear. It let out a few whining bleats, then seemed to shrivel into itself, shrinking to its original negligible size.

Brennan started to go upstairs, then remembered Mother and the homunculi in the basement. He hesitated, cursing himself, then headed back for the corridor that led to the basement storage room and the chamber below.

The corridor was thick with smoke. Brennan ran, bending below the acrid fumes, found the open trapdoor, and went down the ladder. The air suddenly became searing hot, and Brennan knew that the fire had spread to the storeroom above. Manikins were scurrying from Chrysalis's secret chamber, wailing and crying like lost cats.

Brennan looked inside. Mother had pulled away from the wall and was flopping and squirming on the floor like a living mattress. Most of the homunculi had pulled away from her, but those attached with umbilical cords were as trapped as she was.

Brennan hesitated, almost turning and leaving; then a vast tele-pathic wave of fear and desperation washed over him, so powerful that even his nonreceptive mind could sense it. Whatever she looked like, Brennan realized, however hideous and inhuman her shape, Mother was still a person.

He didn't know if he'd be able to drag her away with only one arm, but he knew that he had to try. He took a deep breath of the smoke-fouled air, gritted his teeth, and stepped into the secret chamber.

"I'm coming," he called.

He ran into the chamber and managed to tip up a corner of Mother's rectangular body. Her flesh was warm and rubbery and pulsating, and it had a pleasant, somehow soothing smell even in the smoky chamber. He got down on his knees and somehow managed to hoist her onto his back.

Sparks sprinkled from the ceiling and smoke rolled into the chamber like thick fog.

"It's all right," Brennan shouted. He caught his breath at the horrible pain in his broken arm. "We're going to make it."

Then the ceiling fell in.

11:00 P.M.

The sound of singing floated through the night, a ragged drunken harmony in a couple different keys. The lyrics were something about hanging Leo Barnett from a sour-apple tree. The path curved off to the left, but Jay cut across the grass and through a stand of trees. Blaise followed desultorily, kicking at the occasional rock.

The fire was out; the only light came from a few embers glowing feebly amidst the ashes. It wasn't until they were quite close that Jay realized the group of jokers squatting by the tent wasn't a group at all. Or maybe it was, if you count Siamese quints as a group.

By then the singing had stopped.

All the eyes were looking at him. The five bodies were twisted and malformed, flesh flowing into flesh in places and ways that made Jay want to turn his head. He wasn't even sure you could really call them quints; there seemed to be five bodies, but they shared four heads and maybe seven legs between them. On the other hand, they'd come out way ahead on the arm-and-tentacle count.

"Oh, gross," Blaise said with astonishing tact.

Jay ignored him, and hoped the jokers would, too. "Maybe you could help me," he said. "I'm looking for a friend of mine, name of Sascha. Skinny, slicked-down hair, kind of a fussy dresser. Has one of those little pencil mustaches like you see on desk clerks in old movies." No response. "No eyes. Did I mention that? Just skin."

Four mismatched faces regarded him dully. Jay couldn't decide if they were stupid or hostile or what. He waited a long awkward moment and tried again. "Maybe you don't know him. He used to work at the Crystal Palace. You guys from New York?"

"I can make it answer," Blaise said eagerly. "Just watch. I'll make it get up and do a little dance."

"They don't talk," a woman's voice said from behind them.

Jay turned around. He could barely make her out, just a shadowy form sitting under a tree. "I heard them singing," he said.

"They sing," the calm voice replied. It was a young woman. Through the branches, he could see the moonlight reflected on pale white skin. Her dress was unbuttoned down the front, and she was cradling something in her arms. "They sing, but they don't talk."

"Oh," Jay said. He stopped a few feet away from her. He could see one breast, pale and cone-shaped. A baby was nursing at the other. She stroked it gently as it sucked. She looked very young, no more than eighteen, sad and pretty. Her baby in her arms was a round red thing, like a bowling ball made of flesh. "I'm sorry," Jay said. "I didn't mean to intrude. . . ."

"I know where Sascha is," the woman said.

In the darkness behind her, someone moved. Jay looked up, saw eyes peering out of the bushes. They were pale green, and burned with a dim feral glow. He was staring at them when he heard a soft footstep behind him. The hairs on the back of his neck stirred. There was a sudden overwhelming sense of being watched, and all at once Jay was terrified.

He backed away from the woman and the sad twisted creature in her arms, trying not to show any of the fear that was tearing at his guts inside. "Blaise, we're getting the fuck out of here," he said. He turned.

Sascha stood behind the boy, his eyeless stare fixed on Jay. Ezili was there, too. He could see her body, full and lush. She was naked, and in the darkness, her eyes glowed red, brighter than the embers in the fire. She smiled at him and said nothing.

Jay must have made some kind of noise, because Blaise turned around. He saw Sascha, but then his eyes went to Ezili and got big. He grinned, then gave a low hoot of approval that Jay knew he hadn't learned from Tachyon. The boy had no idea of the shit they were in. "Sascha . . ." Jay began.

"No," Sascha replied. "Now it's too late for talking."

A man with a club came sliding out of the darkness, his feet bare, silent as a shadow. He swung, missed, Jay danced aside, and made his gun with his fingers and popped him away. Someone leaped onto his back. He went down hard and rolled. Long fingernails raked across his face, clawing for his eyes. Jay caught the hands, pried them loose, tried to untangle himself. He got his right hand free just in time to pop off a small girl who was coming at him from the right, but by then the woman had sunk her teeth in the fleshy part of his left hand just beneath the thumb.

He cried out. Blaise finally took his eyes off Ezili's tits long enough to see what was going on. "*Hey!*" the boy called out.

The woman worried at his thumb with her teeth and tried to kick him in the balls at the same time. Jay slapped her hard alongside the head, got his hand loose, and popped her right out from under him. Sascha shouted out, "Stop it! Leave them alone!"

It was enough to freeze everyone for a second. Blaise was staring at Sascha with fierce concentration, holding him in the palm of his mind. Behind him, Jay saw the vast shadow of the Siamese quint lurch unsteadily to its feet and stumble forward. Oh Jesus, he thought. "*Run!*" he screamed at Blaise.

He saw motion out of the corner of his eye, and whirled. The thing with the pale green eyes had emerged from the bushes and was gliding silently across the grass, five feet off the ground, like some obscene manta ray with a semihuman face. It was naked, its skin pale and pimpled. Male genitalia drooped from the center of its face beneath those hideous eyes. Jay fought to keep down his lunch as he sent it away, but behind it came others. The looming joker with flesh soft and dark as blood pudding, the boy with the ice pick, the human centipede skittering forward with knives in half his hands. They were all around him.

He got rid of the ice pick when he saw the sad-voiced young

woman coming at him, her baby lifted over her head like a weapon. It made him hesitate, only for a second, but it was enough.

A dozen strong hands seized him from behind, the ground dropped away under his feet, and pain erupted everywhere.

Sunday
July 24, 1988

3:00 A.M.

HIS ARMS WERE ON fire.

He didn't remember waking up. He wasn't sure he had. For a moment he thought he was dreaming, his nightmare come to haunt him once again, only this was a new part, after the cone-faced thing began to howl. He tried to open his eyes, and saw only darkness. The world had a damp, fetid smell. He couldn't move his fingers. He could feel burning in his shoulders and his wrists, but otherwise his arms were numb. He kicked feebly, and his body began to twist. He was suspended somewhere, adrift above some vast black abyss.

Far off in the darkness he heard coarse laughter and dim, whispering voices. The cone-faced things were talking about him, Jay thought. He remembered his name then; somehow that helped. He tried not to listen to the voices. They reminded him of the trees in his dream, whispering secrets, terrible secrets he did not want to hear.

Then there were footsteps coming up behind him, and the fear rose in his throat. They were coming after him, and when he tried to run, his legs pumped uselessly against nothing.

The blindfold was ripped off his face. Sudden light stung his eyes. Jay closed them, whimpering feebly. "Cut him down," a familiar voice said, close at hand.

Someone grunted. Against his best instincts, Jay opened his eyes a crack. His vision was blurred and painful. The room took shape around him. A basement, he thought groggily. He was hanging from a pipe, swaying in the air, dangling by his arms. A human centipede advanced toward him, hands full of shiny metal, while a man with an eyeless face watched from below. Sascha, he thought, but when he tried to say the name, nothing came out.

Then he was falling. His legs tangled under him, unable to support his weight, and he collapsed, his head hitting the damp stone beneath a solid crack as he fell. Jay groaned.

"Give him another shot," a distant voice said. "I don't want to take any chances with him until we reach Ti Malice."

No, Jay tried to say. All he produced was a moan. Someone kicked at his broken rib, rolling him over with a foot. Then there was a bright light shining in his eyes, a sharp pain inside his elbow. After that he slept.

11:00 A.M.

Chrysalis smiled at him. Brennan thought it was strange to see her again, because he was pretty sure that she was dead. Or maybe she'd just been out of town.

He smiled back tentatively. Now that she was back, how would he explain her to Jennifer? And vice versa? He decided to worry about it later and reached for her. They embraced and he pulled back to arms' length to look at her. His smile froze.

Chrysalis was deteriorating before his eyes. Her crystal flesh clouded with corruption and fell away from her face and body in rotten chunks. Blood ran in sluggish tears from her eyes, her breath whispered in a ghastly rattle from her laboring lungs. He held a corpse in his arms. He felt guilt tear angrily at him and with her last gasp she said, "Brennan," and he awoke soaked with sweat and shaking from horror and anesthesia reaction.

"How do you feel?" someone asked from his bedside.

"Fine," Brennan lied. "Where am I?"

Brennan turned and looked at the speaker for the first time. He was a young man in a white lab coat with a stethoscope around his neck. He looked like a cross between a surfer boy and a palomino pony. Dr. . . . Finn. That was his name.

"The Jokertown Clinic," Dr. Finn told him.

Brennan nodded wearily.

"You know," Finn went on, "it's most astonishing that you're with us at all."

Brennan nodded again. He was groggy and disoriented, but he was starting to remember things. The fire. Mother. The ceiling collapsing.

"It seems," Dr. Finn said, watching him closely, "that a fireman found you in a secret subterranean room when looking through the wreckage of the Crystal Palace. Apparently you were saved from the flames by . . . something . . . that was only a charred, fleshy mass covering your back when the fireman discovered you."

"Mother," Brennan whispered. His mouth felt as if it were full of wet cotton batting and his right arm was a hunk of unfeeling meat encased in a plastic cast. He sat up and swung his legs onto the floor, fighting sudden vertigo that made his head swirl as if he were in the middle of a three-day drunk. His arm was totally numb, but he knew that the numbness would wear off unfortunately quickly. "Where are my clothes?"

"You're in no condition to leave the hospital," Finn said gravely. "Your arm was broken pretty badly, and you've lost a lot of blood. You've also got some burns on your hands and face. You should rest for at least a day."

Brennan shook his head. "I've no time to rest."

"I can't be responsible if you leave the clinic," Finn said, his tail twitching in distress.

"You're not responsible for anything. I am." Brennan stood, and almost immediately collapsed again when he was struck by a severe attack of vertigo. "Now, where are my clothes?"

Finn shook his head. "If you're really determined to leave, I won't stop you. Wait here a minute and I'll find your clothes. It may take a while because everything's a mess this morning."

"The fire?" Brennan asked.

"No. The Crystal Palace was destroyed, but there were actually very few injuries from the fire. It seems that half the staff was up all night partying with the rest of Jokertown, and the other half is being run ragged trying to treat the results of that partying."

"Partying?" Brennan asked. "Why?"

"Oh, I guess you couldn't have heard. Senator Hartmann was nominated for the presidency last night. All of Jokertown's gone Hartmann crazy."

♠

Somewhere in the darkness, the voices were arguing.

"It's not fair," the first voice said. "We need the kiss, too. He spends so much time with *him*. How long is he going to keep us waiting?"

"As long as he desires," the second voice said. "It is not our right to question the master's comings and goings. Ti Malice does things in his own time, for his own reasons."

"We ought to kill them both," the first voice said. "They're dangerous."

"No," said a third voice, a woman's voice, "not these sweet ones. The master will want to taste them, to ride them, to feel them beneath him. The master will want to hear them scream."

That was enough to open Jay's eyes.

"What about *us*?" He saw the centipede man pacing, his voice high and nervous. "What if he likes them better than us? We'll never get the kiss. I can't stand it when he goes off."

Jay lay facedown on a decaying, foul-smelling couch, his head turned to one side, arms tied behind his back. At least he hoped they were tied behind his back; he couldn't feel them anymore, and when he tried to move his fingers, there was only numbness. The upholstery smelled of piss. His head was pounding, and his ribs screamed at the slightest motion. He was still in the same dank cellar. He could see an old hot-water heater a few feet away, its pipes eaten by rust. Beyond it was a second room, larger than the one he was in, where shadowy figures waited in the faint light that poured through grime-encrusted windows. Jay tried to count them, but there were too many, some of them moving around. When he tried to concentrate, his skull felt like it was about to split open.

He must have groaned, or whimpered, or somehow given away the game. The argument stopped suddenly, and he heard footsteps. Rough hands turned him over toward the ceiling. Sascha stood above him. The telepath looked a little worse for wear. His hands were trembling, and strands of dark hair were plastered to his pale forehead with sweat.

"What," Jay said. It was all he could manage. His lips and throat were dry and raw. "What," he repeated.

"Get him some water," Sascha said.

A moment later, Ezili knelt beside him, holding a glass to his lips. Her hands were hot, but the water was cool and Jay gulped it down greedily and let it run over his lips and chin. "Suck," Ezili whispered in his ear, laughing, and Jay could smell her, and feel the heat that came off her skin in waves.

"You should never have followed us to Atlanta," Sascha said.

Jay sputtered through the last of the water. "My arms," he managed. "The ropes . . . cutting off my circulation. Let me loose."

"I'm blind, not stupid," Sascha said. "You can't use your power with your hands tied. You need to point your finger, to make believe your hand is a gun."

"He's trying to trick us." The human centipede stepped up behind Sascha. He was tall and stooped, hunched over like a question mark, his face a pinched afterthought on a narrow hairless head. All his arms were grotesquely long and thin, skin pulled taut over bone and muscle. But there were so *many* of them. "I told you he was dangerous," the joker said. "Kill him." He had a long serrated knife in one of his myriad hands.

"No," Sascha said. "He's too valuable."

"A treasure," Ezili whispered.

"You know how the master feels about aces," Sascha said.

"Ask the others!" the centipede man insisted.

"Do I get a vote?" Jay wanted to know.

Ezili laughed, and Sascha turned his eyeless face toward Jay. "You'd vote for life," he said solemnly. "Stupid." His fingers rubbed idly at a large scab on the side of his neck.

"You've been a bad boy," Ezili said teasingly. "What did you do to them, eh? All our lovely friends . . ."

"I told you," Sascha said. "He teleported them away. To New York City."

"The master will be angry," Ezili said. She ran a finger lightly down Jay's cheek, delicately circled his ear. "So many mounts, gone. You'll have to be punished."

"The master," Jay repeated. "Who's that? Hartmann?"

Ezili looked at him blankly.

"The Puppetman," Jay said, remembering the name Tachyon had used. The centipede glanced at Sascha in confusion.

"Is that what this is all about?" Sascha said. "You poor sad fool. You have no idea what you've blundered into." He gave a short, sharp laugh that had no humor in it. "But then again, few of us did," he added bitterly.

"I want to play with him," Ezili said. Her hand worked at his belt and slid into his pants.

"Not tonight, honey," Jay said weakly. "I've got a headache."

Ezili smiled and took her hand off his cock. "When he kisses you," she whispered, "then you will be mine again. He likes to have the new mounts fuck me. He will ride you and you will ride me."

"Some fun," Jay said.

Ezili ran her tongue across her lower lip.

There was a scab on her neck, too.

Jay had seen it before, the night they'd balled on her carpet, but he'd forgotten about it. Now it was right there in front of him, an old sore, crusted over with a scab, just like Sascha's.

He looked up at the centipede. The hole in his neck was open and raw, the skin around it red and inflamed.

All of them, Jay thought wildly. Not joker terrorists or militant Hartmann fanatics but . . . something else.

Something terrible.

His stomach clenched inside him, and again he had a sick feeling of vertigo and a sense of unspeakable dread, as if he had just dropped into his nightmare.

"You won't get away with this," Jay said with all the bravado he had left. "Blaise will tell them what happened. They'll come after you . . . Tachyon, Hiram . . ." He tried to think of who else might come looking for him, and couldn't come up with any names. "I'm a popular guy, Sascha," he finished weakly. "They're not going to let you fuck around with me."

Ezili thought that was hilarious. Her laughter was almost hysterical. The centipede joined in.

"The boy won't be telling anybody anything," Sascha said almost sorrowfully. He reached down and grabbed the front of Jay's shirt and jerked him upright to a sitting position. "There."

Behind the sofa, a monstrous shape filled the gray shadows along the wall. In the dimness, Jay saw arms, tendrils, claws, flesh twisting into flesh. And eyes . . . It wasn't until the creature moved that Jay recognized the Siamese quint.

Blaise was slumped unconscious on a mattress at its feet, wrist and ankle shackled to nearby pipes. His face was battered and bruised, and dried blood had caked over one eye, sealing it shut.

All Jay could think was that Dr. Tachyon was going to be *really* pissed.

NOON

Brennan headed immediately to Our Lady of Perpetual Misery. As he crossed Jokertown he could observe the tail end of the mass party that Finn had told him about. Drunks were still staggering about the street wearing Hartmann–Jackson campaign buttons. Hartmann banners festooned practically every building, having appeared magically overnight like mushrooms sprouting after a rain. Hartmann posters were stapled to every flat surface. You couldn't go anywhere without seeing his smiling face. His omnipresence was almost eerie, and for the first time Brennan felt some misgivings about such an uncritical, overwhelming passion.

Father Squid was still conducting Mass, so Brennan slipped in the back of the church and waited, trying to make himself as inconspicuous as possible. The joker sitting in the pew next to him glanced over once, saw the state of Brennan's clothing, then decided that it was far more important to pay attention to what was happening with the Mass than stare at the bloodstained nat who'd sat down beside him.

Mass lasted only a few more minutes, but the church took a long time to empty. Brennan caught the priest's eye as he was surrounded by members of the congregation who wished to talk to him—mainly, it seemed, about the coming of Hartmann and the expected golden age—and Father Squid called Quasiman over and whispered a few words to him. Quasiman shuffled off and Father Squid gestured significantly to Brennan.

Brennan slipped out of the church and went around to the back, where Quasiman was unlocking the rectory.

"I hope you're all right," Brennan told the joker. He could see a series of deep scratches running down Quasiman's face.

"Sure," Quasiman said. "Do you think you'll be needing me soon?"

Brennan looked at him. Quasiman looked back with deep, intelligent eyes that held no memories at all of the events of last night. "I—no, I'll think I'll be able to handle things now. But if I do need you, I'll let you know."

"Okay," Quasiman said. "I'll be ready."

He opened the door to the rectory and Brennan went quietly inside. The shades were drawn and Jennifer was still asleep on the couch. Her face looked smooth and serene as that of a child. Her skin color was good, her chest rose and fell with easy regularity. She looked well on the road to recovery, but Brennan didn't want to jeopardize her health by waking her.

He quietly tiptoed to the hallway that led to Father Squid's little bedroom. His bag was sitting by the bedroom door. He took off his battered, bloody clothes and discovered how hard a simple thing like changing pants can be with an arm in a cast. Once he accomplished this, he closed the door behind him, and sat down on Father Squid's water bed and rested for a moment.

He took a deep breath. Dr. Finn had been right. He was worn out already. He hoped the rest of the day would be easy on him. Right now he didn't have the strength to fight half his weight in puppies.

He picked up the phone by the bedstand and dialed a number that had been given him by a cat. It rang once, then a recorded message came on that said, "We're sorry, the number you're trying to reach is no longer in service."

He hung up the phone. Fadeout worked fast. He even had the telephone company jumping. Brennan sat on the bed, thinking for a moment. Kien might know where Fadeout's headquarters were, but the thought of going to his enemy for help made Brennan gag. He would do it if he had to, but there were others he could see first. There was one other he was particularly eager to see.

He put the last weapon he had, a snub-nosed .38, securely in the waistband of his fresh set of jeans, and went out into the living room.

He watched Jennifer sleep for a moment and resisted a powerful urge to kiss her. He walked through the living room without making a sound and closed the door silently behind him.

Quasiman was sitting in the grass, listening to whatever thoughts they were that drifted like clouds across his mind.

"Tell Father Squid I'll be back," Brennan said, but Quasiman gave no sign that he'd heard. Brennan smiled to himself, well aware how lucky he'd been that Quasiman had responded when he'd needed him the night before.

As he went through the churchyard to the street beyond he wished that he could always be that lucky. He stepped to the sidewalk just as an empty cab went by. Brennan whistled shrilly and the cab stopped a little ways up the block. Maybe, he thought, my luck has shifted.

"Twisted Dragon," he said to the cabbie, who nodded, flipped the flag with his flipper, and pulled off down the street.

The talkative cabbie was festooned with Hartmann buttons, and Brennan let him jabber on about the crucial events in Atlanta while putting in only an occasional grunt to sustain his end of the conversation.

"The fur," the cabbie said, "is really gonna fly now. Hartmann versus Bush. Oh, boy. And if Hartmann don't win, Jokertown is gonna go crazy. I don't think Tachyon will be too welcome around here. Why do you think he done it?"

The cab pulled up in front of the Twisted Dragon.

"Why do you think Tachyon turned his back on us?" the cabbie asked Brennan again.

Brennan would have shrugged, but the cast made that difficult. "I'm sure he had his reasons," he said, only vaguely aware of what the cabbie had said, and not at all sure of what Tachyon had done or hadn't done. The answer didn't please the cabbie, who burned away from the curb despite the twenty that Brennan handed him.

Brennan went inside the Dragon, dismissing the political maneuverings from his mind. He had more immediate problems to worry about, and so did Lazy Dragon, whom Brennan spotted drinking at the bar.

The Twisted Dragon was as crowded and noisy as it usually is, which is saying a lot on both accounts. Brennan simply walked up behind Dragon, who jerked with surprise when Brennan stuck a knuckle in his back, simulating the barrel of a gun.

"Nice to see you again, pal," Brennan said. "Shall we have a little chat?"

Dragon nodded once, and his hand started to go slowly to his jacket pocket, until Brennan jammed the knuckle a little harder into his back.

"Relax. Keep your hands in sight. I don't want you turning into a teddy bear and scaring all these people."

"All right," Dragon said quietly, his hands resting flat on the bar. "What do you want?"

"I could want your ass, chum, but you saved my life once, so we'll call it quits. If you tell me how to get in touch with Fadeout."

"All I have is a phone number," Dragon said. "The one I gave you a few days ago."

Brennan shook his head. "It's no good anymore."

"Then I can't help you."

Brennan stared at Dragon, who returned his gaze steadily. "All right. But if you're lying, if you know how to get in touch with Fadeout and warn him that I'm coming, then it's open season on dragons. And I've got my hunting permit right here." He increased the pressure with his knuckle.

Dragon shrugged, feigning nonchalance. "Why should I care what you white dudes do to each other?" he asked.

"Good attitude," Brennan said, and faded into the crowd.

Cross Dragon off the list, Brennan thought when he hit the street. It was time to visit the Magic Kingdom again.

♥

"*Blaise*," Jay said in an urgent stage whisper.

The boy's eyes were closed, but Jay could see the tension in his muscles. He was conscious, Jay was convinced of it; groggy maybe, terrified almost certainly, but conscious.

In the next room, Charm was singing. That was what the others called the Siamese quint; Jay had a sick feeling he knew what that was short for. Sascha had left twenty minutes ago, after saying something about needing to get a new boy. From the conversation, Jay gathered that he had popped away the old boy last night in the park. He wasn't quite clear what they needed a boy for, but it seemed to have something to do with the master's travel plans.

Sascha's telepathy would have made any attempt at escape futile. If they were going to make a move, they had to do it now. As near as Jay could determine, there were only five people left in the other room—six if you counted the grotesque infant nursing at its mother's breast. He figured he could discount the mother and child. Ezili and the joker who looked like a sack of blood pudding shouldn't be too dangerous either. That left only Charm and the centipede man. The centipede sat beneath a window in the other room, a whetstone in one of his left hands, a half-dozen knives in his rights, the arms on the right side of his body moving with a strange rhythmic grace as he sharpened the blades. The sound of steel against stone lent an eerie counterpoint to Charm's singing.

"*Blaise*," he whispered again. "C'mon, dammit. Wake up."

The boy opened his eyes. All the arrogance was gone from them now. Even in the darkness, Jay could see how scared they were. The contemptuous junior mentat had turned back into a little boy on him.

"We got to get out of here," Jay said, trying to keep his voice low. "This is the best chance we're going to get."

"They *hurt* me!" Blaise said. His voice cracked with pain. He spoke much too loud. For a moment Jay stiffened, but the singing went on in the next room.

"I know," Jay whispered. "Blaise, you have to keep your voice down. If they hear us, we're fucked."

"I'm scared," Blaise said. His voice was softer, but not soft enough. "I want to go home."

"Pull yourself together," Jay said. "I need you. You have to mind-control one of them."

"I *tried*," Blaise said. "Last night . . . I had Sascha, but they didn't listen to him, and then that thing . . . that joker . . . too many minds, I wasn't even sure how many, and some of them . . . it was like an animal mind, only smarter, and it kept sliding away from me, I couldn't get a grip . . . they *hurt* me." He was crying now. A line of red ran down one cheek, where his tears mingled with the dried blood that had closed his eye.

"They're going to hurt you a lot worse if we don't get out of here," Jay said. "You don't need to mess with the big ugly one. Just grab the guy who looks like a centipede. Make him stand up and say, *I'm going to go check on the prisoners.* You got that?"

"I'm going to go check on the prisoners," Blaise repeated numbly through swollen, cracked lips.

"Casual," Jay stressed. "Make it real casual. Then get the fucker back here with one of his knives and have him cut me loose. Once my hands are loose, we're home free. I'll pop you back to the Marriott and you can bring the cavalry. Okay?"

"I don't know," Blaise said.

"I thought you were part Takisian," Jay whispered with all the scorn he had in him. "You guys good for anything but crying?"

Blaise blinked back tears, then nodded slowly. "I'll try."

The boy's battered face twisted in concentration. Jay held his breath. The singing went on for what seemed like an eternity. Then a chair pushed back and he heard a thin voice announce, much too formally, "I'm going to go check on the prisoners."

The singing stopped. Jay heard footsteps.

Too many footsteps.

The centipede crossed the cellar like a sleepwalker, knelt down in front of Jay, groped behind him, and started sawing at his bonds with a knife. From the sound it made, Jay had the sick realization that his hands were bound with wire, not rope.

Charm came in just behind him, lurching forward with a ponderous stumbling gait. One head glanced over at Jay and the centipede, and ignored them. All the other eyes stayed fixed on Blaise. "No," the boy whimpered as the joker's vast dark shadow fell across him. He tried to scuttle back on the mattress, but there was no place to hide.

One of Charm's hands reached up into the pipes that ran along the ceiling and emerged with a baseball bat. The first swing caught the boy's head with a *crack* that made Jay nauseated.

2:00 P.M.

This time Brennan's approach was straightforward. He knew where he was going, he knew what he wanted to do. Quinn's garden was gorgeous in the afternoon sunlight. He either had tremendous horticultural skills or had hired a superb landscaping service. Brennan wouldn't mind talking gardening with the Eskimo, and if things went right, he'd have his chance.

He cut through the poppy bed and approached the caterpillar sentinel from the rear. As it had done the first time he stumbled upon it, the machine turned its head slowly, grinned, welcomed him, then dispersed a billowing cloud of gas in his direction.

Brennan fell, artistically he hoped. He winced when his right arm hit the turf and twisted so that his left hand was under his body. He held his breath as the gas dissipated, and took shallow, cautious breaths when he had to. He got a little dizzy from the residue gas, but then he was still feeling woozy from his medical treatment, anyway.

He lay there for ten minutes before he heard approaching footsteps and a grumbling voice. "Sunday afternoon," it was saying, "Sunday afternoon. Can't a man be left in peace to enjoy himself even on the weekends? What's this world coming to?"

The grumbling stopped and through slitted eyes Brennan saw Quinn staring down at him.

"Now who's this?" Quinn continued his monologue. "Who's caught in the web spun by my caterpillar? Wait a minute. Caterpillars don't spin webs, do they?"

"That's right," Brennan said, sitting up and pointing his gun at Quinn. "You're thinking of spiders."

"You're unconscious," Quinn said. "You can't talk."

Brennan could see that the Eskimo was badly ripped, but that wasn't unusual. He peered doubtfully at Brennan, seemingly not even cognizant of the gun Brennan was pointing at him.

"Running downs through your system this afternoon, Quinn?"

He nodded tranquilly. "Quaaludes."

"Lucky me. Now here's what we're going to do. We're going back to your place, then we're going to call up someone else and have a little party. That all right with you?"

Quinn nodded agreeably. "Sure. Sundays are boring anyway. There's usually nothing on television worth watching at all."

"You first," Brennan said, waving his gun at Quinn. He didn't want to get within reach of the doctor in case Quinn realized what was happening and tried to sink his finger needles into him again.

Brennan got a better view of the inside of the mansion than the last time he was there. Whatever taste Quinn had in landscaping didn't extend to interior design. The inside of his Magic Kingdom was decorated in what could best be called exotically eclectic taste. The entrance hall was lined with portraits of famous drug addicts of the past, including Edgar Allan Poe, Sherlock Holmes, Elvis Presley, and Tom Marion Douglas.

The room Quinn led him to had a group of display cases that housed, among other things, a collection of Chinese opium bottles and antique Turkish water pipes. Against one wall were terrariums with rare and delicate species of fungus and cactus, against another were aquariums with various species of puffer fish.

"Quite a place you've got here," Brennan said, gazing about in wonder.

"Thanks." Quinn beamed. "It's thematic, you know."

"Yeah," Brennan said. "Now I want you to make that phone call."

"Who are we calling?"

"Fadeout. I want you to get him here fast. Tell him you've discovered something new. Something important that he has to see right away. Can you handle that?"

"Hey!" Quinn stood straight up. "Sharp as a tack!" But he stopped and peered at Brennan. "But why should I?"

Brennan decided that subtlety was out of the question. "Because I got a gun," he said, pointing it at Quinn. "And I want you to."

"Hey," Quinn said, backing away. "I was only asking." He went to the telephone, and Brennan kept pace behind him, out of arms' reach. He peered at the number that Quinn was trying to dial. It was different than the number that Fadeout had given him, as Brennan had suspected it might be. He didn't think Fadeout would hand out his secure number to just anyone.

Quinn, meanwhile, was having difficulty dialing, but finally made it through on the third try. Brennan positioned himself before Quinn, where the Eskimo could see his gun.

"Hey, hey!" Quinn said into the receiver. "Guess who? . . . That's right. Coo-coo-ka-choo . . . No, wait a minute. That's the walrus. . . . Anyway, it's me, Quinn. Yeah, listen, Phil old boy, I was fooling around in the lab today and came up with something you've just got to see. . . . Sure I'm sure. . . . Everybody's gonna jump for joy. . . . Hey, has the Eskimo ever let you down? . . . Well, recently, I mean . . . Okay . . . okay . . . When you can make it . . . Sure . . . Adios."

He hung up the phone.

"Well?" Brennan asked.

"He's got some stuff to do, but he'll be by in an hour or so. Say, want to see my greenhouse? I've got a great collection of marijuana plants."

"Sure," Brennan said. "Why not?"

3:00 P.M.

The sound of footsteps on the stairs made Jay open his eyes.

It was very quiet. He had been sleeping . . . or drifting in and out of consciousness, it was hard to be sure. He glanced over toward the mattress and saw Blaise staring at him. The boy's eyes were wide open, fixed in terror. A froth of blood bubbled out of his mouth where Charm had knocked out some teeth. He didn't seem aware of it. He didn't seem aware of anything.

The footsteps got louder. Jay squirmed along the couch, his useless hands still bound behind his back, and tried to get a good look into the next room.

Hiram Worchester stepped into the basement.

Jay blinked. For a moment he thought he was hallucinating. Then he gathered all the strength he had in him and screamed. *"Here!* Hiram, I'm back here!"

Hiram's head snapped around. Charm lurched to his feet and moved slowly out of the shadows. "Watch out!" Jay yelled.

He heard Ezili laughing.

Hiram was carrying a suitcase, huge and black, closed with three bright brass hinges. It was so large it was almost a trunk, but he carried it as easily as a normal man might carry a briefcase, and Jay realized he had made it light. Charm took it from him and set it on its end, reverently. Six hands began working simultaneously on the latches.

Jay Ackroyd went cold all over.

Hiram looked at him across the length of the basement. The ace looked rumpled and tired, his impeccably tailored suit stained with sweat. Jay met his eyes; they were full of pain, and shame, and something that might have been terror. He looked as though he was going to cry. When he raised a hand in a gesture that had grown all too familiar to Jay and rubbed at something on the side of his neck, Ackroyd wanted to cry himself.

Sascha stepped into view beside Hiram, his head moving slowly from side to side in tiny birdlike motions as his telepathy tested the waters. It was safe; Sascha nodded. "Open it."

Charm opened the suitcase.

Inside was a young girl, no more than four or five. She was tiny, fair-skinned, blond, naked. And smiling.

Clinging to her in an obscene embrace was a thing that looked like a cross between an aborted fetus and the biggest maggot Jay had ever seen. Its mouth was pressed to the side of her neck, and in the sudden quiet Jay could hear faint sucking sounds.

But its eyes were alive and alert. They found Jay in the darkness and considered him hungrily.

My nightmare, Jay thought wildly. He almost expected it to howl. Warmth spread across his thighs as his bladder let go.

"He is very afraid, master," Sascha said.

"Later I will taste his fear," the little girl replied. She climbed awkwardly from the suitcase and put a dainty hand on Charm to steady herself. She had a voice out of a Shirley Temple movie, but the words belonged to the thing on her back.

"Hiram," Jay pleaded. "Do something."

"There's nothing to be done, Jay," Hiram Worchester said softly. "I'm sorry."

Jay twisted helplessly against his bonds, trying to wrench his hands free. It was useless. He couldn't even *feel* his hands; for all he knew, they had fallen off an hour ago.

"They are strong, master," Ezili said.

"Both aces," Sascha confirmed.

Hiram looked as though he was going to say something. Instead he turned to stare at a wall. Jay called out to him. "Make a fucking fist, Hiram. These guys are nothing compared to you. Pile on the weight until the goddamn leech is a thin film on the floor!"

"You don't understand," Hiram said. "Ti Malice is my master. I couldn't live without his kiss. How could I hurt him?" His huge body shook. "I could . . . never . . . hurt him."

"I will try the boy first," the little girl announced.

If Blaise heard or understood, he gave no sign. They came into the room one by one; the girl first, with the creature Hiram had called Ti Malice glistening against her flesh, then Sascha, Ezili, the centipede, even Charm and the others. Only Hiram remained back in the other room.

Blaise stared up at them blankly, then seemed to wake, as if from a deep sleep. "No!" he shouted, scrambling back across the filthy mattress, as far from Ti Malice as he could go. It wasn't far enough. "No, please."

"Interesting," the girl said. "I can feel it touching the mount's mind, trying to push her away." Stunted vestigial limbs stirred feebly as Ti Malice prepared to move to a new host.

"Not the girl," Jay screamed, "the thing on her back."

Blaise gave him one quick, desperate glance, and in that moment, Jay truly knew the meaning of fear.

"Hold him for me," Ti Malice told Charm with the mouth of its child. The huge joker shambled forward.

The boy's violet eyes went back to Ti Malice and narrowed in a last desperate act of courage as his mind reached out for the parasite's.

Then Blaise began to scream.

4:00 P.M.

Brennan peered through the peephole when the doorbell rang. It was Fadeout, looking bothered and impatient. Brennan smiled and opened the door.

"All right, Quinn," Fadeout said as he stomped into the entranceway to the Magic Kingdom, "what's all this . . . about . . . ?"

His voice faded as he spotted Brennan standing before him, and so did he. But Brennan was ready.

He slammed the door behind the ace, and as Fadeout disappeared, Brennan threw the contents of the metal canister he'd been holding right at him. A fine white powder fluffed out from the container, coating Fadeout from head to toe and sprinkling the floor all around him.

Fadeout blinked astonished eyes, and sneezed. His tongue came out and licked the corner of his mouth. "Jesus Christ!" he exploded. "That's cocaine!"

Brennan nodded.

"Do you know how much money you just threw at me? Jesus Christ! We're talking millions!"

Brennan dropped the canister and drew and aimed his .38 right between Fadeout's eyes. "We're talking dead," he said flatly.

Fadeout backed away with enough white powder clinging to him to make him look a six-foot-tall sugar donut. "You're angry," he said to Brennan.

"You're right," Brennan said. "Calm me down."

"What do you want?"

"Chrysalis's diary." Brennan gestured with his gun. "Or your head, either one. I figure you've read it already. I figure that I can find Dead-head somewhere. I figure he's hungry."

Fadeout barely suppressed a shudder at the mention of Deadhead, the psychotic ace who could access people's memories by eating their brains.

"Well, okay, I guess we can come to some kind of accommodation. It's at my apartment. We can go and pick it up—"

"You can call and have it delivered."

"That's fine, too."

"This way." Brennan gestured with his gun, and Fadeout walked ahead of him, slowly and carefully. "In here," Brennan said.

He led the way to Quinn's combination boudoir and rumpus room, where Quinn himself was already installed in the chair that Brennan had once been held captive in.

"Bummer," Quinn said when they entered the room. He apparently was off his 'lude low and his brain was functioning somewhat normally.

Fadeout fixed him with a steady glare. "We'll talk later," Fadeout said.

"Sit there," Brennan ordered.

Fadeout sat on a chair next to Quinn, and Brennan tossed him a straitjacket he'd found among Quinn's collection of bondage devices. Fadeout slipped it on wordlessly, then Brennan awkwardly tied him into it. To make doubly sure, he further tied Fadeout into the chair using some leather restraints that were also part of the Eskimo's unusual collection.

"Now, about that call," Brennan said.

Fadeout, who by now had given up all pretense at invisibility, grumbled, but did as he was told.

Brennan sat and watched the two as they waited for the delivery to be made. Once or twice Fadeout tried to start a conversation by offering apologies and excuses, but Brennan was having none of it. A look at his face was enough to shut Fadeout up.

Finally the doorbell rang, and Brennan went to answer it. A Werewolf in a Mae West mask was at the door. He handed Brennan the leather-bound journal and looked at him expectantly.

"That's it," Brennan told him. "You're not a delivery boy. You don't get a tip."

The disappointed Werewolf went down the driveway as Brennan went back into Quinn's bedroom.

"Well, it's been delivered," Fadeout said. "How about letting us go?"

Brennan turned to Quinn. "You have servants?"

"Yeah, man. Sunday's their day off."

"So they'll be back tomorrow?"

Quinn nodded.

"They'll let you loose then," he said, and turned to go.

"Okay by me," Quinn said. "Guess I'll cook some acid and meditate on the lessons I learned today."

Fadeout, though, was not so phlegmatic. "Hey, Cowboy!" he called. "Let me loose!"

Brennan shook his head. "Don't push it. You're lucky I'm not leaving you dead."

"Come on!" Fadeout implored, but Brennan just kept walking. "You bastard!" Fadeout yelled, and then he broke into shrill, mocking laughter. "You think you're so damn smart! You'll see what good that stupid book does you!"

Brennan kept walking and left the house, leaving its door open, hoping against all odds that some burglars would come by and empty it. He stopped before Fadeout's brand-new BMW and decided to take it back to the city. He thought about Fadeout's mocking words as he hot-wired the car, and his curiosity compelled him to open the journal.

As he scanned the pages, he realized that in a sense Fadeout was right. There was not a single fact, a single piece of concrete data in the whole book. It was a personal journal where Chrysalis had kept her thoughts, where she wrote in clear, plain, feeling words about her doubts, fears, and anxieties.

Brennan turned to the entry for the day, well over a year and a half ago, when he had offered her his protection and love and she'd turned him down. That was the last day he had seen her alive.

"What," she had written, "am I so afraid of? I'm not afraid to show my hideous deformity to the world every day—in fact I revel in the discomfort my appearance causes, in the revulsion it evokes. *I have to live with it every day; so should everyone else.*

"I make men make love to my ugliness as the price for the information they seek. Why can't I give myself to one who might love me for myself? Is it fear? Fear that he doesn't really care, that he's using me, that he'll drop me the moment he achieves all he wants?

"I'm such a coward.

"Good-bye, my archer, I shall miss you. I shall miss what might have been between us."

The journal hung loosely in Brennan's hands. He didn't want to read any more. He hadn't the right. No one had. He only skimmed the last few entries to make sure they contained nothing that could possibly relate to her death. Then he took the cigarette lighter out of Fadeout's brand-new BMW and burned the journal to ashes there on Quinn's thick, green lawn.

♣

"So fresh," Blaise said. "Intense. Exquisite."

He was naked on the mattress, Ezili spread out beneath him, cocoa-colored thighs spread, her legs locked around his waist as he thrust into her heat. She was covered with a fine dew of perspiration, and she screamed every time the boy pushed into her.

"Slowly, my precious one," Blaise commanded, but of course it wasn't him at all, it was the creature that clung to him like a pale white leech, its mouth pressed to his neck, its tiny eyes closed so it might better enjoy the sensations flooding through the boy's body. "This mount has never known a female," it said. "It grows very excited. Slowly, Ezili-je-rouge, slowly."

Obediently, Ezili slowed beneath them. She showed her teeth when she laughed. "I will make it last," she promised. Her fingers reached up and played with the boy's nipples.

Jay turned his face away from the tableau and found Hiram Worchester standing above him. The huge ace looked as anguished and helpless as Jay had ever seen him. "Untie me," Jay whispered. "Now, while they're occupied."

Ezili was screaming again, her voice husky with pleasure.

For a long time, Hiram Worchester said nothing. There was only the wet, angry sound of flesh on flesh, and Charm's guttural singing from the next room. Finally Hiram turned away and walked off without saying a word.

"Now!" Ti Malice said in Blaise's voice. The boy's body jerked in orgasm. Ezili's legs tightened around him, and she laughed.

5:00 P.M.

Jennifer was awake when Brennan returned to Father Squid's. She and the priest were playing chess. When she saw him, she stood and threw her arms around him and kissed him, then held him at arms' length. "Why did you let me sleep through all the excitement? You almost got yourself killed without me!"

"Almost," Brennan agreed. He threw himself down on the sofa and sighed deeply.

"What's the matter?" Jennifer asked.

Brennan shook his head. "It's all gone. I've used up all the possible clues. There's nothing left to investigate. Bludgeon, Oddity, Wyrm, Morkle, Quasiman. None of them did it. Her journal was no help. Her . . . files . . . have been burned. Everything and everyone else has vanished into thin air. Sascha, Ezili, her master . . ."

Jennifer sat down beside him and laid her hand on his cheek.

"Is there no one else to question?" Father Squid asked.

Brennan shook his head wearily. "I don't think so, Father."

"There's me," a small voice peeped.

Everyone turned to see one of the homunculi come out shyly from behind the couch.

"How long have you been there?" Father Squid asked.

"Awhile. I was watching. There is nothing else I can do."

"Can you help?" Brennan asked, desperate for any information. "Have you heard of any of those names?"

"Ezili," the homunculus said. "I've heard that name."

"Yeah," Brennan said. "A lot of people have. Only no one knows where she is."

"Perhaps she's at the loft."

"Loft?" Brennan said, suddenly sitting upright on the sofa.

"Yes. When Sascha started acting strange, the Lady wanted to know about this woman he was seen with. We followed her to a loft near the East River. Two of my brothers went there, but they never came back."

"Do you remember this address?" Brennan asked in a low voice.

"I think so," the homunculus said.

Jennifer looked at Brennan. "You're not going alone this time," she said.

Brennan nodded. It was only a few hours until dark.

◆

"I'll make it get up and do a little dance," Blaise had said when he'd first seen Charm in Piedmont Park. The memory had still been there, in the back of the boy's mind, and his master had found it and been amused.

Charm had been dancing for almost forty minutes now. One of the pairs of legs, attached to the female body in the middle, had stopped moving twenty minutes ago, but the rest of the joker continued its grotesque shuffle.

When Charm finally collapsed in exhaustion, the huge body slumped against the couch, jolting it sideways almost a foot. The silence that followed was profound and frightening.

Sascha and the centipede man entered the room. "Does it please you?" Sascha asked.

"Very much," Ti Malice replied through Blaise. "It feels intensely, and when its mind takes hold of another's, it feels the other's emotions as well as the physical sensations . . . so much to savor, all at once . . . flavors, colors . . . the textures of two or three bodies . . . exquisite . . ."

"A treasure," Ezili said. She sat on the mattress, one arm coiled around the boy's skinny leg. Both of them were still naked.

"His powers will be useful, master," Sascha pointed out. "Any mount you might desire is yours now, even the most powerful of aces. The boy can bring them to you, and hold them still, helpless, while you take them."

"Yes," the creature had Blaise say. "You've done well. You shall have the kiss soon, my dear one."

Sascha looked like a dog who'd just been thrown a SlimJim.

"This mount has known death in a way I have never tasted," Blaise said for his master. "It has joined with the minds of the dying . . . tasted the sweet with the bitter, the killing with the dying . . . sipped at the darkness itself . . . yes . . ."

Blaise turned slowly, studying the others in the basement. The thing that rode him opened its own pale, weak eyes.

"Him," the centipede man said eagerly. He pointed at Jay with half a dozen knives. "Kill him. He sent all your other mounts away, master. He's dangerous."

Eyes fixed on Jay; Blaise's violet and strangely wide, his master's vague and frightening. Jay stared right back at him.

Until Hiram stepped in the way. "No," he said. "Not Jay. He's an ace."

"Ackroyd is powerful," Sascha agreed. "A projecting teleport. When he is yours, you can never be threatened again. He can point a finger and move you to safety whenever an enemy threatens."

"That is good." The eyes began to move again.

They stopped on the centipede man.

It took the joker a long moment to realize what was happening. "No, master," he said. "Not me. I'm . . . I'm useful, too. . . ."

"Only a joker," Ezili said. "He wanted to kill them both. Your new treasures."

"I was afraid," the centipede said. "They were aces, dangerous, I didn't want you hurt. No, please . . . I just didn't want you hurt, master."

"He wanted to keep your kiss for himself," Ezili said.

"In a moment he's going to attack you with his knives," Sascha reported matter-of-factly.

Blaise's eyes narrowed slightly; the knives clattered against the stone floor as they fell from limp fingers.

"Hiram, do something," Jay said.

Hiram turned away.

The human centipede stood immobile, his body frozen by the power of Blaise's mind. But the boy must have left him his mouth, because he was still begging. "No, please, take one of the others," he cried in that high, sharp voice. "Take the woman . . . or the girl. Yes, take her. Or Charm, take Charm, he can't even talk, he's stupid, take him. Please don't hurt me, master. I love you."

"*Blaise!*" Jay screamed. "*Let him go!*"

The boy didn't even turn his head.

The centipede man reached over with a half dozen of his right hands and seized the uppermost of his left arms. "I love you, master," he whimpered. "I love you, I love you." Then the words turned into a high, thin shriek of pain as he ripped the arm right off his body. Blood spurted.

"He loves you," Ezili said, smiling, as the man's blood-soaked hands dropped the severed arm to the floor and seized the one below it. The second arm didn't come off quite so cleanly. The man began to use his fingernails, tearing at his own flesh with all the strength left in him.

Hiram walked to a corner of the cellar and threw up.

Jay couldn't watch. He looked at Blaise. There was a look in those dark eyes that Jay had never seen on a human face before. The boy's penis stirred slightly and began to rise, until a monstrous erection was growing from the tangle of coppery red pubic hair. Ezili noticed it, too, and covered it with her mouth.

But when the joker's second arm came off, she took her lips away from him just long enough to say, "He loves you not."

9:00 P.M.

Someone had broken in here before.

Brennan glanced at Jennifer, who was waiting below him on the rickety fire escape while he considered the bedroom window. One of its panes had been partially removed by a glass cutter. He took a deep breath and rested for a moment.

His right arm, covered from wrist to elbow in a hard plastic cast, throbbed like hell. He'd been careful while climbing the fire escape, but he couldn't keep from banging it around a little.

Brennan tried the window that opened into the second-story loft above a closed-down printing company. It was unlocked. He took a deep breath, lifted the window, and entered the bedroom.

It was dark and quiet. He motioned Jennifer to stay behind. She nodded and Brennan went through the bedroom into a part of the loft that had been subdivided into a number of small rooms. He moved through the darkness, peering into them. They were mostly bedrooms, but one had been soundproofed and turned into a torture chamber. Thcy were all empty.

A lavish kitchen was opposite the warren of rooms. A huge living area with white carpeting formed the other half of the loft. Brennan crept down the hallway and peered into the living area. It, too, seemed empty. He flicked on the light switch. The walls were covered with weird, painted designs.

Brennan approached one to look at it more closely, and a hideous, flat flap of flesh rose into the air from where it had been resting out of sight on the sofa, and swooped at him with the speed of a diving falcon. The joker's face, located on its underside, was almost human, except for the male genitalia that hung below its pale green eyes.

Brennan ducked, instinctively throwing his arm up to protect his face, and the joker rammed it, sending a wave of agony lancing through his system. He fell and lost his gun.

The thing made a tight turn and came back at Brennan again, its skin pale and pimpled, an erect spine from its underside pointing at Brennan like a lance.

There was a loud explosion, reverberating endlessly in the living room, and the thing jerked away, keening a loud cry of anger and pain. Brennan glanced up the corridor at Jennifer, who was standing braced, her pistol out and smoking.

The manta-ray joker swooped at her like a spinning, rolling airplane, and she ghosted. It cut right through her and darted into the bedroom from which they'd entered. There was a crash of shattering glass as it broke through a window and escaped.

"What was that?" Jennifer demanded in a shaking voice.

"I don't know," Brennan said. "A guard?"

"Well, it didn't do a very good job," she said, coming down the corridor and helping Brennan to his feet.

Brennan recovered his gun and focused shakily on the designs painted on the walls of the living room. "What is that stuff?" he asked.

"*Veve,*" Jennifer said. "Haitian religious designs. Symbols of the *loas,* the voodoo gods."

"I see," Brennan said, though he didn't. He especially couldn't understand what any of this had to do with Chrysalis's death. He moved almost aimlessly through the living room, tired and numb with pain and failure.

"What should we look for?" Jennifer asked.

"Anything," Brennan said in a voice with little hope. "Anything that might somehow shed light on these insane happenings. Anything that might lead us to Sascha."

He opened a door and found himself staring in a hall closet that was jammed with clothing, mostly coats of all kinds for both sexes and all sizes. The Oddity, he remembered, had been looking through Chrysalis's bedroom closet, perhaps searching for the mysterious coat that had been mentioned in Chrysalis's will.

"Give me a hand," he said over his shoulder to Jennifer. "Maybe there's something . . ."

He was reaching for a mink coat when he noticed a lightweight linen jacket dangling from the hook on the inside of the closet door. He took the jacket down instead, frowning as he looked at it. It was pure white linen, clean and spotless, except for an almost unnoticeable spray of bloodstains near the bottom edge. He stared at it for a long moment and then reached into its pockets. The left one was empty. The right one contained a pack of antique playing cards. He shuffled through it. The ace of spades was missing.

He looked at Jennifer. The pain, weariness, and frustration was gone from his face. His eyes were hard, his voice soft and dangerous.

"Chrysalis's killer," he said quietly, "is in Atlanta."

10:00 P.M.

"Bring me my cloak," Blaise said.

The boy's mouth still glistened from Ezili's juices. Ti Malice, his eyes alive and avid, clung to his neck, talking with his tongue. When it grew quiet, you could hear a faint sucking sound, like an infant nursing at its mother's tit.

Hiram came forward with the cloak. It was heavy purple felt, the inside lined with black satin. He helped Blaise into it, fussing with the drape the way he sometimes fussed with Jay's suits. The cloak was too long for Blaise; the end of it trailed in the dirt. Hiram made adjustments. Then he lifted the voluminous hood, pulling it forward over the boy's head, concealing the bright red hair and the thing riding on his back. With the ties knotted around his throat, his face shadowed, Blaise looked like a hunchback.

"I will ride this mount into the world," Ti Malice announced through Blaise. "Ezili, you will accompany me. Dress."

Ezili rose from the mattress, sleek and lazy as a cat. Her smooth, coffee-colored skin was still spattered with blood. She saw Jay watching her, smiled, and ran a tongue across her lips as she bent to pick up her dress.

"Hiram," Jay said, begging, "*please.*" The thought of Blaise wandering through the streets of Atlanta, with his awesome mind-control powers at the disposal of Ti Malice, frightened him witless. "You don't realize how powerful Blaise is. You don't know what you're turning loose."

Ezili laughed as she slipped into her dress, pulled it down around her breasts. "Are you sure of that, little one?"

Hiram didn't hear a word. "When will you return?"

"When I grow bored with the new mount," Ti Malice replied in the boy's familiar voice. Blaise reached up, touched Hiram's beard, gently stroked his cheek. "You shall not want for my kiss," he promised. Hiram smiled.

"What about Ackroyd, master?" Sascha asked.

Blaise turned his body. The boy's violet eyes stared at Jay, and he could almost feel the other eyes on him, the ones hidden in the blackness beneath the hood. "I will try the other mount when I return," Blaise said. "Keep it safe for me."

Jay tried once more. *"Hiram!"* he yelled.

Hiram opened the cellar door. Blaise swirled his cloak around him as he turned, and climbed up into the Atlanta night.

Monday
July 25, 1988

THE NIGHTMARE CAME AGAIN. The woods, the steps, the cone-faced thing turning, turning. . . .

Jay woke in darkness, screaming.

"Jay?" a deep voice asked. "Are you all right?"

Dimly, through the dark of the cellar, he could see Hiram looming above him, a vast shadow. Jay struggled against his bonds, gave it up, slumped back with a groan. "No," he said in a hoarse whisper. Ti Malice had been gone for hours. "I'm not all right. I'm tied up in this stinking cellar, I had to watch some poor bastard rip himself apart with his bare hands, Blaise is out doing God knows what, and in a little while a giant maggot is going to fasten itself to my neck and suck my blood, so *I'm not all right.*"

Somewhere in the middle of that Jay's whisper had turned into a scream. He heard Charm stir, woken from sleep. Then the joker began to sing "The House of the Rising Sun." It was just what Jay needed.

Hiram sat on a corner of the old sofa, shoulders slumped. "I'm sorry," he said weakly. "If there's anything I can do . . ."

"You can untie me," Jay said quickly.

"Sascha would know the moment I began," Hiram said helplessly.

"So?" Jay said. "What's Sascha going to do? Charm's strong, but you're an *ace*, dammit. You can handle him. This is the best chance we're going to get. Once my hands are free—"

"I *can't*, Jay," Hiram said, cutting him off in a voice thick with despair. "I would if I could, but . . . Jay, I'm sorry. I never meant for any of this to happen, you have to believe that."

"I believe it," Jay said gently. Hiram sounded weary, and heartsick, and full of pain. There was a long silence. "How long?" Jay finally asked.

"A year and a half," Hiram replied. "It happened on the tour. In Haiti. Ezili was his lure. I deluded myself into thinking I was seducing her, but of course it was the other way around. Afterward, when I'd dozed off, she opened the door, and the master took me in my sleep. Once I was his, he used me to smuggle him into the United States. I had money, influence. It wasn't difficult at all."

"This is your chance to break free," Jay urged. "Use it."

" 'It's been the ruin of many a poor boy,' " Charm sang softly. " 'And me, by God, I'm one.' "

Hiram could not look at him. He shook his head.

"Untie me," Jay whispered. "That's all you need to do. Simple. I'll handle the rest, just get my hands free. You don't even have to watch. I'll pop you to the Jokertown Clinic, you can get treatment for . . . for whatever he's done to you. Do it now, Hiram. We don't know how much time we have left."

"You'd *hurt* him," Hiram said. His voice broke. "You don't understand . . . his kiss, it's like . . . words can't describe it, Jay. When you're part of him, it's as though you're alive, for the first time in your life. You feel such intense pleasure. Food, drink, sex, even the simple act of breathing, it all becomes intoxicating . . . but when he leaves you, when he moves to another mount . . . that's like *dying*, Jay. The world turns gray, and after a week or so, the physical withdrawal sets in. You can't imagine the pain. You *crave* him. It's a hunger, and if it's not fed . . ." He looked up, his eyes imploring understanding. "Besides, he's not evil, not the way you and I understand it. Without his mounts, he'd die. He needs us, just as we need him. It's just that his morality is . . . different than ours."

"In New York," Jay said, "after Sascha had run to Atlanta with your little pal, I found a torture chamber in his apartment. Not to mention a body in his bathroom."

"Yes," Hiram said. He looked away again. "A mount. One of the jokers." His voice was so low that Jay could barely hear it over Charm's singing. "Sometimes . . . pain is different from pleasure, he says, but just as . . . as interesting. The sensations of death are . . . especially . . . especially . . ."

"I got it. He tortures his more expendable mounts to death to get a few jollies, right? But he's not bad, just misunderstood." He snorted. "Hiram, that thing *defines* evil."

For a long time, Hiram Worchester said nothing. There was only Charm's guttural singing from the next room. But finally Hiram's lips moved, so weakly that Jay did not catch the words.

"What?" he whispered.

Hiram turned his head. "Foul . . . oh God, Jay, you don't know what it's been like . . . so many times, I just wished for it to be over . . . that he'd kill me the next time . . . but I'm too powerful, you see. I'm an ace. He wants aces . . . wants the powers . . . I'll never be free. And you . . . it'll be the same. . . ."

"No way," Jay said. "Hiram, don't let him take me."

"I can't hurt him! I *told* you."

"Then hurt me," Jay said. "Kill *me*, if it comes to that. But don't let him take me." He never thought he'd hear himself beg for death, but his flesh was crawling at the very thought of Ti Malice. It would be like his nightmare, but this time he would never wake, this time it would go on and on forever.

Hiram Worchester stared at him with sudden wonder on his broad face. "Kill you," he murmured. His fingers flexed, closing slowly into a fist, then opening again. "He would be angry, Jay . . . so very angry, you can't imagine. Perhaps . . . perhaps then he might . . . free *me*."

Jay knew what he meant by "free."

7:00 A.M.

They waited at the airport all night for the first available flight to Atlanta. Jennifer fell asleep around midnight, but Brennan could not. He sat up all night meditating on a playing card, an ace of spades, left him in a will.

When it was time to board the flight, he slipped it into the breast pocket of his denim jacket where it would be close at hand.

9:00 A.M.

When the door opened, Jay caught a brief glimpse of pale, thin sunlight filtering down from above. Blaise stepped into the cellar, stumbling on the last step, almost tripping over the end of his cloak. The boy looked dead on his feet, his face drawn and pale. He'd been ridden to exhaustion, and beyond.

Sascha stepped forward to remove the heavy felt cloak. "We were concerned for you, master," he said as he undid the ties. "We heard sirens . . . screams in the night. . . ."

Ezili laughed from the doorway. "The night was magic, Sascha," she said, running a tongue across her lower lip. "Hartmann went mad. We watched it on the television. A circus of blood. Then the jokers went mad, too. We wandered in the park and played with them all night long. No one noticed." She shut the cellar door behind her, and darkness resumed its reign.

"This mount is tired," Ti Malice announced in Blaise's hoarse, weary tones. "It is time to try the other. Bring it."

Everyone looked at Jay.

Sascha folded the cloak, set it aside, turned his face toward Jay. There might have been pity in his eyes, if he'd had eyes. He nodded at Charm, and the huge joker shambled forward.

"Can't we talk this over?" Jay asked.

Charm ignored him. Hands grasped his legs, shoulders, feet, and jerked him into the air. Charm flung him over a shoulder, carried him across the cellar. The place still smelled like a butcher shop. Flies swarmed around decaying pieces of human flesh. Charm tossed Jay down on the mattress. Ezili bent over him and kissed him lightly, her lips wet and hot. "Soon," she said.

"Prepare it for me," Blaise's voice commanded.

Charm grabbed a handful of Jay's shirt and yanked sharply. The fabric tore with a loud ripping sound, until it got tangled in the jacket.

"Its bonds are in the way," Ti Malice noticed. "Untie it. Strip it."

"Master," Sascha cautioned, "he is dangerous when his hands are free."

"I can't even feel my fucking hands," Jay complained. He tried not to think about what he was thinking about.

Sascha picked right up on the thought he was trying not to think. "He thinks he'll have a chance once he's untied."

"Is it afraid?" Ti Malice asked.

"Of you, very much. Of being a mount. And there is some other fear, an older fear. . . ." The telepath frowned. "A dream he's had. You remind him of this nightmare, master."

"Free its hands," Ti Malice said. "This young mount has the power to hold it still."

Charm turned him over, slammed him down into the mattress, and pinned him with a boot while hands fumbled behind his back.

Jay's wrists had been bound for so long he couldn't feel any difference when they were free. Charm kicked roughly at one arm, and it fell heavily to the side. His shoulder shrieked with pain. Roll over and get the hand up, he thought, but Charm was pressing down on him. He couldn't move.

Then something else grabbed him, something stronger and harder and more powerful than Charm's twisted body would ever be.

Blaise's mind.

The foot went away. Jay stirred, but it was Ti Malice who moved his arms, through Blaise. When he rolled over, they were right there, kneeling beside him on the mattress.

The boy was still smiling. His master peered over one bare, bruised shoulder. Jay could hear the faint sucking sound, could see the boy's blood pulsing through pale translucent veins in the creature's glistening flesh.

The boy spoke. "Strip him."

Charm peeled the jacket off Jay's back. It was damp with sweat and spatters of blood. The joker ripped away his shirt. Now he was bare-chested, his throat and neck exposed to the demon's kiss.

"He's trembling," Ezili said. "Trembling for the kiss."

Jay felt a faint tingling in his hands. He tried to move them, to make a gun, to point. He couldn't move. Blaise's power and his master's will held him perfectly still. Jay's eyes flicked down to his hands. They were pale, bloodless, his wrists bruised and purple. He looked like he was wearing fish-belly gloves, and there were dark red lines in his skin where the wires had cut deep. He tried to flex his fingers, make the feeling come back. Nothing.

"Master," Hiram said.

He stepped out of the corner, looming over the mattress behind them, his shadow almost as huge as Charm's. Ti Malice looked at him with Blaise's eyes, but Jay couldn't even turn his head. He felt Hiram's presence more than he saw it. His hands were full of pins and needles as his circulation returned.

"Master," Hiram repeated. He sounded frightened. "Please. Let this one go."

"Why?" Ti Malice wanted to know.

The tingling in Jay's hands had begun to turn to pain. The pins and needles were replaced by knives and pincers. He gasped in sudden pain, and the noise made him realize he still had control of his voice. Of course, he thought. Like the centipede man. Ti Malice liked to hear them beg.

"He is . . . a friend," Hiram said. "I've never asked you for any-thing before. Please."

Ti Malice turned to Sascha. "What will it do if I take this new mount."

The telepath turned his head toward Hiram. "Nothing," he re-ported after a moment. "He could never hurt you."

Ti Malice turned back to Jay as if Hiram Worchester no longer existed. "Down," he said.

Jay lay down on his side so his master would have easy access to his back and his neck. Blaise stretched out beside him on the mattress. He was so close Jay could smell Ezili on him, close enough for their bare chests to touch lightly, close enough for a kiss.

His hands were on fire, the blood rushing through his fingers like white-hot wires. It was an effort not to faint.

Ti Malice pulled its mouth away from the boy's neck with a soft wet sound. The creature began to wriggle up and over Blaise's shoul-der, toward Jay. Its own limbs were stunted. It writhed forward like some huge worm, an inch at a time, tiny three-fingered hands grasping feebly at the boy's flesh for purchase. Blood trickled weakly from the ragged hole it had left behind. Jay forced his eyes away from the horror coming toward him and looked into the boy's eyes. Blaise seemed dazed, lost, and Jay remembered what Hiram had said. *When he leaves you, it's like dying.* "Blaise," he said urgently. "Let me go."

Those deep violet eyes blinked once, twice, tried to focus. "He . . ." Blaise said. It was his own voice, his own words, and for a split second Jay dared to hope. "He said . . . hold you."

He felt the cold wet touch of Ti Malice's flesh on his own as the thing's withered hand pulled at a shoulder. Don't look, Jay told himself. Like in the dream. Don't ever look up at the moon; if you do, you're lost. He had dreamed that dream a thousand times; he knew better than to look.

He looked.

The creature's mouth was round, like the mouth of a fish, and as it slid forward in jerks and starts, its tongue moved in and out. Its tongue was round, too, flushed with blood, red and glistening, like some obscene blind snake.

Its eyes were wise and cruel and terrible.

Blaise was fucking hopeless. "*Hiram!*" Jay screamed.

Hiram's voice came from a long way away. "I can't hurt him."

Ti Malice's atrophied legs kicked feebly at Blaise's face as it moved off the boy and onto Jay. It must have kicked too hard. Blaise winced. For a moment, Jay felt his fingers flex.

The thing was crawling across him, his flesh crawling beneath it. But there was something important. . . . "Shit!" Jay said.

"*Master!*" Sascha cried out in alarm.

Jay drowned out his warning with a shout. "*Hiram!*" he screamed. "*Hurt Blaise, dammit. Hurt Blaise!*"

Hiram kicked the boy in the head.

Charm was stumbling forward, Ezili, Sascha, but they were all late, too late. Jay had his body back. He rolled to one side and came down flat on his back, with Ti Malice clinging to his chest, thrashing as frantically as a worm impaled on a hook.

His hand came up, but his fingers were like wood.

Ti Malice slithered up his chest, looking straight down into his eyes.

Jay folded back three fingers, stuck one out, lifted his thumb, tried to point. His hand was shaking.

The blind snake came coiling out.

Jay stuck a shaking finger into Ti Malice's eye.

There was a short, crisp *pop*.

Jay felt a sharp pain, and blood began to spurt from the hole in his neck, but he hardly noticed. The weight was off his chest.

Ezili screamed.

"Oh, God," Sascha said.

Blaise began to weep uncontrollably.

And behind him, he heard Hiram Worchester say, very softly, "It's over."

10:00 A.M.

The Atlanta airport was crowded with weary delegates heading for home, still buzzing about a convention that no one was ever likely to forget. Brennan pushed through them, uncaring and unseeing, with Jennifer in his wake. They didn't even stop to join the crowd watching a midget being cut out of a cat carrying case. He staggered out, rumpled and red-eyed, croaking, "Water, water!"

They were nearing the end of the line, but Brennan was feeling no elation. His anesthesia-provoked dream of the night before was still vivid in his mind. Intellectually he didn't blame himself for Chrysalis's death, but he realized that emotionally he did. He remembered the line from Tachyon's eulogy about the harsh expectations Chrysalis's ghost would have, but he knew that Chrysalis's ghost wasn't driving him. It was his own savage ghost, fueled by his unrelenting memories of her. He wondered if he'd ever be able to lay her to rest.

They caught a cab downtown and stopped at a pawnshop to buy two guns, a Walther PPK automatic for Brennan and a Smith and Wesson .38 Chief Special for Jennifer. He paid cash; the proprietor didn't ask any questions.

NOON

The hospital wanted to admit all three of them, but Jay was having none of it. He hung around just long enough to answer a few questions, cadge a fresh supply of painkillers, and make sure they were going to take good care of Blaise. Then he grabbed Hiram and had the nurse phone for a cab.

The cellar of the burned-out ruin where Ti Malice had set up housekeeping was almost an hour's ride from the center of Atlanta. Hiram stared vacantly out the window as they drove. Every now and then he had a fit of uncontrollable trembling, and a look of panic came into his eyes. "I'm all alone now," he said once. Jay didn't reply. Conversation would have required more energy than he had right now. He stretched out and closed his eyes.

The next thing he knew, Hiram was prodding him gently in the ribs. "We're here," he said.

Jay sat up groggily, fumbled for his wallet. It was empty. "I've paid the fare already," Hiram said. He helped Jay out of the taxi and into the hotel.

An alarm was screeching in the Marriott lobby; one of the elevators was stuck between floors. Jay winced; his headache was already a blinding band of pain behind his eyes, the noise was the last thing he needed. He jabbed at the call button savagely, and they took a different elevator up to Tachyon's floor.

Jay unlocked the suite with Blaise's key, turned on the lights, and went to the bar to mix himself a stiff one. Hiram poked his head into the bedroom. "Tachyon?" he called out. There was no answer. "He's not here," Hiram said, returning to the living room.

"Yeah," Jay said. "I figured." He sat down to wait.

Hiram moved to the bar and looked at the bottles, but made no move to mix himself a drink. He just stood there, staring, like a big lost child. Then he started to tidy up. He rinsed out a couple of dirty glasses, picked up an ashtray full of cigarette butts, looked around for a place to dump it. There was a jar full of ashes sitting on the bar, next to the liquor. Hiram peered into it curiously for a moment, shrugged, and dumped the butts in there.

They both turned at the sound of the door opening.

Dr. Tachyon sat in a wheelchair, his bandaged stump cradled in his lap. Behind him, pushing the chair, was Jack Braun.

"You," Braun said, glaring at Jay. "We've been turning over half the city looking for you. Where the hell have you been?"

"Jay, Hiram," Tachyon said. He started to rise from the wheelchair. "What's happened? Where's Blaise?"

"The hospital," Jay admitted.

Tachyon made a choking sound. "Is he all right?"

"He has a small fracture of the skull, and he's lost a few teeth, plus some bruises and abrasions, and a bad case of shock. But the doctors figure he's going to be okay. The hospital wanted to keep him under observation for a few days, that's all."

Dr. Tachyon staggered as if Jay's words were a physical blow. Jack Braun clouded up like a thunderhead and came storming forward. "You goddamned jerk. He's only a kid, what the hell did you think you were doing, dragging him into some sleazy—"

Jay pointed, Jack popped. Maybe Braun finished his thought center stage at Freakers. Then again, maybe not.

"Sorry," Jay mumbled to Tachyon. "My head's about to split open and hatch, I just can't take any more right now. Should you be out of that wheelchair?"

"It was Jack's idea," Tachyon said. Jay could see how weak the little man still was. When he stumbled, he put out a hand to steady himself, but there was no hand there. His bandaged stump fetched up hard against the back of the sofa, and Tachyon gasped.

"Sit down," Jay said.

Tachyon sat back down in the wheelchair, cradling his stump in his lap. Jay turned back to the bar. "What are you doing?" Tach asked.

"Pouring you a drink," Jay said. "You're going to need one."

He filled the second tumbler up with bourbon and ice cubes, brought it to Tachyon, and put it into his unresisting left hand. "I don't . . . I don't drink bourbon," Tach said.

"Drink it," Jay said.

Tachyon drank it, his pale lilac eyes full of dread. "Tell me," he said when the glass was half-empty.

Jay told him all of it.

To his credit, the alien listened without interrupting. Tears began to roll down his cheeks when Jay reached the part about the centipede man, but still he held his tongue.

"Once Ti Malice was gone, the fight went out of the mounts. Ezili pitched a screaming fit, and the other woman, the girl with the baby, made a break for it. The rest just gaped at us. It was like they couldn't quite comprehend what was happening. I was going to call the cops, but Hiram stopped me."

"Hiram?" Tach said, looking over at the big ace.

Hiram nodded ponderously, as if his head were almost too heavy to move. "We had all done . . . vile things. Myself included. What purpose would be served by imprisoning the mounts? We were only his instruments, his hands, his mouth, his eyes. It was Ti Malice who murdered, not your grandson. I told Jay there was no sense in bringing Blaise to trial. The real murderer was already gone. And the rest of them . . . were they any different? You knew Sascha long before Ti Malice took him, doctor. He was never an evil man. Ezili was the worst, but even there . . . how much was Ezili and how much was the master? She had been his prize mount her entire life."

"They're all going to be living in hell anyway," Jay said.

"With me," Hiram added darkly.

Tach looked from one to the other. "Without the kiss . . ."

Hiram nodded. "You . . . you cannot imagine."

"Oh, Hiram," Tachyon said, his voice thick with pity for his old friend. "You should have come to me."

"There are a lot of things I should have done," Hiram said.

"Anyway," Jay said, "I let the mounts go."

"All of them?" Tachyon said, astonished.

"I didn't figure I had the right to pick and choose," Jay said. "Charm was the only one I thought twice about. He was the one who killed Chrysalis."

"Charm?" Tachyon said. "But why?"

"Chrysalis knew everything about everybody. Ti Malice depended on secrecy for safety. Exposed, he was pitifully vulnerable. She must have found out about him somehow, but what she didn't know was that Sascha was already his. The way I figure, her trusted telepath told his master that Chrysalis was getting close, so Ti Malice sent

Charm to take her out. It adds up. The killer *had* to be someone Sascha knew, otherwise he would never have gotten inside the Palace without being detected. Maybe Ti Malice rode Charm personally that morning, to experience the sensation of beating someone to death. Or maybe not. I don't suppose we'll ever know."

"All this time searching for the man who killed Chrysalis," Tachyon murmured softly, "and yet you chose to let him go."

"Charm's fucked up enough," Jay said. "Besides, it wasn't Charm, it was Ti Malice. And Ti Malice is gone."

Dr. Tachyon sipped from his drink and thought about that for a long time. Finally the alien gave a short, curt nod. "So much blood," he said. "So much killing. It has to stop, Jay."

"Yeah," Jay said. "Maybe Barnett is right."

"No," Tach said.

Hiram Worchester stood up suddenly. "I should go. I have to pack . . . check out. . . ." His voice trailed off.

"Of course," Tachyon said.

"Go on," Jay told him. "I'll come down in a minute."

Hiram nodded and stepped out into the hall. When the door closed behind him, Ackroyd turned back to Tachyon. "He's going to need your help, doc. He's an addict, and from what he says, the kiss is a hundred times more addictive than heroin."

"Hiram will have all the help he requires," Tachyon said. "I owe him a debt I can never repay. A blood debt. My grandson's life." The alien shook his head. "I could have helped him," he said plaintively. "Why didn't he tell me?"

"There's a better question. You're supposed to be Hiram's friend. So am I. So how come, all this time, we never noticed that anything was wrong?"

Dr. Tachyon just looked at him. Tears welled up in his eyes, and behind them, guilt.

"Shit," Jay said. He was tired of tears, tired of guilt and shame and fear and pain. "Just forget it, okay? There's nothing we can do about it except try to get him through. Hiram used all the strength he had left in him to kick your grandson in the head. He's going to need us."

"Then we must not fail him," Tachyon said.

Jay nodded. Suddenly he felt very weary. "I better go down and keep Hiram company," he said. "He's still pretty shaky."

"Of course," Tachyon said.

But when Jay opened the door, Hiram was right there, in the hall. His huge body was trembling, and he looked up at Jay from forlorn eyes. "Hiram, what's wrong?" Jay asked.

"It's . . . nothing," Hiram began. "I suppose . . . an anxiety attack." He blinked, as if to clear his head. "Jay . . . if you wouldn't mind . . . could you . . . come down to the room with me? It's just that I . . . would rather not be alone right now. Can you understand that?"

Jay nodded. As he took Hiram by the arm, Dr. Tachyon rose unsteadily from his wheelchair. "We'll both go," the little alien announced in a tone that brooked no dissent. Hiram looked at them both gratefully. Jay figured they must have made quite a sight as they limped off together.

While they waited for the elevator to arrive, Tachyon turned back to Jay. "One thing," he asked. "You never said where you teleported Ti Malice."

"Funny thing about that," Jay said. "The way my power works, I have to visualize a place real good before I can teleport anyone there. I have to be able to get a clear picture in my head, really see it in my mind's eye. I got a bunch of places like that, places I know inside out. Sometimes it's just reflex. I don't have time to think about what I'm doing or where I'm going to send someone. I just point, and they wind up the first place that pops into my head."

"Yes?" Tachyon said politely.

"I made a lot of phone calls from the hospital. Ti Malice hasn't shown up in any of my usual places. Somehow, though, I didn't think he would. I looked right into that son of a bitch's face when he was crawling toward me, and the only thing that popped into my mind was this nightmare I've been having since I was a kid." Jay coughed apologetically. "I know that place *real* well," he said. "So you figure it out."

Dr. Tachyon thought about it for a moment. There was the sound of a chime. The elevator doors opened. Tach nodded slowly to Jay, turned, and entered the car.

1:00 P.M.

Brennan heard the outer door to the suite open, tired voices, then the door close. He stood up, framed in the doorway leading into the bedroom portion of the suite, gun in hand. Tachyon, Ackroyd, and Worchester stood clumped together, astonishment on their faces as they saw Brennan.

"Daniel! What are you doing here?"

Brennan knew that Tachyon had lost a hand, but that knowledge didn't prepare him for the pale, drawn, bedraggled figure before him. Tachyon had obviously been through a lot the past week, but, Brennan thought grimly, it wasn't quite over yet.

"Tracking Chrysalis's killer," Brennan said grimly.

Tachyon's bloodshot eyes went wide with astonishment. "Surely—"

"What the hell are you talking about?" Ackroyd interrupted. He looked a little worse for wear, himself. His face was puffy and bruised and he seemed to be favoring one side.

Brennan shook his head and gestured with his gun. "Sit on the bed," he said in a cold voice, "and I'll tell you a story about a murder."

Hiram hung back for a moment, then did as Brennan ordered. Ackroyd sat down next to Worchester and kept his hands carefully in his lap.

"Oh, God," Hiram moaned. "Will this never end?"

"Let's give him a chance," Tachyon said.

"Why?" Ackroyd asked truculently.

"Because I know who killed Chrysalis," Brennan said softly.

Ackroyd frowned. "It was Malice's joker goon. Chrysalis had discovered him—"

"No, it wasn't." Brennan took a deep breath so that he could speak in a calm, even voice. "I was Chrysalis's lover," he said. "Perhaps even her friend. That alone might have brought me back to track down her killer. But the murderer added insult to that injury. He tried to frame me for her death." He stared unblinkingly at Ackroyd. "Even you admit that was a clumsy job."

Ackroyd nodded reluctantly. "Yeah. It had me going for a while, but it didn't take me long to realize it was a setup."

Brennan nodded, switched his gaze to Tachyon. "I had no idea why Chrysalis had been killed. Any number of things could have triggered the murder. I couldn't isolate the motive, so I concentrated on finding an ace strong enough to crush Chrysalis. But that, too, proved to be a blind alley, because Chrysalis wasn't killed by an ace with super strength."

"What?" Ackroyd said. "That's ridiculous."

Brennan shook his head. "I knew something was wrong at the crime scene when I first saw it, but it took me a while to figure it out. There was very little blood in Chrysalis's office. She'd been killed before being pulped. Her heart had stopped pumping so there was no blood sprayed on the walls, desk, or floor."

Tachyon nodded. "That makes sense."

"Someone was covering his tracks again, pretending that Chrysalis had been battered to death by an ace with extraordinary strength. But who?" Brennan shook his head. "The list of suspects had again become endless, but I thought I could narrow it down by questioning Sascha. He was a telepath, he'd been on the murder scene, and he was acting peculiar. I figured he knew more than he was admitting. He'd disappeared, but I thought I could track him down."

"You couldn't have found him," Ackroyd said. "He was here in Atlanta."

"That's right," Brennan agreed. "But during the investigation I found out that he was in thrall to a mysterious master, someone called Ti Malice. Then I found Malice's apartment, and in the apartment was a closet, and in the closet was a coat, and in the coat were these." He carefully reached into his hip pocket with his broken arm and took out a deck of playing cards. They were ornate, but worn and tattered and of great age and apparent delicacy.

"So what?" Ackroyd asked with a frown.

"These are the cards," Brennan explained, "that Chrysalis played solitaire with, the deck from which the murderer took the ace of spades to frame me. The deck he then absentmindedly put in his coat pocket and took with him after he left her office. Isn't that right, Worchester?"

Brennan stared grimly at the huge ace. Hiram tried to speak, but no words would come out. He stuttered, sputtered, and fingered the angry sore on the side of his neck, his face pale and beaded with sweat, his hands trembling.

Brennan dropped the cards on the floor and took from his jacket pocket the ace of spades that Chrysalis had left him in her will. He scaled it at Hiram. The card flew true, struck Hiram's broad chest, and tumbled to the floor where it landed faceup, black and ominous against the carpet.

♠

"Cute," Jay said as the card fluttered to the floor at Hiram's feet. "That mean you're going to start killing people now, or what?" He started to get up.

"I told you not to move." The barrel of Brennan's automatic slid a few inches to the right, until it was fixed on Jay.

"So shoot me," Jay said. He got to his feet, looking right at Yeoman. "You got *any* idea what Hiram has just been through?"

"I don't care what he's been through."

"Aren't you the fucking soul of compassion?" Jay said.

"I don't waste my compassion on killers," Brennan said.

"Oh, I forgot, you're Mother Teresa," Jay said with bitter sarcasm. "Well, pardon the hell out of me. Thing of it is, though, seeing as how you hate killers so much, I can't help noticing you're the only one in the room with a gun in his hand."

"Jay, Daniel, *please*," Tachyon pleaded. His good hand cradled his bandaged stump, and he sounded weak and sick at heart. "Can't we work this out like civilized people?"

"He's trying to protect a killer," Yeoman said icily.

"You got a hell of a lot of nerve calling anyone a killer, Danny boy," Jay snapped back.

"This isn't about me," Yeoman said.

"*Stop it!*" Tachyon cried. He looked over at Brennan. "Daniel, there must be some mistake. I know Hiram Worchester. I have known him for close on two decades now, in good times and bad. He is a good man. Even if I believed for a moment that Hiram was capable of such an act, he was here in Atlanta at the convention while Chrysalis was being murdered in Jokertown. He *couldn't* have done it."

Jay glanced back at Hiram uncomfortably. "Well," he admitted with vast reluctance, "that's not quite true. I checked the airline schedules. If he took the last flight out and the first flight back, he'd never have been missed. But Carnifex could have caught the same flights. Same for Braun, or any of them."

"That can easily be verified," Tachyon pointed out. "Even if Hiram used an assumed name, a man of his size would have been noticed."

"Then check it if that's what it takes to convince you," Brennan said. "I have all the proof I need."

"What about a motive?" Jay demanded. "Or don't you bother with things like that? Motives, chains of evidence, courtrooms, what a fucking nuisance, right? Your way is a lot simpler. Danny Brennan says he's guilty, time to kill the poor bastard."

"I have evidence," Brennan replied curtly. "Enough to convince me that it's true."

"As far as I can see, you don't have jack shit except for a deck of cards you found in some coat pocket," Jay said.

"Jay makes a good point," Tachyon put in. "Do you have any proof that Hiram brought the cards to this apartment?"

"The kitchen cabinets were full of expensive gourmet foods. There was every kind of utensil you can imagine, everything a gourmet cook like Worchester would need. And the jacket was white linen, expensive, fashionable, custom-tailored. Size 68 long. Chrysalis was killed by an ace. How many aces wear that size?"

Silence filled the room.

Jay turned to look behind him. Hiram still sat on the corner of the bed. He was not using his gravity power; the mattress tilted ominously under his massive weight. His face was pale and damp, his shoulders slumped, his eyes still fixed on the ace of spades that lay at his feet.

The stillness lasted an eon. All three of them were looking at Hiram now. The big ace seemed oblivious until Tachyon finally, softly, said, "Hiram?"

Then he looked up, and sighed hugely. His eyes were sad and sick. "Yes, doctor?" he asked.

"Are you all right?" Tach asked gently.

"No," Hiram said. "I haven't been all right for some time."

"This is crazy," Jay said. "Hiram, don't just sit there. Tell him that he's wrong."

"I wish I could," Hiram said with quiet dignity. "You don't know how much I wish that."

"What are you saying?" Tachyon asked, dread in his voice. "You don't mean to say that these accusations are true?"

Hiram nodded, his eyes far off and full of pain. The big man seemed to be having trouble speaking. "I . . . I'm sorry."

Then it was Jay who had no words.

"There must be some explanation," Tachyon said. "I cannot accept this. You're a good man, a man of courage and integrity."

"Ti Malice," Jay blurted. "That fucking *thing* was riding you, using you, your powers, your body." He swung around to face Brennan. "You don't understand the situation. Hiram was a victim. Even if he did do it, he was only the instrument."

"No, Jay," Hiram interrupted quietly. "I appreciate your loyalty, but . . . it wasn't like that. It was me. Just me. God help me." He fell silent again, eyes turned inward.

"Hiram, tell us," Tachyon implored.

For a moment Hiram didn't seem to hear. Then the big ace began to speak. His voice was weary, so quiet they had to strain to hear. "I needed the kiss," he began simply. "That was why I flew back to New York that night. The last flight out, just as Jay surmised. You don't know what it was like to go without the kiss . . . I needed it badly.

"So I flew back up, and went to him secretly. There were always other . . . other mounts about. Ti Malice was never alone. When I arrived, he was mounted on Sascha. But my . . . my master was pleased to see me. He left Sascha and gave me his kiss.

"That was when Sascha told me. He was angry. It was an act of spite. I'd taken Ti Malice away from him, you see, and there is nothing so awful in the world. He wanted to hurt me, so he told me that Chrysalis had hired a man to assassinate Gregg Hartmann. He knew how hard I'd worked, how much hope and faith and trust I'd put in Gregg. Sascha had picked it out of her mind just that morning. He was only a skimmer, you know, the poorest kind of telepath, but her plan must have been right there on the surface of her mind.

"It didn't bother me, not then. When Ti Malice honors you with his kiss, everything seems just as it should be, and nothing can bother you. But after a few hours, the master bestowed his kiss on Ezili, leaving me alone again. That was when I finally grasped what Sascha had said. I couldn't believe it. It seemed so monstrous, so obscene. I knew Chrysalis. Not well, but I knew her, we'd spent five months together on the *Stacked Deck*. I couldn't believe she would do such a thing. I had to confront her. I dressed and went down to the Crystal Palace.

"She was alone in her office, playing solitaire. You have to believe me, I never intended to hurt her. I told her what I'd heard, demanded to know if it was true. She didn't deny it. She didn't say anything. She looked up at me once, suspiciously, then went right back to playing solitaire. When I pressed her, all I got were evasive, meaningless answers in that infuriating fake accent of hers. If only she'd talked to me, told me what she knew about Gregg, what she'd seen . . . perhaps I wouldn't have believed her at first, but I would have listened. Dear God, why wouldn't she *talk* to me?"

"She didn't trust you, Hiram," Jay said, with a sad certainty. "That was how she was. She didn't trust anybody."

"I tried to make her see . . . how important it was. What a good man Gregg was." Hiram laughed bitterly. "I talked about his principles, his courage, his commitment to all of us, jokers and aces alike, how he was our last hope. Dear God, what a fool she must have thought me!

"I begged her." Tears were running down Hiram's face. "If it was true, what Sascha had said, I . . . I *begged* her to call it off. And all the time she just played cards, turning them over one by one, putting them down in place. They made a little snapping noise when she flipped them off the deck, I remember. Black on red, red on black. Her face . . . like a skull. I couldn't tell what she was thinking. She reminded me of death, sitting there playing cards while her hired assassin went out to do her killing for her. By what *right*? I asked her that, and she had no answer. I was very angry then. I made accusations, threats, told her I would go to the police. She just looked up and said that I'd do no such thing, that she knew a few things about me, too, and I knew she was talking about Ti Malice. Then she told me to get out. I refused. I begged her to talk to me, to listen to me. She just laughed, and started to get out of her chair. That was when . . . when . . ."

His voice trailed off. Hiram Worchester looked down dully at his hands, resting on his knees. The fingers of his right hand closed slowly into a fist, then opened again, just as slowly. "I tried to make her sit back down," he said, his voice a hoarse whisper. "I just wanted to talk to her, that's all. I swear it. She was going to walk out on me, and I couldn't stand it. So I made a fist and tried to slam her back down into her chair. I'd done it dozens of times, hundreds . . . just hold her there with my power, that's all I wanted to do, make her talk to me, make her tell me the truth . . . tell me who the assassin was, so we could stop him. I just wanted to make her sit down and *listen* . . . but . . ."

Hiram broke down, choking on his own words, his immense body shaking with dry sobs. But Jay didn't need to hear any more. He remembered Chrysalis as he had found her. Her chair splintered beneath her, her bones shattered. He could imagine the rest. A fist closed in fury, a mind blinded by rage . . . How much had she weighed in that second? A thousand pounds? Two thousand?

"You left out the last part," Brennan said. "After she was dead, you weren't through. First you gathered up her cards, all except the ace of spades, which you dropped on the body to make them think it was me. But that wasn't quite enough, was it? An autopsy would show how she died, and that would point right at you. But the broken bones, the shattered furniture, that suggested a fight, so you did a little more damage to the office. And then, just to make sure, you knelt down and made your fist heavy so that when you hit her, it would look as though her head had been crushed by someone with superhuman strength."

Hiram sagged. "I . . . I couldn't let myself be caught. Without the kiss . . . I couldn't face that. And there was the campaign . . . I was an ace, a Hartmann delegate, if it got out, it could destroy everything. Barnett might even win the nomination. So much was at stake, I just . . . panicked." His thick fingers pulled nervously at his beard. "It wasn't like you said . . . so cold . . . calculated."

"Wasn't it?" Brennan said. "You commit murder, try to pin the crime on someone else, and now you say it was all a mistake. I didn't notice you confessing when you thought you'd walked away clean." His gun was aimed at the center of Hiram's chest. "You were willing to let me pay for your crime, and when the cops grabbed Elmo instead, you didn't say a word." Brennan's voice was flat and calm, but Jay could hear the fury behind the words, implacable and deadly.

Hiram dropped his head again. "No," he muttered, low under his breath. "No, I didn't." His shame was written all over his face. "If you're going to kill me, get on with it."

That was when Jay Ackroyd made up his mind and stepped between Hiram Worchester and Daniel Brennan.

"Get out of the way, Ackroyd," Yeoman said.

"Daniel, Jay, please," Tachyon said weakly from the chair where he sat huddled in pain and misery. Both men ignored him.

"You claim Chrysalis was your friend," Yeoman said. "Why are you trying to shield her killer?"

"It was an accident," Jay said. "You heard him. You heard how it happened. Have a little goddamned mercy."

"Mercy is God's business," Brennan said. "Mine is justice."

"Tell me about it," Jay said scornfully. "Better yet, tell all those guys you've killed. Tell their widows and girlfriends. Tell their parents. Tell the kids some of them may have left behind."

"They knew the risks they were taking. The men I've killed would have killed me just as fast if I'd given them half a chance. I've never murdered an innocent woman."

"Chrysalis was a lot of things," Jay said, "and one of them was my friend, no matter what you think. But she was never innocent."

"I knew Chrysalis," Brennan said. "She did what she had to."

"Fuck that," Jay said. "She did what she *chose* to. What she chose to do was send a hired assassin to Atlanta. By last count, two Secret Service agents, a hotel manager, and a journalist are dead as a direct result, and we came *that* close to adding Jack Braun's name to that list. I'm not defending what Hiram did, but in my book, his hands are one hell of a lot cleaner than yours."

"Jay," Dr. Tachyon interjected softly, "Brennan's killings are an affair of honor. A blood feud. On Takis—"

"That's Georgia outside the window, not Takis," Jay said. "Why the hell are you defending this homicidal loon?"

"I owe him a life," Tachyon replied.

"You owe him a life," Jay repeated with disgust. "Real good. Well, you owe Hiram a life, too, remember? Not to mention the life you owe me. Come to think of it, you owe fucking *Gregg Hartmann* a life, if it really went down in Syria the way the papers said. Then there's the Turtle, Golden Boy, Straight Arrow . . . is there anyone you *don't* owe a life?"

"I owe Brennan two lives," the little alien said feebly. "I could never betray his trust."

Ackroyd wanted to scream. Instead he turned back to Yeoman. "Well, *I* don't owe you shit," he said. "You want justice? Fine. We'll take Hiram to the police, and he'll go on trial. But let's make it a two-for-one sale, shall we? You're great at serving up justice, how about you try a nice big spoonful yourself. Turn yourself in along with Hiram. Stand up in front of a fucking judge and tell him about your *war*."

"I answer to my own conscience, Ackroyd, and frankly, I don't give a damn what you think about it," Brennan said. "I'm not turning myself in. Now, for the last time, get out of the way."

There was a long moment of silence. Jay stared at Brennan. Brennan stared back. Tachyon looked helplessly from one to the other, then struggled to rise from his chair. With only one hand, it was a painful, clumsy process.

"I can get a finger up pretty damn quickly," Jay said to Brennan.

"The moment you even start to lift that hand, I'm going to squeeze this trigger," Brennan told him. "What are the odds on you being able to teleport a bullet in flight?"

"A million to one," Jay admitted. "But only if you don't hesitate. A split second of indecision, and you'll be shooting through the bars in the Tombs."

"Do I look like the hesitating sort?" Brennan asked quietly. His hand was very steady.

Jay thought about that one and didn't much like what he came up with. He risked a quick glance back over his shoulder. Hiram sat slumped on the corner of the bed, staring off into space, completely out of it. Whatever the hell was about to go down, it didn't look like the huge ace was going to be much of a factor.

"There's someone else," Tachyon said softly. His head moved slowly from side to side, searching. "Another mind. In the wall."

"Real good," Jay said sourly. He felt ill, but he should have seen it coming. "The phantom bimbo, right?"

"Changes the odds a little, doesn't it?" Brennan said, smiling.

Jay flexed his fingers and stared down the barrel of Brennan's Walther. It reminded him how much he hated guns, and the kind of assholes who carried them around. From the look in Brennan's cool gray eyes, he had just about run out of time. There was nothing left but to go for it.

♥

Brennan felt a vise clamp down on his brain. For a panicked moment he thought he was having a seizure of some kind, but then he realized that it was Tachyon. Tachyon's mind control. He raged against it, pushing with all the strength he had in mind and body. But it was useless. The only part of his body that he could move was his eyeballs. He glanced around the room and saw Jennifer walk woodenly out of the walls.

"Nice work, doc," Ackroyd said. "Now—"

"No."

"Look, goddammit—"

"Decisions must be made. *Discussed* and made."

"I've made my decision."

"And I don't agree," Tachyon said flatly. "Grant *me* a little consideration in this, Ackroyd. I stand between three friends."

The detective stared at Brennan. "Friends," he snorted.

Tachyon lowered himself slowly back into his chair. Brennan could see the strain on his face, but the mental vise he'd placed upon Brennan's mind still held. "We will talk," the alien said, "but peace will lie upon this room."

Bending, Tachyon pulled his dagger from its boot sheath and dropped it on the carpet at his feet. Jennifer walked woodenly toward

Tachyon and dropped her gun next to the knife. Tachyon turned to Brennan. "Daniel, will you lay down your weapon?"

There was no sense being stupidly stubborn. There was no way he could break Tachyon's mind control, and there was no way anything further would happen if he insisted on keeping his gun. He nodded, almost imperceptibly.

"And Ackroyd?" Tachyon asked. "What about you?"

"I hate this Takisian bullshit."

"I could take control of you and make you a dummy in these talks. I would prefer not to."

"Yeah, well, okay."

"Hands in pockets, please."

Tachyon released Brennan. He stepped forward and dropped his gun at Tachyon's feet. He looked at the alien with anger and bitterness in his eyes. "You betrayed me," he said.

"I prevented murder," the alien snapped.

"Self-defense—"

"*Oh, please!* We bandy with words. Killing, it's *all* killing! You kill Jay because he attempts to put you in the Tombs. You kill Hiram because *you* get to mete out justice. The end result is all the same— death! And it's *got to stop!*" Tachyon pressed the heel of his hand against his head as if trying to push back agony. He turned to Worchester, who had been a mute witness to this all. "Hiram, what do you intend to do?"

"That's already been decided," said Jay. "We'll take—"

"*Shut up!* Hiram?"

"I'll return to New York and turn myself over to the authorities."

"I'll accept that," Brennan said. It was a reasonable end to their difficulties. It was a solution Chrysalis would understand.

"I don't recall him asking your fucking opinion," Jay gritted.

"He'd better take it into consideration," Brennan said. He turned to face Worchester. "If you get to the airport and change your mind, if you decide to run, you'd better know now that you'll never have another day's peace. I'll be coming for you."

"You utterly amaze me, Daniel, with your rigid, self-righteous certainty," Tachyon said. "Who made you God? Who gave you the right to place your judgment above all others?"

Brennan barked a short, harsh laugh. "That's funny coming from you, Tachyon. Release Jennifer."

"No," Tachyon said, shaking his head.

"Why not?" Brennan asked, flaring with anger he could no longer suppress. "We have an agreement."

Jay plunged forward. "We've agreed to nothing. Hiram stands trial and maybe goes to prison for a *mistake*, while this guy walks free? Fuck that! If his little war excuses him, then Hiram should be completely exonerated."

"Jay," Tachyon said, shaking his head, "you've allowed your anger to replace your brains. Elmo stands accused of a crime he did not commit. Hiram has confessed to it. He must stand trial."

"Yeah, but we're talking involuntary manslaughter here. Voluntary manslaughter, tops. Hiram may walk out of that courtroom with probation." Jay jerked a thumb at Brennan. "How's Danny Boy gonna take that?"

"We'll all have to see, won't we?" Brennan said coldly.

"To hell with that," Jay said. "Why don't we let Hiram write out his confession and then get on a plane to Tibet or wherever the hell he wants to go?"

"He'll die before he ever reaches that plane," Brennan said softly.

"Not if you're behind bars."

Hiram stirred and got off the bed. He no longer looked lost, victimized. It seemed as if he'd made a decision and was determined to carry it through. "You can talk until you're both damned," he said. "This is *my* decision to make, and I will go to New York and stand trial because I choose to." He looked directly at Brennan. "And not because I'm afraid of you. I'm not."

And Brennan could see that that was true. Hiram had been through the fire and emerged cleansed. He looked as if he feared nothing now.

"Hiram—" Jay began.

"Jay, your friendship warms me, but I must do this. I've been a puppet for too long. First with . . . him . . . then with Ti Malice. Well, it's all over. I'm through being a puppet."

"Hiram's right," Tachyon said passionately. "Don't any of you understand? Hiram's trial is critical, not only for Elmo or Hiram, but for *all* of us. The law is the witness of our moral life. Its history is the history of the moral development of your race. But my race upset the balance. We created superhumans, and the result has been a growing chaos. The Turtle assaults with impunity because he is armored literally and figuratively with the secret of his identity. I invade people's minds. You, Jay, violate their civil liberties. And Daniel, you kill them. If we don't demonstrate our willingness to abide by the rule of law, then we are everything Barnett says we are. We are dangerous and heedless and deserve to be controlled since we are unwilling or unable to abide by the rules of civilized society."

"That's fascinating," Brennan said dryly, "but you missed something. I'm not a wild card. I'm just a nat."

Jay whirled on him. "You bastard. Tachyon, all you've done is convince me that I'm right, and that this killer should be behind—"

Jay cut off in midsentence. Brennan looked at Tachyon, pale and shaken, who had half risen out of his chair.

"Yes," Tachyon said wearily. "I am once again playing God. Go, Daniel. Take your lady and go. Never return. If you do, know that I will not aid you."

Jennifer swayed drunkenly when Tachyon released her. Brennan caught her, supported her. He looked back at Tachyon once before he left the hotel suite, and Tachyon looked back.

Neither parting glance was kind.

♣

When Brennan and his girlfriend were both gone, Tachyon finally released his iron grip on Jay's body and mind. The alien was trembling, his brow beaded with sweat.

Jay ran to the door, jumped out into the hall, looked up and down. There was no one waiting for the elevators. He made a dash for the stairwell, slammed through the fire door, breathing hard. The stairs were empty, silent. They were gone.

Swearing loudly with disgust, Jay turned on his heel and stalked back to the room. He slammed the door shut behind him. The noise made Tachyon wince. Jay pointed at him, his arm trembling with tension. "I hope you realize what you've done," he said bitterly. "You've just let another Demise out onto the streets."

Tachyon looked at him for a long moment. Then the wide lilac eyes rolled up into his head, and the little alien fainted dead away.

"Oh, hell," Jay said. The perfect ending to a perfect week. He gave Hiram a weary look. "C'mon," he said, "help me tuck the little fuck into bed."

10:00 P.M.

Sometimes, Brennan thought, duty was never ending.

He and Jennifer had left Atlanta immediately. They retrieved Brennan's van from the airport parking lot and drove to where the Crystal Palace used to be. Brennan got out and walked over to the ruins.

It was dark. There were few pedestrians on the street. There was nothing to bring them here now that the crystal lady was dead and her palace was gone. Brennan stared at the wreckage for a long moment. The stench of burning was still in the air, the tide of memories still flowed in his mind. He turned and stood before one of the piles of debris that had been around since the Jokertown riot. He waited until he saw eyes blinking inside it.

"How are you?" he asked.

"Sad. Our lady is gone and our home is burned."

"I didn't want that to happen," Brennan said.

"But it did," the voice replied accusingly.

"Yes," Brennan said, "it did. Have you found anyplace else to go?" The tiny head shook no.

"Yes, you have," Brennan said softly.

11:00 P.M.

Digger Downs was typing furiously on a laptop computer, so engrossed that he didn't notice when Jay stepped into his apartment. "You forgot to lock your door," Ackroyd announced loudly.

Digger glanced up from the screen, startled, and stared at Jay with a guilty look on his face. The reporter was four feet tall, going on five. He looked like a child playing with a Speak 'n Spell. "You," he said.

"Me," Jay admitted. "You really ought to lock your door. Never can tell when someone might break in and trash all your stuff." He looked around pointedly. Digger's apartment was just the way that Mackie Messer had left it.

"You have a hell of a lot of nerve showing up here," Digger said. "I could of died in that goddamned cat box. They sent me all the way to *Alaska*."

"Alaska, Atlanta, hey, that's close enough for government work," Jay said. He smiled. "At least you don't have to eat that airline food."

"It's not funny! I ought to sue you," Digger bitched. "By the time I finally got to Georgia, I was so big they had to cut me out of the goddamned box."

"If it's any consolation, I didn't have a whole lot of fun myself," Jay said. He crossed the room, stepping gingerly over the debris. "Anybody ever tell you you're a shitty housekeeper?"

Digger scowled. "I'm not touching a thing, not till the photographer's been here."

Jay sighed. "I was afraid you were going to say something like that," he said. "What are you writing?"

Digger hurriedly hit a key, storing the file he'd been working on, then slammed down the top of the little laptop computer so Jay couldn't read the file names off the screen. "None of your business," he said. "How'd you know I came home?"

"I'm a detective, remember?" Jay said. He cleared himself a space on one end of the sofa and sat down. "Let's not make this any harder than we have to. I just want to get the hell out of here, check myself into a hospital, and take some serious painkillers for about a month."

"So who's stopping you? Go."

"Not till we get something straight. You're not writing anything about Gregg Hartmann."

Digger laughed. "The hell I ain't. This is the story of my life. I'm writing it *all* . . . Syria, Berlin, Mackie Messer, the Crystal Palace, *everything*. . . . I'm going to hang him out and watch him twist in the wind. I figure a special issue of *Aces* with nothing but the Hartmann exposé. Or maybe I'll sell it to the *Washington Post*, really show that bimbo Sara Morgenstern a thing or two." He slapped the computer with his hand. "When this thing comes out, Greggie'll be lucky if they don't lynch him."

"Real good," Jay said wearily. "So how many other wild cards will get lynched in his place? Ever think about that?"

"That's not my concern," Digger said. "I'm a journalist, that's all. I just tell the truth and let the pieces fall where they may."

"Yeah," Jay said. "Funny, the truth wasn't so important when there was a chance those falling pieces might be coming off your body." He held up a hand before Downs could interrupt. "Just hear me out," he said. "I've already gone over this with Tachyon. He was right—this is a story that can't ever be told. There are reasons, Digger." He went over them, one by one.

Digger was unmoved. "You're asking me to be part of a cover-up," he said when Jay had finished.

"Real good," Jay said. "You got it."

"No way," Downs said with righteous indignation. "I got ethics. Besides, what about *me*? Why the hell should I let Hartmann off easy, he tried to have me *killed*! Forget it, Ackroyd."

"I know who killed Chrysalis," Jay said. "He's going to turn himself in tomorrow morning at the Jokertown precinct house. If you agree to drop the Hartmann exposé, you can have that story instead. I'll arrange for the killer to give you a complete confession before he goes to the police." Jay had already talked it over with Hiram on the flight home. Hiram had agreed; Hiram was in a frame of mind to agree to most anything that might possibly spare further bloodshed. "It's quite a story," Jay said. "It's got blackmail, drugs, sex, death, aces, jokers, the works. Juicy." He ought to know. He'd helped Tachyon work out the details. What it didn't have was any mention of Gregg Hartmann or James Spector. Ti Malice was villain enough. "You can have an exclusive," Jay promised Digger. "In fact, how's this, I'll arrange for the killer to turn himself over to *you*, and you can deliver him to the cops."

For a moment, Digger looked tempted. Then his child's face screwed up in a frown. "Do I look stupid or what? The Hartmann thing is headlines coast to coast, talk shows, books, hell, a Pulitzer for sure, maybe a *Nobel.* No way am I gonna swap that for some penny-ante Jokertown murder. I mean, gimme a break, *Chrysalis?* Who cares? She's just another dead joker."

"I'll throw in some money," Jay said.

Digger got indignant. "Hey, I don't take bribes, you got it? You can just keep your goddamned money, the American public has a right to know the truth."

Jay sighed deeply. He was running out of ammunition. "Okay," he said. "Have it your way." He stood up. "Once you run your little scoop, it's going to get real cold out there for wild cards, but if you think you can stand the chill, hey, who am I to argue?" He started for the door.

"Me?" Digger said. "Why should I have to stand the chill?"

Jay turned and looked back at him. "You're an ace, aren't you?" he said innocently. He touched a finger to the side of his nose and raised a meaningful eyebrow.

"But no one knows that," Digger said.

Jay smiled.

"You wouldn't," Digger said, horrified. "I told you that in confidence, man. If anyone found out, I could be in a world of shit."

"So true," Jay said sympathetically. "You know, if it was up to me, I'd just as soon keep a lid on it, but . . ." He shrugged. "The American public has a right to know the truth."

His hand was on the doorknob when Digger called out after him. "Ackroyd."

Jay looked back over his shoulder. "Yeah?"

Downs regarded him thoughtfully. "How *much* money?" the reporter asked.

MIDNIGHT

They stopped at the Red Apple Rest, a twenty-four-hour restaurant on Route 17. Brennan got out and went inside.

"I need seventeen cheeseburgers, twelve foot-long hot dogs with chili, three with mustard and sauerkraut, twenty-six large fries, fifteen Cokes, ten Seven-Ups, and one large coffee. Black."

"Jesus, mister," the counterman said, "what ya got in your van, a pack of starving animals or something?"

"Just a few friends," Brennan said, laying his money on the counter.

Brennan turned as the counterman went to fill his order, and looked back over the parking lot. The moon had nearly set. Hanging on the rim of the horizon, it looked to Brennan like a skull, smiling. It took little imagination to add eyes of deepest blue and lips of coral red. He smiled back as it slipped below the horizon, and said softly, "Good-bye."

♣   ♦   ♠   ♥

CLOSING CREDITS

STARRING	created & written by
Jay (Popinjay) Ackroyd	George R. R. Martin
Daniel (Yeoman) Brennan	John Jos. Miller

CO-STARRING	created by
Jennifer (Wraith) Maloy	John Jos. Miller
Thomas (Digger) Downs	Steve Perrin
Hiram Worchester	George R. R. Martin
Ti Malice	John Jos. Miller
The Oddity	Stephen Leigh
Dr. Tachyon	Melinda M. Snodgrass
Mother and her Children	John Jos. Miller

FEATURING	created by
Charles Dutton	Walton Simons
Lazy Dragon	William F. Wu
Ezili je Rouge	John Jos. Miller
Det. 3rd Grade Thomas Jan Maseryk	Chris Claremont
Det. 2nd Grade Harvey Kant	Walter Jon Williams
Big Joe Jory	John Jos. Miller
Quasiman	Arthur Byron Cover

Father Squid	John Jos. Miller
Fadeout	George R. R. Martin
Sascha Starfin	John Jos. Miller

WITH	*created by*
Doug Morkle (Durg Morakh)	Victor Milan
Elmo Schaeffer	John Jos. Miller
Jack (Golden Boy) Braun	Walter Jon Williams
Billy (Carnifex) Ray	John Jos. Miller
Robert (Bludgeon) Seivers	George R. R. Martin
Tripod	John Jos. Miller
Nephi (Straight Arrow) Callendar	Walter Jon Williams
Stigmata	Stephen Leigh
Squisher	John Jos. Miller
Jube (Walrus) Benson	George R. R. Martin
Doughboy	Victor Milan
Charm	George R. R. Martin
Wyrm	John Jos. Miller
Mackie Messer	Victor Milan

SPECIAL APPEARANCE BY	*created by*
Chrysalis	John Jos. Miller

ABOUT THE AUTHORS

GEORGE R. R. MARTIN is the author of the international bestselling A Song of Ice and Fire series, which is the basis for the award-winning HBO series *Game of Thrones*. Martin has won the Hugo, Nebula, Bram Stoker, and World Fantasy Awards for his numerous novels and short stories. Visit his Web site at georgerrmartin.com.

JOHN JOS. MILLER is best known for his involvement as a contributor to the Wild Cards universe. He also wrote GURPS Wild Cards, a supplement for the GURPS role-playing system.